LORDS & LADIES
COLLECTION

Two Glittering Regency
Love Affairs

Lord Hadleigh's Rebellion
by Paula Marshall

&

The Sweet Cheat
by Meg Alexander

The Regency

LORDS & LADIES
COLLECTION

The Regency

LORDS & LADIES
COLLECTION

Paula Marshall &
Meg Alexander

*M&B™ and M&B™ with the Rose Device
are trademarks of the publisher.
Harlequin Mills & Boon Limited, Eton House,
18-24 Paradise Road, Richmond, Surrey TW9 1SR*

First published in Great Britain in 2001 and 1995

THE REGENCY LORDS & LADIES COLLECTION
© Harlequin Books S.A. 2008

The publisher acknowledges the copyright holders of the
individual works as follows:

Lord Hadleigh's Rebellion © Paula Marshall 2001
The Sweet Cheat © Meg Alexander 1995

ISBN: 978 0 263 86704 6

052-1008

*Printed and bound in Spain
by Litografia Rosés S.A., Barcelona*

Lord Hadleigh's Rebellion
by
Paula Marshall

Paula Marshall, married with three children, has had a varied life. She began her career in a large library and ended it as a senior academic in charge of history in a polytechnic. She has travelled widely, has been a swimming coach, and has appeared on *University Challenge* and *Mastermind*. She has always wanted to write, and likes her novels to be full of adventure and humour.

Prologue

Spring, 1817

'**O**h, damn and blast everything,' Russell Chancellor, Lord Hadleigh, exclaimed aloud as he walked along Bruton Street, causing several passers-by to look at him in some alarm.

The more he thought about his current errand, the worse he felt. It wasn't as though he hadn't been thinking recently of breaking off his long connection with Caroline Fawcett, but he had hoped to do so gradually so that when the end came it would not be too much of a shock for her.

Instead, though, that very morning his father, the Earl of Bretford, had issued an ultimatum to him in such strong terms that there was no denying him—unless he were ready to find himself turned into the street, penniless, with only his title left to him and nothing else…

He had arrived home from the Coal Hole just before dawn, thoroughly out of sorts with himself, having drunk too much and, for once, gambled too much. He had scarcely had time to lay his throbbing head on the pillow before Pickering, his valet, was shaking him awake.

'What the devil are you at, man?' he exclaimed. 'Don't you know that I arrived home only an hour ago?'

'Yes, m'lord, but your father sent for me not five minutes gone, saying that the matter he wished to discuss with you was urgent. He demanded that I inform you that he wishes to see you in his study immediately and will not brook any delay.'

'Did he, indeed?' Russell swung his legs out of bed, which set his poor head protesting in the most unkind way. 'Have you any notion of what has brought this about?'

'None, m'lord, except…' and his valet hesitated.

'Except what, Pickering? For God's sake, have you caught my father's habit of being unable to finish his sentences?'

'No, m'lord, only that he seemed to be rather more angry with the way the world wags than usual.'

At this dire news, for his father's foul temper was notorious throughout society, Russell gave a slight moan before allowing Pickering to help him to dress. On the way out of the room he caught sight of himself in the looking-glass on the tall-boy opposite to his bed, and decided that he looked more fit for the grave than enduring the roasting which he was sure his father was going to give him.

I'm over thirty years old and he treats me as though I were a boy in his teens, was his last unhappy thought before the footman opened the double doors to the study where his father was impatiently pacing the room. It was small wonder that the carpet was showing such visible signs of wear.

'There you are, Hadleigh. By God, at the rate you're going your rowdy life will soon begin to show on your face—' He stopped abruptly before adding, 'I never cease to wonder how unlike you are to your brother, Richard—'

He stopped again.

The sense of being second rate, a disappointment and a failure, was so strong in him that Russell could not prevent himself from filling the gap which his father had created.

'I am not so far gone that I cannot remember my brother's name, sir. Nor that I am somewhat surprised that you should send for me at this ungodly hour to tell me what I already know.'

At this weary piece of impudence his father's face turned from red to purple.

'You are pleased to be insolent, Hadleigh. I have had enough of you. You are so lost to everything but pleasure that I tremble to think of what might happen to the estate when I am called to my last rest and you inherit. Although there is no male entail attached to the estate, it has always been the custom of the Chancellors to pass it on to the elder son without a quibble. I, however, am beginning to quibble. Nay, more than that—' He stopped again.

'More than what, sir? I am all agog to learn the end of the sentence.'

Remembering his unpleasant riposte later, Russell flushed with shame. At the time his disgust with himself seemed to have translated itself into a disgust with everything.

'It is this, Hadleigh. I am serving you with an ultimatum. I wish you to marry and settle down. To begin with, you are to dismiss that woman you have been keeping, immediately, this morning, if possible. I would have you marry some decent young woman—someone like your brother's wife, Pandora. His judgement in marrying her is as sound as yours is faulty. If you refuse me in this, I shall immediately send for the lawyers and arrange matters so that Richard inherits everything but the title. I shall also at that point discontinue your allowance. You would then have to fend for yourself.

'I am not, Hadleigh, about to condemn you out of hand. I shall give you three months to marry someone who will bring honour to our name, provide the Chancellor family with more male heirs, and settle down to bring honour to it yourself. Failing that, I shall turn you away.'

White to the lips, Russell asked, 'Does Ritchie know of this, sir? After all, he has already provided you with a male heir.'

'Indeed not. It would not be proper that he learn of it before you have had a chance to redeem yourself. As for him providing me with a male heir—you know as well as I do that a man of sense would wish to have as many grandsons as possible, the death rate among little boys being what it is.'

Ritchie had once said to Russell that he had lived in his older twin brother's shadow all his life. The truth, he thought, was somewhat different: he had lived in Ritchie's. Ritchie, who had become his father's darling, Ritchie, the soldier-hero, the serious man, the man of duty. Ritchie, who had already fathered a son.

'I wish I had been the younger twin of whom nothing was expected,' burst from Russell's lips almost without him willing the words.

'That, Hadleigh, is what I complain of—your innate frivolity. I have no more to say to you, except that I expect you to do as I ask—or face the consequences. I have been corresponding with my friend, General Markham, whose only child is a daughter and consequently his heiress. He and I hope to arrange a match between the pair of you. He is giving a house-party at Markham Hall next week, and I would wish you to join it so that you might become acquainted with her. I hope you grasp that the matter is urgent. I am not prepared to allow you to continue your irresponsible way of life any longer.

'You may leave. I want no verbal assurances from you, only deeds.'

His father sat down and began to write, lifting his head up only to say, 'You know where the door is, Hadleigh. Kindly use it. I have no wish to see you again until you have done all that I have just asked of you.'

So, here he was, several hours later, about to give Caroline her *congé*, not as he had once imagined, at his wish, but at his father's. If I had any courage at all I would have told him to go to the devil and set out to make my own fortune. But how? I am trained for nothing. I wanted to be a soldier. That was denied me. I was the heir, Ritchie was to be the soldier. I asked my father to allow me to manage our estates at Eddington in Northumberland, but was told that that was cousin Arthur Shaw's job. What's more, he said, he had no wish to deprive him of it in favour of an untrained, overgrown schoolboy.

Russell's unhappy train of thought stopped at this point. He had no mind to revive for himself the misery which had resulted from his father's other brutal interference in his life thirteen years ago. Not that that was entirely his father's fault, but had he been kinder then…who knows, things might have been different.

No, I will not think of that… The past is dead and gone and that time will not return again. What time *had* done was to bring him to Caroline's door before he was ready to face her. The unhappy truth was that he disliked the notion of telling her that he wished to end their liaison so much that he had continually put it off. Now his father had forced his hand and he must bite the bullet.

Somewhat to his surprise there was a hackney carriage standing in the street outside and Caroline's little page was loading bags into its boot. He ran briskly up the steps, his door key in his hand and let himself in, calling her name with an urgency which surprised him. He was even more surprised when the drawing room door opened and Caroline, looking as lovely as ever, walked into the hall, dressed for the street and carrying a large leather bag.

'You?' she exclaimed. 'I thought that you had forgotten that I lived here. Have you any notion of how long it is since you last visited me?'

Shame struck Russell all over again. It was truly his day to feel like a cur! Oh, he would pay her off with a lump sum, but the cruel fact remained that he was casting her off.

'Not lately, I know,' he almost stammered. He had stammered as a boy until a tutor with a cane had banished it— lately it had begun to come back again.

'True,' she said, smiling at him coldly. 'Well, I will relieve you of the need to visit me again. I have tired of your capriciousness and have decided to leave you. I was about to post you a letter informing you of my departure. Fortunately that will no longer be necessary since I can now tell you so in person.'

'Leave me?' he heard himself saying witlessly.

'Yes, leave you. It has been borne in upon me for some time that you have tired of me and did not know how to tell me so. I entered on our liaison for the foolish reason that I was in love with you. Oh, I knew that you would never marry me, but you assured me that you had decided that you would never marry anyone. I stupidly believed that that meant that we could play house together until we became Darby and Joan. I am still in love with you, but I refuse to be a millstone around your neck. I have recently met a worthy merchant who has decided to make an honest woman of me. We are to marry next week.

'And, no, I want no farewell presents from you of any kind. The one wish that I have to leave you with is that I hope that you may never suffer as I have done in loving someone as hopelessly as I have loved you. Farewell, Lord Hadleigh. Let us remember the happy days we had together and wish each other well. Now I must leave. The carriage, and my new life, awaits me.'

'No,' he said. 'Not like this.'

'You mean that you would have preferred to cast me off, and not me you?'

'No,' he said again, but, of course, she was right.

She reached up to pat his cheek with her gloved hand. 'Remember me a little, is all I ask.'

With that she was gone, out of the house and out of his life.

The decision had been made for him, but Russell felt no better for that—only worse, seeing that this was the second occasion on which a woman had abandoned him. Between his father and his mistress he had been shown a vision of himself with all his shortcomings made plain. All that remained was for him to go to Markham Hall to court a woman whom he had no wish to marry in order to recover his father's favour. Woman was perhaps a misnomer. He seemed to recall that Angelica Markham was only eighteen years old.

He arrived home to find that his father was out, so he could not inform him that his long-standing affair with Caroline Fawcett was over. At a loose end—as usual, he thought bitterly—he wandered into his father's study, intending to ask his secretary, Mr Graves, when he would return. The secretary was not there, either. He began to leave, but something, he never knew quite what, led him to walk to the secretary's tall desk, which stood before the window, to examine the papers on it.

There was a small pile of them that contained the accounts and the other details of the family estate at Eddington. Moved, again by he knew not what, he began to inspect them, the accounts first.

When he was at Oxford he had discovered that he had a bent for mathematics. Where others of his age found the subject boring and spent more time either amusing themselves or preparing for a political life by concentrating on the classics, he had played with numbers. They had always fascinated him. He remembered Dr Beauregard saying…

No, forget that, forget everything to do with Dr Beauregard, particularly his daughter.

He could not, alas, forget what lay before him while he rapidly totted up the lines of figures. Now, having done so, he thought, nay, he was sure, that something was wrong. He added them up again, to reach the same answer and to turn back to an earlier sheet. He had just finished checking that when the door opened and Graves came in.

'Ah, m'lord, were you looking for me, or your father?'

'My father, but I find that I do have a question for you about these accounts.'

'Indeed, m'lord. I wonder what you think that you have found.'

'If I am not mistaken, Graves, there are some discrepancies here which I ought, perhaps, to discuss with you.'

Graves, who was well aware of the lack of consideration and respect which the Earl had for his heir, always addressed Russell in a manner which showed that he shared his master's opinion of him. He shook his head and there was a slight hint of mockery in his answer.

'I, too, have checked these figures and have discovered nothing untoward. I fear that you must be mistaken.'

'I, however, fear that I am not,' returned Russell in a voice which Graves had never heard before. 'You will do me the courtesy—'

Graves did the unforgivable: he not only interrupted his superior, but refused to do as he had been ordered. 'I am a busy man, m'lord. I have gone through these accounts and reports most carefully and find nothing wrong with them. May I suggest that you raise this matter with your father, who, I assure you, has the utmost faith in my ability and my integrity. He, too, always checks my work, and that done for him by Mr Arthur Shaw, his agent at Eddington, and so far all has been to his satisfaction.'

For a moment Russell was tempted to seize the impudent swine before him by his cravat and threaten to throttle him if he continued to refuse to discuss the matter. Only the thought that his father would be sure to take Graves's part prevented him. Yes, he would speak to his father, but he knew full well that his answer would be the same as his secretary's: a refusal to listen to what his son might have to say.

And so it proved.

His father had been quite jovial at dinner, so much so that over their port at the end Russell had felt able to lean forward and remark, 'By chance, sir, I saw the accounts from our estate at Eddington. I thought that I detected evidence of something wrong there. I wonder if you would allow me to—'

He stopped. His father's face was rapidly turning purple with anger, as it had done so often when he had been a boy, and his old helplessness in the face of that anger had returned to plague him.

'Come, Hadleigh, what do you have to say to me that is so urgent that you see fit to badger me over a glass of port? Why do you hesitate? Pray continue.'

'I was wondering, sir, whether you would allow me to go there and see if all is well. As I recall, neither you nor any other member of the family has visited Eddington, preferring our home in Norfolk instead. Perhaps it is time that one of us did. You are occupied in government, Ritchie is reorganising the estate he has inherited, so that leaves me.'

'So it does, Hadleigh, and why in the world you think yourself fit to go to Eddington and trouble my good agent there is beyond me.'

'But I am your heir. My name is Hadleigh, which is taken from a village not ten miles from Eddington and I have reason to believe, from looking at Mr Shaw's reports, that it might be useful if I visited the land to which I owe my name.'

Russell knew, by the expression on his father's face, that it was hopeless to continue: his final words confirmed that he was right.

'Confine yourself to matters of which you might know something,' his father almost snarled. 'Arthur Shaw is a good, hard-working fellow—unlike yourself—and I will not have him distressed by your meddling in affairs with which you have nothing to do, and of which you know nothing. That is my last word to you, sir.'

Russell was tempted to try to continue to plead his case. Unfortunately his scrutiny of the accounts and reports had been cut short by Graves so that he had been unable to gather enough evidence to convince his father that he had right on his side. He was also dismally aware that even if he had his father would continue to snub him. To press the matter further might, he feared, result in him saying something unforgivable, but what would be the point of that in the face of his father's intractability?

Fortunately he would shortly be out of the house for some little time, even if the errand he was sent on to Markham Hall was not one which he would have chosen. At least, while he was there, he might forget for a time that he was not only unloved, but also despised.

Mary Wardour moved a chess piece on the board which stood beside her before beginning to fill yet another sheet of papers with numbers and arcane signs. She was halfway down it before there was a respectful knock on the door.

She sighed. Gibbs, the butler, of course. What was it *now*? Was she never to have a whole afternoon of quiet and peace?

'Come in,' she called, laying down her quill pen on the stand before her.

Gibbs entered, looking rather more solemn than usual. 'A lady to see you, madam,' he began, but got no further before the lady in question pushed urgently past him.

'No fuss,' she trilled. 'I will announce myself. You may leave us.'

Mary gave an inward groan. Of all the people in the world who had to interrupt her just when she had thought that she was about to solve the tricky problem of the knight's move, this particular woman was the last she would have welcomed.

'Lady Leominster,' she said, rising. 'Pray be seated. I quite understand that your fame is such that you need no announcing.'

The Lady chose to interpret this as a compliment.

'Oh,' she declaimed, 'and I am sure that you will be delighted to have a short rest from your labours. I am, I own, a little surprised that you should frowst indoors on such a fine sunny day. But no matter, I have come to reprimand you, you naughty thing. It is a godmother's privilege, after all. You so seldom go into society these days that you are in danger of becoming that strange thing, a female hermit. This will never do. To that end I have prevailed on my cousin Markham to invite you to his grand house-party next week.'

Mary's expression was so mutinous that she raised her gloved hand. 'No, do not refuse me. It is high time that you married again.'

She put her head on one side and studied Mary's face as though it were a fine painting brought out for her to admire.

'Quite lovely,' she murmured. 'Yes, quite lovely. With that complexion, those dark eyes and even darker hair, any man would be proud to call you wife. And your fortune, of course. We mustn't forget that.'

How many more of society's taboos could the old trout ignore or break? Wasn't it enough that she had burst into the room without so much as a by your leave when Gibbs must have assured her that the mistress was not at home?

'Yes,' said the Lady, and then, as though issuing an order from on high, 'Yes, of course, you must marry again. Thirty is not such a great age for a widow.'

'Heaven forbid,' exclaimed Mary and goodness, where had

that come from? After all, her marriage to Dr Henry Wardour had not been an unhappy one, despite the great difference in their ages and that it had been arranged between him and her father and presented to her as a *fait accompli*.

'Do admit that it must have been off-putting' exclaimed her tormentor, 'to marry an old fellow like Dean Wardour. I suppose that is why you feel condemned to carry on his work.' She waved a disparaging hand at Mary's pile of papers and the chessboard, having ignored another taboo—that one did not raise such intimate matters as the nature of a couple's married life with one of the partners in it.

She was so determined to make her point that she leaned over and struck Mary smartly on her writing hand with her glove before continuing with increased vigour. 'It's all very well for an old codger to trouble himself with such abstruse matters as mathematics. A handsome young man would soon give you other things than *that* to think about. All the more reason, then, to accept the General's invitation.'

The only reason which Mary could think of which would make her accept the invitation was that it might enable her to dismiss the old harpy sitting opposite to her so that she could get back to continuing her late husband's work—which was also her work.

'How long would I be expected to remain at Markham Hall? Not too long, I trust.' If that grudging acceptance made her sound nearly as elderly as her late husband, then so be it. Fortunately it seemed to please the harpy if her crocodile's smile was any guide. And there's a couple of mixed metaphors which would have set my late husband grieving if he had heard me utter them!

'My dear, I am up in the boughs, I do assure you. I will

inform the General myself that you will be delighted to renew your acquaintance with him and dear Angelica. You do remember dear Angelica, don't you?'

If dear Angelica was the girl who had sulked and moped her way through her come-out party, which Mary had unwillingly attended only after another session of bullying from the formidable lady opposite to her, then Mary remembered dear Angelica.

'Oh, yes, Lady Leominster. Of course I remember her.'

Who, indeed, could forget her tantrums? One could only pity the unfortunate man who might lead her to the altar. Fortunately again, the Lady took her utterance at face value, leaving Mary to regret being such a cat when thinking about, and speaking to, others, but happy that she was able to disguise her true feelings.

Her reward was a smacking kiss from the Lady, who rose and announced dramatically that she was off to persuade— by which she meant bully—her niece Phoebe Carstairs to visit Markham Hall as well. 'Another gel who does not know what's best for her,' she sighed.

If I knew what was best for me, then I wouldn't even consider putting a foot in Markham Hall, let alone visit it, was Mary's rebellious thought before resuming her work with a brain that was now more concerned with how she was to endure a week of total inanity when she might be enjoying herself by finally getting this confounded white knight to behave itself.

The black knight had been much more obliging.

Chapter One

Markham Hall was a truly beautiful building. It dated back to early Tudor times and was a dream of rich crimson and gold bricks and mellowed stone. All the later improvements, designed to increase the comfort of the family and the family's guests, had been added at the back so as not to spoil the illusion that the Hall was still an Early Tudor fortress that had been transformed into a mansion.

It was said that good Queen Bess had lived here for a short time when her Catholic sister Mary had been on the throne, but no proof of this had ever been offered except a contemporary portrait of her as a young woman which hung in a prominent place in the Great Hall.

A large number of visitors were arriving that late April afternoon. There were several carriages on the gravel sweep before the main doorway, which was actually a gate which opened on to a quadrangle around which the original house had been built. A bevy of footmen, grooms, coachmen and various servants were carrying luggage into the Hall.

Two footmen, one of them carrying a large green umbrella,

ran forward to greet Mary's driver and to open the door of her chaise for her so that she might descend and be escorted indoors, together with her maid, Jennie, and her companion, Miss Eliza Truman, away from the light rain which had begun to fall.

Inside all was beauty and comfort. Mary's suite of rooms overlooked the rolling countryside where a folly in the shape of a ruined miniature tower stood high on a hill. Peter's Place, it was called, after a fabulous huntsman who had run with the Quorn Hunt, Leicestershire's pride, two hundred years ago.

Mary had scarcely time to change out of her travelling clothes into a light mauve gown and settle herself on the sofa in her little withdrawing room before the butler and a footman arrived with the tea-board.

'Lady Markham thought that you might care for some refreshment after your journey from Oxford. We dine late here in the Great Hall. The General likes to call it supper. The family and the guests assemble in the Stuart room at the sounding of the first bell and meet to converse before the meal.'

'Very civilised,' murmured Mary, eyeing the teapot and the biscuits known as Bosworth Jumbles.

The butler bowed. 'The General and his Lady send word that they hope that you will enjoy your first visit to Markham Hall. They are looking forward to meeting you again. Should any of your wants remain unsatisfied, then you have only to ring for the housekeeper, Mrs Marsden, and she will look after you.'

'Well,' said Miss Truman when the butler had bowed himself out, 'I have encountered less state when my late patron visited royalty. The tea, however, is most welcome.'

Mary had forgotten what visiting her wealthy contemporaries was like. She was not sure that she wished to live a life of such formality, if only for a fortnight. She had brought her work with her, but doubted whether she would ever find time to solve the latest problem which she had encountered. Her companion, though, obviously revelled in being waited upon so assiduously, suggesting that they might ring the house-keeper for more hot water when they had drunk their first cup.

The rain outside had stopped and the sun was shining. Mary said, 'Do so, by all means, but I should wish to take a walk in the grounds. If *you* wish to rest after our journey, there is no necessity for you to accompany me.'

'At least take your maid with you. It will be expected.'

Mary sighed. Peace and quiet was all that she wanted. 'Indeed, no,' she replied gently. 'I am sure that I shall be per-fectly safe.'

'But who will carry your umbrella?'

'Why, I shall. Now, will you please excuse me? I shall not be long.'

Her umbrella in her hand, a short jacket over her dress, Mary made her way downstairs and out into the open after asking a somewhat surprised footman the best way into the gardens. He escorted her to a large door at the back. One path from it led to the stables, another to a series of formal gardens before taking a sharp turn into the Park itself.

The gardens had been improved during the last century, almost certainly by Capability Brown, Mary decided, before she ventured into the Park where she admired in turn the or-namental bridges, the artfully placed stands of trees, and the lake and its miniature stone quay where two small pleasure boats were moored.

Mary was compelled to admit that everything she saw pleased her, particularly the fact that she was the only person present to admire the unfolding vistas which Brown had so carefully devised. The scene before her was so beautiful that she began to wish that she had not left her sketchbook and water-colour paints at home. For a time she sat on a rustic bench placed exactly where the view before her was at its most lovely, and it was with a sigh that she rose and returned to the Hall.

A different route back through the formal gardens seemed a good idea until she heard men's voices coming from one of them when she approached the trellised archway which led into it. She was about to turn and retrace her steps in order to avoid them when she heard a voice which memory told her was familiar.

No! It could not be him! It could not!

He spoke again, and laughed at the end of a remark which set the rest of those present laughing, and this time she was sure that she recognised the voice of the man who had made it. Whatever the cost she must find out if her supposition was correct so that she might be prepared when she met him later at dinner. To have come upon him without warning would have challenged even her own calm self-control which was legendary among those who knew her.

She moved forward in order to look into the enclosed garden so that she might see the company assembled there, but not be seen by them. And yes, it was indeed Russell Hadleigh whom she thought that she had heard, whose pleasant baritone voice she had immediately recognised, even though it had been thirteen years since she had last listened to him speaking.

He was seated among a group of young men before an iron table on which stood, not tea, but bottles of port, Madeira and white wine. Unbuttoned might be the best word to describe them all, including Russell, Mary thought wryly, especially, perhaps, Russell. She also recognised Peregrine Markham, her host's son and heir, but the other young bloods were unknown to her. It was, perhaps, fortunate, she thought later, that she was not near enough to hear what they were saying—which, judging by the nature of their laughter, was not very proper.

Peregrine Markham suddenly stood up, which set her moving away before she could be seen and recognised. She had no wish to speak to any of them, let alone Russell Hadleigh, before she had had time to compose herself. Indeed, how she made her way safely back to her room she never knew, her brain was in such a whirl.

Mary had hoped never to see him again, and had she known that he, too, was going to be a visitor at Markham Hall, she would never have given in to Lady Leominster's bullying and agreed to go there. By great good luck, though, seeing him without his being aware of her presence meant that she could prepare herself for the inevitable moment when they would meet before dinner. It was essential that he should not know how much the mere sight of him still had the power to disturb her.

The disturbance was, of course, ridiculous. How could his betrayal of her thirteen years ago still have the power to upset her? Worse than that, how could the mere glimpse of him set her heart beating so rapidly as though it were only a day since he had last walked away from her after giving her such a loving kiss?

The Judas kiss of treachery, she had thought later. The memory of it had caused her so many bitter tears until, as the years passed, she began to forget him and his broken promises— which made her present strong reaction to him so unexpected.

I grow maudlin, to allow him to affect me so powerfully. Why, I even started to ask myself whether he would recognise me, as I recognised him. Oh, he has changed. He is no longer a handsome, slim boy, but a man with a cynical face, all that charming innocence which he once possessed has quite gone.

'My dear, have you been over-exerting yourself?' asked her companion when she re-entered their drawing-room. 'You look quite flushed. I do believe that it was a mistake to undertake a walk after a hard day's travelling.'

'Not at all,' Mary replied, a little distressed that her recent experience had overset her to the degree that Miss Truman was able to remark upon it. 'What you are seeing is merely the glow of exercise'—and what a lie that was! 'The grounds are quite remarkable and worthy of the brush of a master painter.'

'Indeed,' said Miss Truman, quite deceived by this explanation. 'I have read about their excellence, and now I am privileged to enjoy it. I have also heard that the General's chef is known for his excellence and I am looking forward to dinner— or supper, as always he calls it—with the keenest anticipation.'

Would that I were, was Mary's internal reaction to that!

Russell Hadleigh was not feeling much keen anticipation, either. He had not yet met the young woman whom his father, and hers, intended that he should marry, but was shortly about to do so. He had met her brother, Peregrine, always known to his associates as Perry, several times before, and had taken him in mild dislike. The notion of him as a brother-in-law did not attract.

Perry Markham was a gambler who took losing badly. Despite his recent bout at the tables, gambling was not an addiction with Russell. He could take it or leave it. It occasionally served to relieve a little his boredom with his empty existence. He could not understand a man allowing it to dominate his life as Perry Markham allowed it to dominate his. He wondered whether the General knew exactly how much his son was losing at the tables—and how much he was drinking to cover the pain of his losses there.

Russell had forsworn drinking that afternoon for the amusement of watching the others indulge themselves overmuch. It was during a pause in the idle conversation of young fellows with too much time on their hands, and too little to do in it, that he had seen a female hovering near the arch which led into the garden in which they sat. He could not quite see her face, but he thought that she looked young—or had he hoped that?

He *had* hoped that she might enter and bring a little brightness to an afternoon which was dull despite the sun which had begun to smile on them all. Alas, the sight of so many young fools—and he counted himself among them—must have caused her to turn away and deprive them of the pleasure of her presence.

Now his valet was dressing him for the evening with his usual loving care. It was an odd existence, he thought, which turned so much on dress and the other minor minutiae of a man's existence. He had recently asked his father if, when the next election came along, he might be allowed to stand at one of the seats which the family controlled—a small borough whose name gave him his title. To become an MP would give him an interest in life and allow him to bring some experience of power and management to the time when he finally inherited.

'You are not ready to do that, sir. Nor steady enough,' his father had growled at him.

'I am older than Lord Granville was when he first went into Parliament, and quite as steady,' he had replied.

'But you are not Lord Granville,' his father had snorted.

What could he say to that, other than, 'But I understand that he was only in his early twenties when he became an MP and I am over thirty. By then he had been an Ambassador to Russia.'

This did not answer, either. He wondered afterwards why his father had taken him in such dislike that he would not give him the opportunities which other heirs to noble names had been offered. Had what had happened thirteen years ago been enough to damn him as a serious person? Surely not—but the thought was always there.

Instead he was at Markham Hall to propose marriage to a young woman whom the *on dits* said was a frivolous, flighty piece—and that solely to please his father and not himself. Well, he was about to find out whether the *on dits* spoke truly or were simply baseless rumours.

Downstairs he found himself before the Tudor drawing room which opened on to the Great Hall where the General and Lady Markham, Perry and Angelica standing beside them, were receiving their guests. Angelica was pretty enough and fortunately bore little resemblance to her brother Perry, whose looks were not of the first stare, to say the least.

'I understand that you are acquainted with my son, Peregrine,' the General said, 'but I believe that you have not yet been introduced to my daughter, Angelica.'

Russell allowed that he had not and turned his attention to her—to find that she was a beauty in the current mode, with bright blue eyes, flaxen ringlets and a prettily rounded figure beneath a pink silk frock decorated with cream rosebuds. She offered a curtsy to his low bow and simpered at him, saying in a little girl's fluting voice, 'So happy to meet you at last, Lord Hadleigh. I have heard much of you from my brother.'

Had she, indeed? And was that a recommendation or not?

'And I am delighted to meet you, Miss Markham.'

'Oh, please call her Angelica,' interrupted Lady Markham cordially. 'We are all friends here, I trust.'

'Angelica.' He smiled and bowed again. 'So I must be Russell.'

It was the least he could say. He could only wonder what her conversation would be like. Well, he would shortly find out, for his valet had informed him that the Servants' Hall had it that he was to sit next to her at dinner. Her conversation? Had he run mad? Persons of his rank married young women for their dowry, not their conversation.

He gave a bow and a nod to Perry, who also simpered at him. After the General and his Lady's enthusiastic reception of him, Russell dismally realised that they, and his father, and now Perry, had settled between them that he was to marry Angelica. He wondered what all the hurry was about.

At last he was free to enter the drawing room, which was rapidly filling up with the General's guests, most of whom knew one another. It was his duty to be pleasant to the other guests, and one thing which Russell did know was how to be pleasant. He thought that he might even be able to do it in his sleep!

It was when he had finished talking to the Honourable Mrs Robert Chevenix, whose husband was a crony of his father's, that he saw a young woman sitting beside a middle-aged female who was obviously her companion. The young woman's dark head was turned away from him, but there was something strangely familiar about her whole posture. It was not until she turned towards him, and he at last saw her face, that he knew who she was.

Mary Beauregard! Mary, his lost love whom he had last seen thirteen years ago. Somewhat to his surprise, she was still very much like the young girl he had once known. Oh, her face had matured, but in the doing had served only to add to her quiet beauty, not detract from it. Her skin was as creamy as he remembered it, and her dark eyes…

Those dark eyes in which he had once drowned—he would never forget them. Those eyes that, alas, were faithless like the lips which had promised him eternal love when he had last seen her. An eternal love which had only lasted a week.

Now, thirteen years later, he ought to be able to look at her coldly without the sight of her enchanting him as it had once done, but he couldn't, and what sort of man did that make of him? It was a question which he did not immediately answer, because at that moment she saw him. Instead, a new question sprang into his mind.

What did she see when she looked at him?

Was she as inwardly disturbed as he was?

Only the eye of love, or of hate, could detect the faintest quiver of her mouth, or the hand which shook when she raised it to smooth down the fichu of her dowdy dress, but Russell saw both telltale signs and wondered which of the two contrary emotions was afflicting him and, quite possibly, her.

He bowed, his face, usually so mobile, a mask—the impassive mask which he wore when he chose to play cards. He said as coolly and distantly as common politeness would allow, no more, no less, 'Mrs Wardour, I believe. We meet again after many years.'

Mary looked up at him. Near to, as he had seen the changes time had wrought in her, she saw more plainly those which had altered him. One thing that struck her again was the cynicism written on his face, in the curl of his lip, in the knowing eyes which looked at her, and seemed to dismiss her.

'Yes,' she replied, as cool as he. 'I am, however, now the widow of Dr Henry Wardour.'

This statement shocked Russell out of his deliberately chosen indifference to her and the company in which they found themselves.

'I must commiserate with you upon his death, he must have been a good age.'

'But not so very old,' she riposted. Mary would never have supposed that she could outface her one-time love to the point where she retained her self-control and he did not. 'He was only in his early fifties. Such a difference in age on marriage is a commonplace in our society. Indeed, I gather that you are here invited here as a possible suitor for Miss Markham so I find your surprise at my marriage a little misplaced.'

What in the world had happened to the ardent young woman whom he had once loved that she could speak to him in the tones of a cold shrew?

'Your rebuke is a just one,' he admitted, and could not say more, for at that point they were joined by Perry Markham, since the Markhams' reception line had ended and dinner was almost upon them.

'So, Hadleigh, you have already made yourself known to Mrs Wardour, but then, no pretty woman ever fails to gain your attention, eh,' and he poked a stiff finger into Russell's ribs which set him moving away.

'You mistake, Markham. Mrs Wardour and I knew one

another many years ago—and we were renewing an old acquaintance, were we not?'

Mary's response to that was to offer both men a stiff smile.

'Too many years ago for us to be able to claim that we are old friends,' she said.

If this frosty answer surprised Perry Markham it did not surprise Russell.

'Well, in that case, old fellow,' went on Perry, smiling at Mary, 'I shall not be encroaching on a long-time friendship if I inform you that I am to escort Mrs Wardour into dinner. But fear not, you are to take in my sister Angelica, who cannot wait to further her acquaintance with you. She will be along any moment to claim you, so you will forgive me if I ask Mrs Wardour to join me so that I may show her my father's famous collection of porcelain.'

Both Russell and Mary were only too pleased to end their unwanted and unhappy tête-à-tête—with the exception that Mary had no wish to become more intimate with Perry, and Russell was not greatly looking forward to squiring Angelica, whom he suspected was exactly the kind of vacuous young creature whom he had always tried to avoid.

However, they both separately thought that in an imperfect world one cannot always have exactly what one wants—which was a conclusion which they both took into dinner with them!

The Great Hall was justly named. It was hung with faded banners covered with the honours of bygone battles. The dining table ran the length of the room before a giant hearth. On the wall facing the hearth were placed antique Tudor settles before low wooden tables. Flambeaux provided light even on this spring evening for the Hall's windows were high and small and their glass panes were dull with age. All in all it was scarcely a friendly place, and the formality which seemed a feature of the Markham household was very present in it.

Matters were not helped for Russell by Angelica having been placed on his left hand and Mary on his right. Mary had Perry Markham on her right and he was monopolising her attention while Angelica was doing the same for Russell. Unfortunately, her conversational powers were as limited as he had feared.

Having assured her that he had been to Astley's Amphitheatre, the home of horses, and acrobatics, but not lately, he then had to confess that he had not been overly impressed with Master Betty, the famous boy actor. Yes, he had seen the ballet at the Opera House, but no, he was not greatly taken by that either.

'What, then, do you prefer?' she simpered at him.

'Shakespeare,' he told her, 'in particular when Kemble plays the great parts, such as Othello, Hamlet and Macbeth, but his brother Charles is also admirable in lighter roles.'

'Oh, Shakespeare!' She pouted. 'I was taken to see *Macbeth* in my come-out year. What a disappointment! Everyone was ranting at everyone else and people were being killed on stage. I wonder that anyone should pay to go to see such dreadful things.'

She ended with a delicate shudder and a widening of her blue eyes. 'On the other hand, I quite liked *As You Like It* when they made it into a pantomime. The clowns were so funny, much better than all that boring talk. Have you visited the Prince Regent's home at Brighton? They say it is most fantastic. I confess that I was greatly surprised when I was presented to him. He was so fat and ugly—and so old. I cannot abide old men and women.'

'Yes,' Russell said, 'I have visited the Pavilion and quite

like it. As for the Regent being old, I fear that, if we live long enough, we all come to that in the end.'

Angelica's shudder was a prolonged one this time. 'Pray do not let us speak of it. Tell me, have you read *The Secret of Harrenden Castle*? Now there is a horrid book which I do like—you never actually *see* the bodies in it.'

So this was the woman whom his father wished him to marry! Had he given up his lively Caroline for this vacuous young thing? He thought of his brother's wife Pandora with her frank ways and her keen interest in everything about her. Now *there* was a treasure if there ever was one, even if she were something of a surprising treasure for quiet Ritchie to have won.

Angelica, who, to give her her due, was finding it as difficult to talk to Lord Hadleigh as Lord Hadleigh was finding it difficult to listen to her, gave up at this point. Why did her papa wish her to marry this dull old man? She had imagined that he might be a jolly fellow like Perry and his friends, but no such thing. He was as solemn as a judge and as dreary as the parson on Sunday morning when he was droning on and on in his sermon.

All in all, it was a great relief for them both when the dinner ended and the ladies withdrew to leave the gentlemen to their cigars and their port. But not before Russell, the devil prompting him, had leaned sideways to whisper in Mary's pretty little ear, 'Are you finding all this as tedious as I am?'

Mary, who had been as bored by Perry as Russell had been by his sister, said sharply, 'Indeed not, and if I were it would be a gross insult to our hosts' hospitality to say so.'

Russell bowed his head and murmured, 'Rightly rebuked. You were always much more aware of the niceties of life than I was.'

'Was I, m'lord? I fear that I have quite forgot the details

of any conversations which we might once have had,' and she turned away from him to address Perry again, as though to speak to him was wearisome.

The anger which seemed to overcome Russell these days was upon him again. He murmured to her back, 'Now, madam, that I do not believe, nor should you ask me to believe it.'

Mary's head swung sharply round. 'What you might believe, m'lord, is a matter of total indifference to me. Pray allow that to terminate our conversation,' and she turned away from him again to address a bemused Perry.

'I had not understood that you were so well-acquainted with Lord Hadleigh, Mrs Wardour.'

'Once, long ago,' she replied as carelessly as she could, and, more to punish Russell than because she wished to ingratiate herself with Perry Markham, added, most graciously, 'Pray call me Mary, Mr Markham.'

'Only if you will address me as Perry,' he responded gallantly.

Angelica had found the young Honourable Thomas Bertram, known by his friends as the Hon. Tom, to be a more amusing dinner companion than Russell, who now whispered into Mary's ear, 'If we are all to be so informal, Mrs Wardour, then you might oblige me by calling me Russell—as you once did.'

She swung round again, to murmur under her breath so that Perry might not catch what she was saying, 'Certainly not, you forfeited that right long ago. Pray cease to badger me: it is not the act of a gentleman to twit a lady so mercilessly.'

Well, that was that, was it not? And Russell, who was already regretting his baiting of Mary, said slowly, 'I apologise, Mrs Wardour, but the temptation to address you as I might once have done was too great for me.'

How dare he? How dare he after he had treated her so

lightly all those years ago! Mary turned away from him for the last time, saying, 'I would be extremely happy, m'lord, if you refrained from addressing me at all,' and gave Perry her whole attention for the rest of the dinner.

She would not be drawn into conversation with him, not now, or ever again. He deserved nothing from her, and nothing was all that he would get. She had done her duty to her hosts by speaking to him at all and from this evening onward she would be careful to avoid his company.

Russell ate the rest of his dinner in silence and it might as well have been straw that he was consuming. Angelica offered him the odd word now and then, and it was a great relief when the meal ended, the ladies retired, cigars were offered, and the port began to circulate.

Talk became general, and, as Mary had earlier thought, the men being alone together it became unbuttoned. The younger men at the bottom of the table began to talk prize-fighting, their seniors, politics. Russell, caught between the two, said nothing.

Presently Perry, avoiding his father's eye, leaned forward and said to his fellows, *sub rosa*, as it were, 'To avoid the stifling dullness of the Leicestershire countryside in spring I have two diversions to offer you, gentlemen. Tomorrow a Luddite is to be hanged at Loughborough for an attempt on the life of a local mill-owner. I thought that we might make up a party and compare how these matters are organised in the country compared with those in town.

'On the following day there is to be a mill not far from here between two bruisers, both from London. One is Sam Tottridge, who gave Tom Cribb a hard time before he lost—and Tom's a tough customer, being champion of England. T'other is a man of colour, known as Yankee Samson because he comes from some godforsaken corner of the States. What say we make up another party to watch that? I'll run a book on the match if that is agreeable to you all.'

He turned to Russell, who had sat there quietly trying to make his one glass of port last until it was time to join the ladies. 'How about you, Hadleigh? Are you game?'

'Not for the hanging,' said Russell as coolly as he could in an effort not to give offence to his host's son. 'I find no pleasure in watching a man being strangled to death to the cheers of his fellows, particularly when the man in question is a poor devil who has lost his livelihood. As for the boxing match, I shall decide that on the day. I prefer to put the gloves on myself occasionally rather than applaud a man who does it for me.'

'Oh, well, suit yourself, Hadleigh. Tottridge is worth watching, believe me, and the black has a good reputation, too. As for murdering Luddites, I beg to disagree with you there. Hanging's too good for them. Not turning parson, are you?'

It was plain that Perry Markham had drunk more than he ought. Russell smiled. 'Not at all. Merely growing old, I suppose.'

'Doesn't seem to take others that way. Never mind, though. You can always stay at home with the ladies and play back-gammon and help to wind their wool for them.'

Several of Perry's hangers-on laughed sycophantically at this. Russell merely smiled, and answered him, again pleas-antly, 'What a splendid notion, Markham. I thank you for your suggestions on how to pass my time. You have, I believe, a good library, and that might serve to catch my interest.'

Several of his hearers sniggered at this, and Russell was relieved that the General ended this rather unpleasant conversation by announcing briskly, 'Time to join the ladies. They will be wondering what has become of us.'

I doubt that, thought Russell, watching the rest of the party stagger rather uncertainly towards the drawing room, although some of them might welcome our arrival to save them from boredom.

I also wonder whether Mary will be kinder to me after dinner than she was during it!

Chapter Two

Russell was among the last to arrive in the drawing room where some of the ladies were busily talking, others were playing a hand of whist, and the quieter souls were happily engaged in their canvas work, Mary Wardour among them.

There was a chair near to her and on impulse he walked towards it, and pulled it round so that he half-faced her and her companion, who was also stitching purposefully away. Thus placed, he had quite deliberately trapped her into a situation where their conversation would be so public that she would be loath to rebuke or reprimand him as she had done at dinner.

'Mrs Wardour,' he said, smiling at her.

Mary looked up at him and, despite herself, it was as though something wrenched inside her. She was a girl of seventeen again and her young lover was smiling at her: his mouth had a little curl at the end and his eyes…

She shook her head. What in the world was she thinking of? Lord Hadleigh was no longer her young lover and she had tried to forget him and all his works. Alas, here in this crowded room, surrounded by the curious, careless and the malicious, she must say and do nothing which would damage her own reputation.

'Lord Hadleigh?' she said and inclined her head.

'Mrs Wardour,' he said again, as though he were memorising her name, 'we were well-acquainted long ago, I believe, and we meet again after many years. I think that we should be doing one another a kindness if, from now on, we behaved as though we were meeting for the first time.'

Was he drunk, to make such a monstrous proposition to her? He looked and sounded sober, unlike Perry Markham, who had obviously over-indulged and was lurching into the room and now trying to avoid her, probably as the result of finding her a dull partner at dinner since she had shown no interest in racing or the delights of the London stage.

Russell Hadleigh was plainly waiting for an answer from her. What could she say to him? Not what she wished to, here in public, that was for sure. To have exclaimed, 'Go away and cease to trouble me,' would certainly set society's tongues a-wagging, and no mistake!

Instead she said, as coolly as she could. 'If that is what you wish, m'lord, it would only be civil of me to agree to such a polite request.'

'Splendid,' was Russell's answer to this rather cold concession. He leaned forward a little confidentially, adding as he did so, 'Then if I proposed that we should take a circuit of the picture gallery together, you would not refuse me, I trust. I understand that you have visited Markham Hall before and would surely be qualified to show its treasures to me.'

'I, m'lord?' Mary could not help replying. 'Would it not be more appropriate for you to ask Miss Markham to display the family treasures? After all, I gather that she is the real reason you are here.'

Good God! Had rumour already given Angelica Markham to him as a bride? Rumour also said that Mary Wardour had been invited for Perry Markham's sake. Was that as false as the one relating to Angelica? If he had been dubious about making her Lady Hadleigh before he had met her, now that he had, any dubiety he had previously experienced had been reinforced: he had not the slightest intention of marrying the girl. He was only too happy that the moment the Hon. Tom Bertram had arrived in the drawing room Angelica had made a dead set at him. They were each well suited to the other.

'Oh,' he said, as carelessly as he could, 'you should take no note of gossip of that nature. I am here—why am I here?' he continued. 'I am not quite sure, but looking for a bride is far from my mind at the moment,' and he gave her his most dazzling smile again, a smile which poor Mary remembered only too well.

'Nor am I looking for a husband,' returned Mary shrewdly, for she knew full well why she had been invited and Perry Markham was certainly not to her taste.

Miss Truman, who had been listening to their odd conversation with some interest, now took a hand in it.

'I think, my dear,' she said to Mary, a light note in her voice, 'that it would only be proper to introduce me to Lord Hadleigh, seeing that you have had such a long acquaintance with him.'

Now, what to say to that? was Mary's somewhat frantic thought. She could scarcely tell her companion the unhappy truth of her first acquaintance with Russell, who had now risen to his feet, waiting for the introduction which would inevitably follow.

The rapport between him and Mary, once so strong, but now almost forgotten, was strongly revived. He grasped that she was somewhat overset by her companion's innocently made remark and, however badly she might have treated him in the past, he had no desire to embarrass her in the present.

He bowed to both women. 'My friendship with Mrs Wardour was long ago, when we were little more than children. We have, alas, seen nothing of one another for many years, until this very day.'

Mary and Miss Truman both rose on that, and Mary, thankful for Russell's intervention, if for nothing else, did the pretty by making her companion known to him.

'I believe, m'lord,' Miss Truman said, 'that I had the honour, some years ago, of being for a short time the companion of your brother Richard's wife, then Miss Pandora Compton. Circumstances parted us and we lost touch. I trust that she is in health.'

'Very much so. She is now the mother of a lively and handsome boy.'

'Which does not surprise me,' Miss Truman said, 'since my dear Pandora is both lively and handsome herself.'

Russell gave a smile of such pleasure on hearing this that Mary was bitten by a sudden sharp and unwanted pang. What in the world would make her indulge in such folly as being jealous of the unknown Pandora Chancellor? she asked herself furiously. Lord Hadleigh could compliment the whole female sex and bed whom he chose. It was no business of hers if he admired his brother's wife. But, alas, it seemed it still was, since she was being weak-minded enough to allow him to charm her all over again. It was as though thirteen years had never passed.

'Indeed,' he replied, serious now.

'And I am sure that my dear Mary would be happy to show you the picture gallery. She is extremely knowledgeable about such matters. You could not have a better guide.'

It was quite plain to both her hearers that Miss Truman was busy matchmaking. She had already decided that Perry Markham was not a person whom she could recommend her employer to marry. Lord Hadleigh, now, was quite a different matter. Not only was he handsome, but she had already been informed that he had been decent enough to refuse to join the party which was attending the hanging on the morrow while, on the other hand, the wretched Perry was the ringleader in the unhappy affair.

As for Mary, after such a recommendation from Miss Truman, she had no choice but to agree to Russell Hadleigh's wish to have her as his escort and the pair of them rose to carry out Miss Truman's bidding.

The eyes of most of the room watched them leave it. Later, General Markham was to say fiercely to his son when he cornered him in his room, 'You must know how essential it is that you offer for Mary Wardour. Most of our problems would be solved by such a marriage. But instead of fixing your sights on her, you fool about with a pack of young men whom you have brought here against my wishes. As a result of that, you have allowed Hadleigh to corner her when I wished to fix his interest on Angelica. Do you wish to live permanently in Queer Street?'

Perry hissed back at his father, 'May I remind you, sir, that it was not I who lost the family's money by gambling on Boney winning at Waterloo, but it is I who will have to pay for it by marrying a blue-stocking of a widow who is older than I am and has no interest in any of the things which amuse me.'

'Delay much longer in offering for her,' his father exclaimed, trying to goad his son into doing as he wished, 'and the whole world will soon know that we are bankrupt. So far I have been successful in staving off ruin, but my creditors are growing weary of waiting for pay day.

'As for her lack of interest in your idle life, what has that to do with not wishing to marry her? Get her with an heir or two and you and she may go your own separate ways. No need to wish to play Romeo and Juliet together. After all, I am the heir to my cousin, Viscount Bulcote, and since, unfortunately, he is as poor as a church mouse, too, we have no salvation there. On the other hand, Mrs Wardour might care to be called Lady Bulcote—if Russell Hadleigh hasn't snapped her up first.'

Russell Hadleigh wasn't snapping anyone up, least of all Mary Wardour. In fact, he wasn't sure exactly what he was about. He had told himself to avoid her, that he had nothing more to say to her, nor could she have anything to say to him, and yet, when dinner was over, the mere sight of her had set him mooning after her as though he had been twenty again!

Once they were out of the room and in the vast Entrance Hall, one door of which led to the picture gallery, Mary turned to him and said in the frostiest tones she could summon up. 'You can really have little wish to spend the next half-hour in my company inspecting paintings about which you must care little. May I suggest that we part—possibly to return to our suites and then, after a decent interval, to the drawing room.'

'Indeed not,' was his answer to that. 'Not only do I have no wish to return to the drawing room, other than in your company, but I do wish to see the General's paintings. I missed the Grand Tour because of the war, my Oxford education was ended prematurely for a reason of which you are well aware, and, as I grow older, I have become determined to fix my interest on other pursuits than gambling, drinking and attending race meetings and boxing mills. An idle life is beginning to tire me.'

Whatever could he mean by speaking of his education ending prematurely for a reason which she well knew? Had he not ended it himself when he had abandoned her so cruelly?

She was about to tell him that in no uncertain terms when something about him stopped her. The empathy for her which Russell had experienced a little while ago—that memory of their lost happy time together—now overcame her. Whatever else, she knew that he was not lying to her. After all these years he wanted her company. Not only that, his interest in the paintings was genuine, not a trick to enable him to begin deceiving her all over again.

'Very well, since you put it so movingly, Lord Hadleigh, I will do as you ask. You must, however, remember your request that we meet as strangers and practise a self-denying ordinance, as the saying has it. Refer to the past again—however remotely—and I will leave you at once.'

'So noted,' he replied in a comic parody of a clerk registering the commands of his superior, and again it was as though the years had rolled back and he was teasing her as he had done then. 'Lead on, Mrs Wardour. You may begin my education.'

He had not been lying to her when he had said that he wished to see the contents of the picture gallery, or else he was a superb actor. He showed a keen interest in the paintings, which ranged from a fourteenth-century panel of the Madonna and Child by a pupil of Duccio to the latest works of the

English masters. Lawrence had painted the General himself and they debated briefly whether he deserved to stand alongside the great masters of the past.

'Reynolds, perhaps, or Gainsborough at his best may merit such an honour,' was Russell's verdict, 'but Lawrence is an extremely competent journeyman, no more.'

'I think that you know more about painting, Lord Hadleigh, than you suggested earlier.'

'That is my brother Ritchie's influence,' he confessed. 'He is a gifted water-colourist—but then he is a gifted everything, unlike his slightly older brother.'

There was no bitterness in Russell's words, nor in his voice, but there was something there which told Mary not of envy or of jealousy, but of a certain wistfulness, of something missed and lost.

'I have not had the good fortune to meet your brother,' Mary said, surprised at how easy talking to Russell had become. 'I remember that he went to Oxford a few years before you when I was still little more than a child.

'Oh, few people have met him. He resigned from the Army after Waterloo in order to restore the estate which had been left him while he was still a serving officer. He spends most of his time in the country and visits London rarely. As for Oxford, he was excessively precocious and was only fifteen when he matriculated. My father also thought it best that we did not attend there at the same time.'

Again there was that odd note when he referred to his brother. A mixture of pride and something else, hard to judge.

By now they had completed their tour. Russell motioned to a long sofa which stood in front of one of the glories of the collection: a Tintoretto showing the god Jupiter in the shape of a bull abducting Io. The sky above them was a miracle of colour.

Once seated, Russell stared at the painting and a thought which was difficult to resist popped into his head. *I ought to have behaved like Jupiter all those years ago and carried Mary off before she had time to change her mind about me. Had I done so, we should not now be sitting primly side by side—and like Ritchie I might be starting a little family of my own.*

What would happen if I tried to kiss her now—which would be much less than Jupiter did to Io, of course—but it would serve for a new beginning with her. Merely to sit by her has my unrepentant body behaving as though I am twenty again.

No, I must not! I promised to behave myself, and behave myself I will.

Mary, seated beside him, her hands in her lap, and her mind a whirl of conflicting sensations, was also affected by the painting's subject. She tried to drive both memory and desire from her. In an effort to banish the unwanted feelings which were beginning to overwhelm her, she turned towards Russell in order to say something banal to him which would return her wandering senses to their proper condition of calm self-control.

She began to speak.

Only to discover that Russell was also turning to her and also beginning to speak.

What they were about to say was never to be known.

As many times before in their lost past when they had found themselves similarly afflicted, they began to laugh. Laughter released them from the unnatural state in which they had been living since they had found one another again.

Russell gave a little cry, something between a moan and

an exclamation of exaltation, and put one arm around her. With the other he tipped her face towards him and began to kiss her on the lips. Mary responded by kissing him ardently back. The kiss, which had, at first, been a gentle one, began to change its nature and ascend into passion. That, and their sudden unwanted recollection that they were in a public room where they might be discovered by their fellow guests at any moment, ended the kiss abruptly and left them staring into each other's eyes aghast.

Laughter and passion had alike flown away.

'Forgive me,' said Russell hoarsely.

'I cannot forgive myself, let alone you,' Mary said breathlessly. 'Whatever possessed me to make me start kissing you back? No, do not speak of the past,' she went on, 'I see by your expression that you are about to.'

Well, that was true enough, particularly since the present had become unbearable. It was a long time since merely the presence of a woman had roused Russell so rapidly. Even with Caroline true passion had been missing—something which explained why their relationship had deteriorated so rapidly.

He thought of Ritchie's eyes following Pandora around the room: his rapt expression when she had been cuddling their child. He cursed himself. What was the matter with him that Ritchie and his doings seemed to exist as some kind of reproach to his own empty existence?

Mary saw his face change and, before she could stop herself, put a hand on his arm.

'What is it, Russell? What troubles you?'

'Nothing,' he said abruptly. 'Only that I am selfish to tease you so, and to jump on you just now, without warning. Whatever could you think of me?'

Honesty won, as it usually did with Mary. 'I thought how much I was enjoying being jumped on. I suppose that means that I wasn't really thinking of anything at all. Until I remembered our situation.'

Russell began to laugh and his body began to behave itself. He remembered that one of the reasons why he had loved Mary was her transparent honesty—which made her subsequent behaviour so surprising.

'You did not find me repellent, then?'

Truth won again. 'No, I never did.'

The smile which she gave him served to set his recovering body on edge once more.

This would never do. Russell rose, put out his right hand, said, 'Allow me,' and lifted her. 'Is it your wish that I escort you to the drawing room?'

Before Mary could answer him, the door to the gallery was opened by Perry Markham, followed by the Hon. Tom Bertram and a giggling Angelica.

Perry made straight for them, saying, his voice lurching like his walk, 'We have come to see what could be occupying you so. Not the paintings apparently, Hadleigh, since you had your back to them.'

'On the contrary,' said Russell, raising the quizzing glass which he rarely used and inspecting Perry through it. 'I have been admiring your Duccio, a very rare specimen that, and the Tintoretto behind me. That, too, is a nonpareil, or so both my brother and Mrs Wardour assure me. For my part, I prefer something less showy, like the tiny Watteau—a great favourite of yours, I dare swear.'

Perry goggled at him. Dutch O, What HO, and Tint O—whoever he was! What in the world was the fellow spouting about? Perry Markham might be the heir to rooms full of rare paintings, but he knew nothing about any of them.

'You see how well Mrs Wardour has been instructing me,' continued Russell sweetly, using all the charm for which he was justly famous. 'Pray do tell me, which is *your* favourite painting? I would be delighted to inspect it.'

Perry gazed wildly around the room before pointing at a Fragonard oil of a pretty courtesan and saying, 'Oh, that, I suppose.'

'Really,' teased Russell, swinging around and bringing his glass to bear on it. 'I can't read the painter's name from here. Do tell me who he is.'

Perry continued to goggle helplessly at him. Mary, to save the poor wretch from further embarrassment, said helpfully, 'It's by Fragonard and its title is *Girl with One Slipper*.'

The Hon. Tom, not so fuddled as his host's son, exclaimed, 'I like it, but it's a trifle warm, is it not? Shouldn't be hung where the ladies can see it.'

'Really!' exclaimed a tittering Angelica, who was behaving as though she, too, had spent the evening drinking, 'Do let me look,' and she swayed over to the painting, past the amused Russell and inspected it closely.

'It looks quite ordinary,' she announced disappointedly.

Mary, whose attempt to spare Perry from Russell's naughtiness had backfired badly, and who was determined to reprimand him in private for roasting the poor ignoramus so mercilessly, announced, 'Oh, dear, Lord Hadleigh, I am most dreadfully thirsty. I should imagine that by now lemonade and other light refreshments will be being served.'

'Quite so,' agreed the Hon. Tom. 'We came here to get away from them.'

Russell, bent towards her and put out a gallant arm. 'Allow me, Mrs Wardour. I, too, feel in need of light refreshments. I have no wish to be overset by the heavy.'

'Stop it,' Mary hissed furiously into his ear when she took his arm. 'I am having difficulty in keeping a straight face while you engage in your nonsense—and he is our host's son.'

'Delighted to oblige you,' Russell almost carolled, so pleased was he that Mary was at last treating him as a fellow human being and not an obstruction in her path. 'You must continue to instruct me in proper conduct during the remainder of my stay here, most improving, exactly what I need.'

'Did he really mean that?' asked a baffled Angelica when Russell and Mary had disappeared through the door. She was the only one who had heard Russell's reply to Mary. Fortunately, she had not heard Mary's remark which had provoked it.

'Mean what?' asked Perry, who was now fuddled in a double sense. Firstly through the amount he had drunk and secondly through Russell's nonsense about painting and artists.

'About Mrs Wardour instructing him.'

Perry shook his head—and then wished he hadn't. He thought that it might be about to fall off. The Hon. Tom, who was uneducated, but not a fool, said slowly, 'He didn't mean any of it. He was roasting us.'

'Was he, by God!' exclaimed Perry making a staggering run for the door. 'I'll teach him what's what and no mistake.'

'No, you won't,' said the Hon. Tom. 'In the condition you're in he'd make mincemeat of you. They say he's as good with the gloves, the foils and the pistols as that brother of his. Besides, you'd only be proclaiming that he'd riled you. Refuse him the satisfaction. What's more, your pa wouldn't like it.'

'Pa never likes anything Perry does,' offered Angelica helpfully.

'There!' said the Hon. Tom. 'Leave it. You'll have forgotten everything by morning, I dare swear.'

'He always has done before,' was Angelica's brutal finale
to the whole unhappy encounter. Did they really want her to
marry someone who spent his time admiring paintings?

Which, if Mary and Russell had heard her, would have had
them agreeing that it was the most sensible thing anyone by
the name of Markham had said, or thought, all night!

'That was really exceedingly naughty of you,' Mary told
Russell reprovingly, once they were safely out of the picture
gallery. 'You must have gathered by now what a nodcock
Perry Markham is, but there was no need to have made a fool
of him quite so mercilessly.'

'No?' replied Russell, haughty eyebrows raised. 'He began
the whole wretched business by jeering at me and mocking
me, most mercilessly, after dinner for not wishing to see that
poor wretch hanged tomorrow. I was only giving him a taste
of his own medicine—and before two others, not before the
entire assembled men of the company. I consider that he got
off lightly—but I promise not to do it again if it distressed you.'

'And you really are not going to watch the hanging
tomorrow?'

'By no means. I take no pleasure in behaving like the
ancient Romans in the Colosseum who cheerfully watched
gladiators slaughter one another, even if I do admire their
architecture and their writings. By the by, I hope that none of
the ladies will be in the party, although I suspect that quite a
number of women will be present.'

Mary shuddered. 'It is bad enough speaking about it without being there. Will all the men be going?'

'Most, I suspect. But let us speak of more pleasant things before we rejoin the others.'

'Indeed. There is one question which I should dearly like to ask you, and that is, did you ever meet Lord Byron before he started out on his travels again?'

'Several times. I heard him make his speech in the Lords on behalf of the hand-loom weavers who were losing their livelihood because of the new machines. I thought it very fine. I also think it is a great pity that he never bent his energies more towards politics than pleasure. After all, he is his own man, unlike others who have their choices made for them. I agree that he writes some immortal poetry, but his private life of unbridled pleasure does not bear inspection. I gather that now he is in Europe he still mixes writing divine poetry with living a sybaritic life.'

How easy, Mary mused later, while retiring for the night, it had been for them to fall back into the half-serious, half-jesting mode of conversation which they had enjoyed before their affair had come to its sorry end. There was no doubt that their minds worked in harmony. Earlier that evening Miss Truman had commented that Lord Hadleigh had the reputation of being a lightweight in life and love.

After talking with him again, Mary thought that she was wrong. She was, however, gaining the impression that something was awry in Russell Hadleigh's life, and that he envied his younger twin, Ritchie, not only for his happy marriage but for having a settled aim and career. He must also have watched Ritchie achieve a certain amount of justly earned fame for his exploits as a soldier, leaving the Army with the rank of colonel and a reputation for courage and enterprise.

She shook her head. Why should she waste her time thinking about the problems of her one-time lover, however much, if truth were told, he still attracted her?

But the past was the past and must remain dead. A thought which she took to bed with her after reading a little of one of Mr 'Monk' Lewis's lurid romances, a Tale of Terror called *Feudal Tyrants*. Mary had a passion for such novels, which had shocked her husband whose taste in literature was fixed on the arid and the philosophical. He considered it to be her one weakness.

Whether it was Mr Lewis's vivid descriptions of past times which excited her brain, or whether it was meeting Russell Hadleigh again that did the damage Mary could not decide on the following morning. Whichever it was, during the night—was it in a dream?—she found herself walking in the gardens of her father's home in Oxford. She was seventeen again and beside her was a handsome young man who had arrived that morning to be her father's pupil.

Dr Beauregard was not one of Oxford's official dons, but he was a mathematician with a European-wide reputation and it was a habit of some of the professors to send their brighter pupils to him for further training.

'I am expecting a new young man this morning, Mary,' her father had earlier told her, 'so I am afraid that you must forgo your work with me today. Wilkinson thinks that he has a very good mind and would profit from spending some time in my company. What is surprising about him is that he is a young nobleman—it is not often that they display such rarefied talents, although one must not forget Henry Cavendish, of course.'

He was, Mary knew, referring to Henry Cavendish, the grandson of the second Duke of Devonshire, who had made some remarkable discoveries in chemistry.

'No, Father,' she replied, teasing him gently. 'No, I promise not to forget Henry Cavendish.'

He fixed her with a stern eye. 'See that you do not, my dear. Knowledge must always be treasured and never lost. The young man to whom I have referred is the heir of the Earl of Bretford. His name is Russell, Lord Hadleigh, so you must address him as m'lord. He has a courtesy Viscountcy, I understand. I think, that after I have assessed him today, it is likely that you may both profit from taking your lessons together with me. We shall see.'

Lord Hadleigh! What a delightful name. It was like those in the Tales of Terror which her father grudgingly allowed her to read. 'All work and no play makes Jane a dull girl,' he had said once.

Well, she wouldn't be a dull girl with Lord Hadleigh as a fellow pupil—although whether she would enjoy taking her lessons with him was quite another thing! She had learned— to her distress—that if she ever told anyone, male or female, of any age, that her papa was teaching her advanced mathematics and that delightful piece of arcane mystery, calculus, they were sure to look at her as though she had sprouted two heads.

Aunt Charlotte Beauregard had once told her never, ever, to let any young man know how clever she was, for that was sure to end any chance of marriage for her. Years later, Mary learned that an extremely clever mathematician and geometer named Annabelle Milbanke had succeeded in marrying Lord Byron despite that; but since the marriage had proved to be an absolute disaster, perhaps Aunt Charlotte had been right.

At the time of Lord Hadleigh's arrival, however, such warnings troubled Mary not at all. When their maid, Polly, arrived in her room to tell her that her papa wanted to see her in his study downstairs, Mary had run down eagerly, knocked on the study door and found her papa seated behind his desk. A tall young man was standing facing him.

He turned and bowed when Mary entered. She was immediately struck dumb at the sight of him. He was so extraordinarily handsome: a cross between the statues of the young Hercules and the God Apollo who stood in the entrance hall of the Beauregards' home.

But Russell, Lord Hadleigh, possessed one great advantage over them:
he was warm flesh and blood, not cold stone. He had fair waving hair—he had removed his mortar-board with its nobleman's gold tassel when she had entered—and bright blue eyes above his classically handsome face.

Her father was saying something: introducing him, no doubt. Mary curtsied in a kind of daze. She thought that he was informing m'lord that he and she were to study together with him and, if so, how would she ever be able to say anything sensible before such masculine perfection?

It was almost as though he knew how overthrown she was, for he was saying in a voice as beautiful as he was, 'I am delighted to meet your daughter, Dr Beauregard. It is rare to find such intellect as she must possess and such beauty combined in one person,' and he bowed to her at the end of his speech.

'No doubt,' said her father drily, 'but, if you are to study together, looks must give place to diligence and, dare I say it, inspiration. Mathematics needs that as much as poetry or painting.'

Lord Hadleigh nodded solemnly. 'Indeed, sir, and it shall be a pleasure to try to discover it from your teaching.'

That was the beginning. Lord Hadleigh was to arrive on the following morning for an hour's teaching for as many weeks as her father cared to instruct him. He was not so advanced as Mary was, but it was amazing, she thought, how quickly he caught her up. He did not pass her. They cantered together along the paths which earlier mathematicians had laid down for them. Isaac Newton was Dr Beauregard's God. Once he had hoped to surpass him. Now he devoted his life to trying to find someone who might overtop even Newton.

The morning of Mary's walk with Lord Hadleigh he had rubbed his eyes halfway through the lesson and exclaimed, 'At the rate we are progressing I fear that the pupils may yet outclass the master. Perhaps that is not surprising: after all, Newton was a very young man when he had his most original ideas. Mary, my love, I grow tired. Take Lord Hadleigh on a tour of the gardens; by the time you return I shall doubtless be refreshed.'

When she recalled this detail of her dream Mary grasped, for the first time, that her father was beginning to succumb to the illness which was, in due course, to carry him away from her forever. In her dream, though, which was not really a dream but time recalled, she thought nothing of this, only that she would be alone with her new friend.

He was, however, already more than a friend. They had sometimes been playfully naughty in their supposedly serious discussions with her father. At first he had reprimanded them; later he had encouraged them, for in it he could see forming the inspiration which had left him, but which he hoped he was passing on to them. So, on that late spring morning, walking in the garden, something more than scholastic inspiration was beginning to pass between the pretty seventeen-year-old girl and the handsome twenty-year-old boy.

They walked down a pleached alley to a herb garden, where later all the scents of summer would fill the air, but which, like the pair of them at present, only offered hints of a beautiful maturity.

Lord Hadleigh duly admired everything, although an older Mary ruefully knew that her father's garden was but a miniature of those gardens he must have known which surrounded his father's great country houses.

They looked into one another's eyes. Russell, for so she was coming to think of him, was not innocent. He had already learned the delights which came from pleasuring women—and being pleasured by them. But Mary was, and knowing that he went slowly with her. Not only had he no wish to seduce his tutor's daughter, but he was beginning to care for her for her own sake. Such charming innocence, allied to such remarkable learning, was not to be besmirched. Both were to be respected.

So he sat by her on a rustic bench and they talked together of small things. She asked him what it was like to belong to a family since she was an only child whose mother had died young.

'A large family?' he replied, and there was a note in his voice similar to that which sounded when the older and more disillusioned Russell Hadleigh spoke of his brother and of his sister, long married to a Scots laird and long lost to him. 'My father is not what is known as a family man, you understand. Ritchie and I were friends when we were boys, but he saw fit to part us when we grew older. Twins should not be over-dependent on one another, he said, but must learn to live alone in the world.'

'I would wish to have had a sister, or a brother,' she told him. 'Someone to whom I could talk freely.' She gave him a shy glance. 'As freely as I find that I can talk to you.'

Something happened to Russell then, she was sure. For his face grew shuttered and what he then said surprised her at the time, although later she understood, or thought that she understood his unspoken meaning. 'I do not wish to be your brother.'

This declaration, she remembered, saddened her a little at the time, but she continued to talk to him. He had a dog at home, he told her, one Rufus, which had grown old and which he had left behind when he came to Oxford.

'Father will not allow me to have a dog or a cat,' she said sadly. 'He does not approve of pets. He calls it light-minded to wish for one.'

'And you do wish for one?'

'Yes, very much.' She wanted to add, I should not feel so lonely, but thought that it might be weak-minded of her to confess such a thing.

'If I were your papa,' he said, smiling at her, 'I would allow you to have any kind of pet you wanted. A bird, perhaps. Ritchie had a parrot until it died of old age. Being Ritchie, he taught it to speak a little.'

'How kind you are,' she told him, before looking at the little watch which hung from her waist. 'I think that it is time that we returned. Papa considers punctuality to be one of the great virtues. He says that most females do not treasure it.'

'Nor most males, either,' returned Russell, which set her laughing and saying,

'You see, that is what a kind brother would say.'

Mary did not remember exactly what had happened on that long-ago spring afternoon, only that it was the start of something which in the end became more than friendship, more than the love of brother and sister, but which ultimately became more powerful and dangerous than either.

Now, older and wiser, she contemplated the day ahead. The women of the party, deserted by their men, had arranged to visit a neighbour who had recently improved his gardens. Rumour claimed that they were magnificent, including not only a cataract tumbling down an artificial hill, but also not one, but three, follies.

I'm not really in the mood for follies, Mary thought. Instead I'll cry off and spend a quiet day in the library with my chess set for company. I grow tired of female small talk. Once there she could hide away from everything, including a past whose happiness had not yet been touched by pain.

Chapter Three

Russell Hadleigh yawned and put down his book. The morning was not yet half-gone. He had arrived down to a late breakfast to find that, for once, the other men in the house party had forestalled him. They were all agog and all eager to be off to the hanging. Thinking of it certainly wasn't putting them off their fodder, the Honourable Thomas told Russell a trifle gloomily.

'Put you off yours, has it?' asked Russell, contemplating the Honourable Thomas's half-empty plate.

'Doesn't do to say so,' was the rueful reply. 'A fellow's supposed to look forward to such things. I'd cry off if I could, but they'd all jeer at me for being lily-livered.'

'Well, by that I am lily-livered,' said Russell. 'For, as you know, I've no intention of joining the party.'

'Well, you're Hadleigh, Bretford's heir, and even if Perry does come on a bit strong with you, you're grand enough to do as you please. I'm only a wretched younger son, tolerated because I'm one of the crowd who makes up the numbers. Doesn't do to offend—though I suppose I might kick over the traces one day.'

Enter assorted gentlemen, thought Russell, remembering the instructions in various stage plays: courtiers and hangers-on of the great, the rich and the powerful. He shivered a little. I suppose that I have them, too—or would if I liked the notion of a crowd of sycophants walking around me all day. He disliked the thought: it was yet another thing which Ritchie didn't have to trouble about since he was a younger son who did have money—but not enough to attract the parasites.

'So there it is,' moaned the Hon. Tom dolefully, adding another slice of ham to his plate. 'What will you do while we are junketing?'

'Read a little, walk a little, ride a little: admire the scenery.'

'Leicestershire doesn't have scenery,' said the Hon. Tom. 'It only has countryside. Countryside ain't scenery.'

With this last remark he wandered off towards where Perry was holding court: something which he would not be able to do if his father were to be gazetted bankrupt.

Really, Russell thought gloomily, all that he was doing at Markham Hall was practising idleness in different surroundings from those he was used to.

His valet fetched him nuncheon some time after noon, and he ate it in his room, looking out over the park and towards some low hills in the distance.

I am becoming solitary. I think I'll go and be solitary in the library.

Yes, the library *was* solitary. Not a soul was in it. It was a typical gentleman's collection, he saw, his eyes roving along the shelves and his hands thrust in his pockets. He was bored with himself and, to that degree, was bored with life—until he reached the table in the window.

On it stood a small and exquisite chessboard, whose finely wrought miniature men were set out as though in the middle of a game. On one side of it was a pile of unused paper, on the other, another, smaller pile on which had been written lines of what appeared to be mathematical symbols.

Intrigued, Russell picked them up and studied them. It soon became plain to him, although it would not have done to many, that the symbols were the complete record of the game on the board until it had been abandoned for the time being.

The piece that was being studied on the last page was the white knight, and the calculations on the paper showed all the different consequences of moving it from its present position on the board—and the consequences for all the other pieces if each possible move it could make was analysed!

Russell could not prevent himself from picking up a clean sheet of paper and the pencil which had been left on the table and begin to list the further changes which followed on from those on the last sheet of paper. He was so absorbed in this task that he did not hear the door open and someone enter.

A cool voice said in his ear, 'Pray, what are you doing with my work, m'lord?'

Russell started up. It was Mary standing beside him, Mary who had left the chessboard in the library, secure in the knowledge that no one would visit it, or, if they did, would stare goggle-eyed and uncomprehendingly at both the board and her papers.

'Nothing,' he said, his mind still on the ramifications of the latest move. 'I am merely doing my own work—and not interfering with yours.'

She gave a little laugh which was neither kind, nor unkind, but neutral. 'Then you haven't forgotten our numbers since we worked together with my father.'

'Indeed not, Mary, although I own I am a little rusty—but the rust is fast disappearing as I begin to work with them again. And pray call me Russell as you used to when we last played with numbers.'

'I was not playing with numbers today, *m'lord*, I was working with them.'

Mary's stress on the word *m'lord* was slow and deliberate. This troubled Russell not at all. Since he had sat down in front of the chess board something had happened to him, something which he had not felt for years. He felt not only liberated, but full of a sense of power, of achievement. The ennui which had marred his recent life had disappeared. He felt himself equal to anything.

'Nor am I playing with numbers today, Mary. I am fascinated by what you have been doing, which is, I suppose, trying to work out a logical means of countering every move your opponent makes in a real game. That, if you could succeed, would be an achievement worthy of Newton or Pascal themselves. I have, in my own small way, been trying to see if I could join you in your exercise.'

His face was so eager, so alight with interest that for a moment time disappeared and they were boy and girl in her father's study again. Time re-ordered itself, but the effect of that brief spasm was to set Mary answering him as she would have done then.

'Perhaps you would allow me to examine your work, Russell?'

Russell! He had seen the slight quiver that had passed across her face before she answered him—and then she had called him Russell! He had said, or done, something which had unwittingly restored some of the rapport which they had once shared.

'Willingly,' he said, and handed her the sheets of paper which he had filled with his calculations.

Mary sat down beside him and began to inspect them. Presently she laid the papers carefully down on the table and looked at him for a long moment before saying slowly, 'How long did it take you to do that, Russell—I mean, m'lord? I have only been absent a short time—' She stopped and shook her head.

Russell was suddenly overwhelmed by a great sense of anticlimax. He took Mary's shaking head to mean that she was disappointed by what he had done. The feeling was the more acute because he thought that what he had written down was worthwhile, the logical conclusion of her own calculations.

'I'm sorry,' he said humbly, 'if what I have just done was all a nonsense. It is a long time since I did any serious work with numbers…' Mary, her eyes shining, had put her hand on his arm to stop him from explaining himself.

'Not at all,' she exclaimed. 'If you haven't done anything like this lately then what you have accomplished here is re-markable. I could not have done all this in twice the time. It is an area where you always surpassed me in the past. I was better at looking at the principles involved, you were more ac-complished with the detail. That is why Father said that we made such a good team: our strengths differed.'

She was speaking with all the eagerness of the girl who had sat by him in her father's study. It was as though for Russell, too, that time had returned. He leaned forward, sharing her eagerness, saying, 'You really mean that, Mary? You are not deceiving me to keep me in countenance?'

'Not at all. Oh, if we could only work together again… what could we not do.' Now it was her turn to stop briefly, before saying, 'Forgive me. I am talking nonsense. You have a life of your own and we parted for good long ago.'

He wanted to say, I have no life which holds any meaning. Instead, without thinking, he took the hand which she had used to check him earlier and kissed it.

'Tell me the ultimate of what you are trying to do, Mary, and perhaps, while we are at Markham Hall, we might find time to work together again.' She made no attempt to resist him, but the light which had filled her face and make her look almost a child again was gradually fading.

Mary said sorrowfully, 'You know full well, m'lord, why we may not do that. Any opportunity we once had to work together disappeared long ago.'

'That was then, Mary, this is now.'

Russell's ardour was all the greater because the strange combination of mathematics, the presence of Mary, and the notion that they could be together again, was having a profoundly erotic effect on him. He knew that most men and women would be amused by the notion that anything so dry, so abstract, as the higher mathematics could rouse a man as he was now roused!

Later he was to tell himself that power, and the sense of power, is an aphrodisiac, and if excelling at playing games with numbers made him feel powerful, then it was neither strange nor unnatural, but only to be expected, that he should become roused. When, added to all that, the woman who was with him was, in her quiet way, as beautiful as she was clever, it was no wonder that his breathing had begun to shorten dramatically.

He was a boy again and the world was opening up before him as it had done then.

'You have just said that you were favourably impressed by what I have already done—how much more, then, could we not do if we worked together? Before we do, however, I think that we ought to play one another at chess. I have to confess that it is many years since I last engaged in a game.'

The sad truth was that after Mary had left him the mere sight of a chess board had been enough to distress him. They had played so many happy games together, encouraged by her father who thought that the brain was excited by it: that it acted as a form of inspiration.

What to say? He looked so eager, so pathetically eager, and if the truth were told she was remembering that the game which had once been such a source of pleasure to her had become just another chore, an intellectual puzzle to be solved. To sit opposite to him again would be like revisiting her lost girlhood. On the other hand, if she allowed him to tempt her into giving way on this, was she simply paving the way for yet another piece of treachery on his part?

Why she agreed to play against him Mary never knew.

'Very well, but it will only be one game, I am not promising anything more than that.'

It *was* a surrender, though, and they both knew that it was.

'Allow me to record the state of the current game first,' she said and, taking his answer for granted, rapidly wrote it down before rearranging the pieces.

'You may have white,' he said, once the pieces were rearranged.

'Indeed, not,' said Mary haughtily. 'I want no favours from you.'

Russell laughed. 'How that takes me back. I remember that you never did. Shall we let chance settle the matter?' He took a coin from his pocket and saying 'Heads or tails? I say heads,' he prepared to toss it up.

'No,' said Mary, laughing across at him as she had done so long ago. 'Allow me to inspect the coin first. I seem to remember that you had two and one of them possessed two heads and the other two tails. You played that trick on me once, but never again.'

'Oh, ye of little faith,' Russell grinned back at her and threw the coin to her. 'It is a good one and you may do the tossing. Am I right to trust you?'

Oh, yes, it was just like the old days when laughter and banter had filled their time together after the hard work of study was over.

Mary said reprovingly, 'You know that I never cheated you. There,' and she tossed the coin up, caught it on the palm of one hand and covered it with the palm of her other.

The smile she gave him when she exclaimed, 'Now, Lord Hadleigh, which is it? Heads or tails?' nearly destroyed him.

'Tails,' he finally achieved.

'Tails it is,' she announced, lifting her hand. 'Why is it that you always win, even when you are not cheating me?'

He could not prevent himself from saying, now suddenly sober, 'Now Mary, you know as well as I do, that I did not always win.'

Either she did not take his meaning—that she had ended their affair and married another—or she preferred not to. She swung the board around to give him the white pieces and said quite simply, 'Let the battle begin.'

That, too, was said in memory of the old days and with the same calm amusement which she had used then. It was for her beautiful quiet that he had always loved her. He had been a noisy boy—unlike Ritchie—and he was fascinated by her calm self-control and wished that he possessed it.

Time and the passing years had sobered him, and he was not sure that it had been for the better. Meeting Mary again, though, had revived some of his old exuberance, his zest for life, the sense that anything was possible for him if only he put his mind to it.

'Prepare to be dealt with as the Romans dealt with Hannibal,' he announced grandly, 'particularly as you have no elephants.'

'But I have knights instead,' and she moved the Black one—to which Russell countered with his White—and battle was fairly joined.

The afternoon flew by. Early on someone—who?—looked in on them and retreated at the sight of their rapt faces, at the fair head and the dark bent over the board.

Once Russell raised his head to stare into Mary's eyes. 'You are bamming me,' he said accusingly as she moved a minor pawn. 'What the devil—if I may be so frank—did you do that for?'

'Since you read my notes you should know exactly why—and the devil had little to do with it.'

Oh, but he had, thought Russell a few moves later. He desperately wanted to win this game. To prove what? That he might have lost to her years ago, but he could not lose now—although it seemed likely that he was just about to do exactly that.

And then he saw a way out of his dilemma when he was on the point of being mated. Mated! There was a double meaning there, was there not? Mate in chess meant death—but in life it meant the possibility of birth. Which one was this? And if he were not to win, for he could not, might he not force a draw and in the doing hold both death and life in balance: the perfect equilibrium! He moved his White knight for the last time.

'Stalemate!' he announced triumphantly.

And so it was.

Neither of them had won—or lost.

The perfect ending.

Mary did not think so. 'That was not supposed to happen,' she exclaimed, indignant for once. 'I must have made an error in my calculations.'

'Ah,' said Russell, laughter on his face. 'But then you were playing yourself, not me. I think the ending is perfect, for neither of us have lost face.'

'Or both of us have,' countered Mary, beginning to smile herself. 'I wonder what Father would have said.'

'That we are well matched, but then, we always were.'

Mary's smile disappeared. 'I think that we ought to stop now,' she said. 'The others will be returning at any moment.'

'But you will give me a game again tomorrow, will you not? And allow me to assist you with your calculations?'

His face when he said this was as earnest and serious as he could make it. To be with her again was all and more than he might have expected. It was not simply that she stirred him as no other woman had, but their meeting of minds was something that he had never experienced with anyone other than Ritchie when they had been boys together.

She could not refuse him. Forgetting everything which had earlier passed between them, she remembered only the exhilaration of the last two hours—and gave him the reply which he so dearly wanted.

'If you promise to behave yourself and not pester me about the past, then yes, we may do as you wish, only providing that you are reasonably discreet.'

'Bravo!' was his response to that. 'As we have already

noted, the men of the party are preparing to journey to the boxing mill so we might as well agree to meet here at two of the clock. I see that there is a chess set and board on one of the cupboards which looks as though no one has used it for years. I propose to take it to my room and engage in a little useful practice. You will not find me such an easy mark tomorrow, I hope.'

'That remains to be seen,' returned Mary saucily. 'For the present then, adieu. I shall expect you here on the hour tomorrow,' and she left him to pick up the spare chessmen and the board, wondering what kind of a fool she was to put him in a position where he could let her down all over again.

Eliza Truman was waiting for her in their suite. She said nothing at first, but after Mary had rung for the tea-board to be brought up to them, she remarked, her voice as neutral as she could make it, 'By chance I visited the library and saw you there with Lord Hadleigh, playing chess. It is not for me to advise you—you are, after all a widow, no longer in the first stare of your youth—but are you wise to allow him to cultivate you? His reputation is that of a man who has no wish to settle down.'

'In that,' returned Mary, 'he is like many others.'

'Indeed, but those others are not pursuing you.'

Mary sat down and stared at her companion. 'What makes you believe that *he* is pursuing me?'

'The way he looks for you—and after you. And you are surely not pursuing him.'

Mary's answer was not as totally honest a one as those she usually made. 'I am not sure what his motives are for seeking me out. Other than that in our long-ago acquaintanceship we frequently played chess together and, since he was at a loose end, as I was, we agreed to play a game. That is all.'

But enough, perhaps, was a comment which Miss Truman was wise enough not to make. Instead she asked, a little pointedly, perhaps, 'May I enquire who won this suddenly decided-upon match?'

'No one. It was a draw. Ah, splendid, here comes the tea-board, now we may refresh ourselves,' which, Mary thought, was as good a way as any other to put an end to that line of conversation.

Before dinner, Perry Markham, in high spirits after the hanging, was entertaining a few of his cronies in his room. It was quite a merry affair since port and wine were circulating freely. 'Can't wait until after dinner to down a few glasses, can we?' being part of Perry's cheerful invitation to his small court. 'Hanging's thirsty work. Astonishing how many of the plebs were drunk before it began, wasn't it? It's a wonder they were wide awake enough to enjoy themselves when the fun started.'

The Hon. Tom, who had been quietly sick in the middle of the so-called fun, had blamed his own malaise at the hanging on too much ale in order to keep up his reputation for being part of Perry's hard-living set. In consequence he had felt compelled to refuse to drink in the evening. He sat in a large armchair looking woebegone.

'Not too set down to miss picking a few pockets, though,' he said mournfully. 'I lost my purse and my handkerchief.'

'Oh, come on, Tom, do cheer up,' roared Perry. 'I've a fine piece of news, hot from my man Dawson, to pass on to you all. It seems that m'lord of Hadleigh, who was too fine and delicate-minded a gentleman to come to Loughborough with us, spent the afternoon with Mrs Wardour playing chess—in the library of all places. Didn't know anyone used it these days.'

This, as he intended, drew a great deal of appreciative and already tipsy laughter.

'Thought she was invited here for you, not him,' said one would-be know-all, 'and that Angelica was his target. Not like you, Perry, to let another put his oar in before you.'

'Game's not over yet,' spluttered Perry, 'and it's not chess I'm talking about. As for Angelica, she's more interested in Tom, isn't she? But there's no hope for you there, old chap— the General wants a richer prize than your good self, more's the pity. I'd prefer you as a brother-in-law rather than that high-minded ass, Hadleigh, who looks down his nose at me every time we meet.'

The ringing of the first bell for dinner, informing the guests that they were to meet in the drawing room, ended this Parliament of Fools. There was a rush for the door as a result of which the Hon. Tom was last out, still nursing his grievances against life and hoping that the sight and sound of Angelica would cheer him up.

He was lucky. Angelica was standing before the hearth, admiring herself in the huge mirror which stood above it, while ostensibly chit-chatting with Mary. She saw the Honourable Thomas reflected in it when he came through the door. Ignoring all the conventions relating to politeness and good manners, she broke off her conversation with Mary in mid-sentence, turned and almost ran to him.

'So there you are, at last. I thought that the hanging was over before noon. We all expected your party back in the mid-afternoon, but no such thing. It has been a most boring day. I have seen enough gardens and follies to last me for the rest of my life!'

'Come to that, my dear girl, I never want to witness another hanging, but we won't tell your brother so, will we?'

'Mrs Wardour must have had a dull day, too. Or at least a dull afternoon. I gather, that of all things, she spent it playing chess against Lord Hadleigh.'

The Hon. Tom was left to reflect how rapidly gossip ran round a country house. He wondered uneasily whether his pursuit of Angelica had been watched closely enough for the news to reach her father. It wouldn't do for him to open a real campaign for her hand until Lord Hadleigh had left without making an offer for it.

Lord Hadleigh had watched Miss Angelica with a mixture of amusement and relief. Thank God he was not her target, and that she had made it easy for him to approach Mary, whom she had left at a loose end, since Perry Markham was too far gone to remember his duty to his father, and the estate, to seize the opportunity to charm her.

'I think that I am more than happy that you didn't go to watch the hanging today,' Mary whispered to Russell, 'since most of those who did go have arrived back on their very worst behaviour. Does it usually have such an effect?'

'Oh, I think that it was the drink before, during and after, which has made them all so infernally jolly,' Russell whispered back. 'Don't look, but the General has a face like thunder this evening. Expect lightning during dinner, if not before.'

Before was the truest word Russell had spoken. The General, after a word with his wife, walked up to Perry and began to expostulate with him in a whisper—which was not the best mode of speech to employ with his overset son.

Finally the General seized Perry by the elbow and gently tried to urge him to the door.

'I think,' announced the General loudly enough for the rest of the company to hear him, 'that you and your friends who went to Loughborough today might like to dine in the Small Hall and join the men after the ladies have left us. I shall ask the butler to arrange matters. In the meantime, you might wish to adjourn to the small drawing room.'

He did not add, if you can still walk, although Russell, amused, considered it likely that Perry and his friends might be legless after they had dined on their own—if not before.

Only the Hon. Tom was unhappy at this turn. He was stone-cold sober and still to be deprived of Angelica's company. It was too bad, but he—and Perry and the others—still retained enough sense to do as the General bid them, even if they grumbled gently all the way to their new rendezvous. Only Russell, of the younger members of the party, was left to join his elders, something which did not trouble him in the least. This was particularly true after the General had informed them that dinner would be delayed for a short time while the table was re-laid.

He was right not to be troubled. He had Mary on his right, and she had no Perry on her left to try to monopolise her, only elderly Brigadier Sykes, who was slightly deaf and whose conversation was limited to military matters and asking women how their children were faring. Neither of these conversational ploys would serve to enable him to entertain Mary for more than a few moments.

'My lucky day,' Russell whispered to Mary, 'since I have been gifted with your company during most of it.'

'We must behave ourselves,' Mary whispered back. 'You must not ignore Angelica and I must try to convince the Brigadier that although I am Mrs Wardour I have neither children nor a husband. He seems to be having some difficulty in grasping the nature of a widow.'

'Point taken,' responded Russell in his best Parliamentary manner before turning to Angelica and asking her how she had enjoyed her afternoon.

'Not at all,' she pouted. 'I was the only lady present who wasn't married or past her last prayers. Our hostess seemed to think that it would entertain us to learn all the Latin names of her plants and animals. She had a small menagerie of rather smelly monkeys and a creature called a hamster: a horrid little thing which resembled nothing more than an over-sized rat with nasty front teeth. She actually offered it to me to hold.'

'Really?' asked Russell, intrigued by this sad recital. 'And what did you do when she handed it to you?'

'Screamed and dropped the wretched animal—and then there was an awful to-do with everyone running round trying either to dodge it or catch it. The gardener finally picked it up—and then, of all things, *he* tried to give it to me. At that point I fainted and a footman carried me into the house where they restored me with tea. I'm sure that I shan't have any appetite tonight.'

How he kept his face straight during this mournful tale, Russell never knew, particularly since Angelica was attacking her dinner as though she had been starving for weeks. He heard Mary stifle a muffled giggle, and to cover it, remarked, 'Perhaps the animal was as frightened of you as you were of it.'

'Surely not,' exclaimed Angelica, between spoonfuls of asparagus soup. 'One good thing came out of it, though. I was able to remain in the house and was spared any further lectures or possible attacks by ravening beasts.'

'There was that,' agreed Russell solemnly.

His duty being done, he turned towards Mary, who was

scarlet-faced from suppressing her laughter, and said in as low a voice as possible, 'Do you remember the day that I introduced you to a guinea pig?'

'Indeed I do. I was so entranced by it that you had difficulty in taking it away again with the result that Father came home before you had gone and raised the roof about the inadvisability of keeping pets. Once you—and the guinea pig—had been banished, he made me go and have a bath in case I had caught some dreadful disease from it.'

'He and Angelica would have a great deal of common ground there, if they had none elsewhere,' Russell could not resist remarking. Yes, it was just like old times again when they had teased one another unmercifully.

'I said that we must behave ourselves,' Mary told him severely after that. 'To that end you must entertain Angelica again, and I will ask the Brigadier about the campaigns he engaged in during the last war. That is another of his favourite topics for conversation.'

So, it was all downhill, particularly when, once dinner was over, Mary and the women departed and the refugees from the hanging returned to the dining room in their place. Their presence was enough to drive a man to drink and no mistake. Fortunately Russell's newly made resolution not to overdo things held good and he returned to the drawing room quite sober and ready for another bout of jousting with Mary.

Unfortunately, Mrs Markham, in the good cause of persuading Lord Hadleigh to offer for her daughter, button-holed him the moment he was through the door and rounded him up for a game of spillikins with Angelica and some other youthful members of the party who had arrived at Markham Hall not long before dinner.

It was all enough, thought Russell morosely, playing the mindless game with several giggling girls and the Hon. Tom, to make him wish that he had broken his resolution and was in no better state than Perry, who slouched in an armchair in the corner of the room, his legs spread out before him and his head on one side, like a drunken idler who had escaped from Hogarth's great series of prints: *Marriage à la Mode*.

By the time that the noisy game had ended, Mary, and her companion, had gone to bed—a place to which Russell finally retired. He would have gone there much more cheerfully, was his final judgement after a night of so-called merriment at Markham Hall, if Mary had been waiting for him in it.

Alas, Russell's stay at Markham Hall improved not a jot. Both the General and Mrs. Markham were determined to throw Angelica at him, and short of being rude to his host and hostess there was nothing he could do about it. The one thing which kept him from inventing some reason for leaving was Mary's presence.

Even that, though, was soon to be denied him. One afternoon, in the library, to which they repaired whenever they could escape the iron clutches of the Markhams—for Mary was also being relentlessly pursued on Perry's behalf—she had bad news for him.

She had just trapped his Black King in the inescapable corner to which she had driven him when she announced mournfully, 'This game must be our last for the time being. I have just received a letter from my Aunt Charlotte Beauregard, in the north, asking me if I would visit her as soon as possible.'

Russell stared at her, dumbstruck. He had begun to congratulate himself that, little by little, he was melting the ice around Mary's heart. Yesterday, for instance, she had laughed up into his face, and put a congratulatory hand on his when a clever move on his part had driven *her* King into a fatal position.

He had taken the hand and kissed the palm of it, and she had made no move to reprimand him. On the contrary, she had left her hand in his so that he had kissed it again, his eyes fixed on hers.

'Mary,' he had said hoarsely, 'it is time we spoke of the past. We cannot go on pretending that what happened, did not happen...'

'No,' she told him, but she did not take back her hand which he kissed again. 'It was you who suggested this prohibition. Without it we cannot go on.'

'*I* cannot go on like this,' he murmured. 'It is killing me. What I felt for you when I was little more than a boy is as nothing to what I am feeling now.'

'No,' she had replied, at last retrieving her hand. 'We are friends now, not lovers. Let us remain so.'

'Alas, Mary, I can never be merely your friend.'

Had she not been so determined that she would not mention the past she would have replied, Then you must have changed greatly, since if in the past you were more than my friend, you would not have abandoned me so lightly.

But since she was so determined, she said nothing although, if she had, the trouble which lay between them might immediately have been resolved. As it was she merely smiled and shook her head so that Russell, despite his growing desire for her to be to him what she had once been, fell silent also. If he could have nothing else from her, then he might be able to live with her friendship, however barren that might seem to one who loved her so ardently.

'Aunt Charlotte was my father's sister,' she explained to him when telling him that she must leave. 'She is one of my few relatives, but she lives so far away—near Newcastle, in fact—that we rarely meet. Consequently when she asks me as a favour to visit her as soon as possible I feel it to be my duty to go.'

Russell was struck by this piece of news. 'Near Newcastle, you say—exactly where?'

'By some coincidence, not far from the little town which gives you your name. I suppose you know it well.'

'I don't know it at all,' he was compelled to confess. 'For some reason my father never visits Eddington House, our country house there, and neither Ritchie nor I have ever been further north than Doncaster, where he has a small country house which is used once a year to visit the races there. My father is passionately devoted to the breeding and running of racehorses.'

Something in the tone of his voice set Mary remarking, 'And you are not?'

'Not to the exclusion of everything else.' He did not say that it was a pity that some of the affection which his father showered on his horses might have been better employed in caring more for his children.

Mary did not pursue the topic and they spent the rest of the afternoon in experimenting with the chess set, working out all the different moves which might result from the moving of minor pawns.

'I shall be lonely when you have gone,' he told her before they parted. 'I shall have to think of some excuse for leaving. If you thought that I was invited here so that I might make an offer for Angelica, you were right. Since it is plain that we have nothing in common, I must not remain to raise false hopes in the General's breast.'

'Well, I was invited for Perry,' returned Mary frankly. 'And a less suitable match for me I cannot imagine. However, I am my own mistress and so nothing can compel me to marry someone whom I dislike.'

'If, by that, you mean that I am not my own master, then you have hit the nail on the head once again. I came here at my father's behest; he thinks that it is time that I married. What he does not know is that the one woman whom I might wish to marry has decided to remain merely my friend. I fear that he will be most displeased when I return without fixing myself on Angelica.'

Mary scarcely knew how to answer him, so decided to say nothing.

They sat for a moment in silence. Mary was collecting the chess pieces, Russell was arranging the sheaf of notes which they had made between them, preparatory to handing them to her.

He said suddenly, apropos of apparently nothing, 'In two days' time I think that I shall make my adieux and pay a visit to my brother. He is the most sensible creature I know and his advice is always worth having. What I will ask you to do is give me your northern address so that I may write to you. I promise that the letters will be those of a friend. I will also send you some further calculations about the chess game after I have begged, borrowed or stolen Ritchie's set.'

Mary hesitated; Russell thought that she was about to refuse him.

'At least grant me this,' he said earnestly. 'It is little enough.'

She nodded. It was another surrender. Later, much later after he had left Markham Hall, Mary decided that Russell was behaving like the Roman general, Fabius Maximus. Fabius, always known as the Cunctator, or The Delayer, had defeated the invading Hannibal by withdrawing before him, destroying his position little by little, leading him on until he had defeated the invader in one last great battle.

Would there be one last great battle between herself and Russell, and if so, who would win it? More to the point, what would either winning, or losing, really mean?

Chapter Four

More than once, on his way to Ritchie's home at Liscombe Manor, Russell asked himself if he had taken the coward's way out by deserting Mary before she had left and before matters had been resolved between them.

On the other hand, he had, almost without knowing it, allowed the influence she still possessed over him to lead him to make up his mind to do something about the bad blood which existed between him and his father.

Whether it was her renewed admiration of his mathematical and philosophical powers, which, despite the length of time during which he had not practised them, were still there if only he cared to call on them, or whether it was the memory of the bright future that he had thought he once had with her which had done the trick, Russell could not decide.

What he *did* know was that, rightly or wrongly, Ritchie might be able to give him the kind of advice which would set him on the way to ending the pointless life to which his father's treatment had condemned him.

* * *

Ritchie was in the stables when he arrived at the Manor. He was breaking in a young horse, but was doing so without the brutality usually inflicted on the animal. He must have seen Russell arrive, but made him wait while he patiently whispered in the horse's ear, led him gently around the yard, and then mounted him in one easy movement.

After that he cantered slowly around, raising the whip which he never once used, to acknowledge Russell's presence before dismounting, handing the animal over to a watching stable lad and greeting his twin with an uncharacteristic and demonstrative arm thrown round his shoulders.

'You look done up,' he said calmly. 'Surely the journey from Markham Hall wasn't quite so demanding.'

'Not at all,' Russell riposted, standing back, 'but…' and he shrugged his shoulders '…I am at a kind of *point non plus*, and it is beginning to trouble me. I thought that you might be able to help me.'

'Point taken,' said Ritchie, punning a little in his dry way. 'But not here and not now. Later, after dinner, unbuttoned and a bottle of port between us, would be more suitable. For the meantime, come in and meet Pandora and the brat. I have a horrid feeling that he's going to look more like you than me. On the other hand, he behaves like me, quiet and contemplative. Nurse says that she's never known such a well-behaved child, most unnatural.'

'And on the other hand, again,' quipped Russell, walking beside his brother into the sprawling Tudor building, 'I'm sure that you're happy that he doesn't look like you, and behave like me. I seem to remember that I was always a noisy boy.'

'To say the least, and point taken again.'

He was leading Russell into a large room with an old-fashioned fireplace, above which was an intricately carved representation in wood of herons in flight. Pandora sat before it with a sleeping child on her knee. Motherhood had made her lovelier than ever and had given her a new steadiness.

'Welcome,' she mouthed at him, waving a hand at the child who stirred a little and turned his face into her breast. 'I've just finished feeding Will. Nurse has gone to fetch him a shawl before she puts him down for his afternoon sleep.'

No wet-nurse for Mrs Ritchie Chancellor then, thought Russell, somewhat amused, but the amusement was mixed with jealousy. Ritchie had married his true love, but he had been denied his. And the result was the handsome boy on his wife's knee.

As if he had known what his brother had been thinking, Ritchie said gently, 'Why not give Uncle Russell the brat to hold, my love? A little practice for him would not come amiss.'

'Surely,' said Pandora with a grin, 'but if he wakes, then he must do the soothing.'

Will did not wake, and Russell found himself doing something which he had not foreseen when he had left Markham Hall: holding a warm male infant, and—most surprisingly—wishing that the little bundle was his.

'Well, what is it that brings you here?' asked Ritchie when Pandora had left them to their port that evening. 'I thought, from Father's letter, that you were off making an offer for young Miss at Markham Hall.'

'Not I,' said Russell fervently. 'She was to my father's taste, not mine, so I am doomed to disappoint him once again. How I am to tell him without the heavens falling on me is at least one part of my worries.'

Ritchie held his port up to the light and stared at it.

'May I enquire who, if anyone, is to your taste?'

'Mary Beauregard, who is now the Widow Wardour. I don't suppose that you remember her.'

'Just, although I never met her. She is back in your life, then?'

'Yes, but that is not what I particularly wish to speak to you of, delighted though I am to meet her again. It's Father. What the devil is it that I have to do to satisfy him?'

'He gives me no responsibility, leaves me to rot in idleness and when, by accident, I thought that I had found that there was something odd about the reports and accounts from Eddington he sent me away with a flea in my ear. I'm damned sick of it all and I don't know how to remedy matters. I may be his heir, but…' and he shrugged his shoulders again. 'Perhaps you might be able to tell me what I could do to please him.'

'Nothing,' said Ritchie. 'He's determined not to be pleased by you. Why not try pleasing yourself? That's more to the point we keep running around.'

'That's easy for you to say. You're of independent means, I'm not.'

'Agreed.' Ritchie was thoughtful. 'Of course, you could throw everything up and enlist as a private soldier—but I wouldn't recommend it.'

'Exceedingly helpful of you, I'm sure,' sniffed Russell. 'I'm absolutely sure that something is going badly wrong up north—but I'm helpless…'

His voice trailed off. Why was Ritchie looking at him like that?

'Really?' said Ritchie. 'Tell me, are you going to spend the rest of your life feeling sorry for yourself? It's time you defied the old man, took the initiative.'

'Now, how the devil do you propose that I do that? He's warned me off.'

Ritchie looked sideways at him. Oh, Russell knew that look. He'd seen it often enough when they were boys.

'Your trouble,' his twin told him, 'is that you're too easy-going. You want people to like you. I don't. You're so good and truthful it's almost nauseating. Why don't you go up north, to Eddington, and try to find out what is happening there? Question old Shaw, ferret about. After all, you are the heir. Tell him that you're Father's agent, or emissary, what you will. Smile at him and ask him to show you round, explain things, go over the books.'

'But suppose he refuses to oblige me and asks for evidence? A letter from Father giving me the power to question him, for instance.'

'So, tell him that as you're the heir you don't need one.'

'But that would be lying,' said Russell, staring at Ritchie who, his face impassive, was carefully inspecting the ceiling.

'So lie, then. If I hadn't told a good few in my time I wouldn't be sitting here trying to advise my Don Quixote of a brother—I'd be six feet under. Everyone lies if it's in their interest. Go to the House of Commons and listen to them doing it all day long. Why should you be the only honest fool in the world? Try being a dishonest one for a change: it usually answers better.'

Russell was fascinated. Was this Ritchie speaking? Of course it was. He'd been one of Wellington's agents in Spain, had single-handed broken up a smuggling ring in Sussex and had doubtless done more beside. That he always looked as if butter wouldn't melt in his mild mouth must invariably have been an asset in the dangerous life he had led.

'My life has always been too easy,' he said at last. 'Being the heir, I've never really had to try, have I?'

'True,' said Ritchie, transferring his attention from the ceiling to Russell's face via his glass of port.

'So I go north and pretend I'm you?'

'If you like. Trying to be the man you might have been if our father hadn't unmanned you somewhat might be better. We are alike in some things, but not in all. I'm a rogue, you're not. On the other hand, your honesty might just be an asset in certain circumstances. You'll have to work out for yourself which they are.'

Russell, whose glass was empty, poured himself a large jorum of port. 'I think, little brother, I'll get halfway drunk as a preparation for being halfway honest.'

'Excellent,' said Ritchie. 'I'll drink to that, too.'

Russell was remembering this conversation when he was being driven north. After a happy fortnight spent with Ritchie, he had arranged to leave all his retinue—such as it was— behind at Liscombe, taking only his valet, Pickering, with him and his elderly coachman, Needham, who had known him since he was a lad. It would look odd if he were to travel completely on his own, but the less everyone knew of what he was about to do, the better.

'I'll send you the bill if they eat me out of house and home,' Ritchie had murmured as a last fond farewell—adding 'Good luck,' before Russell climbed into the heavily loaded post-chaise. The other chaise he had with him was left, together with its driver, with his accommodating twin.

The journey north was uneventful until they reached a small posting inn on the far side of York. Another chaise stood in the yard. A stable lad was leading its horses away. Pickering, sent to commandeer a room for his master, returned with a rueful look on his face.

'It seems, m'lord, that the best rooms have already been taken by a lady and her retinue, travelling north.' He hesitated, coughed and added. 'I enquired as to her identity and was informed that she was a Mrs. Wardour, a lady of substance. She is on her way to Ancoates, near Corbridge.'

'The Mrs Wardour who is travelling from Markham Hall, I trust?' said Russell. Well, he might have lost the best rooms in the inn, but he was going to have the bonus of meeting Mary again.

'Indeed, sir. I saw her lady's maid myself. A fine young woman with whom I became acquainted at Markham Hall.'

'Very fortuitous, then,' said Russell with a grin. It seemed that both master and man were in luck.

Pickering inclined a respectful head. 'True, m'lord. I have asked for supper to be served at not too late an hour.'

'Splendid—and while you're about it, see if there is a post-boy available to help Needham, who is feeling distinctly under the weather.'

So, Mary was here! Russell's worries about what to do when Eddington was reached flew away. He was on the verge of whistling when he entered the inn, but restrained himself. Persons of his standing were expected to maintain a due decorum—on public, at least.

He wondered how long it would be before he would meet her, and once again he was in luck. Walking into the parlour, he found that she was already seated there, her maid by her side. It was the maid who saw him first. She bent her head and whispered to her mistress, who rose in one graceful movement.

'Lord Hadleigh. I am surprised to see you here. I had thought that you had returned to London after visiting your brother.'

Russell bowed. 'That was my original intention, I do own. However, I changed my mind and decided to visit Eddington. You may remember that I spoke of it. I had a mind to see the place, particularly since I have never travelled further north than Doncaster.'

He did not add that another reason was the thought that he might see her again since her destination was so near his—although their present meeting was, gratifyingly, much sooner than he might have expected.

'Then we shall be near to one another once we reach journey's end,' murmured Mary. She was not sure how to greet this news. On the other hand, she could not deny that the moment she had seen him her heart had begun to beat faster and the journey north, hitherto rather dull, now took on a different complexion.

Russell, as if picking up her thoughts, offered, 'We could do it in tandem, could we not? I have been feeling rather bored with no company other than Pickering who, good fellow though he is, is rather lacking in the conversational line.'

'Why not?' agreed Mary, wondering what she was letting herself in for. Was this another part of his campaign to charm her again—something which she had sternly told herself after she had left Markham Hall that she would not allow him to succeed in?

Making decisions in his absence was one thing: holding on to them when she met him again was quite another.

'And since we are both lodging here this evening, would it be too much to ask that we might take supper together? It would be easier for the landlord and more pleasant for the pair of us. I know that Pickering will certainly be sharing his with your little maid.'

What could she say but yes when he smiled down at her in that winning way? If he had been charming in youth, he was overwhelming in maturity. Russell was simultaneously thinking the same thing of Mary. Even a tiring and lengthy journey north had not dimmed her attractions.

The landlord was only too happy to accommodate them at the same table. The food he supplied was, like his rooms, plain, but excellent. Roast beef, followed by a syllabub, with a bottle of excellent wine, were the perfect ending to a tiring day. The only thing lacking, Russell thought, was that Mary would not be sharing the bedroom with him.

Whether it was the food or the wine which was the cause, her manner to him had never been so easy. They laughed and talked like old friends who had not seen one another for years rather than the fortnight which had elapsed since he had left Markham Hall. It was as though they were young again, experiencing the new delights which leaving childhood behind had brought them.

'Miss Truman is not with you, I collect.'

'Unfortunately, no. Just before we were about to leave Markham Hall she received a letter from her elder sister—or rather from her elder sister's lawyer. It seemed that she was on the point of death and it was essential that Miss Truman should repair at once to Norfolk, where her family has lived for some generations. She was reluctant to leave me, but I pointed out that my maid could take her place on the journey and that my coachman and my footman would guard us both. Besides, once I had arrived at my Aunt's home, I should not lack for company. Were you lonely on your journey? I see that you have not brought along with you the grand train which was yours at Markham Hall.'

'Sometimes I'm quite happy to be alone,' replied Russell truthfully. 'Particularly since I have recently been taking stock of my idle life and deciding to do something about it. Discovering at Markham Hall that I had not lost my mathematical bent was a useful beginning.'

'You have not entered Parliament, then? Heirs to great names often do.'

He shook his head. He could not tell her of his father's contemptuous dismissal of that wish. Instead he murmured, 'Somehow, it never seemed…àpropos.'

Mary was shrewd. 'To you—or to your father?'

She knew at once that, somehow, she had said the wrong thing. He looked away, and the subtle rapport which, despite all, they still shared, told her that she had said something to disturb him.

He turned his head towards her again and smiled his beautiful smile. 'Both, perhaps,' which was as far as he dare go. He was not about to whine to her about his miserable life. Ritchie had told him to lie whenever it was convenient, and so he would offer Mary half a lie.

But he did not think that he had deceived her.

Silence fell.

The meal was ended, the small fire which had been laid for them was dying down and it was time to retire.

Mary was the first to rise. She picked up the shawl which she had discarded during the meal and prepared to make her adieux before leaving. Russell rose, too. For a moment they were face to face before the door.

She licked her lips nervously. Russell took a deep breath

at the sight, and before he could stop himself took her into his arms, bent his head and kissed her, not as once before on the lips, but oh, so gently, on the cheek. Some instinct told him not to frighten her. As before, merely to touch her roused him.

Mary's response was even more eager than the last time—but her behaviour at the end of a few stolen moments was exactly the same. She drew back, placing her right hand over his mouth and saying, 'No. You no longer have the right to do that—nor do I wish it.'

Russell, his eyes hard on hers, knew that if he had uttered half a lie a few moments ago, Mary was now offering him a whole one. Her tongue said one thing, her face and the posture of her whole body told him another.

'No,' he said, and his 'no' was quite different from hers. 'You do not mean that. You love me still—as I love you.'

'You forfeited my love.' She was trembling as she spoke and looked away from him lest the mere, and dear, sight of him broke her resolve. 'You said that we were to be friends, only friends. More than that I do not want and cannot give. Break that resolve and we must part, never to meet again. Now, pray allow me to leave. I have had a long and difficult day—as have you.'

Russell swallowed. 'Very well. Let us meet again at breakfast—as friends.'

She inclined her head, hiding her glorious eyes from him. 'If you will behave yourself.'

He said, and it was, in some odd way, the hardest thing he had ever had to say, 'Yes, I will behave myself, at breakfast—and all the other breakfasts and suppers until we take our separate ways at journey's end.'

'If you will—but only and always as friends.'

Russell bowed to her. He had given way and in the doing a strange thought crossed his mind. He had never really asked himself exactly what had happened, what had been said, and done, that she should have thrown him off all those long years ago and which had left her so obdurate where he was concerned. Tonight, when he reached his room, he would attempt to recall those long-lost days and so discover what had caused her change of heart.

Once alone, though, his memory refused to obey him. He had tried so hard to wipe out his love for Mary that to live again those idyllic days was almost impossible. In the end he lay down to sleep, distressed. He had always prided himself on his memory—even Ritchie could not excel him there: in that, they were equals. He had never thought that it would let him down so badly.

For a time he dozed before falling into a restless sleep from which he awoke some time in the small hours, just before the summer's dawn. He stared at the opposite wall—he had not drawn the bed-curtains, and suddenly his memory, hitherto so lacklustre, returned in full force and in full colour, unlike many of his dreams which were in dreary black and white.

Her father had driven them to a great house not far from Oxford in order to meet a savant, a learned man, whose great-grandfather had been a friend of Isaac Newton. Mary's father had boasted to the savant about his two youthful prodigies and he had asked to meet them.

After a happy morning spent displaying their skills, the savant, whose name still eluded Russell, said, 'Now I wish to talk of private matters to my learned friend, Dr Beauregard, so perhaps the young people might like to repair to the library.

It's not a suggestion which I would make to many of their age, but I believe that they might enjoy themselves.

'I have an Orrery there, and laid out on the library table some plans, calculations and diagrams which I have drawn up in an attempt to build a clockwork machine which would be able to add, subtract, multiply and divide, thus saving our brains as well as our energy. We would then have more time to engage in important work based on what our mechanical servant has already accomplished for us. I would value their opinion on my efforts.'

Thus dismissed, they had walked down a long corridor filled with the portraits of the learned man's ancestors—and what the devil had his name been? No matter, they had arrived at the library and did, indeed, enjoy the time they spent there— if not always quite in the way which their host had intended. They had played with the Orrery, watching the planets, including their own, revolve around the central sun, before examining the savant's work and marvelling at its complexity.

'Do you think that we could ever be able to do anything which might rival this?' Mary had asked him.

Russell, whose time had been spent between admiring the savant's intellectual prowess and Mary's face, alight with eager interest, answered her with, 'Why not? I doubt whether he was any more advanced in his skills when he was our age than we are now.'

He felt a dreadful shame on remembering his answer. What had he, Russell Hadleigh, done but neglect the skills which he had acquired in early youth, wasting his time in pleasure instead? Inevitably, since he was at bottom a man of sense, aimless pleasure had begun to pall, leaving him with nothing since his father had closed before him every avenue which he might have explored. Had he continued with his studies as Mary had done, who knows what he might have accomplished? Instead, once she had thrown him off, they had seemed barren, a symbol of all that he had lost—and wished to forget.

At this confrontation of the past Russell Hadleigh with the present one, his mind almost betrayed him. His revived memory began to slip away in a haze of regret and pain. To regain it he admonished himself sternly. What had she said then? How had she answered him? Immediately he was with her in that book-lined room and once more her voice was in his ear, as clear and youthfully excited as though he had truly recovered that lost time. He saw her face again, alight with the joy which had sprung out of their mutual intellectual passion.

'I think,' she was saying, 'that if we continue to work together there is nothing that we might not do.'

His other passion for her, which had been growing during the weeks which they had spent together, came into full flower at that moment.

'Oh, Mary,' he exclaimed, 'I know that you are speaking of our studies, but is there not also something else lying between us?—this, for instance,' and he leaned across the table to kiss her on the brow.

'Tell me, I beg of you, my darling girl, that you have come to feel for me, as I feel for you.'

He had drawn back so that he might speak to her from the heart, and she, her eyes, shining like stars, which told him as much as any words that he was not alone even before she said, 'I had not dared to hope…I, too…'

She stopped.

The older Russell, remembering this, knew that Mary had led a quiet life, away from the society of those of her own age and consequently the feelings which she then had for him were so new to her that she did not know quite what to make of them.

Was it normal, or usual, she must have asked herself, for a young woman to feel such strange excitement in the presence of a young man; to long to see him when they were apart; to have such a lift of the heart when he came into the room? Russell knew of her inexperience and was tender with her. He had no wish to exploit it in any way. To have done so, to have played with her feelings, even if he had stopped short of seducing her, would have been the act of a cur.

More than that, though, was his own understanding that what he was beginning to feel for her was more than simple lust, but something deeper. It was an understanding that here was the other half of himself whom he had been fortunate enough to meet before he had wasted his youth dallying with other women after whom he might lust—but never love.

He remembered that, mesmerised, they had stared at one another across the table.

'Perhaps I should not have said that—' she began.

He would not let her finish.

'No, Mary, you're wrong. When I told you what I felt for you I was neither lying, nor flirting, nor passing an idle moment by trying to please the young woman I was with. I truly meant it. When we are both a little older I shall ask my father—and yours—for their permission to marry you. That is, my darling, if that is what you wish.'

Her face told him that his wish was granted, before her words.

'In the meantime,' he said slowly, 'we must behave ourselves. Your father trusts us, and we must not betray that trust. We have all our lives before us, and we must remember that if we are tempted to anticipate our love.'

Oh, what a pompous young ass he had been! Yet he had meant every word he had said, particularly since he was convinced that the world lay all before the pair of them. If he had forgotten his father's demeaning of him, or that Dr Beauregard might have other plans for his daughter, glorious though a marriage to Bretford's heir might be, that was the privilege of his eager, innocent youth, not his disillusioned maturity.

A little chaste loving which might not rouse him overmuch seemed now in order, and so he kissed her gently, put his arms round her and petted her as innocently as he could, so that she turned her star-struck eyes up to him, and stroked his cheek in her turn.

Fortunately, they both drew apart before matters became too ecstatic, and when Dr Beauregard and the savant returned to talk to them of the savant's plans, they were behaving themselves. Mary was inspecting one piece of paper, and Russell another—and there, for the time being, his memories ended.

Were they memories? Or was it a dream? Russell was to ask himself these questions the next morning. Or was it a mixture of both, since immediately before he fell into a deep and contented sleep, he remembered the name of the savant: it was Dr Henry Wardour.

What he had not yet remembered was all that had led up to that dreadful day when he had learned of her betrayal, but he would—he was sure that, given time, he would.

Chapter Five

Mary had thought that breakfasting with Russell might be different, but no such thing. To her surprise they were as easy together as though they had been Darby and Joan themselves, the mythical husband and wife whose marital bliss had been a by-word.

Pickering, Russell's post-boy and the two drivers had already had a self-important conference in which they had agreed the route north until they were near Newcastle upon Tyne. The post-boy had been able to advise them on the best inns, and which shortcuts to avoid.

He had put a grimy finger by his nose and told them to avoid all the minor roads: it was safer on the main ones.

'Less likely to be attacked by the gentlemen of the road—or stray Luddites trying to stop and loot a passing coach,' he had finished.

Told of this by Pickering, Russell remembered that Ritchie had handed him a pair of pistols and an elegant-looking, but deadly, French sporting gun for protection. 'Better be safe than sorry,' had been his farewell words.

'These days even the Home Secretary carries a brace of pistols in his carriage when driving around London—and you will be driving across the moors both before and after York. Keep them with you so that you can use them in an emergency.'

'Come on, brother,' Russell had protested. 'I'm not off to the wilds of Spain and having to worry about dodging Napoleon's army.'

'True, but these days travelling in England is not as safe as it was, believe me. If it were ever really safe, that is.'

So far, at least, he had met nothing untoward on his journey north other than small crowds of ragged boys running and shouting after the chaise once it had left the stable-yard of the post-house. He would be sure to rag Ritchie about his dooming once he had arrived safely at Eddington.

In the meantime, they drove north in tandem so that the journey became for both Russell and Mary something out of time. In the evenings they played chess and renewed their friendly rivalry in the world of numbers to the bemusement of their fellows in the common room of whatever post-house they were lodging in. Neither Russell nor Mary dared trust themselves to seek privacy in the other's bedroom. Simply being together, even in company, was disturbing enough without tempting fate further.

Pickering, for one, could not believe what was happening to his master.

'Can't think what's come over him, never seen him so happy before,' he confided to Mary's driver with a knowing wink, 'unless it's your missis, of course. Not that he suffers from the blue devils, you understand,' he added hastily, 'just not very cheerful. Always considerate, though, many aren't.'

'You're right there,' said the driver. 'My missis is a good 'un, too.'

* * *

It was on their way from the last post-house before their roads diverged that Mary and Russell's time in Arcadia ended. The previous evening Mary had come to believe that perhaps, after all, she might consider forgiving Russell for his past behaviour.

Her marriage had been happy enough, even though Dr Wardour had been old enough to be her father, but it had only been a meeting of minds. If she were honest she had endured his love-making, tepid as it was, rather than enjoyed it. With Russell, though, she was beginning to grasp that their relationship was so powerful that it encompassed both the mind and the body.

If their hands touched over the chessboard, it was, indeed, as though their whole bodies were engaged. If Russell so much as looked at her in a particular way, with his startlingly blue eyes hooded, her response to him was strong enough to frighten her. From his behaviour Mary was compelled to believe that she was having the same effect on him. It was all quite different from her sober games of chess with Henry Wardour!

If they were both so profoundly moved by such slight things as these, what would happen if they were to engage in the final act itself? She had listened to other women talking, and had been surprised that they could find such pleasure in it—but now she found herself wondering what it would be like if she and Russell...

At this point in her musings Mary put up her hands to cover her hot face. What had come over her that she should think such things?

But she knew.

It was meeting Russell Hadleigh again and discovering that the current which ran between them was so strong that if she ventured into it, she would drown, as surely as she would drown if she walked into the Thames in London. But if drowning there brought death and oblivion, what would drowning with Russell Hadleigh bring her?

Sleep that night was long in coming, and her dreams took her into the past again, the past where they had walked in the garden together, happy in each other's company. She would not allow herself the nightmare of reliving the past where she had lost him, but would remember only the happy, earlier part of it and the increasingly joyful present.

And if she were a fool to indulge herself in that, then she was a fool and so be it.

'There will be no chess game for us tonight since our roads divide this afternoon,' Russell said at breakfast, 'but when we reach our destination we shall not be so far apart that we may not arrange another, either at Eddington or at Ancoates. The road between them is not too difficult for a chaise. Or a man on horseback.'

'True,' agreed Mary. 'And that being so, we must arrange a meeting as soon as we are settled in.'

Russell thought that these were the kindest words which she had spoken to him, seeing that it was the first time that she had initiated a meeting between them.

'Indeed,' he said eagerly. 'As soon as possible, although I am not quite sure what kind of welcome I shall get when I reach Eddington.'

Mary's rather surprised expression told him that he needed to explain himself a little.

'I fear that they have had no warning that I am coming. It was a spur-of-the-moment arrangement—but it is strongly approved of by my brother Ritchie. He thinks that I need occupation and that visiting Eddington, and learning how it is managed, will be of use to me.'

This was another half-lie, but he did not wish to tell Mary of his suspicions about the running of the Eddington estate until he had had time to inspect it. It would not be right to criticise Shaw if he were mistaken—although he was pretty certain that he was not.

Their chaises were being made ready for the journey in the stable yard. Both Mary and Russell were finding it difficult to say goodbye. Russell dearly wished to kiss her before they parted, and Mary was, to her own surprise, wishing that he would take the initiative and do so. After all, he had twice kissed her without any encouragement from her, and now, after almost living together for several days, they had fallen into the carefree camaraderie, if not to say love, which they had enjoyed in youth.

'Soon,' said Russell, bowing over her hand. 'I shall arrange to visit you soon. You will allow that, I trust?'

'So long as you do not take advantage of me when you do.'

'No, indeed, you will be quite safe since your aunt will play duenna.'

Still they did not move away, and still Russell held on to her hand. The post-boy gave a preliminary toot on his horn to recall them to the rigours of the day.

'Adieu,' he said at last, and this time he did kiss her, on the hand—but the effect on them both was as strong as if he had kissed her on the lips. Only after that did he, reluctantly, release her hand, and Mary, equally reluctantly, moved away.

'Until we meet again,' he breathed, before allowing Pickering to come up to him and say briskly,

'Time we left m'lord. We have a somewhat longer journey than Mrs Wardour after she takes the by-road to Ancoates.'

Reluctantly they parted. Even the knowledge that they might meet again soon was not enough for either of them. Mary resumed her seat in the chaise, filled with a vague unhappiness. The certainty that they would not meet again that evening weighed on her mind as heavily as a burden she had taken up would lie on her shoulders.

Again and again in her musings she returned to the same conclusion: how strong must their mutual passion be if the passing years had not been sufficient to dim it? Once they had met one another again, the miseries of her forsaken past had been swept away. The quiet life which she had lived with Henry Wardour seemed empty and barren—even though when she was living it it had seemed sufficient to her needs.

Russell was experiencing similar feelings. He must, he decided, clear up this odd business at Eddington quickly so that he could concentrate on winning Mary back again. With her by his side, stalwart and true, he believed that he could face anything, including his unloving father.

Halfway between the post-house and the parting of their ways one of Russell's horses fell slightly lame and slowed them down, with the result that Mary's chaise, which had started ahead of them, was soon out of sight. Needham and the post-boy decided that they would take on a sound horse at the next inn they reached—which would delay them even further.

Russell had half-hoped for yet another farewell at the moment of their final parting—and having taken on a nag which looked distinctly seedy, but proved to have unexpected stamina, he was still in hopes that Mary might wait for him to catch her up, even if it delayed her quite considerably.

He was surprised, however, when after a sharp bend in the road, her carriage came into view, and even more surprised to find that it had ended up in the ditch, half on its side. Its two horses had been cut loose by a pair of ill-favoured fellows who were leading them away. The driver was lying on his back in the road and the post-boy was nowhere to be seen.

Mary and her maid were standing in the middle of the road, being harangued by another ill-looking fellow who, Russell saw when his own chaise neared the scene, was threatening them with a pistol.

His chaise jerked to a stop before he could even give an order for it to do so. Russell's post-boy had seen what was happening even before he did, and was, Russell was to discover later, already reaching for a rusty blunderbuss which he always carried with him.

Russell leaned forward to take his own pistols from where they had been stored for easy use. He handed one to the startled Pickering, put his own into the waistband of his breeches and picked up the French sporting gun which Ritchie had lent him. Seen at a distance, it looked exactly like one of the new Baker rifles which the British Army had adopted.

'Enough to strike terror in anyone's heart,' Ritchie had said in his quiet way.

Russell jumped out of the chaise. Pickering followed him as he had been instructed before they left Liscombe: he was gingerly holding his pistol away from him as though it might, by accident, fire in his direction rather than at the enemy.

Russell strolled leisurely forward, the sporting gun at the ready, stopping some distance away from the armed man so

that his likelihood of being shot by him would be low since
the robber's pistol looked more like an antique than a dangerous weapon.

He could see that it was Mary and her maid who were in
the most immediate danger so he knew that he must go carefully. He was ruefully aware that he was appearing to be much
braver than he actually was in trying to act as he thought that
his twin might when in a tight corner.

'What's this, then?' he asked in as unthreatening a
manner as possible—but keeping the rifle trained on the
armed robber.

'What does it look like?' snarled the robber, backing away
a little. 'We wants the missis's money and her hosses. Yours,
too, as well.'

'This says you won't get either,' drawled Russell, raising
his sporting gun and sighting along its long, elaborately
carved barrel.

'Try to fire that and I'll shoot the missis,' threatened the
robber, pointing his pistol at Mary. Had he seized her, and then
made the threat, Russell would have had no alternative but to
give way at this point and try to work out another stratagem for
rescuing her, but the robber could see what Russell could not.

Not only had Pickering, following his master's example,
raised his pistol menacingly, but Russell's post-boy was also
advancing on him, his blunderbuss in his hand. Worse than
that, the robber's two cohorts had decided to save themselves
by mounting the horses they had been holding, and were
riding rapidly across the scrub which lined the by-way and
into the trees, away from possible death or capture.

Deserted by his accomplices, the robber still tried to hold
his ground, waving his pistol between Mary and Russell, who
was busy holding *his* ground.

Mary, without turning her head towards him, shouted, 'Be careful, Russell, he might kill you instead of me.'

'Yes, do be careful,' mimicked the robber. 'It's a pretty choice for me, ain't it?'

'Point non plus,' murmured Russell to himself. Aloud he said, 'Don't be a fool, man. It's a hanging matter if you kill any of us—and all for nothing. If you kill the lady with your one bullet, I shall certainly shoot you. On the other hand, if you kill me, then my servant here will shoot you. Not a pretty choice at all, I would say.'

'Damn you!' howled the robber. 'What have I to lose? It's a hanging matter or death whatever I do. I *will* kill the doxy,' but before he could swing his pistol in her direction Russell tightened his finger on the trigger of his gun and fired himself.

The robber dropped to the ground, his pistol still in his hand. Blood was pouring from his shoulder. He tried to sit up, but failed. Russell walked forward, kicked his pistol away, and turned to Mary, who was white-faced and trembling, but who had remained quite calm during her ordeal.

'You're neither of you hurt?' he asked, stopping himself with a great effort from taking her into his arms to comfort her. 'I shouldn't have let you go on unescorted.'

Mary said, her voice shaking, 'No, but I was very frightened—until you came.'

She looked down at the man on the ground. 'Russell, he's going to bleed to death unless we do something for him.'

'So, as one might expect,' Russell said, 'you are merciful as well as brave. Pickering,' he shouted, 'you can put down that pistol, get one of my shirts from my luggage and we'll see if between us we can't make some impromptu bandages. Needham, go and see if you can do anything for Mrs Wardour's driver. Meantime I'll take Mrs Wardour and her maid to the chaise and open the bottle of brandy I always keep in it for emergencies. That should put some colour in their cheeks.'

Mary gave a strangled laugh at this sally designed, she was sure, to steady her shattered nerves. Her maid, over whom Pickering had been hovering protectively, and who had said nothing so far, murmured, 'You were very brave, m'lord.'

'Not I,' said Russell, leading them over to where his chaise waited, the post-boy standing by the horses. 'I was lucky rather, and need to thank my brother who armed me so well.'

Presently, after he and Pickering had bandaged the would-be robber, Russell checked with Needham that Mary's driver was slowly recovering from the fall he had taken when the shot from the robber's first pistol had killed one of their horses, thus landing him—and the chaise—in the ditch. The chaise had lost one of its wheels and would have to be abandoned for the time being.

'But never mind that,' Russell said, continuing to take charge and order matters clearly and lucidly after a fashion which surprised him when he thought about it later and which impressed Mary at the time. 'One way or another I'll see that you reach Ancoates—but what are we to do with our murderous friend?' He pointed at the robber whom Pickering had propped up against one wheel of Russell's chaise.

'Nothing,' the man moaned. 'You've done for me, now leave me here to die. I'm only an old sojer, turned off after Waterloo. Who's to care about me?'

Russell looked down at him—and thought of the distance, and difference between them. There was no sentimentality in his conclusions: the man had threatened to kill both him and Mary, but he felt compelled to ask himself how he would have coped with the bad hand which fate had dealt to the man before him had he been in his position.

His own worries about his life seemed mean and stupid in the face of this. Starvation and ruin would never be his lot: his life had been cushioned from birth. He had never even had to contemplate what Ritchie must have done daily when he was in Spain: his own death or mutilation.

Nevertheless, the man had threatened to kill Mary and he must be handed over to the authorities to be dealt with.

The post-boy, who had shown remarkable presence of mind during the whole wretched business, and who possessed a great deal of local knowledge, took a hand again by solving the problem of where to deliver the robber.

'There's a post-house back on the road north in a village not far from here where the Squire has his big house in the main street,' he offered eagerly. 'I mind me that he's a magistrate. If you allow me to drive you there, you can hand this fellow over to him. Mr Needham and Mr Pickering can look after the ladies and Mrs Wardour's injured driver if you leave some of your arms with them.'

'Excellent,' said Russell. 'I am supposing that once we arrive at the post-house we can hire a chaise to come back and pick them up. One thing is for sure, my chaise isn't big enough to hold everyone—even merely to take them to this village. Besides that, we shall certainly need another post-chaise if I am to escort Mrs Wardour, her servants and her luggage safely to Ancoates, seeing that her own is so badly damaged. We shall also need to hire labourers from the village to pull her coach out of the ditch so that we can unload it.'

Mary had walked over to Russell's chaise, her maid following.

'If you could leave two of your rugs behind, Lord Hadleigh,' she said, 'We could use one of them to sit on the grass by the road while you are gone and my poor driver, who still seems overset, could lie down on the other until he recovers. I am sure that both Pickering and Needham will be able to keep guard for myself, Jennie and my driver until you return.'

'You could, of course, come with us to the inn,' Russell offered. 'I do have room for just one more.'

'I haven't the slightest intention of deserting Jennie and the others,' she announced. 'The weather is fine, and the scenery, now that I have the time to inspect it, is wildly beautiful and well worth a more prolonged look. I suggest that you make all speed to this village and settle matters there.'

She was rewarded with Russell's most brilliant smile. 'I should have known that you would always consider others before yourself,' he murmured. 'I have no doubt that you are being a most splendid influence on me.'

Her smile for him was equally dazzling. 'I have to say, Lord Hadleigh, that judging by your recent behaviour you really need no guidance on how to act both bravely and promptly. Here comes Pickering with the rugs. Now you may safely leave us.'

Between them Pickering and Russell manoeuvred the barely conscious robber into the chaise where he lay full length along the seat opposite to Russell's, moaning gently all the way back to the main road and from thence to the village of Coatsburn, which was, as the post-boy had said, at no great distance from the attempted robbery.

The Squire's house was indeed in the centre of the village, facing the Market Cross. Its gardens were all behind it and ran down to a tributary of the Tyne. A supercilious butler answered the door and stared at Russell as though he were a hawker come to sell pins and needles.

'Yes?' he enquired, his lip curling.

'You may inform your master—whoever he might be— that Lord Hadleigh of Eddington wishes to speak to him on a most urgent matter. Since speed is of the essence here, I trust that you will not delay further.'

'Of course, m'lord, pray enter.'

Before the butler had time to leave the entrance hall, a door at the side opened and a large gentleman in country clothing entered and stared at them both.

'What is it, Peters? And please introduce me to this gentleman before you begin any explanations.'

'I have the honour to introduce my master, Sir Ralph Cheyney, to you, m'lord Hadleigh. Lord Hadleigh says that he wishes to speak to you most urgently, Sir Ralph.'

The large gentleman, who appeared to be in his middle fifties, said drily, 'Does he, indeed? Pray, what can I do for you, m'lord?'

'I am sorry to intrude,' Russell began, 'but I regret to inform you that an attempt was made to rob a lady travelling north, apparently on her own. I was travelling a little behind her, and was sufficiently fortunate to prevent the attempt from succeeding. I have in my chaise one of the robbers who was badly injured when I fired at him to prevent him injuring the lady. On being informed that you were a magistrate, I have taken the liberty of driving the wretch here and asking you to dispose of him. I could scarcely leave him bleeding to death on the road.'

'No, indeed,' replied Sir Ralph, again dry. 'Most messy—

and inconsiderate for other travellers, too. Peters,' he said to the butler, 'ask Mr Williams to come to the study. Please, m'lord, do me the honour of accompanying me there so that we may make arrangements to dispose of your prisoner. A Luddite, perhaps?'

Russell shook his head. 'No, Sir Ralph, an old soldier turned off after Waterloo.'

Sir Ralph shook his head. 'That's too bad, but he shouldn't have turned robber—but who knows, he perhaps had no other skills.'

'Possibly not.' They were now in Sir Ralph's study, where a large desk stood in front of a magnificent hearth flanked by bookshelves which were filled from the floor to the ceiling with imposing-looking tomes.

'We magistrates meet here,' Sir Ralph explained. 'Now, m'lord, is there anything else I might do for you?'

Russell told him of Mary's predicament, and how he proposed to deal with it, Sir Ralph nodding the while.

'I think that I might be able to help you here. I will send my wheelwright and a carpenter to examine the chaise and find out whether it is repairable. Unfortunately, the only post-house in the village is a poor one. It may be able to supply you with fresh horses, but the accommodation it offers is most unsatisfactory. It would please me to entertain you and the lady overnight—she must be suffering from shock and a night's stay would be a great restorative.'

He looked hard at Russell. 'I knew your father, Lord Bretford, long ago when we were young together. You are not very like him. We might have been relatives once—but that is an old story. Since you are still Lord Hadleigh, I take it that he is alive and well.'

'Indeed,' Russell replied. He had heard his father speak several times of old friends of his youth, but he had never mentioned a Ralph Cheyney. 'It is kind of you to offer shelter and I am immediately prepared to accept it on behalf of myself and the lady. She is Mrs Mary Wardour, the niece of Miss Charlotte Beauregard who, I gather, is settled not far from here.'

'Yes, indeed. I have met the lady and will be pleased to assist her niece.'

Russell told Sir Ralph that Mary was waiting patiently by the roadside. Sir Ralph immediately arranged for his own coach to be sent forth on the instant to bring the whole party to Cheyney Court, as his home was called.

'After that, m'lord, I will arrange to have nuncheon served. Nothing like good food to soothe the nerves, eh? Do you wish to accompany the coach and direct my man to where your party is to be found?'

Russell allowed that he did. Sir Ralph, who seemed to be a bustling gentleman, next turned his organising energies on Mr Williams, and made arrangements for the robber to be removed from Russell's chaise and transported to the local gaol where a doctor would examine him. 'Mustn't have him die on us,' he roared cheerfully, 'before we hang him.'

If he hadn't been given such a talking to by Ritchie about his soft-heartedness, Russell would have deplored Sir Ralph's cheerful coarseness: as it was he found himself being amused by it.

'Quite so,' he said, his face as straight as he could make it. Wouldn't do to antagonise such a helpful fellow who was making sure that not only would he be able to rescue Mary without delay, but was also offering her shelter for the night.

* * *

Mary was prepared for a long wait and could only hope that the robbers would not return to finish what they had started. She was not overly worried for, even if Pickering seemed a trifle unhappy about his role as her protector, both her driver and her post-boy seemed quite cheerful now that they had been left armed with the reloaded sporting gun and the two pistols. On the contrary, her driver kept muttering that if they reappeared he was ready and waiting for them this time.

What had surprised her about their recent adventure—or misadventure, she was not sure which it was—was the speed and courage which Russell had shown from the moment he had arrived on the scene.

He had told Jennie that he had not been brave, but he had strolled forward, holding his gun at the ready, as though it were something he was used to doing every day. All his charming indolence of manner had disappeared. He had told her that his brother had been a soldier, and he had behaved just as she might have expected one to behave.

After he had shot the robber he had organised matters so briskly that she was not surprised to see his chaise returning after a very short time, followed by a wagon and a rather elderly, if splendid, coach with equally splendid armorial bearings on the side. The motto beneath the arms was in English, not Latin, and proudly proclaimed 'Always Ready'!

Russell leaped out of his chaise—there was no doubt that he was ready, too—and advanced towards her, saying, 'We have had a piece of great good luck to counterbalance the bad one we have just suffered. Sir Ralph Cheyney, the local Squire, turned out to be an old friend of my father's and is offering us not only a meal, but also lodging for the night—

and possibly longer if your chaise needs a great deal of repairing. Two of his men are in the wagon and will start work at once to pull it out of the ditch in order to discover how badly it is damaged.'

She had never seen him so animated, so happy. Since she had met him again there had always been a faint aura of restraint about him, almost as though he were not sure of himself. In that he had been quite different from the eager boy she had once known.

'How extremely fortunate we have been,' she exclaimed, once matters had been arranged and she was seated in Russell's chaise being driven back to Cheyney Court. 'We might have been compelled to spend the night in an indifferent post-house. You have not been very long, either. I had imagined that it might be quite some time before you returned.'

'Oh, Sir Ralph is a managing kind of man and was highly indignant at the notion that a lady of quality should be put to any distress by a pack of thieves! He would hang all the highwaymen at his gate-post if he thought that would deter others, were his last words to me before I left. Moreover, since he has had the goodness to put himself and his people about so much, I have arranged that we shall be equally brisk in our return— particularly since he has ordered nuncheon to be prepared for everyone from your good self down to the junior of the two post-boys. I think that we have quite made his day.'

'Oh, the robbers, highwaymen, call them what you will, did that,' Mary riposted, 'except that...' and she hesitated '...except that I am sorry to learn that the wounded man is an old soldier, turned away and left to fend for himself after defending our country. Can that really be true?'

Russell's face was grave. 'I fear so. My brother spoke about it and said that if I had become an MP he would have asked me to raise the matter in the House—he considered it to be a great scandal and a shame.'

'Did you wish to be an MP?'

A shadow passed over his mobile face when he replied, 'I would like to have become one, but my father had other notions about who should sit for the seat he controls. Unfortunately, I'm not sufficiently well known to be able to gain adoption at the few which become vacant and are neither Rotten Boroughs nor in the gift of the great—like my father.'

Mary said robustly, 'My late husband was of the opinion that too few people were eligible to vote. He also thought it was quite wrong that a single person—such as the Duke of Newcastle—would not only be able to compel his workmen to vote for his candidate, but that he also had the gift of a number of Parliamentary seats so that even those who could vote were deprived of choice.'

Russell made a wry face this time. 'I suppose that someone like myself, trained for nothing, is hardly the stuff of a good MP.'

'Nonsense. You have a very good mind—but forgive me if I inform you that something tells me that you have not used it overmuch in the years which we have spent apart.'

Mary thought for a moment that she had gone too far. She was not in a position to offer him such an implied rebuke. Their re-acquaintance was too short for her to judge him without his resenting her frankness. He was so silent after she had finished speaking that she opened her mouth to apologise—only to have him say in a slow, heavy voice, 'You are quite right. I have wasted my time—and it is only recently that I have come to understand that, for my own good, my life must change.

'You are the second person in the last few weeks to tell me as much, and I have resolved to reform myself. In future I shall trust in my own judgement and not depend on that of others.'

He meant by that his father, but he could not tell her so, for that would be a betrayal of them both.

Mary's reply was a measured one. 'I needed to learn that after my husband died,' she told him. 'While he was alive he made all the decisions for the pair of us, even down to what he wanted for dinner and how the house was to be run. I was left to be...not an idle decoration, for he expected me to continue to work on mathematical problems, but someone who obeyed his every wish without question.

'At first, once he was no longer there to direct me, I found it difficult to make my mind up about anything, but after a time I began to find it exciting to be in charge of myself. Although he left me his money and his estate in a trust for me, the income from it is more than enough to enable me to live in comfort, and I find that I like being my own mistress.'

She was not surprised to hear him say, his expression a trifle wry, 'Does that mean that you do not wish to marry again, but would prefer to remain a wealthy widow?'

What could she say to that? She was rapidly growing to believe that she might like to be Lady Hadleigh since Lord Hadleigh was distinguished, among other things, by his kindness, but the past lay between them and would not die. For the first time Mary felt that it was a mistake to pretend that what had happened all those years ago had not happened, that it might be better if they spoke of it.

Consequently her answer was a hesitant one, 'If, and note that I say if, I found someone whom I could trust as well as love, who would not treat me as though I were a child, then I might wish to marry again.'

Russell's face lit up as though she had made him the most splendid present: it was as though he were once again the eager boy he had been and not the blasé dandy which he had become. 'Does that mean that there is hope for me yet?'

It was a measure of how far he had come, both with her and the world, that he could be so abrupt, so sure of himself.

Even when she shook her head and murmured, 'I fear that you are going far too fast for me, Russell,' he was not downcast.

Instead he leaned forward—she was sitting opposite to him—and took her hand, saying, 'I shall not let you escape me so easily this time, my dear. We may be parting soon, but not for long. Eddington is no great distance from your aunt's home and I intend to visit you both.'

He released her hand, partly so as not to seem boorishly importunate and partly because to touch her did dreadful things to him. His smile for her was dazzling, so dazzling that Mary scarcely took in all that he had said. It was only later, alone in her pretty room at Cheyney Court, that she asked herself why he had said, *I shall not let you escape me so easily this time*?

After all, it was he who had abandoned her and not she him. Why should he pretend otherwise? Perhaps he was doing so to win her again? If so, might he not be playing some sort of perverted game such as seducers often engaged in, gaining his pleasure by betraying her rather than winning her?

Not that he had seduced her the first time. It was true that he had never breached her innocence, but was it not a form of seduction to promise her everything—and then leave her without another word until he had walked into the drawing-room at Markham Hall?

Mary put her hands over her hot face. Dare she trust him? Dare she allow the strong attraction which she still felt for him—no, not attraction, Mary, but love—to lead her ultimately to confess that love to him, come what may afterwards? Or should she continue to walk alone as she had done since her husband's death?

And what a barren life that was! No one in her bed, no child, nothing but the cold figures on paper which had been her whole life since she had married Dr Henry Wardour.

Sir Ralph Cheyney had been as good as his word. He found accommodation for both sets of travellers, fed them immediately after they had arrived, bellowing at them, 'I have ordered wine to be served instead of tea, the whole pack of you look quite done up,' which was truthful, but scarcely tactful, being Russell's inward gloss on that.

Immediately after he had promised to visit Mary once they both reached journey's end she had become very quiet. Something told him not to trouble her further, so instead he sat back and drank in her charming face. Her beauty was of the rare kind which consists of character and good bones rather than those more blatant traits which society found fashionable. There was nothing showy about her, nothing of the obvious such as Caroline Fawcett and his other women had possessed.

Was that why he had chosen them? To try to blot out the memory of a piquant face, dark eyes, dark hair and sweet mouth, plus the calm self-command which Mary had possessed even as a young girl. To say nothing of her pretty, trim figure and her graceful carriage. More than that, he could talk to her as an equal and discuss matters with her which had bored Caroline and the others whenever he had tried to raise them.

He thought of her remarks about being an MP and the wrongs of the present system of elections and choosing MPs. Oh, yes, there were women in society who knew of such things, but they were few and far between and growing fewer.

If he married Mary, she would be his friend and companion as well as his lover. They would go through life side by side—and he inwardly snorted his derision at the manner in which Henry Wardour had treated his clever and capable wife.

'There,' announced Pickering, who had been helping him to dress while all these new and powerful thoughts were running through his mind. 'You are now fit to go down to dinner, though, if I may say so, m'lord, I wonder whether any of us will have a great appetite for it, Sir Ralph having served us such a sumptuous collation not many hours ago!'

'True,' said Russell, 'but seeing what a kind host he is, I must try to do his dinner justice. You, being in the servants' hall and not under his kind, if eagle eye, may do as you please.'

Pickering bowed his thanks. It was plain that m'lord was still in the happy mood which had taken him over ever since he had met that woman at Markham Hall. Long might it continue. He was a good fellow and had been the slave of the dismals for far too long.

Mary, sitting in the drawing room listening to Sir Ralph's booming voice, with occasional interjections from his widowed sister, Amelia, who was his nominal hostess, although it was plain that Sir Ralph made all the decisions at Cheyney Court, was quite relieved to see Russell enter.

'Ah, there you are,' said Sir Ralph, rising. 'I was just informing Mrs Wardour that she may stay here as long as she pleases. I would not like her to continue her journey until she is quite recovered from today's untoward events.'

It took all Russell's strength not to reply that he had seldom seen Mrs Wardour look more recovered, but he acknowledged Sir Ralph's kindness with a graceful bow and a murmured, 'I'm sure that Mrs Wardour will accept your kind offer should she need further rest. I trust that she does not object to my speaking on her behalf.'

'Not at all,' said Mary immediately. 'Lord Hadleigh has said for me exactly what I would have said for myself.'

'Excellent!' exclaimed Sir Ralph. 'Now we may sit down to dinner with that settled.'

Mary and Russell were later to agree that, while most of his conversation consisted of exclamations and declamations, he was extremely kind-hearted. He also employed an excellent cook and was a good host even if he did spend most of the meal informing his guests that they really must eat a little more of that—that being virtually every cover placed upon the large table.

'And now,' said Sir Ralph, once the ladies had retired and port and cigars had been produced for him and Russell, 'we may further our acquaintance, m'lord. It has been a great grief of mine that although your father and I were bosom friends in youth we have not met for more years than I care to remember. We were both poor young fellows in those days with no notion that we should both inherit great estates—your father's being the greater.

'Oh, we were carefree then, and what a jolly fellow he was—always joking, always ready for a lark. I mind me the japes he played when we were in London. He was a great one for the ladies until he met my younger sister, Serena. After that he sobered down—we all thought that it would be a match. And then his father inherited the earldom of Bretford when his elder brother died and my jolly friend became Lord Hadleigh, the heir.'

He fell silent for a moment, leaving Russell to mull over the remarkable news that his father had been a jolly fellow in his youth, given to practical joking! Anything more unlike the testy and dour man that he had known all his life could not be imagined. He scarcely knew what to say, but Sir Ralph was a great talker and went on with his reminiscences growing freer and franker as most of the bottle of port went down him.

'The next thing I knew was that he was coming to stay at Eddington, which was the home of Margaret Russell, cousin to me and my sisters. Margaret was the Russell heiress—as you doubtless know, she being your mother—and your father had come to offer for her and marry her.

'Married they were. Serena was heartbroken, so much so that my mother packed her off to Brighton to stay with an aunt—the gossip about the wedding would have been too much for her. I wasn't invited, only my elder brother. He died in a boating accident the next summer, so that I inherited everything. What was even odder was that your father never visited Eddington again, not even after it came to him after old Russell died. In fact, he never spoke another word to either Serena or any of our family from the day we last saw him in London at m'father's place in Russell Square.'

He took another giant swig of port and stared across the room at the ornate hearth as though he were seeing the dead past in the flames of its fire.

'Never did know what to make of that,' he came out with

at last. Then, apparently inconsequentially, 'Still a jolly fellow, your father?'

'No,' said Russell slowly, not knowing exactly how to answer. 'No, no one would call my father jolly. He's the most serious man I know.'

'Jackie Chancellor, serious! You're bamming me!'

'Indeed not. I have never, in all my life, known my father to tell a joke, or even to laugh at one.'

'Odder and odder,' gloomed Sir Ralph. He leaned forward to give the fire a vigorous poke. 'I expect, since I gather that you're off to Eddington, that he might pay us a belated visit, eh?'

'I doubt that very much, sir.'

Russell wondered for a moment whether he ought to be frank with his father's old friend and inform him that the very mention of the word Eddington to Lord Bretford was always calculated to bring on a fit of the dismals. He decided against it. Mumchance was probably better here.

'Hmm!' exclaimed Sir Ralph, staring even harder at the fire. 'It's time that someone ought to visit Eddington. Don't like some of the gossip I hear about young Shaw. Not that I'm a great one for gossip, no indeed! But his father was not what I would call an efficient man and young Shaw is less than that. Things have gone from bad to worse since his father died and he took over.'

Young Shaw! Now here was a turn up for the book. So far as Lord Bretford and Russell, himself, knew, old Shaw was still running the Eddington estate; nothing had reached London about his death or about the son succeeding to his father's place.

Russell remembered his own misgivings about the Eddington accounts which had set him off on his northern odyssey and reintroduced him to Mary, but decided against mentioning them to his host. The news that old Shaw was dead and that his death had been concealed from his father made him more determined than ever to press on to Eddington to find out what exactly was going on there.

He might also try to discover something more of his father's past and the reasons why his character had changed so dramatically. If he did, he would remain mumchance about that, too. I'm learning guile from Ritchie, he thought, damn me if I'm not. He was not sure whether that notion pleased or frightened him.

Pleased would be better—he was beginning to believe that he might need all his twin's steel and ingenuity once he reached Eddington. In the meantime there was Mary to look after and to get to know better, so much better that she might change her mind about him…and then, who knew what might happen…

Chapter Six

They stayed at Cheyney Court for two days while Mary's chaise was repaired. Fortunately it had not been greatly damaged and her—and Russell's—remaining journey north was not very long so that the rather tired nags, which were all that the post-house could supply, would be able to manage it.

'I am quite determined to accompany you the rest of the way to your destination,' Russell told Mary firmly on the evening before they set off again. 'If we travel together we are less likely to be attacked by any wandering Luddites, old soldiers or brigands who might frequent these parts.'

Mary did not argue with him. She rather liked this new downright man—so long as he did not overdo things and turn into a bully, that was.

'Furthermore,' he went on, Sir Ralph nodding approvingly the while, 'I would prefer you to travel in my chaise with our servants following in yours. This would have the advantage that my strong right arm and Ritchie's French sporting gun would both be at the ready should any fool still be determined enough to attack us.'

'Quite right,' roared Sir Ralph. 'Very commonsensical of you, eh, Mrs Wardour? M'lord's strong right arm should always be at the disposal of a fair lady—and you are a very fair lady, if I may say so,' and he winked at Mary. He had already privately decided that Russell and Mary would make 'a handy pair' as he put it to himself in his downright way. The sooner the better, too.

'By the by,' he added, 'that rogue you disposed of, m'lord, is being transported to Newcastle Gaol tomorrow, there to await trial and judgement. You might be needed to attend the trial to give evidence so I have forwarded them your address.'

Russell nodded a trifle ruefully. He could not condone what the fellow had tried to do, but he could understand why he had done it. He would plead for mercy for an old soldier fallen on hard times in the hope that the mandatory death sentence might be commuted to transportation to Botany Bay, but the final word would be with the judge.

He had no doubt that if Sir Ralph still possessed the powers of the old English barony he would cheerfully have hanged him before the gates of Cheyney Court as an encouragement to others not to turn highwayman and murderer. But times were changing a little and the notion that the death sentence was mandatory for all crimes of every kind, including robberies worth more than five pounds, whatever the age of the offender, was coming under attack—particularly now that there was an empty continent in Australia for felons to fill.

He and Mary discussed that, and other serious matters, in the chaise on the way to Ancoates. On the evening before they had left, they had played a game of chess—to the great wonder of Sir Ralph, who had said, most earnestly, 'Surely, m'lord, you will not try a lady's brain too hard by playing such a difficult game with her? I am quite willing to propose myself as your opponent to save her from being overset.'

'Have no fear, sir,' was Russell's reply. 'Mrs Wardour is a mistress of the game and could beat most men of my acquaintance should she care to give them a game. I am reasonably proficient, but I shall need all my concentration when we joust together if I am not to be disgraced.'

The game which followed proved him to be telling the truth. It was a long one and to Sir Ralph's stupefaction it ended in stalemate. He pretended to be reading a local newspaper but every now and then came over to stare at the board and watch a few moves, particularly when it became plain that there was going to be no rapid finish.

'I should not wish to give either of you a game,' he said, melancholy in his voice. 'You had the right of it m'lord, the lady is your equal. Stalemate, eh? Shall you play another game? Stalemate is not a happy ending.'

'On the contrary,' said Mary, smiling at the kind old man. 'It is a very happy one. If no one has won and no one has lost, then honour is equal and no one has bitten the dust.'

She looked across at Russell when she had finished speaking and saw him nodding approvingly. She asked him on the journey whether he really agreed with what she had said, or had nodded merely to make her happy.

'Oh, I agreed, for that game—and also, at the moment, for the game of life, too, in which I am trying to persuade you to think well of me again. Believe me, when that day comes, stalemate will not do. The King must have his Queen—or the Queen must conquer the King. Whichever way one looks at it, there must be an even happier ending—both for the chess game and for us. At the moment, though, stalemate must do.'

'Logic-chopping,' exclaimed Mary joyfully. She seemed to have caught the habit of exclamation from Sir Ralph. 'You are logic-chopping. How pleased my father would have been with you. He always said that you were lacking in that department and what a pity it was that you never exercised your brain enough so that you might excel.'

She coloured. 'I shouldn't have told you that. It was what he said to me, confidentially, in private.'

'Do not reproach yourself, Mary, for breaching his trust, since he often told *me* the same thing in private. I was an idle fellow then, and since. Meeting you again has done wonders for me. We must arrange to meet more often and enlarge on these matters. Your father used to speak to me about trying to invent a machine which would add, multiply and divide of itself, thus saving us all a deal of trouble. Did he do any further work on it before he died?'

'Alas, no. He was struck down when he thought that he was on the verge of solving some of the problems he encountered in it. I know that he hoped that my late husband would carry on his work, but unfortunately he thought that my father was chasing a mirage. Worse than that, he insisted on destroying all my father's papers which related to it, even though my father had arranged my marriage to him so that we could continue it together. So nothing now will ever come of his dream.'

They sat for a moment in silence. One of the things which he liked most about Mary was her ability to sit quietly beside him between their eager bouts of conversation when they spoke of everything under the sun. One thing Russell had kept up was his reading—something which his father heavily criticised him for if he came across him with a book in his hands.

'What an idler you are, Hadleigh! Have you nothing better to do than waste your time reading—the latest novel, I suppose?'

He supposed wrongly. Helped by Ritchie, once he had come back when the wars were over, he had drawn up a reading list of those books which he thought might not only improve his general knowledge, but also those which might possibly help him when he came to inherit.

His father might have been surprised to know that his despised son was diligently reading the papers and reports of the Board of Agriculture and was consequently privately critical of the way in which his father was allowing his lands to be run—even those which did not surround Eddington and which he visited more often.

Talking to Mary was another thing. It was reviving his old academic interests and he found himself looking forward to each new day after a fashion which he had lost many years ago.

They were nearing Ancoates when she asked him, 'Is there any particular reason why you are visiting Eddington? It is a matter of some wonder to the natives around here, my aunt tells me, that no member of the family ever visits the place. The Russells rarely left it, always provided a magistrate, and took a great interest in the district. The village is very run down, she says, which is a great change from the past when the last Russell squire built it, intending it to be a model for other landowners to follow.'

She was trying not to be critical of Russell's father, but not only had her aunt deplored what an absentee landlord had done to the estate, but Sir Ralph had also dropped in her presence some heavy-handed hints to the effect that all was not well at Eddington. Consequently she awaited Russell's reply with some interest.

He was slow in answering her for he was weighing his words with some care, which was yet another change in his habits. He had been impulsive in the past, Ritchie had always complained of it, but the new life on which he had embarked was altering his behaviour day by day, something of which he was not fully aware.

'I have come here of my own volition,' he told her. 'It was my mother's home, and I thought it a shame that neither of her sons has ever visited it. I don't blame Ritchie in the slightest. He inherited a run-down estate from an old uncle of ours and has been busily restoring it for himself and his family. I suppose that watching him at work spurred me on. He made me feel useless—but then, he always did.'

'And you resented him for that?' Mary asked. Since he was being frank with her, she would be frank back. She had already noticed that he rarely spoke of his father. The only time, indeed, that he had done so was when Sir Ralph had been reminiscing about their mutual past.

'No,' said Russell simply. 'I never resented him. I only wished that I were more like him. He is not only clever, but brave and good. I wish…' and he fell silent.

'What do you wish?' Mary made her reply as gentle as possible.

'I wish that I could have gone for a soldier, too. Things might have been different.'

He decided to be honest with her.

'You see, Mary, my father allowed me no other place in life than that I was the heir and would one day inherit—but that day must be far off and I dislike being made to wish that he would die so that I might be free. I can feel deeply how the Prince of Wales must have suffered before his father went mad and he became Regent. He was a clever man and was allowed to do nothing. He was married off, against his will, to an ugly German princess with whom he had nothing in common. I can think of no worse fate. His reply to that was to become totally irresponsible and I do not wish that to happen to me.

'When I reach Eddington I may perhaps find an aim in life, other than being a clotheshorse, going to the races, gambling, attending balls and reviews and talking nonsense to people for whom I don't care and who don't care for me.'

He did not mention Caroline and the other women. He knew that his dear love understood men and the world well enough to know that there must have been women.

Mary was silent again for some time before she said, 'Forgive me if I ask you if one of the things which determined you to visit Eddington was that your father wished you to marry Angelica Markham—someone little suited to be your wife.'

He leaned forward, took her hand again, as he had done the other afternoon, and kissed it. 'I might have guessed that you would have seen that the comparison I drew between myself and the Prince Regent held good there, too. What a wise creature you are.'

'You have shown some wisdom, too,' retorted Mary, a gleam in her eyes. 'At least you have not grown grotesquely fat, taken to the bottle and married someone unsuitable in private. Oh, dear,' she added, teasing him further, 'I am trusting that you have done nothing like that. If you have, pray forgive me, and I will say no more.'

'Witch,' he said, 'to tease me so mercilessly,' and, tempted by her odd mixture of playfulness and cleverness, he leaned forward and kissed her on the lips. He might as well have lit the touch paper of one of the fireworks to celebrate the said Regent's birthday, so strong was their mutual reaction.

"'Where the bee sucks, there suck I,'" muttered Russell, drawing away a little. 'Will Shakespeare was writing about more than bees when he penned that. Let me drink of your divine honey again.'

She had not drawn away from him, rather she was still leaning forward, bemused. Her lips were swollen, her cheeks red and her eyes were bright, glowing at him while he spoke. Her lips did not refuse him when he claimed them again. His hands rose to stroke her neck gently.

Mary gave a little moan. All her resolutions about not allowing him into her life again had flown away. He had trusted her with the most intimate confidences about himself and his life and, by doing so, had disarmed her. That Russell had not made them with that end in mind was not to the point.

For a moment they clung together as they had done so many years ago, both of them frustrated by the knowledge that, for honour's sake, they must go no further. And, more to another point, to go any further in the closed confines of the chaise would be extremely uncomfortable. On top of that they were rapidly reaching journey's end.

In the end, astonishingly, it was Russell who drew back and released her gently. He had always been gentle, she remembered, despite his liveliness. He raised his hand, the one with which he had been stroking her neck, face and hair, and placed a finger on her lips as though to soothe her.

'No more,' he said, 'not here, but God, how you tempt me.'

'As you tempt me,' she whispered.

'I know. Oh, Mary, how did we come to part? With you by my side I could have faced my father.'

It was such a cry from the heart that Mary was moved beyond words. She put up her own hand and stroked his face. If he had felt like that in their lost past, then why had he left her? She was not to know that Russell, also greatly moved, was thinking the same thing of her.

Mary was certain that sooner, rather than later, they must face their joint past before they could, perhaps, move into a better present. Not now, not in the chaise, rapidly nearing their destination, but at some time and place where they could be alone, with nothing to distract them.

'What an adventure, my dear! And what a blessing that you were with Lord Hadleigh, and that he was able to rescue you so promptly. I am not in the least surprised that Sir Ralph Cheyney offered you hospitality and lodgings—he is an odd fellow, to be sure, but most good-humoured in his brash way.'

Miss Charlotte Beauregard always spoke in a grand rush, without drawing breath, but her kindness, like Sir Ralph's, was undoubted.

They had scarcely arrived at her pretty country house on the outskirts of Ancoates before she was serving them tea and begging Russell to stay overnight before driving on to Eddington.

'I have a particular reason for reaching there as soon as possible,' he told her, 'which, regretfully, makes me refuse your neighbourly offer. What I would ask you is that you allow me to visit you, and Mrs Wardour, as often as possible. The ride from Eddington is not far, and, I was told by Sir Ralph, is through some impressively wild country, quite unimproved. He has, I gather, no time for the likes of Capability Brown and his fellows.'

'Oh, yes, he is a real character,' agreed Miss Beauregard 'Do have more tea, Lord Hadleigh, and of course you may visit my dear Mary as often as you please. The door will always be open for her rescuer. You know, Sir Ralph even disapproves of my garden because he says it is too civilised. I ask you, could anything be too civilised! I told him that he would deplore the disappearance of the wild man of the woods, and he informed me that he did. We do have a real hermit, though—some ancient scholar who lives in a broken-down cottage in the woods between here and Cheyney Court—but he scarcely qualifies to be a wild man.'

It was pleasant sitting in the charming drawing room opposite to Mary and listening to his hostess's diverting prattle. Russell almost wished that he had agreed to stay overnight, but Sir Ralph's cryptic remarks about Eddington had piqued his curiosity.

'A hermit in a cottage,' he said, smiling at Miss Beauregard while she energetically bustled about, making sure that he and Mary were comfortable. 'I thought that they always lived in damp grottoes.'

'Not this one. He does have a long beard and hair down to his waist. He seems to be quite harmless, though the village children throw stones at him on the few occasions when he visits Ancoates. Neither they, not their parents, can be persuaded that the poor creature is harmless. I have never met him—I understand that the villagers call him George.'

'So, superstition is as rife in the country as it is in the town,' said Mary. 'One always thinks of the countryside as a haven of rural bliss.'

'Not at all—and more to the point, country poverty is, in some ways, more harsh than town poverty, and there has been a lot of it about lately.' Miss Beauregard looked hard at Russell before continuing, 'Your agent at Eddington has turned a lot of labourers away recently. Is that why you are paying us a visit? It is many years since any member of your family did the honours here.'

Russell shook his head. 'No, this is the first I have heard of men being turned off. I have come because I was curious enough to wish to visit the only part of my father's estates of which he is an absentee landlord. It is quite unlike him. He takes a great personal interest in all the rest.'

'Odd, that,' said Miss Beauregard, echoing Sir Ralph. 'I remember meeting him as a young man when he was staying with the Cheyneys and he seemed very happy here. If you will forgive a personal remark, you are not in the least like him. You are a male version of your mother, and she was a typical Russell, well built and fair like you. I remember your father as being dark. I was once informed that you have a twin brother. Is he your double?'

'No, indeed. He is dark, but he does not much resemble my father, either. A little more, perhaps, than I do.'

Something in his voice when he had ended his last sentence struck both his hearers. There was an ambiguity about it— almost a touch of regret. If so, it was gone in an instant, and Russell was his usual cheerful self again.

After he and his chaise, now shared with Pickering, had left, Miss Beauregard turned to her niece.

'Now there is a young man of whom I approve. His manners are beautiful and he is obviously taken with you. Are you taken with him? You ought to be, you could scarcely do better. There is more to life, my dear, than being the widow of a dour old man.'

Mary protested, but not as vigorously as she might have wished, 'We are friends only, dear aunt.'

'Now *that* I don't believe. I saw the way in which you were looking at one another, and that was not at all friendly, no, indeed. I know what friendship entails and it is far too tepid a word to describe that which lies between you. I assure you that you have only to say the word and that young man would be on his knees before you, proposing—'

'Aunt,' said Mary, desperately breaking all the rules of etiquette by interrupting the old lady when she was in full flow, 'Lord Hadleigh did propose to me once, years ago, before I married Henry Wardour, and as soon as he had done so, he disappeared out of my life, deserting me completely, never to be seen or heard from again until I met him at Markham Hall last month. I had not meant to tell you this, but I would not like you to believe that any strong feelings are left between us.'

'So you say, my dear, but I am sure that there is something more to your story than you know. I pride myself on my ability to read my fellow men and women and I cannot believe that the man I have just met would betray you after such a dastardly fashion. No, indeed, he is a gentle fellow, not a roué or a rake who would betray a woman in any way. I would say that, if anything, he is too kind for his own good. He's not at all like his father—rather he takes after the Russells.'

Her eyes misted over. 'I was to have married George, the last of the Russells. He was my true love from youth, but he was taken with a fever and died a week before our wedding. That is why I have never married. I never wanted another man after I lost him. Lord Hadleigh looks very like him—and talks like him, too.'

Her eyes were glistening with tears and Mary put an impulsive arm around her aunt and kissed her. She said nothing, but she was hoping that perhaps there was some explanation for Russell's behaviour which would account for his apparent desertion of her.

That night, in the half-life which precedes sleep, she was with him again on their last day together.

It was not long after he had first declared his love for her, and he was about to leave Oxford to spend the long vacation in London.

She had been for a walk and had returned to be told by the butler that m'lord was with her father. He had almost winked at her: she knew that the servants were all aware how much she and Russell had come to feel for one another, but she was not sure how much her father knew.

Later, she remembered, she was walking in the garden at the back of the house when she saw Russell coming towards her, his face eager.

'I'm so pleased to have found you alone,' he told her. 'This may be our last opportunity to be together before I leave for London. Rather naughtily I didn't tell your father that I would come looking for you, since there is something I must ask you, and where better to do so than here, in the place which you love so much.'

Mary knew what was coming and her heart beat so fast that she thought that it would spring out of her chest.

'It is this, my darling. Will you marry me?'

He went down on one knee before her and took her hand and kissed it after he had finished speaking. 'I shall ask my father to approach yours in proper form, but I wanted to tell you myself that I wish to make you my wife without the old men coming between us.'

The look which he gave her when he said this was so mischievous and yet so loving that Mary felt quite light-headed with joy—to say nothing of light-hearted.

'There is no reason why we should not marry soon,' he went on. 'My father will be sure to want an heir since Ritchie and I are the last of this branch of the Chancellors, and he dislikes "the other lot", as he calls them, intensely. And when we are married we can play at chess and mathematics to our hearts' content—as well as enjoy ourselves in others ways. For example, like this.'

The mischief on Russell's face increased with every word he uttered and he concluded by taking her in his arms and kissing her with all the passion of youth. Mary's response was equally strong. They stood heart to heart and both believed that there had never been such fortunate lovers.

'Enough,' he said, breaking away from her and panting slightly from the force of his desire. 'We can surely be patient for a little while before I make you truly mine. It will not be long before everything is settled. In the meantime we must write to one another.'

'Every day—or nearly so,' laughed Mary, 'however expensive the post is.'

They kissed again—and parted.

Mary watched him walk away from her. When the path turned to make its way back to the front of the house and the entrance gates, he swung round and waved to her, blowing her yet another kiss before he disappeared.

And that was that.

Mary wrote to him as she had promised, but nothing came back. Her father said nothing of any letter from Lord Bretford asking for her hand in marriage on behalf of his son.

The days which had once seemed so bright with promise turned dull and dark, whatever the weather. After a dreadful six weeks had passed without a word from Russell, she spoke to her father of him, saying, 'When Lord Hadleigh returns, shall we go on to study further in Newton's *Principia*, Father?'

Her father looked up. He had just spent several days in London, visiting the British Museum and staying with an old friend in Bloomsbury. His voice icy, he said, as though she had been impertinent in asking such a question, 'Indeed not, my dear. I had a letter from Lord Hadleigh's father but two days ago, saying that his son did not intend to return to Oxford this autumn, but would continue his studies elsewhere.'

Afterwards Mary was to wonder that she had not fainted from shock on hearing this. Numbly, trying to keep her voice both steady and neutral, she asked, 'Did he happen to mention me in his letter, Father?'

Her father looked up from his work again—he had impatiently resumed it as soon as he had finished speaking. 'No, Mary, he did not. Why should he? His relationship was with me, as his son's tutor. I am sorry to lose him—with guidance to help him steady himself he had the makings of a very promising mathematician. Now I really must cease conversing with you—to go on will mean me losing the thread of the argument which I have been developing.'

Even now, so many years later, she could not keep the tears from falling as they had fallen on that evening long ago when she was at last alone. It was shortly after that that her father had told her early one morning before they had begun to work together that he had arranged her marriage with Henry Wardour.

'But he is an old man, Father,' she had exclaimed. 'Do I have to marry him?'

'Dear child,' her father had said gravely, 'he is not so very old, after all. Furthermore, I have to tell you that the physicians have said that I have not long to live. I do not wish to leave you alone in the world. Dr Wardour is a fine mathematician and you can continue with him the work which we have been doing together on the calculating machine. He is a good man and will look after you. You will oblige me by being a dutiful daughter and marrying him—and you will also oblige yourself.'

'And who knows? I might be lucky enough to see my grandchildren before the Good Lord calls me to my last rest. I have arranged for you to visit my brother in London and you will be married from his home: I shall join you there in time for the wedding. I am fearful that my health will not stand up to the planning and other arrangements if we hold it here.'

Mary was helpless before him. She knew that as his daughter he had the right to give her in marriage to whom he pleased. She wanted to say, He is old compared with the one whom I thought was my true love, Russell Hadleigh—but he has left me without a word, has not acknowledged my letters and, by his father writing to mine to say that he will not be returning to Oxford, has destroyed my last hope of becoming his wife.

His supposed love for her had been a sham. He was nothing but a rich young aristocrat enjoying his summer by pretending to love an old scholar's daughter. And so, because nothing else was left for her, she had married Henry Wardour and tried to forget that golden summer when she and Russell Hadleigh had laughed, worked, played and loved together.

The memory of that betrayal could still bring tears to her eyes and cause her to start up from sleep to ask herself why she should let him into her life again—risking the possibility that he might destroy her happiness once more.

And yet, and yet, the mature Mary who had been in his company and rejoiced in it as she had done in her girlhood, thought that somehow, somewhere, there was a false note being struck.

Nothing that Russell had said or done in the last few weeks had shown him as a man who was careless of others. On the contrary, he was invariably kind and thoughtful to all those around him, not only to his equals, but also to servants, officials and other men whom most persons of his rank took for granted. As her aunt had said that afternoon, he was almost too kind.

Now that she had brought herself to try to remember that lost past, and not forget it, there was another puzzle to be solved also—and that was the speed with which her father had arranged her marriage to Henry Wardour.

He had said subsequently that he had always intended her to marry him so that his work might be continued after his death, but he had never spoken of it to her before that fatal Long Vacation during which Russell had abandoned her.

Mary sat up and peered restlessly into the darkness. Was she imagining things? Was there more to Russell's disappearance from her life than she had at first thought? Was she starting at phantoms, trying to find excuses for him? More than ever she wished to talk to him about why he had left her after promising her so much.

Yes, she would talk to him, and soon. Matters could not be left as they were.

After that she could sleep.

* * *

By a coincidence, which was no coincidence at all, but something entirely to be expected since they had recently spent so many days together working, talking and laughing together as they had done at Oxford, Russell was also revisiting his lost past that night. It was not, however, until after he had been brought up short by the truth of the brutal present.

Once he had found himself on his father's land he was shocked at how derelict it was. Eddington village was particularly run-down with signs of neglect in all directions. Tumble-down cottages with leaking roofs housed a population of ragged and resentful beings. One scrawny fellow spat at the chaise when it rolled along the one main street, another shook his fist at it. It was quite unlike the rural idyll which he had imagined it to be before he had set out from London.

On impulse he stopped the chaise outside the village's one ale house: a place which had obviously seen better days. A battered sign, on which the Chancellor arms could just be made out, hung on a pole over the main doorway.

Pickering said doubtfully, 'You'll surely not be wanting to venture in there, m'lord, it looks none too clean to me.'

'I could do with a pint of ale,' returned Russell, short for once. 'You may stay in the chaise, or come with me, as you please.'

He was not really thirsty, but the day had been a long one and, for some reason he could not explain, he was desirous of finding out how the labourers on Chancellor lands lived when not at work. A group of villagers standing before the doorway watched him climb out of the chaise and walk by them. One man said something beneath his breath and the rest snickered.

Russell ignored him. He was not sure whether it was his

splendid turn-out or the Chancellor arms on the chaise door which was the more responsible for arousing the glares which he was receiving. He pushed the door open and found himself in the most miserable caricature of a village inn which he had ever encountered.

Behind a dirty counter a middle-aged man watched him in silence as did the room's few patrons. One old gaffer sat before a hearth in which a minimal fire burned. Conversation had died at his entry and every eye on him was resentful as though he were some enemy to be faced down.

'A pint of your best ale, landlord,' he said, as cheerfully as he could.

'I have no best ale, young sir,' grunted the man.

'Then your worst will have to do,' returned Russell cheerfully.

The old gaffer snickered. 'Best you don't try it, sir,' he advised. 'Bart, here, used to brew a good tipple, but them days are long gone, more's the pity.'

'He asked for the worst and so he shall have it,' groused the landlord.

Russell offered him his most dazzling smile when he was handed a grimy pewter tankard. He swallowed his distaste at its appearance before managing to swallow the tasteless stuff as well—to the amusement of the old gaffer and the indifference of everyone else.

He waved his tankard at him, saying, 'You seem to be a man of parts, my friend. Perhaps you might be able to tell me what state the by-way to the big house is in. Would my chaise be able to manage it?'

'Just about,' the old man cackled. 'Been right neglected, so it has, since young Shaw took over. Better in summer than in winter when t'mud takes over, too. Visiting him, are you?'

Russell put down his empty tankard. 'You might say so. He's not expecting me, though.'

The old man's gaze on him was suddenly shrewd. 'You've a right look of the Russells about you and no mistake. Some sort of relative of them, are you?'

'Yes,' said Russell, amused by the old man's lack of respect for the gentleman he obviously was.

'Well, don't expect much comfort when you get there. The place has never been the same since the new man took over and that's the truth.' He began to laugh gently to himself.

The new man? thought Russell. Who can he mean? Enlightenment suddenly dawned. I suppose he is speaking of my father who inherited Eddington when the old gaffer must have been in his prime.

He was about to question the old fellow further when the door opened and a burly man, as ragged as the rest of the inn's patrons, burst in.

'So help me Gawd, there's a chaise outside with the Chancellor arms on it—and who the devil can be inside is what I want to know, because if it's one of them I'll be sure to give him a piece of my mind.'

He suddenly saw Russell standing at the bar and began to stutter. 'I meant no offence, sir, no offence at all.'

'I trust not,' said Russell coolly. 'You said a moment ago that you would give one of them a piece of your mind. I am Russell Chancellor, Lord Hadleigh, and you may give me as many pieces of your mind as you may care to offer.'

The old gaffer cackled again. 'That's Josh Whateley, m'lord. Noisy when the gentry ain't about, as quiet as a mouse when they are.'

'I meant no offence, m'lord, none at all,' blustered Josh.

'And none taken, but I would dearly love to know what you might have said—had you a mind to.'

'Nothing, nothing at all,' raved Josh, turning and running out of the door.

The old gaffer cackled again but a dour, burly fellow who had been sitting in one corner nursing an empty tankard which had once held ale, stood up and said, 'If Josh won't say it, I will. The fancy clothes on your back, m'lord, are paid for by the men Mester Arthur Shaw's laid off and who will starve this winter or end up in the workus. Shame on you and the man who owns Eddington and don't care a damn about it. I'd say more except that I'll not risk prison, but I won't stay in the same room as the man who lives off my back.' He brushed past Russell and strode out of the room, slamming the door behind him.

Every fearful eye was on Russell. He scarcely knew what to say when confronted with such shameful poverty. Fellows in London talked cheerfully abut the agricultural depression, but here, in the north, far from London's salons, he was seeing the stark reality of it.

'It's a free country,' he said gently, 'and a man has the right to speak his mind. Until I reach Eddington I shall not know the truth of this matter, but be sure that when I do I will discover it. In the meantime I will bid you all good evening.'

He left a noisy room behind him, but his determination to discover what was going on at Eddington House had been strengthened even more by what he had seen and heard in its village.

Chapter Seven

The drive to Eddington House was through yet more uncared-for land. A few sheep grazed in its park, but nothing like as many as might have been expected. The day had been a dark one and some lights could already be seen in the manor's windows. It was also a bad omen that he had driven through open gates where there was no sign that the lodge beside them was inhabited.

The drive led up to a sweep before an Elizabethan family home which had had been partly improved in the middle of the last century. To its detriment, Russell decided, when he stepped down from the chaise after handing Pickering his dispatch case to carry. The door to the stable-yard was closed and locked and there was no sign of any grooms or outside workers.

Pickering, annoyed by the delay, walked up to the big oak door and hammered on it. Nothing happened. He hammered again, this time with all his strength, but still nothing. Russell, standing beside him, said, trying not to sound too exasperated, 'Why don't you push at the door and see what happens?'

Pickering nodded and obeyed.

To the surprise of them both, for Russell had not really

expected the door to be unlocked, it opened, and they walked in. Immediately the sound of singing could be heard coming from somewhere not far away. There was a big Chinese gong in the dirty entrance hall and Pickering hammered on that with the stick which hung beside it.

Still nothing. The noise the singers were making had presumably been too loud for the gong to be heard. Master and man looked at one another. Pickering said, 'Shall I go exploring, m'lord?'

Russell made up his mind. He would start as he meant to go on. 'No,' he replied. 'This is my home and I mean to find out what is amiss here. The noise seems to be coming from that direction,' and he pointed to the double doors which had faced them when they entered. 'You may wait for me here—and don't let the dispatch case out of your hands.'

He strode to the doors, flung them open and found himself in a huge room with a hammer-beamed wooden ceiling. In the centre of it was a long oak table whose top was being enthusiastically banged by pewter tankards wielded by half-cut singing men and a few half-dressed women. The man seated on his own at the far end of the table, and who was leading his guests in a drunken rendering of 'Do ye ken John Peel', was obviously the host.

He, and his guests, were so intent on their song that they failed to notice that they had a visitor. Russell walked slowly forward until he arrived in the line of sight of the lone man.

'Good evening,' he said in his most pleasant voice. 'Am I interrupting something important?'

The heads of everyone at the table turned to stare at him. The host, putting down his glass—he was the only man there who boasted one—exclaimed in a voice meant to dominate and to cow, 'What the devil are you doing here—and who the devil are you?'

Russell offered him his sweetest smile, the one which charmed everyone he met, but which did not charm this fellow, and retorted with, 'More to the point, what the devil are you doing here? And who the devil are you?'

Arthur Shaw, for Russell was certain that he was the man playing host, turned to a battered old retainer who was standing just behind him, 'Briggs,' he bellowed, 'see this fellow out before I send for the constable to remove him. And you, young man, oblige me by leaving quietly. I've no wish to set the dogs, or the law, on you.'

At the mention of the word 'dogs', a large wolfhound suddenly rose from beneath the table and rushed at Russell, barking madly. He held his ground, saying as commandingly as he could, 'Sit, sir, sit!' before giving its owner another smile when the dog, surprised, obeyed him.

'Oh, I really wouldn't set the law or the dogs on me, Mr Arthur Shaw—for I believe that to be your name—for you would have a deal of explaining to do to the authorities as to why you tried to turn the son of the owner of Eddington House out of his own home. I am Russell, Lord Hadleigh, the Earl of Bretford's son and heir.'

The company, which had been buzzing gently while Russell and Arthur Shaw exchanged words, fell suddenly silent. Shaw himself was nothing daunted.

'That's an extreme claim to make, young fellow. How do I know that you are who you say you are?'

Russell moved forward. 'A good question that. Send Briggs for my man, Pickering, who is waiting in the entrance hall for me, and all shall be revealed.'

'Off with you, Briggs,' snarled Shaw, 'and bring in anyone waiting there so that we may clear this matter up once and for all. By the by, sir—or m'lord, if that is who you are—you may do me the goodness of informing me of how you managed to enter the Manor.'

'With pleasure,' drawled Russell, now in total command of himself and the room. Indeed, he noticed that one or two of the revellers had risen from their seats and were trying to make an unobtrusive exit through the far doors. 'I am not a house-breaker, nor a burglar, I merely walked in by the front door which you had carelessly left open—something which will not make my father happy with your conduct here when I inform him of it.'

This was deceitful of him, since his father had no knowledge of his visit to Eddington and he had no intention of allowing him to learn where he was. In any case, Pickering's arrival, looking highly offended, and holding the ancient retainer by his right ear, cut this dialogue short.

Before saying anything, Pickering handed Russell the dispatch case. 'What is it, m'lord?' he began. 'This man...' and he flung the retainer from him '...has been most offensive, demanding that I prove that you are Lord Hadleigh. Of course you are Lord Hadleigh, who else could you be? There are the Chancellor arms on your chaise and in that case which I have just handed to you are letters and papers which will act as further confirmation of your identity. It also contains a draft from Coutts, a draft which allows you to draw money from most country banks. I can fetch further evidence from the chaise, m'lord, if this insolent fellow is not satisfied by what we already have to offer.'

He waved a lordly hand at Arthur Shaw, who was begin-

ning to look as though he had eaten something which dis-
agreed with him.

Russell's admiration for Pickering grew—why, he was
behaving as haughtily as though he were the accused aristocrat!

'Oh, I think that it might be wise if you brought in further
proof,' he said, still at his most charming, 'and while you are
doing so, Mr Shaw would be wise if he were to dismiss this
unseemly mob who are busy ruining a rather fine table. I see
that several of the roisterers are vomiting on the floor—one of
the kitchen staff present might be good enough to mop it up.'

Arthur Shaw, having taken the dispatch case from Russell
and examined it, sullenly conceded that he accepted that
Russell was who he said he was even before Pickering returned.

'Peg,' he ordered the half-dressed woman nearest to him,
'go to the kitchens and do as m'lord asks. The rest of you go
to the servants quarters, except for my personal guests who
will be staying the night here.'

Peg, thrusting her ample bosoms back into her bodice, rushed
off in her bare feet, to return a little later with a frightened-
looking little maid, two buckets and two mops. By then all of
the revellers had disappeared, save for Arthur Shaw, and Pickering had reappeared with further proofs of Russell's identity.

'Now,' said Russell, seating himself in the high chair which
Shaw had vacated, having motioned him to remain standing,
'you may inform me of what the devil is going on at Eddington.
The Manor appears to be a giant pigsty, the village and the lands
are in ruins and you are conducting a saturnalia in the Great Hall
with the Manor's servants and the cronies whom you call friends.
You are sending accounts to my father which purport to show
that you are making a vast profit while at the same time fields
lie fallow, sheep are few and you are laying off labourers.'

'Oh, I think that you are mistaken, m'lord,' whined Shaw. 'I don't think those who live down south know how bad times are up here. I have had to lay off labourers to make up for the loss in income caused by last year's bad harvest—and I have still managed to increase your father's revenues. Not a bad thing, surely.'

'Bad times up here, are they?' enquired Russell, leaning back in his chair. 'You looked as though you were having a jolly good time when I came in. I suppose those bottles of port, wine and ale all came from my father's cellars. Will their use be featured in your next set of accounts or are they what I believe are called perquisites of office—or perks for short?'

'Oh, yes, m'lord,' babbled Shaw. 'Seeing that I had made a profit on the year and since your most noble father has repeatedly told me that he has no intention of visiting us, I thought that he would not object if I rewarded my servants and friends with a little sup of something now and then.'

'In this case,' said Russell, examining the contents of the table, 'I would describe it as rather a large sup. Never mind, I will pass no judgement on this until I have examined your accounts and estate papers myself.'

'In the morning, m'lord, I take it,' said Shaw eagerly. 'It grows late and I assume that you have had a long journey today.'

'Then you assume wrongly. I have had a short, and pleasurable, one. And no, I don't wish you to bring me the accounts and papers in the morning, I order you, in fact, to bring them to me now. Or rather, I will accompany you to the estate office and there you may hand them over, immediately.'

'Indeed, m'lord, if that is what you wish,' croaked Shaw desperately. He had hoped to do more than a little doctoring of them, but no matter, the idle young aristocrat before him would find dealing with them rather difficult and a little flim-flam might mend all. 'I shall be happy to explain them to you, now if you wish, although morning would be better.'

'My thanks to you,' drawled Russell, standing up. 'But I have no need of your advice. I would prefer to examine them on my own. Now, lead me to your office.'

Arthur Shaw looked wildly round the room. 'But, m'lord, you will not be used to figuring—'

He stopped because Russell was gently shaking his head at him. 'As you wish, m'lord, but I don't use the estate office to work in. During your father's long absence, my father and predecessor, who died three years ago, thought fit to use the study attached to the library—the office was too draughty for an old man, you understand. Besides, you couldn't carry all the papers away, too many…'

He was babbling and knew it, and it wasn't helping him at all. M'lord was looking at him as though he were some species of insect and when he spoke his voice and manner had changed completely.

'I don't think that you understand me, Shaw. Without further ado lead me to wherever your accounts and the estate's papers are kept and hand them over to me at once. If there are too many for me to carry, I assume that you have a few footmen about who aren't too drunk to assist me to carry them. If not, you may have the honour.'

It was hopeless. Shaw's surrender was abject.

'Very well, m'lord. As you wish, m'lord.'

'Oh, I do wish, Shaw. You and your father may have been the masters here for the last thirty years, but no longer; whether or not you remain as my agent is dependent on what I might discover from your accounts and on your behaviour while I am here. Not only that, but I would like an explanation as to why your father's death and your succession were never reported to my father.'

Russell had never in his life spoken to anyone after the fashion in which he was speaking to Shaw. He was discovering in himself a will of iron, a will which he had never been required to use before he had come to Eddington. Here, however, on his own, against his father's wishes, but with a sudden determination to put right—if he could—what was so patently going wrong at Eddington, he was beginning to realise that he was more like his twin than he had thought.

Exhilaration ran through him when he followed Shaw into the study. He had acquired an aim in life, and given luck he might try to act as Ritchie had recommended before his father had the chance to find out what he was up to—and stop him.

Later that night he was not feeling so sanguine. He had been examining all the estates papers—such as they were. From them it was difficult to make out what exactly the financial state of Eddington was—other than that it was not what it was supposed to be. It was obvious to him that the accounts Shaw had sent in were a total invention. He had succeeded in bamboozling his father because he was sure that the old fool—for that was how he was uncharitably beginning to think of him—had, after a cursory examination, thrown them over to his secretary, Graves, as passed.

It was not unreasonable to suppose that, at some point, either his father, or Graves, ought to have realised that what had been paid in to the local bank and what the accounts reported did not match. Apparently the nearest bank was at Ancoates. He grinned a little when he found that out. Here was a splendid opportunity to kill two birds with one stone. It would make it easier for him to visit Mary.

That Shaw had been systematically plundering Eddington for years—embezzling being the more proper term—was quite plain and now he would be able to prove it. Russell laughed out loud. It amused him that the first real use of his mathematical talents, nurtured by Dr Beauregard and Mary, would be to solve the problem of the looting of one of his father's estates.

Before that, however, he must sleep and in the morning he would decide on a plan of action. He yawned. He had been hard at work for several hours and it was now after midnight. His bed was a damp and uncomfortable affair, even in summer, and had scarcely been warmed by the dirty brass warming pan the frightened little maid had brought up after being bullied by Pickering.

Worse, his head was buzzing with figures, making it difficult for him to sleep. In desperation he tried to banish Eddington, Arthur Shaw and the account books from his mind and think of Mary. Not only of the love they had shared, but of what had happened after he had left Oxford and gone to tell his father of his love for her and his wish to marry her…

Like Mary, Russell was not certain whether he revisited the past or was dreaming it. He remembered that last day with her in the garden. He could see her lovely, piquant face which had charmed him precisely because she was so different from all the smooth society beauties he had seen since his father had become Earl.

He had gone down from Oxford in a dream of love. He remembered, wincing, how he had been so stupidly sure that his father would approve of his choice of wife. The Beaure-

gards were an old family, even older than the Chancellors—
their origins dated back to Norman William. They were comfortable, not rich, but surely, he had told himself, the Bretford
Earldom was such a wealthy one that there was no necessity
for its heir to marry a rich heiress—a moderately rich one
would do.

His father's greeting of him on his return was so cold that
Russell thought that it might be wise not to raise the matter
immediately. Give the old man time to adjust to the fact that
he was going to be about for the next few weeks, being his
considered judgement.

Alas, his father grew no warmer towards him, so, not
wishing for further delay, he asked if he might speak to him
of an important matter. He had not yet received a letter from
Mary. He had sent her three since he had arrived home, but he
assumed that it might be some days before she received them.

'Now what important matter can that be, Hadleigh?' his
father enquired nastily.

'It is this, sir,' he began, his manner hesitant. 'I have met
a young lady at Oxford. She is the daughter of Dr Beauregard,
the celebrated mathematician and one-time astronomer of
whom you may have heard—'

'Yes, yes,' his father said testily. 'I have heard of Dr Beauregard. I recently attended a lecture he gave at the Royal Society.'

'Excellent.' Russell beamed in his naïve folly, as he later
glumly recalled. 'Then you will not be surprised to learn that
his daughter is both beautiful and well informed.' He did not
say clever—he thought that his father might not approve of
cleverness in a woman. 'And I have decided that—with your
permission, sir, which I now ask—I wish to marry her.'

'Marry her!' his father snorted. 'What nonsense! I have

higher ambitions than that for you, Hadleigh. There are, at present, few on the marriage market who are good enough in terms of wealth and station for the future Earl of Bretford, but I have no doubt that, if we wait for you to be of a suitable age to marry, there will be plenty to choose from. Why, you are barely out of childhood's frocks and already prating of marrying a nobody of little fortune.'

'The Beauregards are not poor!' exclaimed Russell desperately.

'As I—and my kind—count poor,' said his father, 'poor is what they are. No, no, forget this youthful folly. See the world and other women before you babble of marriage to me.'

The words flew out of Russell's mouth before he could stop them. 'I shall not change my mind, sir. Mary is everything which I could want in a wife. She is good and clever, as well as being beautiful. I can talk to her as I have been able to talk to no other woman.'

His father began to laugh. 'Go to, Hadleigh! Don't prate to me from the depths of your lack of experience of the world about what is desirable in the wife of the future Earl of Bretford. This is the last I have to say on the matter, except that I think it better for you not to return to Oxford. I am disappointed to learn that Dr Beauregard has allowed matters between you and his daughter to go so far as for you to discuss marriage with her. I had thought that you attended Dr Beauregard's home to further your small talent in mathematics, not in the arts of illicit courtship.'

He paused, stared hard at his son and said, 'As my heir, dependent on me, I expect you to do as I wish. You may leave me now, Hadleigh. I shall not change my mind.'

'Nor I mine,' had retorted Russell mutinously. So mutinously that he told himself savagely that his father had not ordered him to stop writing to Mary, and write to her he would. After that—well, after that he would decide what action to take to try to make his father change his mind. If he could be persuaded to meet Mary, that might do the trick. He surely could not behave so harshly once he knew what a treasure she was and what a splendid future Countess she might make.

He ran downstairs to find that the post had arrived and, despite Graves's annoyance, demanded to go through it first to see whether a letter from her was waiting for him. It was not, neither on that day nor on any other.

Shocked and distressed, he wrote to her daily, begging her to write to him—but nothing came back. In the end, damn what his father might say if he knew, he made a clandestine visit to Oxford to try to see her, and to ask why she was not replying to his letters after everything which had happened between them.

It was a wet summer's day when he arrived at the Beauregards' home. He asked the butler if he might speak to Miss Beauregard. The butler looked at him strangely and showed him into the drawing room where he waited eagerly to see her.

Instead, it was Dr Beauregard who walked in. He wore his sternest academic's face. 'I am surprised to see you here,' he said, without further preamble. 'I understood that you had left Oxford for good.'

So his father had already written to the College authorities, telling them that he would not return! Nothing daunted, he said, 'I came to visit Miss Beauregard, sir. I trust that she is well?'

'Of course, she is well. Why should she be otherwise? She is staying with her mother's sister while she prepares for her wedding.'

'Her wedding,' Russell remembered stammering. 'Her wedding! Is she getting married, then?' He knew that he sounded stupid, but the shock of what Dr Beauregard was telling him had sent his senses reeling. Whoever she was marrying, it was not Russell Hadleigh.

'That is the usual reason for a wedding, m'lord. It has long been planned. Her husband-to-be is my friend and colleague, Dr Henry Wardour. She will make him a most suitable wife since she shares his interests and will be able to assist him in his work—and, incidentally, carry mine on when I am gone.'

'But he is an old man,' Russell burst out, 'and I love her.'

Did she love him, though? Was their heavenly summer together just a light flirtation undertaken to pass the time pleasantly before she settled down for life? Was that the reason why she had not answered his letters?—those letters in which he had poured out his love?

His face must have betrayed the agitation which he felt, the sense of betrayal, but it did not move Dr Beauregard for, pulling out his watch, he said impatiently, 'Come, m'lord, come, m'lord, this is childish nonsense after a summer's play which you are engaging in. You are by no means ready to marry, nor would I approve of her marrying you. Nor does she, I may safely say, wish to marry you.

'I have some friends arriving for luncheon. I think that there is nothing further to be said between us. I bid you goodday and wish you well.'

On looking back, now, in the middle of the dark night, Russell was asking himself whether there was not more to this sad story than he was being told. At the time—and ever since—he had taken Dr Beauregard's words at their face value. Now he began to wonder whether he and Mary might not have been manipulated in some way by a pair of fathers who had very different ideas for their children's future than the one which their children had planned for themselves.

Somehow that hopeful thought sent him to sleep. It was hopeful because, if he were to speak to Mary of their past, he would tell her that after he had received no letters from her he had visited Oxford and had had an interview with her father. He had gone there to speak to him of his wish to marry her and that, to his great surprise, her father had told him of her coming marriage. Worse than that, he had said quite plainly that she had no wish to marry him. In no way had he ever betrayed her as she seemed to think.

Was it also conceivably possible that she had not betrayed him?

Mary did not fret when Russell did not immediately pay his promised call on her, but after a week had passed she began to wonder whether he was about to abandon her again.

She said something of this to her aunt, who replied robustly, 'Nonsense, my dear child. Depend upon it, he has probably found that matters at Eddington needed seeing to if all the rumours I have recently heard have any truth in them. Give the poor fellow a few more days and I'm sure that we shall see him again.'

A week later Mary was seated in the garden, trying to decide whether to read Miss Jane Austen's *Persuasion* or to go again through the calculations which she and Russell had made at Markham Hall. Somehow the day seemed too charmingly sultry for her to engage in either and she was falling into a happy doze when she heard footsteps coming, those of her aunt and another person.

Her aunt was talking to a man, and when he replied to her she recognised him as Russell! Sleep flew away. She sat up so sharply that the first volume of Miss Austen's novel and her own papers tumbled from her lap.

'Here he is,' exclaimed her aunt triumphantly. 'I told you that he would come. He informs me that he was sadly delayed by reason of his need to mend matters at Eddington, but has come to apologise for not calling on us sooner.'

Mary, who had risen and was standing in a little sea of scattered papers, said breathlessly, 'No need for apologies. I am sure that Lord Hadleigh was only doing his duty.'

'Alas, yes,' he said. He was standing before her in all his glory, and what glory it was. He had obviously, as he had promised, ridden over from Eddington, and the clothes he was wearing showed off to perfection his athletic body. 'I knew that you would both forgive me if I offered that as an excuse.'

'No excuse,' said Miss Beauregard gaily, 'if what I and half of the neighbourhood have heard of is true. Now, sit down and tell Mary all about it while I go and order tea and Sally Lunns. I fear that, given the weather, ices would be better, but, alas, I have no ice-house. I am informed, though, that the Chinese drink tea in hot weather in order to keep cool, so perhaps we can try a little experiment of our own.'

'I like your aunt,' Russell said, sitting down and stretching his legs before him—which had Mary admiring his boots' high polish and wondering whether it had been achieved by the application of champagne. 'She has a true appreciation of the vital things of life: food, erudition, gossip—and a delightful sense of tact, by which I mean leaving us alone to converse privately.'

Mary smiled back at him. One of his charms was his easiness of manner, plus a sense that he was giving his whole attention to the person he was with. 'Yes, I have been very happy here. Until I undertook this journey north I had not realised how lonely I was in Oxford.'

She blushed after she had come out with this. She had not meant to say anything quite so personal and revealing. His tact was shown by his gravely nodding his head and saying, 'I was sorry that I could not visit you earlier, but things were in a worse way at Eddington than I had supposed, and I felt it my duty to try to begin to clean the Augean stables before I engaged in the kind of pleasure which visiting you would bring me. I can only hope that you approve of my decision.'

'Very much so,' replied Mary energetically, 'although I have to say that you don't look a bit like Hercules, who was the first to undertake that task. All the statues which I have seen of him make him look most wild and ferocious—quite unlike yourself.'

Russell laughed. 'I suppose I ought to take that as a compliment. On the other hand, you have not seen me during the last fortnight when I believe that with the best will in the world I did look rather wild and ferocious at times. It was very lonely, though,' he added, his smile disappearing.

'Would you like to talk to me about it?' Mary asked. 'A problem shared is a problem halved, my father used to say.'

'Yes, I think I would, but on the other hand it is not exactly what I thought that we might talk about when we met again.' He looked down at the papers which Mary had hastily lumped together and said, 'I rather thought that we might talk about that—among others things.' The look he gave her was a meaningful one and Mary blushed again.

'There will be other times when we can talk of those,' she said, 'and since I have experienced loneliness I know that to speak to others of the matters which concern us most is a healing thing, so, if you can bring yourself to tell me a little of your problems at Eddington, pray do so.'

This was a stiff way of speaking, she knew, particularly when what she really wanted was to throw her arms around him—or feel his around her—but with Aunt Beauregard about to return at any moment this was definitely taboo.

'My lady commands,' he said, giving her a low bow without exactly getting out of his basket chair, and he began to tell her of his early days at Eddington and of how he had been trying to mend matters.

'With some little success,' he ended with a sigh. 'After all, I believe that matters were never very good under the long years when Shaw's father was the agent, and since he inherited the post they have gone downhill rapidly. Incidentally, my father is quite unaware that old Mr Shaw had died. The younger one, having the same name, presumably took over without informing him, or Graves, my father's secretary.'

Mary's face was a picture. 'But how could that have happened?'

'Alas, for some reason my father has no interest in anything to do with Eddington, more's the pity.'

'So he sent you here?'

Russell could not lie directly to her, any more than he had done to Shaw, who obviously believed that he was his father's emissary. He had not seen fit to enlighten him because Shaw, being the kind of fellow he was, would probably have written to London and that was the last thing which Russell wanted. He could not imagine his father's reaction if he were to be informed, either by Shaw, or through local gossip, that his son and heir had gone to Eddington and proceeded to turn everything upside down! Even if by doing so he hoped to restore the estate's prosperity.

'Well,' he said, smiling, 'I am the heir,' which was no answer at all. The rapidly growing empathy between him and Mary had her wondering exactly what his answer had meant when a simple yes or no would have done. She said nothing, however. There was something about Russell which was beginning to intrigue her: a hint that he was a sterner, harder man than he had been, and if restoring Eddington was doing that to him then it was all to the good.

'Have you turned Shaw away?' she said. 'Aunt Beauregard said yesterday that the rumour was that you had either dismissed him already or were on the point of it.'

Russell shook his head. 'No—but only on condition that he works with me to remedy matters. You see, I also have to say that if my father had managed his estates as he ought then the Shaws would not have been able to cheat him so easily— if at all. I am certain that Shaw has stolen from us, but it would be damned difficult to prove and would rebound badly on the family name. Absentee landlords are in general not much liked.'

He did not say that, when riding around the estate and through Eddington village and the other hamlets, many men and women had come up to him to try to shake his hand and thank him for coming to save them from the Shaws' exploitation.

'We always knew,' said one old gaffer, 'that some day a member of the family would come up here to put things right. They tell me, young man, that your name is Russell, and it is like having them back again. They were always good to the tenants and labourers. My granddaughter is dressing her third babby in the shawl which the last Mrs Russell gave to my wife when our first child was born.'

Russell did not feel particularly virtuous, rather that in learning how to manage the estate he had found something which he could do, and do well.

'It's odd,' he said, after a short silence in which he had been musing upon the change in his life, 'what started me off on this venture was quite accidental. I was looking at the Eddington quarterly accounts and by using my mathematical skills I realised that there was something odd about them. And then I met you again, and thus not only have I found myself using them at Eddington, but also employing them to help you with your work. I hate to think of all the years I have wasted in empty pleasure when I could have been doing something useful—and being more like Ritchie.'

Mary could not stop herself from leaning forward and putting a hand on his muscular thigh. 'You love, hate and envy him, don't you? But you need not now. What you are trying to accomplish at Eddington is fast becoming the talk of the neighbourhood. I have a confession to make. When you first delayed your visit I began to think that you had deserted me again, but later, when Aunt told me of what was happening there, I knew that I was wronging you.'

Russell picked up the loving hand and kissed it. 'It was the memory of you that inspired me and kept me going at Eddington when things proved difficult. Besides that, there is something else I ought to tell you. I have been thinking of that last summer of ours at Oxford and I believe that we ought to forget our self-denying ordnance and speak of it. There is a false note there, I am sure. I have the strangest feeling that a great wrong was done to us and if we were to speak of what we each thought had happened we might be able to uncover it.

'Not today, though, and not here. In a few days' time I would like to ride with you into the woods. They say there is an ancient cairn there, not far from where the hermit has his cottage. We could take a picnic with us, sit beside it, look out over the quarry, and talk in private, away from prying ears.'

Mary began to laugh. 'Oh, yes. I would like that because my memories are beginning to worry me, too. As for prying ears, I think that we might encounter a few prying eyes if we were to ride out alone—but what of that? I have been a prisoner of convention for far too long and would wish to kick over the traces for a change!'

In her sparkling merriment she was almost the young girl he had once known, and if time had left its marks on them, then it had also given them certain strengths which might have passed them by if they had led too easy a life. Absent-mindedly Russell kissed not only the hand he held, but the pulse-point of her wrist and her arm up to the elbow. They were gentle kisses, but Mary could feel the suppressed passion beneath them.

'It is taking your aunt a devil of a long time to assemble three cups of tea and a plate of crumpets,' he whispered into her ear when his kisses reached the ruffled hem of her short sleeve. 'I mentioned tact earlier—I'm sure that she's practising it, but I must stop where I am lest she find us in what is known as "a compromising position", something which varies between being found kissing on the lips to criminal conversation itself!'

Mary knew that criminal conversation was a polite description of the act of love itself, but she could not object to Russell's indirect reference to it. After all, had she not expressed a wish to kick over the traces? On the other hand she had no wish to kick over the carriage itself! At least, she amended hastily, until after they had had their long-delayed discussion about what exactly had happened—and why—thirteen years ago. In any case here, at last, came Aunt Beauregard with a footman behind her carrying the promised tea and crumpets.

'I do trust,' she said, smiling at her two protégés who were now chastely sitting well apart from one another, 'that you have found plenty to talk about. There were a few problems with the kitchen range, but all is now well. I do hope that you like crumpets, m'lord.'

'Hadleigh will do,' he said, giving her his brilliant smile, 'or Russell, which I think that I would prefer you both to use. And yes, I do like tea and crumpets very much. I'm rather afraid, though, that you are going to find me a constant visitor if you continue to feed me like this.'

'Oh, that won't trouble us at all, will it, Mary? As for Cook, she is constantly complaining that I don't have enough visitors for her to show off her culinary skills—so come as often as you can and make us all happy.'

'Be very sure,' he said, smiling and raising his tea cup to offer them a teetotal toast, 'that I shall certainly accept your kind offer with great pleasure.'

Chapter Eight

'He is coming over this afternoon,' almost carolled Mary, several days later, waving a note at Aunt Beauregard. 'He will be bringing a picnic and we shall make our promised ride to the cairn in the woods. Would you think me very fast if we do not take an attendant with us? I am sure that I shall be quite safe in Lord Hadleigh's company. He has a very strong sense of honour.'

'So do you, my dear,' said her aunt, 'and, after all, you are a widow. Widows are allowed more freedom than single women. When you return he will perhaps stay a little longer— I believe that he will be happy to give you the game of chess which I am too ignorant to offer you.'

Had Mary not, in the past, resolutely refused to consider remarriage, her match-making aunt would not have been so eager to throw her in the way of such an eligible young man as Russell Hadleigh. Particularly when that young man had looked at her so fondly.

He was doing it again when he arrived with an attendant groom who helped Mary on to her horse before being told to enjoy himself in the kitchen at Ancoates. Mary looked particularly splendid in a deep blue riding dress and a little black top hat. Russell, of course, was as debonair as usual. The promised picnic was being carried by a pack horse.

Aunt Beauregard, waving them a fond goodbye from the front of the house, thought sentimentally what a handsome pair they made. Someone ought to paint them—preferably that fellow Lawrence who was all the rage these days; and if Russell thought that Mary looked splendid, she was returning the compliment by thinking the same of him.

The ride to the cairn was not a long one and the path, though rough, was not so difficult that it troubled their horses. It was made in absolute silence—the characteristic of all true woods, Russell remarked to Mary—so much so that conversation and chatter seemed to profane the almost holy quiet. The cairn, when they reached it, was a relic of the Iron Age, standing near a settlement in a small clearing on ground a little higher than its attendant stream, one of the tributaries of the Tyne.

After tethering their horses, Russell lifted down from the pack horse a blanket and the stout knapsack which held the picnic. He spread the blanket on the ground and invited Mary to sit on it.

Mary gazed around her. 'I wonder what they were like,' she said, 'the people who lived near the cairn so long ago.'

'Like us, with different clothing and a different language.'

'Really,' said Mary, 'but their lives must have been so different. Fancy living inside those stones in winter.'

Russell, who was busy unpacking a sumptuous little repast, said, 'You must remember that that is what they were used to.'

'Perhaps people didn't live there at all,' she suggested. 'It might have been a tomb.'

'The locals think not,' Russell said, handing her a pewter plate. 'Apparently the hermit, before he became quite such a recluse, told them that the men who lived here built the cairn because it was isolated, in the shelter of the wood and near a supply of water, oh, and a quarry from which they took the stones to build the cairn and the settlement.

'Here are some sandwiches, madam, with some excellent beef. The cook has suddenly remembered most of her old skills, forgotten since matters at Eddington grew so dire. She has packed us some little cakes which the locals like as well as home-brewed ale and pewter mugs in which to drink it.'

'How are things progressing at Eddington?' Mary asked.

'Slowly,' he replied. 'You must understand that the people living in the house have grown used to an idle life and don't like to be made to live a busy one. On the other hand, I am extremely popular with the tenants and the labourers because they can see that I am beginning to improve matters. Shaw is dragging his feet a little, but I don't like to dismiss him because his local knowledge can be helpful. I have hired some carpenters and builders to repair the structure of the house itself, and begin to paint the outside. Some of the local women have also been drafted in to clean the rooms and make them fit for civilised beings to live in.'

He hesitated a minute, and offered Mary one of the little cakes before going on. 'I know it's an imposition and the place is abominably dirty, but I wondered if you might like to help me to examine what has been stored in the attics.

'For some reason nearly all of the paintings and most of the furniture have been moved there—in order to save the trouble of looking after them, one supposes. I'd like to restore them to their proper places again. I think that a woman's touch might be helpful here. My sister Margaret spends a lot of time buying furniture and rearranging her husband's old home, which had been horribly neglected by his grandfather in his old age.'

'Of course I would, and Aunt Beauregard, too, I suspect. You have only to say the word.'

The eager face which she offered him set Russell all of a-twitch. He had only to look at her these days to desire her. He hadn't felt like this in a woman's mere presence since he was a very young man—since he had last been in Mary's company before their parting, in fact. He told his body to behave itself, but it seemed to have a mind of its own, or rather, to be truthful, no mind at all!

'Very well, then. We shall arrange it before I leave. Now, drink up your ale, it's supposed to be good for you and there is no one here to tell you that young ladies should not drink such a common thing—although your female ancestors did.'

He handed her the pewter mug and, in doing so, their hands met. The wave of passion which passed between them was so strong that for a moment time stopped and they sat there, transfixed, before time began again.

'Now,' said Russell, looking away from his loved one, 'I know why the rule that unmarried men and women should never be alone together was made. I hope that I do not distress you if I tell you that simply to be alone with you has the strongest effect on me—but I shall try to behave myself, although, God knows, it will be even more difficult than it was when we were girl and boy together at Oxford.'

Mary looked away from him and drank some of her ale before saying, 'I think that I ought to tell you that being with you has the same powerful effect on me as it did all those years ago. That being so, I also think that we ought to discuss why you deserted me then, if what you now say is true.'

Russell sat up sharply. '*I* deserted *you*? No, indeed, forgive me for saying so, but you deserted me to marry old Wardour without so much as a letter from you to tell me so.'

The effect of this speech on Mary was so powerful that Russell thought that she was about to faint.

'Dare I believe that you are speaking the truth?' she finally faltered, her face ashen.

Russell, who had been lying stretched out, on one elbow after he had passed her the ale, stood up before falling on to his knees before her.

'Believe that I am telling you the truth. A terrible truth which I have had to live with ever since for, so far as I was concerned, our love was a true and deep one, not that of a boy and girl playing with it for the first time. Why did you desert me, Mary, why? Or ought I to ask you whether you did desert me—for I am beginning to think that we were both tricked. Tell me, did you receive my letters?'

'No,' she replied, her face still white, her whole body trembling. 'No, I received nothing from you, nothing at all. The first news which I had of you came weeks later when my father informed me that you were not returning to Oxford in the autumn. I cannot tell you how strongly that affected me. Even now I have difficulty in holding back my tears.'

The face she showed him told him that she was not lying. Two tears were slowly falling down her pale cheeks.

Russell leaned forward and took her by the shoulders. 'Nothing? You received nothing? And Henry Wardour—how did you come to marry him?'

'My father called me into his study one day to say that he

had arranged my marriage to him. He said that it was a most suitable one, and that he expected me to fall in with his wishes. I was left with no choice. Had I received any letters from you I might have argued with him—but because of that I believed that you had deserted me. Now you tell me that you hadn't.'

She fell silent. Russell, still holding her, said passionately, 'Mary, believe me. I told my father that I wished to marry you and he refused to give me his permission. I didn't allow that to deter me. I came at once to Oxford to see you, but you were not there. You were with your mother's sister, your father told me, arranging your marriage to Dr Wardour. Can you imagine what a blow that was to me? Particularly when he said that the marriage was also your wish.

'So, what is the explanation of these strange events? It now seems that we were writing to one another—but neither of us received any letters. It was the old men, was it not, who tricked us? Your father and mine. For their own reasons they did not wish us to marry, so they intercepted our letters and destroyed them. My father wrote to Oxford saying that I would not be returning there in the autumn. He also told me that I must marry a woman he would choose as soon as a suitable one could be found. Your father married you to Henry Wardour—and consequently we each thought that it was the other who was faithless, and have believed so ever since.'

Still holding her, he kissed her gently on the brow. 'I am not lying, and nor are you, so my understanding of the matter must hold good. Do you believe me now? Do you believe that we were tricked and manipulated?'

'Yes, yes, yes,' Mary said passionately. 'Of course I believe you—look how cunningly they kept us apart.'

The knowledge of the wasted years which they had spent

apart, the regret, the unhappiness, the sense of betrayal and the misery which they had each suffered, caused Mary to shiver violently. She was cold, oh, so cold, and he, the man she loved who, after all, had never betrayed her, was now tenderly holding her in his arms. He was kissing her, and stroking her hands for it was plain that she was so shocked that she was on the verge of unconsciousness.

She had been so brave, as he had been. They had come to terms with life—but at what a price. Slowly Russell lowered her down beside him, so that she lay in his arms, beneath the tender blue of the summer sky. He was murmuring something to her in a low voice but what he might be saying did not matter to her—what mattered was that *he* was saying it.

Mary wished that she could remain like this for ever, lost in time, with no demands being made on her while she came to terms with what their fathers had done to them. She was almost comatose, her eyes closed, her breathing light, but Russell was very much alive, aware of what holding his beloved so closely to him was doing to his self-control, particularly since in the state she was in he ought to say and do nothing which might distress her.

Time passed. So alone were they that they might, Russell thought, have been a pair of Iron Age lovers out to enjoy themselves in the time-honoured way under the summer's sun. If only he could do the same, but a thousand things kept him still and silent while Mary fell at last into a deep sleep.

He heard footsteps, light ones which seemed to be coming nearer and nearer. Dare he, for the sake of Mary's reputation, allow them to be found like this? Before he could answer that question the owner of the footsteps came through the trees to stop, silent, before them.

It must be, it was, the so-called hermit, the wild man of the woods with his long hair, his long beard and his unkempt clothes.

He made no attempt to speak, to walk nearer to them. Moved by some unknown instinct, Russell put the first finger of his left hand to his lips to indicate that the visitor must remain silent. The man nodded his hairy head, and sat down on the stump of a tree, obviously determined to remain where he was.

The magic of the place held all three of them—until Mary awoke and struggled to sit up. Russell disengaged himself, the wild man rose and bowed to her where she sat, bewildered, half-asleep, not sure where she was.

The hermit—his accent was that of an educated man—said in a deep, rusty voice, rusty perhaps through lack of using it, 'I, and the cairn, Mrs Wardour, are at your service—and Lord Hadleigh, too.'

Russell rose and bowed, motioning Mary to remain seated. 'You know who we are, then?'

The hermit's laugh was as rusty as his voice. 'Indeed, there are so few strangers to these parts and you, Lord Hadleigh, are already notorious, Mrs Wardour less so.'

For some reason this answer amused Russell. He threw his head back and laughed. 'Because of my reforms at Eddington?'

'Exactly, m'lord. Dare I ask you both to do the honour of taking tea with me? I see that you have already eaten your nuncheon and the tea-board usually follows it—although I have no board, only tea. My cottage is not far away.'

Mary looked her assent at Russell.

'Assuredly,' he said, bowing again. 'With two provisos: that you offer me your name and that you allow me to pack up the remnants of our al fresco meal before we follow you.'

'By all means. I am George Russell—a relative of yours

on the wrong side of the blanket,' and he threw a comical look at the one which Russell was folding up. 'I was once a scholar and a friend of Mrs Wardour's father and her late husband. I also knew your father, Jackie Chancellor, when we were both young men, so you see that we are not really strangers. You may bring your horses with you—after you have allowed them a drink from the stream.' It was the first time that he had ever offered his surname to anyone local but, after all, Russell Hadleigh *was* a relative of his, the first he had seen for many years and the words had flown out before he could stop them.

Mary, who had resumed her top hat and was untethering her horse, whispered to Russell, 'Do you really believe all that—and by the by, whatever must he have thought when he found me lying in your arms?'

'What a lucky dog I was, I should think,' he whispered back, and when she blushed scarlet, murmured, 'I shouldn't have teased you—but I thought that as "by the bys" went, yours was a bit of a masterpiece. Besides, since we were behaving innocently—to Hades with whatever anyone else might think!'

Their unlikely new friend had walked ahead of them already and could scarcely have heard this by-play. He led them along a narrow track before they came to another clearing where a thatched cottage stood, smoke rising from its one chimney.

'My home is rough but clean,' he told them, 'which also applies to my person. The brook is my bath and serves to wash my clothing,' and he waved them forward into the cottage's one main room.

It was, as he had said, clean if roughly furnished. It was also filled with books. A table, on which were paper, ledgers, an ink well and a quill pen, stood beneath a window, a bed stood beneath another and a fire blazed in the hearth. A kettle stood on the hob. A door opened on to a kitchen and an open storeroom. Beside the fire stood a small side-table on which was a chess board, with a game in progress on it.

The hermit waved them towards two kitchen chairs before seating himself at the one before the table.

'I see that the kettle has almost boiled. I timed my walk quite accurately so that we should return before it did. Having no clock has made me create my own in my head as our ancestors must have done. In these days we gather a great deal of unnecessary paraphernalia about ourselves—but you do not wish to hear of that, I am sure. You do not resemble your father, young man, but I suppose that you have heard that before— you take after the Russells, I think. If I shaved off my beard and hair, you would see a resemblance between us. I gather that you have a twin brother—does he take after your father?'

'No, nor does he look like the Russells. He is dark, intense-looking and wiry.'

'Is he, indeed? Interesting that,' but the hermit did not explain wherein the interest lay. Instead he rose and, carrying the kettle to the kitchen, made the tea, returning after a few minutes carrying three china mugs without handles. A battered tin teapot and a small brown jug of milk arrived after yet another journey.

'I've no sugar,' he announced brusquely, 'nasty stuff. Spoils the taste of everything.' He poured tea and milk into the china mugs and handed them to Russell and Mary, who were both intrigued by the man, his fashion of speech and his way of life. Mary could not resist shooting a few glances at the chess-board. Her chair was next to its table.

The hermit, who seemed to miss nothing, did not miss her interest. 'Play chess, do you, Mrs Mary? And you, Hadleigh?'

Russell was amused to notice that now they were in his own home the hermit was addressing them familiarly. 'Both of us play. Years ago it was our joint passion, but then I gave it up. My passion for it has been revived recently: Mrs Wardour has always retained her interest in it.'

'So I understand. You are continuing your father's work, I believe, Mary.'

Startled, Mary looked across at him. 'You knew of my father's work, sir?'

'Indeed, and that you and Hadleigh here were deeply involved in it years ago. You have renewed that work, I hope, Hadleigh. A pity to waste a gift like yours in unrewarding idleness. I, too, am engaged in working on a noble theory with which I shall not trouble you for you must both resume working on your own when Hadleigh has reformed Eddington. I came here to concentrate on mine in a place where I could forget the world's distractions.

'I would, however, be grateful if you would both look at Black's position and try to discover whether there is any way in which he could avoid what appears to be an inevitable defeat.'

They both rose and strolled over to the table. Mary was the first to speak, looking at Russell before she did so. 'I think, no, I am sure, that Black has a way out. Do you agree with me, Lord Hadleigh?'

She was being formal to try to erase from the hermit's mind his memory of finding her in Russell's arms.

'Yes,' he replied, 'and this is it,' and he moved an apparently innocent pawn.

Mary nodded agreement. The hermit clapped his hands

together in praise and she sketched him a curtsy. 'It was not really very clever of us,' she told him. 'We have been experimenting recently in the hope that one day we might build a clockwork machine which would be able to play chess. This is one of the positions we have studied.'

The hermit clapped his hands again. 'As I thought. You are undoubtedly a pair of prodigies, and you, Hadleigh, are wasting your time playing a reforming agent on behalf of your father, who, I dare swear, knows nothing of what you are doing and probably won't be grateful for it. You should be nurturing your rare talent.'

On hearing this, both heads swung round, Russell's to stare at the hermit and Mary's to stare at Russell. Now, how the devil does he know that? was Russell's furious thought, and, Can it really be true that Russell is here without his father's knowledge—and why? was Mary's response.

'Enough,' said the hermit abruptly. 'It is time that you left. Be sure that I will keep watch for you, Hadleigh. Do not underestimate the hatred which young Shaw must nourish for you. You have stopped his little gallop and no mistake—but take care that, in revenge, he does not stop yours after a fashion which you would not like.'

Russell said coolly, 'I thank you for that warning, sir, and am grateful for your interest in my affairs. May we visit you again?'

'When I send for you,' was the hermit's answer, 'and not before. Now go.'

'Was what the hermit was saying true, Russell?' Mary asked while they walked to where their horses were tethered.

'About what?' he returned stiffly—but he knew quite well to what she was referring.

'That your father does not know that you are here.'

'I am afraid so, yes.'

The very brevity of his reply piqued Mary. She considered her words carefully before continuing. 'Would you care to speak to me of it? It seems such an odd thing to be happening—particularly when you have allowed everyone to believe that you are your father's emissary.'

They had reached their horses. Instead of beginning to untether his, Russell decided on total frankness. After all, he had been deceiving Mary as well as everyone else and she must be finding that hurtful.

'Before we ride back,' he said, 'let us take a short walk. I will be as honest with you as I have previously been dishonest about my reason for being here. When I have finished I hope that you will forgive me. I promise that, in future, I shall have no secrets from you.'

'Very well.'

Russell had never admired her more. The calm way in which she was accepting what she must see as a breach of trust was directly opposite to that in which he knew most women of his acquaintance would have reacted. No reproaches, no sad looks, but the same kind of rational response which she would have given to a problem in mathematics.

As a reward for her he decided on the most complete frankness, beginning with the confession that his relationship with his father had always been a poor one. Slowly he told her everything, ending with the occasion when he had, quite accidentally, come across Shaw's reports and had found them wanting.

'I raised the matter with my father, and he dismissed what I had to say as ignorant meddling. He had absolute trust in old Shaw, he said, and did not wish me to interfere. Needless to say he had no notion that old Shaw had died three years ago and that his dissolute son had taken over.'

'That was very wrong of him, Russell, to ignore your wishes completely. After all, you are his heir.'

'Quite so, but he has always resented me for being the older twin. He has made it quite plain that he would have preferred Ritchie to succeed. Which makes his desire to see me married to some half-witted heiress quite bizarre.'

'No, Russell. He wished to control you, that is quite plain from all that you have said. Why, then, did you secretly defy him by coming north to find out what was going on?'

'Oh, that was Ritchie. I made the mistake of complaining about my useless life to him and he read me the Riot Act and said that only I could remedy my sad situation. He hinted that I ought to defy Father over Eddington and follow my star. You see, he has no wish to be Earl. He has told me more than once that it is not his sort of thing at all and I believe that to be true.'

'I should like to meet him,' said Mary approvingly. 'He seems a man of sound common sense.'

'Unlike me?' But Russell's tone told Mary that he was joking.

'Not at all. From all I hear, you are making a great fist of turning Eddington round. Be sure that I shall not give you away, but I am sorry that you did not tell me the truth earlier.'

'Not as sorry as I am,' Russell said earnestly. 'I think…no, I know that I am still somewhat unsure of myself, but I think that I am improving in that department every day. Mostly because of your influence on me. You inspire me and give me courage because your own is so great.

'Now I am afraid that I must take you home. Aunt Beauregard will be thinking that we have drowned ourselves in the stream.'

Mary began to laugh. 'Not at all. She is a cunning match-maker and the longer we are alone together the happier she is since it means that we are more likely to come to an accommodation.'

They had reached their horses again. Russell turned to her, saying, 'Have we reached an accommodation, Mary? Years ago I asked you to marry me and you answered yes. If I ask you again, will your answer be the same? Even if, because of the peculiar position I am in vis-à-vis my father, it means that we shall have to delay the actual ceremony?

'Since I have just said that you have given me the courage which I was previously lacking I also have to tell you that if he refuses to sanction our marriage and disinherits me for going against his wishes as he has previously threatened, then I shall still marry you and look for work elsewhere. I met Lord Chard for the first time a few days ago. He visited Eddington and began to admire what I have already done. His own land agent is growing old, he said, and he will soon be needing a new one. He joked that it was a pity that I was not looking for work. If I were, he would gladly offer me the position.'

'Should you like that?'

'It would be much better than being Bretford's idle and un-considered heir. He has forfeited my affection and my obedience by his behaviour to me. Nor can I forgive him for the cruel fashion in which he cheated us both. Now let us leave that. For the present I am here and he is there. That being so, when do *you* propose to give me an answer to *my* proposal?'

'Now, immediately! And, of course, the answer is yes.'

Her reward was a quick kiss on her cheek, which was all that Russell dare offer her, but his heart was so full of joy he felt that he was about to burst.

'Splendid,' he managed at last, 'and when will you feel able to visit Eddington's attics and explore them with me?'

'In two days' time.'

Russell groaned. 'I'm not sure that I can wait as long as that to see you again. Before we untether our steeds, do you think that you could allow me a kiss to tide me over until then? I promise to behave myself.'

Mary offered him a subtle smile. 'Suppose I said that I don't wish you to behave yourself? What then?'

Russell gave another groan. 'Don't tempt me. I haven't the patience of a saint, even if I have improved in other ways. What makes matters worse is that we cannot soon be married and in the meantime we must both burn. Are you burning, Mary?'

Of course she was burning! The fact that he had lowered his last defences of all by telling her the truth about his father and himself had made her love him more, not less. That she had been married was not saving her from desiring him more and more each time they met. On the contrary, the supposed passion which she had shared with Henry Wardour was daily being exposed for the tepid thing it was.

'I am not to have my kiss, then,' she said, her eyes teasing him.

Did she know of the terrible effect she was having on him? Of course she did. Mary was no fool and, as a once-married woman, was not a complete innocent. Her pretty mouth had curled up at one corner and her dark eyes were dancing—oh, yes, she was well aware what a temptation she was to him. She was no longer the untried girl of their lost youth.

Russell gave yet another groan and gathered her into his arms. She fitted there as sweetly as though she had been made for that purpose alone. His mouth was as hungry as the rest of him and when hers opened itself to him he teased and played with it as only a man long starved of true love and genuine affection could.

This was heaven, was it not? To taste and savour the loved one, mouth to mouth, heart to heart, body to body, particularly when Russell's, clad as it was in fashionably tight breeches, was telling her of the power of his desire. Her own was revealed by the way she clung to him, by her hands which reached up to stroke the loved face, by the little cries she was making when his hands caressed her back, then her shoulders and finally stole round to fondle her breasts...

Without warning, Russell shuddered and stepped back from her. He had been on the verge of lowering her to the ground in order to consummate finally what had begun so long ago and whose inevitable climax had then been denied them.

'No,' he managed, as Mary tried to pull him back. 'No, for both our sakes we must behave ourselves. Were we able to marry soon then we might continue but, things being as they are, that is not possible. We must be patient, and I, as the man, must be the most patient of all, for it is your reputation and your honour that are at stake here. A man is allowed to be a rake, but a woman, never.'

'I don't care about that,' cried Mary passionately, 'not at all.'

But Russell would have none of it. 'You may not now, but think, later it would be different. I have seen what scandal and gossip have done to women and I would not expose you to them. We must have a new self-denying ordnance and trust that it may not be too long.'

He saw that there were tears in Mary's eyes, and each small pearl reproached him. He should not have touched her, begun to make love to her...but it was stupid for him to repine. He had taken her in his arms and the passion between them, so long lost, had been revived again. It was even more powerful because now they were a mature man and woman, not inexperienced children.

'Come,' he said, not daring to touch her again lest he reignite the spark which had passed between them and which might create a fire which, this time, they could not put out. 'Our horses will be growing tired and I have a mind to enjoy Miss Beauregard's excellent tea and cakes.'

This down-to-earth remark set Mary smiling ruefully. She dried her tears. 'Tea, the universal cure-all,' she said, mounting her horse and turning it towards home. 'I wonder what we should do without it!'

Universal cure or not, it was not tea which was occupying Miss Beauregard when they finally walked into the drawing. Oh, the tea was there, set out and waiting for them with a plate of Sally Lunns which Russell had gravely informed her were his favourites.

No, it was the letter which she was holding which was exciting her. 'Oh, my dears,' she exclaimed. 'Such news as you would never believe. I collect that you both stayed at the Markhams' place in the late spring. I have just received a letter from the General's wife: we were at Miss Pinkerton's Academy together and I think I ought to read it to you. But only after you have sat down and I have poured you both a cup of tea—you must be dying for one after such a long afternoon's ride.'

She waved them to two armchairs—luxurious ones, quite unlike those in which the hermit had already served them tea. Neither Russell nor Mary informed her aunt of that, but after all, he had not served them Sally Lunns, which Russell was eyeing wistfully.

'Now, my dears,' she began, 'listen to this.'

Dear Charlotte,

I have dreadful news for you. We had arranged a splendid marriage between our daughter Angelica and the Marquess of Horsham. They were to be married from the Hall a week ago and a large number of the best-known figures of the *ton* had been invited to be present at the ceremony. The wedding presents were of the greatest magnificence. There was even a splendid one from the Regent who had been a great friend of Horsham's in the days when he was the Prince of Wales.

Judge then, of our horror, when on the morning before the wedding, Angelica's maid had no more common sense than to rush into the breakfast room and inform us, and the assembled visitors, that Angelica was not in her bed, nor was she to be found anywhere, either in her suite of rooms or in the house. Her bed had not been slept in. She had, however, left us a note on her pillow, which the stupid maid had dislodged when she had first realised that Angelica was missing, and it was the next morning when one of the under-servants found it under the bed.

It informed us that she had no wish to marry Horsham, whom she described as an ugly old man, and consequently was eloping with the Honourable Thomas Bertram whose old aunt had died and had left him enough for them to live on. He was bound and determined to marry her, so we were not to try to trace them. The real tragedy was that, due to the idiocy of her maid, we could not hush the matter up. The only good thing about the whole wretched business was that she did not leave Horsham waiting at the church.

I have been ill in bed ever since and the General has been so enraged that the doctors feared an apoplexy. To make matters worse, if possible, Perry had lost a great deal of money at cards to Horsham, and now Horsham is threatening to have

Peregrine sent to a debtors' prison if he does not repay it. He had agreed to cancel Perry's debts once his marriage to Angelica had been arranged.

If you hear anything of my poor child's whereabouts, pray inform me. She could be at Gretna, or in Scotland, or, if the wretch has obtained a special licence, they could already have been married in a church—anywhere!

Miss Beauregard ended this sad narrative with a rueful shake of her head. To her surprise both Russell and Mary began to laugh. It was Russell who recovered first.

'And to think that my father wished me to marry the bolting Angelica,' he choked. 'What an escape for me! I might have been the unfortunate fool left at the altar. She and the Honourable Thomas were casting sheeps' eyes at one another all the way through my stay there. Fortunately, her charms held no attraction for me, or I might have obliged my father by offering for her.'

'This sad story does not surprise you, then?'

'Not in the least. I wasn't aware that if I failed to come up to scratch that Horsham would be the next candidate for her hand. I doubt that the Markhams knew that he was up to his ears in debt—but I suppose turning their daughter into a Marchioness was a great attraction for them, even if he is old enough to be her papa. I wonder where the runaways are.'

Mary said, wiping her eyes, 'Angelica told me that she had a *tendre* for Thomas Bertram, but that her parents were determined to marry her to either money, or a title, or both.'

She looked wickedly at Russell. 'Don't tell me that she held no attraction for you at all. Most of the men at Markham Hall were under her spell.'

'Well, I wasn't. The only woman at Markham whose spell I was under was someone not five yards away from me at the moment—as you well know.'

Mary's smile grew more mischievous than ever. 'Yes, indeed. I have to inform you, Aunt, that Lord Hadleigh has offered me marriage, and that I have accepted. For some good and sufficient reasons we have to delay the ceremony—principally because Russell wishes to see Eddington in better shape before he takes on his marital duties. As a result, this is a private announcement for your ears only.'

She and Russell had agreed on this on the way home. They did not wish to deceive Miss Beauregard while Mary was living with her.

'Oh, congratulations to you both,' exclaimed her aunt. 'I knew the moment that I saw you together that marriage was inevitable. I shall be completely mum, you may be sure, and shall not be writing poor Mrs Markham a letter long enough to surpass her own.'

'That would be difficult, to say the least,' Mary said. 'Would you think me heartless if I told you that I have not a great deal of sympathy for either her, or the General?'

'No, indeed, not now that you have explained matters to me. I collect that you visited the cairn this afternoon. Did you see aught of the hermit? He lives quite near.'

'Surprisingly enough,' said Mary, 'we did. He even invited us into the cottage and gave us tea.'

'And vile stuff it was, if we are to be truthful,' Russell added with a grin. 'Not like your best leaf from China.'

Miss Beauregard looked thoughtful. 'How strange. He has never before asked anyone into his home—rather he has driven them away. Did he offer you any reason as to why you were so honoured?'

'Only that he had the same name as myself. He claimed to be a Russell, George Russell to be exact, born on the wrong side of the blanket. He seemed to know a great deal of what is going on in the district.'

For some reason Miss Beauregard looked quite stricken.

'George Russell,' she said at last. 'I only knew one George Russell and he died long ago. I was to have married him.'

It was Mary's turn to look stricken. 'Dear aunt,' she said. 'We would not have told you of him, but I forgot about your long-ago engagement.'

'No need for you to start repining now,' said her aunt. 'I did all my weeping then. Think nothing of it. I would not like my past sorrow to spoil your splendid news. You must come to dinner soon, m'lord, so that we at least may celebrate it in proper style.'

'Not m'lord,' said Russell, bowing to her. 'Now that we are to be related you must bring yourself to call me by my Christian name—as I believe that I asked you once before. So few people do that I am in danger of forgetting it.'

'Now that,' said the old lady, 'would give me the greatest pleasure, seeing that you will shortly become my nephew-in-law and such a familiarity would become quite proper. It will be particularly so since all my memories of the Russells are fond ones.' She frowned, 'That is why I find it strange that I cannot remember a George Russell other than my own. Of course, it is possible that his existence was kept secret.'

Both her hearers nodded. Most families had such secrets and preferred them to remain so.

'By the by,' Russell said to Miss Beauregard before

leaving, 'I have asked Mary to join me in sorting through the jumble in the attics at Eddington, and she informed me that you might like to help me as well. Would it be an imposition if I asked you to visit Eddington for that purpose in two days' time?'

'Not at all. I had heard that for some reason young Shaw had consigned all the paintings and much of the furniture to the attics when he dismissed most of the staff who were looking after the place when his father died. I take it that you intend to restore the house to its original pride.'

'If I can. I have already had most of the rooms which I occupy cleaned for the first time in years and I shan't rest until the entire house is spick and span once again. I think that I might like to settle here. I haven't enjoyed myself so much in years as I have done since I started to try to restore Eddington, the house and the estate to its former glory.'

He came out with this in such a heartfelt manner that Miss Beauregard grew thoughtful. She said nothing until he had gone, when she asked Mary a question.

'I have the impression that Russell was not particularly happy before he came north. Is that true—or am I being fanciful?'

'Not fanciful at all. Without betraying any confidence he has made me, I gather that he has long felt that he has had no serious interest in his life—and now, running Eddington, he has found one.'

'The talk is that he has already done wonders. The parson only said to me yesterday that it was a great pity that Lord Bretford had not sent him here to mend matters before.'

Sadly, Mary knew that she must deceive her aunt by inference in remaining silent and not telling her that Russell's father had not sent him, but that he had come as a consequence of his own worries about what was happening at Eddington.

'On top of that,' went on Miss Beauregard, 'the whole district is exceedingly happy that a descendant of the Russells has not forgotten us. I only wish that he had made a clean sweep and turned Shaw away—I fear that he may be being too kind-hearted to be wise. I hope that I am wrong.'

Chapter Nine

Russell was not feeling too kind-hearted when he returned to Eddington. It was plain that Shaw had used his afternoon's visit to Ancoates to invite a few cronies over for a drinking party. They were still hard at it when he walked in.

He waited until he had changed into the informal clothing he had taken to wearing at Eddington before he sent for the visibly fuddled agent.

'I believe,' he said coldly, 'that I have already told you that I didn't want Eddington House to be turned into the village taproom either when I am present or when I am absent. By behaving as you have done this afternoon, you are straining my patience, Shaw. I should by rights have turned you away when I discovered your misbehaviour, which I believe to have been criminal, but I wished to give you a chance to redeem yourself by helping me to turn this place round. One more piece of folly like this afternoon's and I shall dismiss you on the instant. Do you understand me, sir?'

Shaw's reaction was to begin to grovel, although beneath his apparent penitence the hate which he had begun to feel for this jumped-up London dandy who had arrived to spoil his little game was slowly turning murderous.

'Yes, m'lord,' he whined. 'I hear you, m'lord. I thought that I might celebrate Jonty Jordan's birthday, but we perhaps overdid things a little.'

'You mean that you were so fuddled that you forgot the time? It might, perhaps, be advisable for you never to strain my patience again by such behaviour.'

'Yes, m'lord, of course, m'lord. Point taken, m'lord.'

'You may go, Shaw. You could better have spent your time in correcting last month's accounts as I directed you yesterday. Your arithmetic was, to say the least, a little faulty. See that they are on my desk by noon tomorrow.'

Russell was well aware that Shaw was beginning to feel a seething hate for him. When the man had left him, cringing and promising to do better on the morrow, he thought of what Miss Beauregard had said, and wondered if it might not have been wiser to dismiss him. To have done so, however, would have left him working in the dark for the wretch did possess a fund of knowledge about local matters which Russell had already found useful. He did rather think, though, that his more ruthless twin would have disposed of Shaw on the spot—but then, he was not yet quite Ritchie's equal in hard determination, although well on the way.

He shrugged his shoulders. He had meant what he had said about dismissing the man and hoped that it might bring him to his senses—if he had any, that was.

In the agent's office, where many of the staff were assembled, Shaw was rapidly proving his master was right. He was busy complaining to Briggs and anyone else who would listen to him about m'lord's dictatorial ways. Some of his hearers were loudly sympathetic; others, like the cook and house-keeper who liked what Russell was accomplishing at Edding-ton, kept their counsel.

'If it might not make matters worse, I'd write to his pa, that I would,' whined Shaw privately to Briggs, his major ally, 'but…' and it was his turn to shrug his shoulders.

Briggs knew what he meant: that the Earl was still under the illusion that it was Shaw's father who was running the estate—and that all was well.

He was in the middle of another tirade about insolent popinjays when the door opened and Russell put his head in. 'Incidentally, Shaw, Mrs Wardour and Miss Beauregard will be coming the day after tomorrow to rummage through the attics with me. I have ordered the housekeeper to have the drawing and dining rooms made presentable and Cook has been warned to be ready with a cold collation around mid-day. The wine which I have ordered from the vintners at Newcas-tle should arrive tomorrow. See that it is stored in the far cellar, the one which the workmen have already cleared and cleaned.'

'Yes, m'lord, indeed, m'lord.' Shaw was so servile that his servility was almost insolent. 'As you wish, m'lord.'

Russell ignored his agent's parody of an obedient servant, but mentally noted it down as another black mark against him.

'Do this, Shaw, do that, Shaw? Does he never stop issuing orders?' grumbled Shaw when Russell had gone.

'He does work hard himself, though,' said a bold under-footman. 'You have to grant him that.'

'I don't grant him anything. I wish to God he'd stayed down south and the sooner he leaves us the better. We were all happy before he came.'

The under-footman, a man in training, one of those Russell

had employed to help to clean and refurbish the house and gardens, opened his mouth to argue with him, but a well-aimed kick in the calf from his neighbour silenced him.

'What'd you do that for, wor Jackie?' he said when Shaw, still fulminating against fate, had left them.

'He's a nasty piece of work is Shaw, best not end up on the wrong side of him while he's still here. I've a feeling young master might get rid of him if he doesn't mend his ways, and then you'll be able to speak your mind freely. Until that happy day, keep mum, and out of his way. He might do you a mischief, else.'

'Still and all—' began the footman.

'Still and all,' mocked his friend, the farrier, also newly employed. 'Besides, who's to know that young master might not grow bored and disappear as suddenly as he came. Least said, soonest mended.'

The older heads nodded wisely at this piece of folk wisdom before making their way to the servants' hall for their evening meal—except for those who were carrying Russell's to the dining room where he sat in lonely, if still somewhat dingy, state.

Mary and Miss Beauregard were alike eager to discover whether all the rumours about what Russell was doing at Eddington House were true. They rode over in Miss Beauregard's modest chaise, clad only in their most down-to-earth and practical clothing. Miss Beauregard had even packed two large brown holland aprons to protect them the more.

'Even in the best-kept houses,' she proclaimed, 'attics are dirty places. One trembles to think what those at Eddington must look like after nearly thirty years of neglect!'

Mary was more exercised about meeting Russell again

than about the condition of his attics. She had spent the previous day working on the problems raised by the chess game which they had started at Markham Hall and, even if she could not discuss them during the visit, she would leave a careful copy of her work with him. It was as though she wished to make up for the years they had spent apart by seeing him as often as possible, never mind that to do so had her all of a quiver—one of Miss Beauregard's favourite phrases.

Their carriage had scarcely had time to arrive on the gravel sweep before the entrance when he was with them. A dirty boy ran up to open the chaise door for them and there was Russell, greeting them as enthusiastically as though it had been weeks since he had seen them, and not a mere forty-eight hours.

He was wearing rough countryman's clothing—as starkly practical as their own, and it suited him, Mary thought, equally as well as, if not more than, the dandy outfits which he had worn at the Markhams.

'What a splendid day you have brought with you,' he exclaimed, giving Miss Beauregard his arm. 'A pity, perhaps, that we have to spend it frowsting in the attics, but alas, duty calls. I gather that there might be treasures to be found there, as well as dust and cobwebs. So, before we start, I have ordered Cook to provide us with tea and my favourite Sally Lunns.'

Mary remembered that, in the past, Russell had always had the power to make even the dullest day interesting and he had certainly not lost that talent. He swept them by a sullen Shaw who had spent the previous afternoon working twice as hard as he had done before Russell's arrival.

'It's rather amusing if a little sad,' Russell told his guests over tea, 'but my valet, Pickering, disapproves mightily of my transformation into Eddington's agent—for that is what I

really am now. He was particularly annoyed this morning
when I insisted on putting on what he persists in calling
"subfusc fancy dress, sir, which is not at all the thing in which
to entertain ladies". My efforts to assure him that what I am
wearing these days is suitable country clothing and that
subfusc refers to a dark or grey costume, nothing like my daily
garments, didn't satisfy him at all. He is pining for the streets
of Mayfair and Vauxhall Gardens, not the scenic delights of
the north country.'

Mary said, 'Papa would have approved of subfusc. He said
it was the only proper wear for a gentleman. He was very
pleased when Beau Brummell introduced the fashion of
wearing black—particularly in the evening. Papa, of course,
wore it all the time.'

'Well, he *was* a reverend gentleman, my dear,' explained
her aunt.

'Russell isn't, though, and contrary to what Pickering
might think, I like you in country clothes, sir.'

He bowed in her direction. 'But you approve of my working
and Pickering does not.' He pulled out his hunter, consulted
it and said, 'Much though I am enjoying our conversation, I
think that we ought to begin work in the attics soon.'

'True,' said Mary, 'and I, for one, am eager to explore
them. Who knows what treasures we might find?'

'I have arranged for one maid-servant to be present to
assist the ladies and two of the stronger estate workers to be
waiting for us should we need to do any heavy lifting,' Russell
said as they walked up several flights of backstairs.

Half of the attic space was given over to the servants'
quarters, although only a third of that was in use because
Russell had not yet completely filled all the vacancies which

Shaw had created. The other half was entered through a door usually kept locked. Daylight came through several windows set in the sloping roof which Russell had recently caused to be cleansed of the grime of the ages. Furniture, china, statuettes, chests and paintings were huddled about higgledy-piggledy. There was barely space to walk between the objects.

Mary and Aunt Beauregard had put on their aprons. The servant girl had brought up dusters, a bowl of water and some clean cloths. The menservants were lifting a tallboy away from the wall for them to inspect. Dusty and uncared for as it was, it was still a magnificent specimen of the furniture maker's art. All three of them stood back the better to admire it.

'Have you any notion why this was banished to the attics?' Russell asked the foremost man of the two whose judgement he had already come to respect.

'Why, m'lord, I believe that Mr Shaw wished to be rid of the furniture so that he might be able to dismiss most of the staff who looked after the house, seeing that empty rooms need no caring for.'

'Well, it can go downstairs again,' said Russell firmly. Mary and Aunt Beauregard were nodding their heads in agreement. 'Move it over to the far wall and we'll arrange for it to be taken there. Have you any notion where it used to stand?'

The second, smaller man said, 'I was the under-butler before I was dismissed. I remember it being in the entrance hall. A black marble bust used to stand on it.'

Russell turned to Mary. 'You and Aunt Beauregard might find it useful to pick out the china and the bibelots which are lying around under the dust. Those you think worthwhile could stand on the tallboy for the present.'

Aunt Beauregard nodded agreement and added, 'Later I

would rather like to identify the paintings, most of which seemed to be leaning against the far wall, behind the furniture. I remember that there used to be a lot of portraits and conversation pieces of the Russell family and I think that I could identify them. There were some beautiful landscapes by Richard Wilson, too.'

They all set to work with a will, growing increasingly dirty in the process. Mary and the little maid washed the fine china which stood in every nook and cranny between the larger pieces of furniture. Aunt Beauregard turned her attention to the little tables, painted armoires, lacquered cabinets and fire-screens on poles—all covered in grime.

It soon became plain that most of the attics' contents were fine enough to return to their original homes—the former under-butler was helpful here. Russell had taken some paper and a pencil up with him and in the intervals of helping to heave furniture about was busy recording where it was to go and any repairs which might be needed.

'And this is only one of the attic rooms where furniture is stored,' Russell exclaimed. 'When it is all back in its proper place Eddington House will be one of the most beautiful in the county. Only Chard's place will be better.'

They worked their way across the room towards the paintings, all of them too excited by the treasures they were uncovering to feel tired. The larger workman had gone to collect a troop of men to carry the selected furniture and objects into the rooms which had been cleaned since Russell arrived. Bedroom furniture they left behind to be moved later since only Russell's, Pickering's and the indoor servants' rooms had been dealt with.

Finally they reached the paintings. Russell directed the

smaller workman, Stubbs by name, to turn them round one by one so that they might all inspect them together.

Aunt Beauregard had been right. There were some splendid landscapes including a small Gainsborough, and two by Wright of Derby. The cream of the collection were, as she had said, the landscapes of Richard Wilson. Finally he began to uncover the portraits. The early ones dated back to the seventeenth century, brown, undistinguished things, but the distinctive face of the Russell family was already present in them, and it rapidly became plain that Russell took after them.

'You have the Russell nose,' Mary whispered to him when a late eighteenth-century grandee had been shown to them. 'To say nothing of the hair. I wonder if the hermit looks like this under all *his* hair!'

So far all the portraits had been those of men, but now a hidden cache of women appeared. These, too, had been carefully stored in chronological order so that it was not until almost at the end when they were presented with a young blonde girl with a pretty eager face.

'Why, I do believe that that is your mother, Margaret Russell, done by Romney, as she was when I was a girl,' said Aunt Beauregard. 'I had thought that that had long gone south with your father. It was a pity that she died so young. I told you that you are very like her, Russell, and that painting proves me right.'

So it did. Mary looked from the pretty girl on the canvas to Russell, and allowed that the likeness was remarkable, even given the difference between their sex.

'Downstairs, at once,' said Russell, his voice cracking with emotion. 'It must go on show immediately. I have never seen a portrait of my mother before. One of my cousins told me that I was very like her, particularly when I was younger, but I could not have guessed how great the resemblance is.'

He wondered why it had been left behind and not taken south—although he was now beginning to recognise that nothing had been taken from Eddington which might remind his father of the family into which he had married.

It was the next painting, though, which was the real surprise. Turned around, it showed a girl who was as dark as Margaret Russell had been fair. She had a thin clever face and glossy black hair dressed in the fashion of the late 1780s. It was another Romney and in many ways was superior to the previous one as though the painter had fallen in love with his subject.

Its effect on Russell, Mary saw, was immediate and surprising. He turned white, his mouth thinned and he said nothing, although previously he had been free with his comments. It was left to Aunt Beauregard to speak.

'So that's where that painting ended up. I wondered what had happened to it. The painter did it as a favour to Serena Cheyney and her brother Ralph. They were as poor as church mice at that time and couldn't afford to pay him. They were Margaret Russell's cousins, but took after their father, not their mother. I remember that your father, Russell, was very taken with her. We thought that they might make a match of it, but when he came back, a year later, it was to marry your mother.

'Of course, by then your mother was the Russell heiress. Serena married Courtney Lascelles a year later. This was after her brother, Ralph, suddenly inherited. Lascelles died when quite young. She never had any children and lives not far from here.'

Russell's face had recovered its normal colour. 'Is this portrait as good a likeness as the one of my mother?' he asked, apparently casually, but Mary could see that something about it had disturbed him.

'Very like.'

Russell said, trying not to sound too moved, although what he was seeing, had affected him powerfully.

'I asked you that because, although I resemble my mother, Ritchie, my twin, by some freak, is a male version of Serena Cheyney when young. We are, after all, blood relatives of hers, but it is still an odd thing that my twin should take after our second cousin, even if we are not identical ones.'

He turned to Aunt Beauregard. 'I hope that this question does not offend you, madam, but was it really true that my father loved Serena Cheyney?'

'Yes, it was really true. In fact, when he returned north we all thought that it was to propose to Serena, but after a few months it was Margaret whom he asked to be his wife. By then, of course, his father had become the Earl of Bretford and your father was no longer poor as he was when we were all young together. It was an odd coincidence that both your father and Ralph Cheyney should suddenly inherit titles and wealth.

'My George Russell was one of our little group of friends: it was because of his death, shortly before your father returned, that Margaret became the Russell heiress and the Eddington estate passed to the Chancellors by her marriage to him.'

She did not add that she had been unfortunate and lost, not only her own true love, but the chance of becoming the mistress of Eddington House. Russell, for his part, was privately beginning to suspect that his father had lost his true love when he became the heir to the Bretford Earldom. Mary, who had been listening carefully to this interchange, was thinking the same thing. Russell was also beginning to see the reason why his father had always favoured Ritchie, the son who looked like his lost love.

They continued to clear the attics, finding one room full of books from the dismantled library and another where fine copper pans, covered with verdigris, lay quite abandoned among the large kitchen furniture. All three of them were pondering on the mysterious workings of fate which had brought Eddington House down to near ruin, as well as the strange behaviour of its owner whose carelessness had allowed it to reach this sorry pass.

'I never thought I should enjoy myself so much,' Mary confessed. 'I'm not sure whether it was finding that fine Meissen porcelain which excited me the most or that lacquered cabinet from Japan. It will be quite wonderful to see them restored to where they can be freely admired when you have finished transforming the house.'

'Which might be some time yet,' lamented Russell. 'But never fear, I intend that, in time, everything will be restored to its proper place—we cannot let such treasures rot beneath the leads.'

'Talking of leads,' remarked Aunt Beauregard, 'when the Russells owned Eddington they used to give tea-parties on the leads—there is a staircase up on to the roof near the servants' quarters. The view from it is magnificent.'

'Excellent,' exclaimed Russell. 'As soon as we have finished all the improvements we shall christen them by inviting half the neighbourhood to one, eh, Mary?'

'What a splendid notion,' she exclaimed, her face rosy with pleasure.

'Agreed, then,' he said, taking her hand and bowing over

it, 'and now let us go downstairs and find out whether my cook can rival Aunt Beauregard's in the tea-and-crumpets line!'

Their excursion to the attics set the tone for their whole happy summer. Never mind that it was one of the wettest in recent history—Russell and Mary's burgeoning love cast a golden glow over it. There were only two flies in the ointment: one was that the rain ruined the harvest, but fortunately Russell had spent most of the estate's surplus from its rents in buying sheep on Lord Chard's advice; and the second was Pickering's desertion.

Russell knew that Pickering was unhappy in the north, 'so far from civilisation' as he once glumly put it, but all the same it came as a surprise when one morning, after laying out Russell's country clothes for the day, he said, his face grave, 'I would have a serious word with you, m'lord.'

Russell, tying a large cream-coloured handkerchief around his neck, riposted idly, 'I thought that you were always serious, Pickering. It is one of your many virtues.'

'Even more serious than usual, then,' said Pickering who liked to bandy words with his master. 'It is this, m'lord. I would ask you to release me from my contract of service with you before quarter-day to allow me to return to London as soon as possible.'

M'lord was so surprised that he dropped his handkerchief. Pickering lifted it from the floor and handed it to him with a bow.

'Really, Pickering, you really wish to leave me? Why?'

'Truth to tell, m'lord, I am not happy here. My home has always been in London and I miss it very much. All my family and friends are there, and besides, you do not need me any more. You live and work in country clothing and the services

I have always done for you are not required. I have been privately training one of the under-footmen to do for you all the necessaries of your new life, for, forgive me for saying so, I think that you intend to remain here—which is why I am asking you to allow me to leave.

'I have always been happy to work for you—as, indeed, have all the servants here and in London. We could not have a kinder or more considerate master, but the city lights beckon, if you will allow me to be poetic.'

'I will allow you anything—even to leave before quarter-day arrives, for I could not have had a more efficient or faithful valet. You will require me to write a reference for you, I suppose, and I shall do so gladly—although I do not gladly lose you. When would you like to leave?'

'By the end of next week, if that is suitable to you, m'lord.'

'Of course it's not suitable, but if you must, you must. I shall miss you greatly, but all the same, I wish you well in the future.'

'Thank you, m'lord, I knew that I could trust you to be kind.'

Kind! thought Russell when Pickering had gone. Ritchie would be sure to say I was too kind in letting Shaw stay on and in allowing Pickering to go when he pleases and not work out his time. The devil of it is, though, the fellow is right: he needs some fine gentleman to look after, not a country fellow dressed in flyaway clothing. For someone London born and bred, the country must seem a dull place.

He was not to know that Pickering's going would make the countryside seem far less dull, if not positively dangerous.

'Leaving us, Mr Pickering, are you?' commented Shaw that night when the valet broke the news to him. 'Can't say that I'm surprised—you're a right regular cockney, aren't you, if you don't mind me saying so. We'll give you a good send-off, though, be sure of that.'

The send-off took place two days before Pickering was due to leave. Privately Shaw had always thought that Pickering acted as though he were superior to them all because he served m'lord directly: to make him drunk thus became a kind of revenge. It also provided for Shaw a bonus which he didn't expect.

They were seated in the servants' hall, the debris of revelry about them. Most of the servants, other than Shaw's crony, Briggs, had already retired. Shaw had rightly judged that m'lord would not object to his faithful valet being given a right royal send-off. Pickering was already halfway to being maudlin when once he and Briggs were alone with him, Shaw began to question him about his life with Russell in London and out of it.

'Bet you were a bit surprised when the Earl sent him up here,' commented Shaw. It was an idle remark with no hidden meaning in it, other than to set Pickering talking in the hope that he might give something damaging away about his master.

Pickering, his senses awry, looked earnestly at his interrogator. 'That's just it,' he said, the drink making him careless—indeed, come morning he had no memory of what his loose tongue had given away. 'The Earl didn't send him here. The talk was that when m'lord asked his father if he could visit Eddington he was expressly told that he would never give him permission to do any such thing. It was the first time m'lord ever disobeyed his dad. The Earl don't know that he's here—my master just came.'

Shaw's jaw dropped. He almost asked Pickering to say all that again so that he was sure that he had not misheard, but Pickering was already near to *point non plus* so far as consciousness was concerned.

'That right?' he managed.

'Jus' said so, din' I? The Earl's no idea he's here, no idea at all.'

Rage consumed Shaw, who had been careful not to drink level with Pickering while he pumped him. So, the damned upstart had no business to be present, had not been sent by the Earl, but had come to Eddington to make trouble for them all on his own initiative. What's more, the bastard had always spoken as though he were his father's emissary!

Shaw's busy and devious brain, honed by a lifetime of dishonesty, was beginning to grasp that he might be able to make use of what Pickering had just told him so that he could regain his one-time virtual lordship here.

'Any idea why he came?' he ventured.

'The gossip in the servants' hall was that he thought that there might be something going wrong here.'

'Such as?' was Shaw's next venture—but he was too late, Pickering slipped sideways from his chair, dead to the world, with no notion that he had betrayed his master and had given his enemy a means of revenge on the man who had spoiled his little gallop at Eddington.

Shaw looked across at Briggs. 'Help me to get him to bed, Briggs, and then you and I will have a little talk.'

They lifted the unconscious Pickering so that he hung between them.

'What did you make of all that about m'lord being here, unknown and against his father's wishes?' asked Briggs once they had deposited Pickering on his bed and had returned to the scene of his recent downfall.

'Hush!' said Shaw, putting his finger beside his nose. 'That's for you and me to know, and not the rest of the fools around Eddington. I've got a right handy notion that we might be able to make good use of Pickering's loose tongue, but the less that others might know about it, the better. If you keep quiet we might both be made for life—best avoid drinking too much from now on or you could give away any little game you and me might care to play when the time is right.'

Briggs nodded agreement and put down his tankard, the ale in it half-drunk. 'Anything you say, Arthur, anything you say, you always did right for us both before that popinjay arrived and spoiled things.'

'Not for much longer,' said Shaw, laughing, 'not for much longer.'

Chapter Ten

September had arrived. Around Eddington and Ancoates the countryside was turning golden and scarlet—when it wasn't raining, that was. In London the Earl of Bretford sat in his study, fuming. It was well over three months since he had heard anything from his son and heir.

He had learned, to his great annoyance, that Angelica Markham had first been betrothed to old Horsham and had then run off with young Tom Bertram. All of which went to show that Hadleigh had disobeyed him once again by not making an offer for the silly chit. It was natural that she didn't want to tie herself to that old roué Horsham, but if she had to run off with someone why couldn't it have been Russell Hadleigh? Not that she would have needed to run anywhere if Hadleigh had had the sense to propose to her.

None of this was worth worrying about while Hadleigh was still missing. What was he doing for money and where was he spending it? Had he been set on by robbers and been done away with? Who was harbouring him? Was he travelling from one country house to another?

The only thing the Earl could be sure of was that Hadleigh was disobeying him. He should have returned to London, after his failed attempt with Angelica Markham, so that he might be told which suitable heiress to propose to next. A more unsatisfactory son and heir than Hadleigh he could not imagine.

He chose for a moment to think of his more satisfactory son, Richard—or Ritchie, as he preferred to be called. Richard, who had already provided the family with an heir if Hadleigh failed, as usual, to do his duty. It was a great pity that he was not the older twin, then he would not be sitting here worrying about what Hadleigh was up to.

An idea struck him. Was it not possible that Richard knew where Hadleigh was? If he did, a visit to him at Liscombe might save a deal of time and worry about the wretch. Besides, it would be pleasant to see young Pandora again and his grandson: better to do that than sit here fretting about Hadleigh.

Ritchie Chancellor was sitting in his study going over his last month's accounts which his bailiff had left on his desk earlier that day when the door opened and his wife, Pandora, burst in. Pandora was given to bursting in: it was one of the things which he loved about her since it contrasted so well with his own complete calm.

'Yes, my love,' he said, smiling. 'What is it this time?'

'It's your father. He's just arrived. Why? How very odd that he should not write to us to inform us that he proposed a visit. He's always so punctilious about such matters. Can anything be wrong?'

Another thing about Pandora which Ritchie liked was her total common sense beneath her apparently flighty exterior.

She was also able to detect the false notes in people's behaviour and certainly his father's completely unexpected and unannounced appearance was very odd.

'Perhaps,' he said, hedging his bets as usual. Pandora was to think later that it was one of the things for which she loved him. 'I take it that his unexpected arrival will not strain our hospitality overmuch.'

'Oh, no. I always have the spare room ready for use and plenty of food and the stables are—' She stopped. 'Ritchie, you are bamming me, are you not?'

'True,' he told her with a grin. 'I know what a splendid housekeeper you are. Now add to your splendour by going to greet Father and put him in a good humour by showing him Will while I finish these books.'

'Done,' she exclaimed and bounced out.

She must have exercised her charms on the Earl with great success, Ritchie thought later, since his father looked very much at ease both that afternoon and later during and after dinner. Particularly since it soon became apparent to him that his father must have had some important purpose behind this impromptu visit. Important because impromptu was usually the last word to apply to any of his father's actions.

Pandora gone, he pushed the bottle of port over to him, saying, 'Now, sir, perhaps you will do me the goodness to explain why you have come here in this ramshackle fashion without giving us warning and in as little state as possible.'

His father laughed and then grunted, 'You should go to Greenwich Fair, Richard, and set up as a mind-reader— much easier than toiling here turning this place into a money spinner.'

'True,' said his son, 'but you haven't answered my question which, I admit, wasn't really one.'

The Earl took a great swig of port, set his glass down carefully and said, 'It's Hadleigh. I haven't heard a word from him since early spring—it's as though he's vanished off the face of the earth. I know he visited you about that time—have you any notion where he might be? If you have, I should be greatly pleased if you would inform me of it.'

'Suppose I told you that he might not wish me to inform you of his whereabouts, what then?'

'Why ever not? And may I remind you it's your duty, as my son, to honour my wishes, and to tell me the truth.'

'Ah, but we have a conflict of interest here, sir. Between father and brother, where does my honour lie?' He lay negligently back in his chair, having said this, his half-drunk glass of port in his hand, and his eyes hard on his father.

'I would say to me. Besides, Hadleigh owes me a duty and you should assist him to honour it, not conceal anything which might enable me to learn what the devil he thinks he is doing. What do you say to that, sir?'

'That I am a free spirit who, for almost twenty years, has not depended on you for support, either financial or otherwise. I admit that I owe you some consideration because you are my father, but that consideration does not extend to my betraying my brother's confidence. If I tell you that I am not sure that I know exactly where he is, but that I could give a good guess, that is as far as I am prepared to go.'

The Earl brought his fist down on the dining table so hard that all the glasses and the remaining cutlery on it rattled alarmingly, and roared, 'Do I take it that you are in a conspiracy with him? A conspiracy to defy me.'

The worst thing about Ritchie Chancellor, everyone was agreed, was that it was impossible to wrong-foot, shake him, or make him lose his temper.

He said, his voice quite agreeable, 'To some extent, yes. I also think that you have kept him on leading strings for far too many years and I am surprised that it has taken him so long to defy you. Russell is no fool, as you would soon find out if you took the care to speak sensibly to him, but he has never been given a chance to exercise his intellect. If he has chosen to do that while he has defied you by disappearing, then you might ask yourself why you have driven him to this pass.'

His father stared at him, his face purpling, 'Why, sir, you are insolent—'

He came to a sudden halt when he saw that Ritchie remained unshaken and was saying, still calm, 'Yes, but truthful, Father. Would you have me lie to you? I am not lying when I say that I know where he might be, nor when I tell you why he might have disappeared. I also believe that he will at some time return, although not, perhaps, quite as the son you have always known, and whom you have consistently bullied and demeaned. That you have favoured me over him does not make me happy.'

His father rose to his feet. 'Enough, sir. I will leave on the instant. I will not stay to be insulted.'

Ritchie said, 'Pray do not, sir. You will distress Pandora, Will and myself. I blame myself that I have never been truthful with you before. Do me the honour of believing that I have no wish to hurt you unnecessarily, but at the beginning of our conversation you begged me to be truthful, and so I have been. I believe that if you stopped to think you might even know where Russell is, and I ask you to do that.'

He saw that his father was struggling with what he hoped was his better self. After a moment the Earl sat down again and said heavily, 'I know you to be an honest man and a brave soldier. That you defend your brother—whose mere existence means that you are denied the title which he now holds and the one which he will one day hold—proves what an excellent fellow you are. No, do not argue with me. I own that I have been hard on him, but there are reasons...reasons which you do not know—'

He stopped and Ritchie saw that his father, surprisingly, was on the verge of breaking down. He said nothing, but allowed him to recover.

'Enough of that. I see that you have, in your own fashion, done your duty to me. Of course I will not leave tonight, nor tomorrow, but I may not stay long because I must find out what in the world Hadleigh has been doing.'

He held out his glass. 'And now, if you will allow, let us drink a final toast together to show that there are no hard feelings between us.'

'Agreed, sir,' and Ritchie picked up the bottle of port to do as his father had asked.

Unaware of his father's worries and Ritchie's defence of him, Russell, with Mary by his side, was surveying the results of his summer's work. The interior of the house was starting to look almost as it had done before the Shaws had virtually dismantled it. The outside was also beginning to show the results of months of work and, if the harvest was proving meagre, the extra sheep, given that they survived the winter, would be bringing in a useful profit by spring.

Eddington village had begun to look more spruce than it

had done on the first day when Russell had driven through it, although to rehabilitate them further, the house, the land and the village would all need a great deal more work done on them, and that would cost money.

'The pity of it is,' Russell was telling Mary on one of mid-September's few fine days, 'that my father has enough surplus cash from his other, better-run, estates and his investments to enable me to finish the work I have begun this year. Alas, things being as they are, it is impossible for me to ask him yet. I want to have set things so much to rights by next summer that I may be able to go to him with the consciousness of work well done and ask him to allow me to stay here as Eddington's master.

'Of course, when—and if—I inherit, that might have to end, but I am not looking so far into the future as that.'

Aunt Beauregard and Mary both agreed that he had done wonders and told him so.

He waved a hand at them, smiling. 'It is far from being all my work, you know. I have had so many willing helpers—including your good selves. Even Shaw, since Pickering went, has been ready and willing to fall in with whatever I have asked. It has been such a transformation that it quite justifies me in keeping him on.'

Aunt Beauregard was not mollified. 'I dislike that man, I really do,' she told Mary while Russell went to the stables to solve a problem which had arisen while they had been working in the library, restoring books to its shelves, even polishing the big desk which had been one of the last things brought from the attic. A fine chess table had been restored to its place by the fire and a battered chess set had been laid out on it. Mary and Russell had already been playing and working there.

'I don't like him much, either,' said Mary, 'but it is true that lately he seems to be quite reformed. Russell says that he could not have done so much without his active help.'

'That's as may be,' her aunt replied tartly, but fell silent when Russell returned and suggested a stroll in the gardens. They had not been improved quite so much as he had hoped— the weather had been too poor—but compared with their condition when he had arrived they were in splendid shape.

'You two young things go,' she said. 'I would like a nice doze in the comfortable armchair Russell has had brought out for me.'

Neither Mary nor Russell argued with her and set off through the herb gardens and on to the much-neglected lawn which one of the gardeners had been scything preparatory to digging the poor thing up and starting again, he had said.

'The trouble is,' Russell began, after they had crossed the lawn and found a broken stone bench to sit on from whence they could see the algae-covered lake whose water was supplied by a tributary of the Tyne, 'I have no wish to wait until next summer before we marry. I really think that to carry on as we are doing would be a drain on my health and sanity! Not only that, I wish to start a family before we both fall into "the sere and yellow leaf", as Shakespeare has it. Am I right in believing that you feel the same?'

Mary nodded. Lately to be with him had become sweet torture. 'Exactly the same. Have you considered what we might do about it?'

'Well, we could get married at any time that we liked, so far as a church service is concerned. The local rector would be only too happy to call the banns. He virtually told me so the other day! The problem there is that a man of my rank and a lady of yours are expected to be married only after the most astonishing legal arrangements are gone through regarding both our finances. That would inevitably mean that my father would have to take a hand in the game since I have no income of my own, other than the allowance which he makes me because the Russells allowed him full access to my mother's money instead of settling anything on her and then, at twenty-one, on me, as is common.

'That is why I have been using the income from the Ed-dington lands to pay for their improvement and my living costs. Before I ran away, for that is what I have done, he told me that he would cut off my allowance unless I married a woman of his choice before three months were up. The three months have come and gone and I have no notion what he might say if I were to tell him that I have found you again and still wish to marry you. Particularly since I have defied him by coming here at all.'

Mary offered him a wry smile. '"Oh, what a tangled web we weave when first we practise to deceive."'

'Exactly. You see my dilemma—which is yours, too.'

'No,' said Mary. 'I love you and trust you. If we married without all the legal piff-paff, I know that you would not cheat me over my money. What troubles me is not that, but that our deceit of everyone among whom we live—other than Aunt Beauregard, that is—would go even further than it already has done.'

Russell took her in his arms and kissed her. 'I am happy beyond belief that you trust me not to exploit you. But not only would the world think that I was a fortune hunter by marrying you if my father cast me off, but I have no wish to live on your money. If it were not my hope that my father and I might somehow become reconciled, I would go at once to Lord Chard and take up his offer to be his land agent so that I might bring something to our marriage.'

Secure in his arms, Mary looked up at his beloved face. It was not her imagination, she was sure, which led her to believe that, since he had arrived in the north and begun to run Eddington, his face had become sterner, stronger and more mature.

He kissed her gently on the forehead—a caress which was almost impersonal, but neither of them wished to go too far since passion was starting to hold them in its thrall and once certain boundaries were passed who knew what might happen?

'Would you marry me if I were only Chard's land agent, Mary?' he asked, bestowing another butterfly kiss on her.

'You know that I would. I would throw away my fortune if I thought that it kept me from you. I would marry you tomorrow without a settlement if that is your wish. I would come to you in rags, or in style if you were in rags, I cannot say fairer than that.'

'Brave girl,' he whispered. 'The time is not yet. If we are still in no-man's land by the time that winter arrives, then we shall think again. We never know what the morrow might bring and it is even possible that our problems might be solved for us, after a fashion which we could not have imagined.'

Later, he was to think wryly that he had spoken truer than he knew, but at the time his words flew away and, lost in a dream of love, perhaps the more powerful for not yet being fulfilled, they sat side by side enjoying one of the few sunny days of that disastrous year.

* * *

Shaw told Briggs of his scheme to be rid of Russell Hadleigh—to Briggs's horror, at first, but the more often Shaw spoke of it the less horrific it began to seem. He had involved Briggs because he needed an ally who was respectable and who could lie as convincingly as himself.

'We couldn't do it if Pickering hadn't left for London,' he said, 'or if the Earl had really sent Hadleigh to check our goings-on. As it is, I can't see any problems for us. We make him disappear'—he never used the words 'kill', or 'dispose of him', in respect for Briggs's more delicate feelings—'and then you drive his chaise, filled with his belongings, into the woods and hide it, telling everyone he's grown bored with playing about at Eddington and has gone back to London.'

'I don't know,' Briggs said. 'I don't like it, too risky.'

'Oh, damn that for a tale,' exclaimed Shaw. 'Think of all the lovely loot we shall get back again. There's another reason we ought to do it soon. I have a suspicion that he's been checking where the money went before he arrived here, so the sooner we're rid of him the better.'

'But what about his woman at Ancoates?' asked Briggs desperately. 'Won't she think it's odd if he takes off for London without her—*and* without telling her he's going?'

'Now, Briggs, you know better than that. His sort takes up and drops women as often as we change our clothes. No, if we do what I suggest then there's no need to worry. We can even give it out beforehand that he's growing bored and talking about going back to the bright lights before winter comes. Who's to contradict us, eh?'

It was probably more the thought of hanging or transportation if m'lord found out, and could prove, that he and Shaw had been on the take which convinced Briggs that he ought to join Shaw in his reckless scheme to make m'lord disappear. Besides, the more he thought about it, the more foolproof the scheme began to seem.

Of course, those locals whom m'lord had recruited or had given their previous posts back would have to be laid off again and would doubtless be noisy about it. As Shaw pointed out, however, all they had to do was blame m'lord for raising their hopes and then leaving them to starve again after he had driven off to the fleshpots of the idle south.

Shaw particularly liked the word fleshpots. He was already practising what he would say when m'lord's departure became general knowledge. Yes, all his troubles would soon be over—and m'lord's too, if it came to that.

Shaw had been right to worry about Russell's investigations into his goings-on before he had arrived at Eddington. Geoffrey Norman, who ran the country bank at Ancoates, had said something which had roused his suspicions about what Shaw had done with the money he had saved by dismissing most of the house and estate workers. That, and Aunt Beauregard's constant moaning about his simple-minded trust of a proven cheat like Shaw, had set him watching the man and listening carefully to what he said and did.

Russell was, as Shaw had suspected, on the verge of being able to tell the authorities of his embezzlement and thus bring about his arrest. In fact, on a fine early October day he saddled his horse to ride over to Ancoates to see, not the banker, but the local solicitor and discuss the matter with him. He had debated with himself whether to drive over to Loudwater and see his new friend, Lord Chard, who was the Lord Lieutenant of the county, but had decided that he would do that after consulting the solicitor.

On his way there, he would, as he had promised her, visit Mary. He had a splendid and elegant new solution to their latest chess problem in his pocket and he wanted to see her face when she read it.

He was travelling down the rutted by-way to Ancoates when he heard the sound of two horses being ridden hard behind him. He turned round in his saddle to see that it was Shaw and Briggs who were following him.

Russell stopped his own horse and waited for them to reach him. Shaw promptly rode ahead of him while Briggs stayed behind so that he was caught between the two of them.

'Might I enquire, m'lord,' asked Shaw swinging his mount around to face him, 'where you are off to this afternoon?'

'To Ancoates,' he replied shortly, 'although it is no concern of yours where I choose to ride.'

'Ah, but if I think it might be,' said Shaw, leaning forward in his saddle, 'what then?'

There was nothing of his usual greasy deference in the way he answered Russell and the expression on his face was a mocking one.

'I have no need to explain myself to you,' Russell replied, and he had never sounded more like Ritchie, 'and you will do me the goodness of removing yourself from out of my way.'

'Now, that,' said Shaw, 'I will not. I am sick of doing you any goodness and I have a mind to put an end to it here and now. Briggs, do as I asked you earlier.'

Behind him Russell heard Briggs give a great gulp before quavering, 'I have a pistol trained on your back, m'lord, and it will stay there until you dismount.'

'For goodness' sake,' said Russell impatiently, without turning his head to look at Briggs, 'the pair of you had better stop play-acting at once. I am a busy man these days and have no time for this. Put your pistol down, Briggs, before you do someone a mischief with it.'

Shaw grinned evilly at him. 'Oh, we mean to do a mischief, both of us…' and he had produced his own pistol to wave at Russell '…so do as you're told, my haughty lordship, and get down at once.'

So, it was mutiny or worse and Russell was blindingly aware that his life was in the balance.

'Very well,' he said, apparently meekly, but secretly determined to do something of which his brother might approve so he dismounted, but the moment he reached the ground he slapped his horse hard on its haunches with the crop which, like Ritchie, he rarely used.

It gave an enraged whinny and bolted—straight at Shaw, who was thrown from his own horse, losing his pistol in the process. Briggs, also taken by surprise, fired his pistol, but hit nothing. Unfortunately for him his own horse took fright at the noise and threw him.

In the confusion Russell ran rapidly through the trees away from the pair of villains whom he now knew intended to murder him. He also knew that he were not far from the hermit's cottage which, if he could reach it and the recluse was there, would mean salvation.

Briggs, the lesser of the pair, at first made no effort to rise, but Shaw, whose determination equalled his cunning, scrabbled around until he found his pistol before running past the prostrate Briggs, roaring, 'Get up, man, go after him, or we'll both hang.'

He then plunged into the woods after the unarmed Russell, who by now had reached the cottage—to find it locked. Desperately looking round him, he decided to run back towards Eddington, taking the short cut home by the quarry in the hope that he could outpace his pursuers.

Behind him Shaw and Briggs panted on, now terrified that if they did not catch their prey it was their lives which would be at stake. The few moments which Russell had spent trying the hermit's cottage door had enabled them to gain on him. Not only that, it had also shortened the distance between them so that he was now in the range of Shaw's pistol if he cared to use it—which he did, although he would have preferred Russell's body to be found without a bullet hole in it.

Russell ignored Shaw's repeated calls for him to stop and ploughed on, widening the distance between himself and his pursuers again until, in his haste, he stumbled over a fallen tree branch concealed by the autumn leaves which were heaped everywhere. Worse than that, he caught his head as he fell and lay there, dazed, in his turn.

'Splendid,' gasped Shaw when they reached their prey as he struggled to rise, not quite certain where he was or what he was doing. 'There's no need to waste a bullet on him after all. Let's knock him on the head and heave him into the quarry. Come on, you lazy devil, we can't afford to let him go now. It's him or us,' he roared at Briggs, who now that the fatal moment had arrived was beginning to regret having become involved in this wretched business at all.

Briggs stumbled forward. Shaw clubbed the struggling Russell with his pistol, caught him under the arms and began to drag him to the edge of quarry. 'Take him by the legs,

Briggs,' he howled, 'and be quick about it. We don't want that damned hermit finding us.'

Galvanised both by fear of Shaw and by fear of hanging, Briggs did as he was bid. Together they heaved Russell over the edge and watched him tumble down, to be trapped by some bushes halfway down to the quarry's floor.

Shaw dusted his hands together.

'Home now, Briggs. Remember—he went off to London this afternoon.'

'But there's them as knows he didn't, and what will they think?'

'Nothing, Briggs, nothing. I've sent the groom who brought his horse round for him today over to the farm Hadleigh way as soon as he'd mounted m'lord. They wanted another labourer there. He grumbled a bit, but I told him it's his duty to go where I send him. That leaves only the pair of us to give evidence of his whereabouts—and who's going to put their living at risk by questioning anything we might say. Besides, by the time m'lord's been gone forty-eight hours they'll have forgotten that he was ever here.'

Privately Briggs doubted that, but Shaw seemed so certain that all would be well that he kept his own counsel. After a short search they found Russell's horse contentedly cropping at some sparse grass and led him back to Eddington House, fortunately meeting no one on the way back.

Unknown to them both, they had been watched by the hermit who had heard Briggs's accidental firing of his pistol and wondered what was up. He had walked towards his cottage in order to avoid trouble, only to stop in the trees, hidden by them but near enough to hear Shaw and Briggs talking before they had heaved Russell's unconscious body into the quarry. He was fearful that if he interrupted them at their deadly business they would make short work of him, too.

Once they had gone he walked over to the quarry and looked down. He gave a short exclamation: m'lord was stirring and was like to fall to the quarry floor at any moment and so finish himself off for good. The question was, how to rescue him? He pondered this for a little, went back to his cottage and found some rope. Had he still the strength he had once possessed which would enable him to tie the rope to a tree, lower himself down and bring the half-conscious man back up to safety?

George Russell had spent the last thirty years avoiding his fellow men and doing nothing for them. He never knew what stirred him to try to rescue Russell Hadleigh. Perhaps it was some dim memory of happy days long ago with Jackie Chancellor, the imperilled young man's father, which caused him to set about his near-impossible task.

Mary had looked forward to Russell's visit that morning. He had seen her two days ago and had promised to look in on them after he had consulted the solicitor at Ancoates. He had told them nothing about the visit itself: he thought the less said about his decision to cast off Shaw before he had taken legal advice, the better.

At first she was not surprised that he was late, but as the day wore on and he never appeared she began to worry a little. On a previous occasion when he had had to cry off at short notice he had sent her a message by a groom with his apologies and his promise to call on the morrow. She knew that as the acting manager of the Eddington lands he was occasionally confronted with crises which required him to act immediately.

Her worries, and to a lesser extent, Aunt Beauregard's, grew stronger the next day when she still received no message from him.

'He's probably busy, dear,' her aunt said. 'I expect he'll come tomorrow.'

But he didn't and Mary began to grow a little frantic. She remembered only too well how she had felt all those years ago when he had deserted her the first time. Had he simply invented a convincing explanation to account for his earlier desertion and now that he had grown tired of his duties in the north, and of her, had he deserted her again?

She did not want to think so, but the burned child fears the fire, as she told Aunt Beauregard on the fourth day.

'Come, come,' said her aunt. 'This is foolish. The sensible thing would be to take Payne and ride over to Eddington. He might be ill—or Chard has called on him to carry out some of his new plans for the county. Best to find out what might be going on.'

Mary with Payne, the groom, riding behind her, set out for Eddington House early the next day. She arrived on the gravel sweep before its main doors with her heart in her mouth. She asked Briggs, who answered her determined knocking, if Lord Hadleigh was in.

She thought that Briggs looked at her oddly before he said, 'Please allow me to escort you to the drawing room, madam. I had better fetch Mr Shaw to speak to you.'

Shaw came in almost immediately. 'Ah, Mrs Wardour, Briggs said that you were asking to speak to Lord Hadleigh. Did he not inform you that he was returning to London? He set out at dawn three days ago.'

Her face white, Mary said as calmly as she could, 'Did he not leave any message for me, Mr Shaw?'

He shook a regretful head. 'I'm afraid not. I never thought to ask him if I were to send you one. I assumed, seeing as you were such friends, that you were already aware that he was returning south.'

How she rose to her feet without falling over, Mary never knew. Russell had done it again. He had left her without a word after all his protestations of eternal love. If she had been shattered by his previous desertion, it was as nothing to the effect of this one.

Twice! He had deceived her twice! What a fool she had been—and Aunt Beauregard, too, who had been so sure of his integrity.

Were all men lying traitors? And he the worst of them all?

'Thank you, Mr Shaw,' she managed. 'I expect that I shall be hearing from him when he reaches London.'

'Possibly so, madam, possibly so.'

He bowed her out. To return to Ancoates and her aunt, not to cry, not to revile him for his treachery, but to tell her as simply as she could that he had deserted her again and this time possibly for good. What a fool she had been to believe him when he had told her that they must have been tricked. Trickery there had been but it had been his.

Her tears were threatening to fall, but she would not cry, she would not. She would get on with her life and try to forget him.

If she could: it was going to be difficult.

Chapter Eleven

At the end of the first week when Briggs and Shaw were congratulating themselves that their murderous plot had succeeded, Mary went for a ride in the woods on her own. She had refused Payne's offer to go with her. She said that she needed to be alone.

When she had returned from Eddington with her sad news, even Aunt Beauregard had been compelled to agree with her and admit that she had been mistaken about Lord Hadleigh.

'I would never have thought it of him, never,' she was constantly saying, 'but, there it is, history seems to be repeating itself. The only thing that I can say to comfort you is, that given everything, you are well rid of him.'

This, of course, was no comfort at all. Nor did the passing days bring any kind of peace to Mary—rather the contrary. Instead of trying to forget him, her wretched memory insisted on going over and over again the events of the past summer and the love they had seemed to share. Somehow this second desertion without a word of warning seemed worse than the first. It indicated a callousness which she would never have dreamed he possessed.

Had all her time with him been an illusion?

One afternoon she was picking flowers in the garden when Payne, the groom who had accompanied her to Eddington, came up to her and asked for permission to speak to her.

'Of course,' she told him. 'What is it you wish to say to me?'

'Only this, Mrs Wardour, I know that it is no business of mine, but one of the servants at Eddington told me yesterday that he thought that there was something odd about m'lord's going. I thought that I ought to tell you of it—you and him being so friendly, like.'

'Something odd,' she repeated numbly. 'What kind of odd?' She did not tell him that it did not seem odd to her since history had simply repeated itself.

'Just that he left some of his clothes behind, and a rifle which he treasured. He went very suddenly, too, without saying a word about his going back to London at such short notice to anyone but Mr Shaw. All the servants at Eddington think that it was very unlike him: he had always been a most kind and considerate master. They would have expected to have had a few words in farewell from him—particularly since he had arranged for most of the books and furniture to be taken down to the library the following day. Most eager about it he was.'

'Is that all?' she said. 'There's probably a simple reason for his behaviour—that he was desperate to return to London.'

'Perhaps so, madam,' he said and bowed. 'But I thought you ought to know.'

She could not take comfort from anything as tenuous as

that, but would behave with the same stoicism which had supported her before, although every time that she looked at her chess set in the window and remembered him sitting there opposite to her, and smiling, the treacherous tears threatened to fall.

That night Mary awoke in the small hours—she had been sleeping badly—but this time the memory of her dreams brought her neither pain nor anguish.

For some reason in one of them she had been with him again on their trip to the cairn, before the hermit had surprised them. They had been discovering how they had been tricked by their parents and she had been so overwhelmed that, afterwards, she had fallen asleep in his arms. And he had made no attempt to seduce her but had just comforted her. Surely, a true villain, a villain who would have deserted her, would have cold-bloodedly exploited her vulnerability, not repressed his own desires, but attempted to fulfil them.

She would not have resisted him then, and he must have known that. There was more to puzzle her—Shaw and Briggs's behaviour when she had called at Eddington House, and now, this afternoon, Payne telling her how out of character his desertion of the folk at Eddington had seemed to them.

Russell had mentioned the word trust to her on several occasions and now Mary asked herself, as the dawn light grew stronger and stronger in her bedroom, Had she been wrong not to trust him?

No, she told herself firmly, I cannot believe that the man I have come to know this summer would ever betray me. If I believe that to be true, as a consequence, I must then believe that he has never left for London and therefore has not deserted me.

This, however, presented another problem for her to solve. She had to admit that his departure seemed plausible enough, but if, as she now believed, he had not left for London, then where was he? More than that, Shaw and Briggs must have been lying, not only to her, but to everyone else.

Mary's logical mind, trained by her father and then her husband, had her asking herself who might stand to gain by his disappearance and the answer was the pair who were lying to her. Russell had stopped their looting of Eddington, but they had probably been unable to plot against him because they had believed that he was his father's agent.

But supposing that they had discovered that he was not. What then?

Which raised the fearful possibility that he might be already dead.

No, she would not believe that, she would not. She would have known. In any case, there must be something she could do to discover the truth, and, if Russell had truly deserted her, then she must let him go and try to build her life anew.

She could not tell Aunt Beauregard of any of this. Much though she loved her, Mary recognised that she was the prisoner of her emotions. No, the best thing, perhaps, was to visit Lord Chard at Loudwater and tell him of her suspicions. He was the Lord Lieutenant of the county and she knew that she could depend upon his judgement.

After deciding this she fell asleep at once, but not before deciding that she would rethink this whole wretched business in the daylight away from her aunt, away from everyone and then map out a plan of action. She would go to the cairn where she had been so happy, sure of only one thing: that Russell had not betrayed her after all.

* * *

'Go riding on your own? Is that wise?' her aunt exclaimed.

'I must be out of the house,' said Mary, as calmly as she could, 'and try to work out what I shall now do with my life.'

This was no lie, but it was an evasion of the truth which her aunt had to accept. In the event she was never to reach the cairn. Before she did so, she had to pass the hermit's cottage. For once, he was outside in the little garden at the back where he grew a few herbs and simples and, at the right time of the year, potatoes. The moment he saw her he waved at her urgently. She waved back, but continued on her way, respecting what she had come to know was his wish for solitude.

This time, however, she was mistaken. He ran after her, calling her name so urgently that she stopped.

'Yes, Mr Russell, what is it you wish of me?'

He had reached her and put out a hand to grasp her horse's reins, so determined was he that she must stay and speak with him.

'I am most happy to meet you, Mrs Wardour. You have saved me a visit to Miss Beauregard, a visit which I did not wish to make because it might have caused gossip.'

He paused for breath as though the effort of speech had been too much for him. Mary said, surprised by his continuing urgency, 'Well, I am here now and you may speak to me. I can always give Miss Beauregard a message from you.'

'No! no!' he exclaimed, more urgent than ever. 'It is you to whom I must speak, not your aunt. And not in the open where we might be seen or heard—too dangerous. Pray come to my cottage as you did once before where we may speak in private. I promise you that you will not regret it.'

Well, here was a thing! What could the poor man mean?

Had solitude driven him mad? He was pulling on the reins now, and lest he frighten her horse which was beginning to grow restive Mary decided to brave all and do as he wished.

'Very well,' she said, once down. 'I'll come with you.'

'Good, excellent,' he said, 'allow me to lead your horse. A gentleman should always make a lady's life as easy as possible. You see that I have not lost all my manners.'

The way back to his cottage was not far, but Mary was already starting to regret that she had agreed to accompany him, but he kept such a firm hold of her horse, tying it carefully to the fence, before taking her arm and leading the way into his humble home as he described it when he opened the door, that she had no option but to obey him.

Inside it was as dark as Mary remembered it to have been, but much tidier. The hermit still held on to her arm, saying, 'Come with me, I have something to show you,' and then led her across the room to his rude bed in the corner.

For one ghastly moment Mary thought that he was about to assault her, but then she saw that the bed was occupied by a man whose head was turned away from her and who seemed to be sleeping.

Why have you brought me here? she started to ask, but only managed to get out the word 'Why' when the hermit, releasing her arm at last, bent over the bed, and shook the man by the shoulder, whispering, 'I have brought her to see you—as I promised.'

The man gave a short exclamation, sat up and turned his face towards Mary—and it was, of all people, Russell, her Russell! She would have recognised him anywhere, even if he was greatly changed with his bruised face and a week's growth of beard.

Her head whirling, she stared at him and of all things was only able to say, mindlessly, and in the circumstances, stupidly, even as she fell on her knees by the bed, 'But you have not gone to London after all!'

Russell smiled at this, and it was his special smile for her. 'So that is what they told you. I prayed, and have been praying since George brought me back to life, that you would not think that I had deserted you again, if that was their explanation for my disappearance.'

He tried to raise himself more, but fell back on his pillow, too weak to do so, his eyes closing.

Mary, the tears beginning to fall, bent down to kiss his cheek.

He opened his eyes and said, 'Are you truly·here? George said that he would fetch you soon, but he did not wish to leave me alone while I was so weak in case my would-be murderers by some sad chance found me and finished me off this time.'

'Shaw,' Mary choked out, 'and Briggs, too, I suppose. I knew that there was something odd about Briggs's manner to me when I called at Eddington House to find out why you had failed to visit us, as you had promised. And Payne, my groom, told me some of the servants there thought your desertion of them—for so they thought it—peculiar. God forgive me, at first I thought that they were wool-gathering, but then, when I began to think of our happy time together this summer, and the vows which you had made to me, I knew that there was something wrong, that you would never betray me by leaving without a word. I was going to visit Lord Chard this afternoon and ask him for his advice.'

Russell was struggling to sit up again. 'Oh, my darling, you have made me so happy that in the end you ceased to doubt me. What else could I think, though, when I could think again, which was only three days ago, but that you would certainly believe me traitor? I worried more about that than how soon it would be before I recovered enough to be able to confront those who have tried to kill me.

'They were Shaw and Briggs, as you rightly suspected. They waylaid me not far from here, knocked me unconscious and threw me into the quarry. By the grace of God, George found me there and got me out, the good lord knows how, and then nursed me back to near life—as you see. I am most eternally grateful to him.'

He sank back, exhausted, on to his pillow again. The hermit said gruffly, 'I couldn't let Jackie Chancellor's son die without trying to save him. Now that you have seen him, Mrs Wardour, I will leave you alone with him for a time. I believe that your presence will be as good a restorative as medicine for my poor patient.'

After he had left them, Mary sat on the stool beside the bed. Her relief was tempered with shame that she had ever doubted him—even for a short time. She leaned over to stroke his forehead, which was as cold as ice. He opened his eyes and smiled at her, 'You have no notion how pleased I am to see you again.'

'And I you,' she said. 'I began to fear that you might be dead. I was riding to the cairn to work out in peace what I should say to Lord Chard.'

'That's my clever darling,' he said, and began to shiver. He gave her a rueful smile. 'Ever since George brought me round I have been unable to get warm. Ritchie told me once that soldiers injured in battle often suffer in this way. I suppose that the attack on me has had the same effect.'

To Mary's shock his lips were turning blue.

Oh, he must not die now, not now that she had found him again! She would not let him. She would warm him and to the devil with all the constraints which society put on women's behaviour. Later she was even to wonder whether the hermit had intended this when he had left them alone.

She leaned down, pulled off her boots and with one swift movement she threw back the covers, slipped into the bed beside him, drew the covers over them and put her arms around him.

'Come,' she said. 'I will warm you. It is the least that I can do after failing to trust you when you disappeared. Remember how you warmed me on the day when we worked out how our parents had deceived us.'

It was true that he was cold, so cold, but she was warm, and she was Mary his love, and after a little time he ceased to shiver and then put his arms around her and she felt him drift off into sleep. She was not to know that it was the first peaceful sleep he had had since the hermit had brought him back to consciousness again.

And as he became warm and slept, Mary, too, held so innocently in the arms of the man she loved, also slept. And there the hermit found them, chaste in each other's arms, the man on his way to recovery and the woman doing sweet penance for ever having doubted him for a moment.

On the evening of the day on which Shaw and Briggs had pitched Russell into the quarry m'lord the Earl of Bretford was still fuming over the fact that October had arrived and he had still heard nothing from his wayward son.

Despite Ritchie having told him that if he thought hard enough he would be able to guess where his brother was, he still had no notion of where he might be. That morning he had snarled first at his valet, then at Graves and finally at the butler. While never a very even-tempered man, he had always been reasonably considerate of those who served him and his own loss of control vexed him nearly as much as it did them.

In the evening he went to a reception given by Lord Sidmouth, preparing to be horribly bored, which he was. Until, while walking from one overcrowded room to another, he was accosted by someone whom he had not seen for years.

'Damn me,' announced a cheerfully rotund gentleman, 'if it isn't my old friend, Jackie Chancellor, after all these years. I have to say you've worn better than me and no mistake.'

The Earl put up his quizzing glass and said in a tone of deadly indifference, 'Do I know you, sir?'

'Well, I'm aware that I've changed, but I hadn't thought I'd changed so much that you wouldn't recognise me,' the fat man said, no whit flustered by m'lord's arrogant dismissal of him, 'but surely you're the Jackie Chancellor who let a bear loose into the Fellow's common-room at Oxford as I'm still the Ralph Cheyney who helped you.'

The Earl lowered his quizzing glass. 'Yes, you are Ralph Cheyney, I see that now, and, by God, you *have* changed, sir.'

'Sir Ralph now, too, not plain Mister. Like you I came into what I hadn't expected. But if I've changed in looks I'm still a bit of the merry-andrew I always was while you've turned into the sort of solemn chap we used to avoid like the plague. Never mind that, let's find a corner where we can talk about old times,' and Sir Ralph, without waiting for an answer, set off through the double doors to do exactly that.

Resignedly the Earl followed him until they arrived at a quiet ante-room away from the crowd, where Sir Ralph sank gratefully into an armchair and invited the Earl to do the same in another.

'By the by,' he began, 'before we begin reminiscing I ought to tell you that I met your son and heir, Hadleigh, last spring. Sterling fellow, isn't he? With a bottom of sound common sense. I hope he marries the pretty little mathematician who was travelling north with him.

'Added to that, I've heard nothing but good of what he's been doing at Eddington. You should be proud of him and for having the common sense to send him there to mend matters. Ever since old Shaw died a few years ago that wastrel son of his has been ruining the place. Let the House go to rack and ruin, turned staff away and let the lands go to rot as well. I wondered what he was doing with the rents. But I suppose that's why you sent Hadleigh there. He's done marvels in a jolly short time, they say. You wouldn't recognise the place. He put the locals back to work, improved everything beyond belief, Chard told me just before I came south. Chard was most impressed by him and he isn't impressed by many or by much.'

The Earl stared at the gossiping fool, rendered almost dizzy by this cascading mixture of idle joviality and unbelievable information. Sir Ralph looked keenly at him.

'I say, old friend, are you feeling quite the thing? I thought that you were going to have a funny turn there for a moment.'

'No, no,' said the Earl hurriedly. 'I'm a little tired, perhaps, that's all.'

Not for a moment would he betray to the half-wit before him that he had not had the slightest notion either that Hadleigh had gone to Eddington or, that he had, improbably, transformed the place. Old Shaw dead! When had that happened? Why had he not been informed? What had young Shaw been doing to the place?

Later, when he had shaken off Sir Ralph who had talked steadily at him about everything and everybody for the last half hour, the Earl remembered something which Ritchie had said to him. That if he thought hard enough he would know exactly where Hadleigh had gone.

Now how the devil could he be expected to know that he had gone north to Eddington, the one place on earth which the Earl detested most of all? Something at the back of his mind pricked him sufficiently for him to shake his head and remember that Hadleigh had made a fuss to him and Graves about the accounts which old Shaw—no, young Shaw—had sent down from Eddington. Hadleigh had even, he remembered now, asked if he might go there to find out what was happening.

Of course, he had refused to allow him to do any such thing.

So! The disobedient swine had set off on his own initiative! Oh, he would have a word with Graves about this in the morning and then, damn him if he would not set off for Eddington himself as soon as maybe and send Hadleigh packing for good and all.

He stopped for a moment—on the other hand, Chard thought highly of him, and Chard was no fool.

No matter, it was not Hadleigh's business to defy his father by meddling with the Eddington estates. Besides, there was another thing. What was all that talk of a pretty female mathematician and some nonsense about Hadleigh marrying her?

Well, he'd soon put a stop to that!

The following morning, after speaking to a friend of Cheyney's who lived not far from Eddington and was also at the Reception, the Earl discovered that matters might be even more serious there than Cheyney had suggested. The Earl walked rapidly into Graves's office. His agent and secretary sat there, working as usual.

He rose. 'M'lord?'

'Graves, I have just discovered that Hadleigh has, against my express wishes, gone north to Eddington and is meddling in things there without my knowledge or my permission. I have a mind to go up north myself and put a stop to it. Order the stables to prepare everything for my journey there tomorrow.'

Had the Earl not been so determined to punish his son he might have noticed the fleeting expression of alarm which passed over Graves's face.

'Is that wise, m'lord? To make the differences between you and Lord Hadleigh so plain to the world? Think of the gossip which might ensue.'

The Earl, who had already begun to turn away, swung on his heel. 'I don't give a damn for gossip. Besides, someone ought to go there. Were you aware that old Shaw died some years ago and that, without informing me and asking for authority to do so, his son took over from him, pretending that his father was still alive?'

Graves put on a shocked expression. 'Indeed not, m'lord. The signatures on the accounts seemed to be in order—as did the accounts.'

'Well, something damned odd has been happening at Eddington if my informants are to be believed. Sounds as though Shaw has been looting the house and grounds. My fault, not yours. I hate the damned place and only Hadleigh's running off to it and this news about old Shaw's death and his son's misbehaviour would take me there.

'Oh, and Mr Richard and his family were due to visit me in a sennight. Write to them explaining that I have been called north on an urgent mission and will entertain them on another date as soon as I return.'

'Of course, m'lord. Certainly, m'lord, as soon as possible.'

'Excellent. I knew that I could depend on you.'

The moment the door had closed behind the Earl, Graves swore a great oath which damned young Shaw and his overdone greed to hell for the devil to deal with him there. He then sat down and began to write a frantic letter to his fellow conspirator, warning him of the Earl's intention to visit Eddington in the somewhat vain hope that the letter might reach him before the Earl did.

Who would have thought that the old man would suddenly throw off the habit of a lifetime in order to travel to a place which he had so often told Graves he would never visit again? Damn Hadleigh and his meddling! Who could have guessed that he was clever enough at figuring to be able to detect something strange about Eddington's accounts and then would decide to drive off and check them on the spot!

If the worst came to the worst his own best plan would be to pack his bags and make off as quickly as possible with his share of the loot from Bretford's northern estates before the Runners arrived to arrest him.

Mary and Russell were playing cards. From the moment of Mary's first arrival he had recovered rapidly, and was almost his old self again. Several days of eating good food had restored the roses to his cheeks. Mary had been smuggling it from Aunt Beauregard's kitchen on the pretext that she was taking it to the poor of Ancoates—making sure that some of it reached them on her journey to the hermit's cottage.

He was sitting in the hermit's Windsor chair, dressed in his own clothing which the hermit had, after a fashion, washed. The hermit had not only shaved Russell's face for him, but he had also cut his own beard and hair and had then shaved himself. The man who had emerged from this shearing had proved to be one who had carried his youthful good looks into old age.

For his part, Russell had never looked less like the London dandy he had once been, but even so his recent experiences, far from destroying his attraction for Mary, had enhanced it by strengthening his face even further. Once his first debilitating weakness had passed, he had had only one idea in his head and that was to bring Shaw and Briggs to justice. Particularly Shaw, because he had repaid the charity and mercy shown to him by trying to murder the man who had offered it.

Unknown to Mary, for the first time he looked like his twin a little. It was more in his expression than in his overall facial structure and colouring where the resemblance lay. Russell now shared the appearance of hard determination which was Ritchie's hallmark. When playing cards with her his face softened a little since their game, played as it was between two such mathematical tricksters, resulted, to the hermit's amusement, in a great deal of mutual teasing.

The game over, they ate the pikelets and biscuits which had come from Aunt Beauregard's kitchen and began to talk strategy. The hermit proved surprisingly strong in this. It was he who had suggested, from the first, that no one should be told of Russell's whereabouts, or of how he came to be thrown into the quarry when all the world thought him back in London.

He was reiterating it now.

'Yes,' said Russell, who had been a narrow winner at piquet, an excellent card game for two sharpers like himself and Mary. 'Giving Shaw false confidence that he has succeeded in his villainy is an excellent notion. By now he will be confident that I am gone for good. Besides, if by some mischance he knew where I was hiding, he would most likely come after me again. In the meantime, as soon as I have recovered, we must all three secretly inform Chard by some means of the plot to murder me. Doubtless he, too, thinks I have tired of reforming Eddington and by now will have been back in London for some time. As Lord Lieutenant he will be best placed to summon up the power and the majesty of the law to deal with them.

'Our biggest advantage will be that of surprise when I reappear again with that law at my shoulder. I trust, sir, that you will form one of our party, for were it not for you I should not be sitting here with my dear Mary, enjoying beating her at cards and eating Aunt Beauregard's excellent provender.'

'May I remind you, m'lord,' replied Mary demurely, 'that since we agreed to play the best of three games, and so far we have only played two and each of us has won one, that last statement of yours was somewhat inaccurate, to say the least.'

'Mere nit-picking,' returned Russell easily. 'I shall of course, win the last one in a canter. Speaking of canter, I can't wait to get on a horse again. All this sitting about is more tiring than I would have thought.'

'When you are quite better,' she told him, 'you may ride again. For the present, concentrate on a complete recovery so that you may be fit enough to travel to Loudwater where you may persuade Lord Chard that you are not, as report has it, enjoying yourself in London.'

Russell leaned over the table and kissed her on the nose.

'Dear, dear, I see that you are determined to nag me even before marriage. What in the world shall I have to endure when you have finally carried me off into unpeaceful domesticity?'

'Nothing, sir, if you behave yourself. As it is, shuffle, cut the cards and deal again.'

'Willingly,' he laughed and his eyes promised her in some near future more than the chaste kiss he had just bestowed on her. Like many men who have narrowly escaped death, Russell was enjoying life more than ever now that it had been given back to him. The best thing of all was that Mary was enjoying it with him.

Dominic Hastings, Lord Chard, one of the great magnates who ruled in the north of England, had just joined his wife and baby son, Henry, in a mid-day meal before retiring to his office to go over the returns from the coal pits and the iron ore reserves which, together with his farming interests, formed the basis of his wealth.

Since inheriting he had, by his own efforts, transformed the Loudwater estates from a position of near bankruptcy to one of great prosperity. His latest venture had been to join with Sir Thomas Liddell in backing the locomotive which George Stephenson, Liddell's engine-wright, had been developing on Liddell's land.

He had been delighted to discover that young Hadleigh, whom rumour had always said was a lightweight, was nothing of the kind. Instead he was doing for Eddington what Chard himself had done for Loudwater. In fact, he had been on the point of visiting him to ask him to join the cartel which Liddell and he had set up when the news had reached him that Hadleigh had returned to London.

He was, alas, probably bored with life in the north, so far from the bright lights of London, one supposed.

Chard had scarcely sat down when there was a knock on the door. He sighed, put down his pen and called, 'Come in.' He prided himself on always being available to his staff.

'Beg pardon for interrupting you, m'lord,' said his butler, 'but a Mr George Russell has called and has asked to see you. He says it is a matter of some urgency.'

He paused, began to speak again, but stopped.

'Well, what is it? Did this Mr Russell give any explanation of his reasons for urgency?'

'No, m'lord,' he hesitated. 'It is not for me to put forward an opinion, but a stranger trio I have seldom seen. By the dress and general appearance of the two men, one would have supposed that the servants' entrance would have been their proper place. The lady with them, however, is dressed in the most impeccable style. Mr Russell is, however, very well spoken. To cap all that, the other gentleman would not give his name.'

His master rose, looking amused. 'Now you have intrigued me. Send them in, by all means. Life has grown a little dull lately.'

'Very well, m'lord.'

Chard walked to the window and looked out across the park where, on this mid-October day, his little family, well wrapped up against the cold, were walking. A moment later, the butler showed in his visitors.

As he had said, the men's clothing was minimally genteel, to say the least. The lady he immediately recognised as that most respectable gentlewoman, Mrs Wardour, and it was difficult to understand what she was doing in the company of two almost ragamuffins!

What was even more surprising, however, was that, after a brief moment when recognition failed him—largely because of his shabby appearance—he knew that 'the gentleman who had refused to give his name' was, in fact, none other than his new neighbour, Russell Chancellor, Viscount Hadleigh!

Of all stupid things he found himself saying, 'Hadleigh! What the devil are you doing here, and in that get-up? I thought that you were in London!'

Russell broke into a delighted grin. How many more times was he to hear that remark before this unlikely adventure of his was over?

'So pleased to see that you can recognise me,' he murmured. 'I had wondered a little whether I was still recognisable! And, no, I am not in London, I am in your study and with the help of my friend and saviour here, Mr George Russell and of Mrs Wardour, I will tell you how I come to be so.'

Dominic Chard began to laugh. 'It had better be a good explanation, but before you begin to satisfy my curiosity, pray sit down, and allow me to ring for some really splendid port. You both look as though a jorum of it would do you the world of good—Mrs Wardour would, I think, prefer an excellent Madeira. You, Hadleigh, look to weigh quite a bit less than you did when I last saw you, so perhaps I had better order you some more solid refreshment when you have finished telling me why you are dressed like one of your lesser servants.'

'Delighted,' said Russell, as they all did as they were bid, 'although I have been doing rather too much sitting about lately. I warn you that my story is somewhat lengthy and very improbable, and that to complete it you will be called upon to exercise your powers as Lord Lieutenant of this county.'

'Now you intrigue me more than ever,' said Chard, assuming his seat behind his desk. 'Pray continue.'

Which Russell did, detailing everything that had happened to him since he had left Eddington on that fatal day. He gave George Russell full credit for saving his life and then revealed Mary's share in helping to hide him from his enemies as well as nursing him so devotedly that he was restored to health sooner than might have been expected.

'You know, Hadleigh, and Mrs Wardour, too,' Chard remarked drily after hearing this, 'women are supposed not to be able to keep a secret, but from the evidence of my life, and now of yours, that is a most thundering lie. As to my own part in this—we must consider it carefully. I think, that for the present, for your own safety, you and Mr Russell must remain here—incommunicado—while we work out our plan of action. Mrs Wardour, I believe that you may be safe at home.'

'Oh, indeed, m'lord. My going innocently about my own business will surely rouse no suspicion—to be busybodying about might seem odd.'

'Exactly,' said m'lord, bowing in her direction. 'Now I agree with you, Hadleigh, that the less Shaw and Briggs know of your resurrection before we move against them, the better. You have explained Mrs Wardour's role in this, and I agree that she must be one of the party which to give evidence against the villains. The more credible witnesses that we have, the better.'

Russell nodded. As he had expected, Dominic Chard had proved, once again, that he was a man of sterling common sense.

'The only thing about accepting your hospitality,' he said, 'is that one of your staff might, without meaning to, give us away.'

Chard began to laugh. 'Not at all. You will be an old friend of mine down on your luck and an invalid who is travelling with another friend who is a doctor. You have appealed to me for help and I am offering you shelter. Your illness means that you will be confined to your room, where Mr Russell here will nurse you as devotedly as Mrs Wardour has done for the few days that we shall need to prepare to spring our trap.'

'More sitting about for me, I see,' moaned Russell, 'but I must congratulate you, Chard—a more ingenious pack of lies I have seldom heard. You even surpass my brother in that department, which is something of a miracle.'

On that cheerful note, and the arrival of an excellent nuncheon and some first-class port for the two gentlemen, who had not recently enjoyed a good meal, and some Madeira for the lady, the serious part of the interview ended.

Chapter Twelve

'I have had another letter from my old friend, Lady Markham,' Aunt Beauregard informed Mary over the breakfast table. 'It seems that her daughter and her husband are still missing. From something that Thomas Bertram said to Perry before he ran off with Angelica, Perry thought that they might call either on me, or at Eddington House. She again asks me to let her know at once if we hear anything of her.'

'Hardly likely that they would visit either place,' said Mary, 'but one never knows. People do the oddest things.'

'They must be somewhere,' said her aunt. 'It makes me almost happy that I never had children. Was there anything interesting in your letters today, my love?'

'Oh, yes. It seems that Lord Chard is about to pay a flying visit to Eddington House and would be grateful if the pair of us would arrange to meet him there for nuncheon on the day after tomorrow. I think, from what he says, that he is unaware that Lord Hadleigh has left for London. Unfortunately, there is no way in which I can inform him of that since he will be calling at Eddington House on the way from Newcastle. He says that he will have a pair of friends with him whom he thinks that we would like to meet, as well as several other important persons in his train.'

Now all of this was in Chard's letter, which had been written after such a fashion as to enlighten Mary as to the true state of affairs without revealing anything to anyone else should it be intercepted. Not unnaturally Aunt Beauregard put quite a different interpretation on it.

'Two friends whom we would like us to meet. What is the betting that Chard is match-making for you?' she exclaimed.

'Most probably,' agreed Mary, her face solemn. Which was not an untruth, since she already knew that Chard's two friends were Russell and the hermit, because she had left them at Loudwater several days earlier and that Lord Chard would be present in his capacity as the legal head of the county.

'You know,' said Aunt Beauregard thoughtfully, 'these great persons never seem to be aware how expensive it is for the people who are expected to give them, and all their attendants, instant hospitality.'

'Oh, I don't think that Lord Hadleigh would mind any expense Lord Chard might engage him in so far as this visit is concerned,' replied Mary—again employing a double meaning.

'One has to hope so. I'm not sure that I wish that Mr and Mrs Thomas Bertram might turn up here—even if it meant that I would be able to set her mother's mind at rest about her whereabouts.'

'And read her the riot act for upsetting all her family so much,' offered Mary with a grin.

'That also,' agreed Aunt Beauregard. 'Meantime, we must decide on our *toilettes* for the day after tomorrow and thank providence that I am not bearing the expense of entertaining Lord Chard!'

Privately Mary thought that Lord Chard might be the one providing the entertainment—but did not say so!

'What the devil does Chard mean by visiting us at such short notice?' grumbled Shaw to Briggs early in the morning of Chard's visit. 'And for what? Some nonsense about employing extra constables to help to keep the peace in these times when riot is becoming commonplace. We have had no rioting—'

Briggs interrupted him. 'There was that fracas at Eddington village, though, when we laid off so many labourers.'

'Maybe, but since that popinjay arrived here and employed most of them again everything has been quiet. I don't like Chard. He thinks that he's better than the likes of us. Oh, well, we must be on our best behaviour and hope that he won't stay too long—or ask too many questions about young Hadleigh. If he does you know what to say—that he should have reached London by now.'

He had barely finished speaking when the under-butler entered in a hideous state of fluster.

'Oh, Mr Shaw, you'd never believe it but a grand coach has just arrived and it's not Lord Chard's. When Thomas, the groom on duty, asked him if he were, the gentleman said that he wasn't, but that he needed to see Mr Shaw immediately. He wouldn't give us his name.'

'Not Chard and needs to see me immediately! Now, who the devil can that be? You go and attend to him, Briggs, and bring him in as soon as he consents to give his name—if he doesn't send him off with a flea in his ear.'

Briggs bustled off, and alas the flea was to alight in Shaw's ear and not the visitor's, for Briggs returned a few minutes later, not in front of, but behind a splendidly dressed large man, whom Shaw had never seen before.

'Your flunkey is insolent, Shaw,' growled the large man, 'for that is who I take you to be. I am Bretford, your employer. I have come here to find out what the deuce is going on at Eddington, but before that I demand to see my son at once. By the by, I find your butler singularly lacking in manners—I hope the rest of your staff are not equally boorish.'

Shaw, disconcerted beyond belief by the sight of the man whom he believed to be permanently and safely settled in London, stammered, 'Oh, m'lord, had he known that it was you he would, I am sure, have accorded you all the honour due to your station.'

'Damn that,' said Bretford pleasantly. 'You should teach him to be polite to every caller, regardless of their station. But this is dilly dally; send for my son at once, I have rather a lot to say to him.'

Shaw gave his employer a melancholy smile, 'Alas, m'lord, I fear that you have arrived too late. Lord Hadleigh left for London well over a fortnight ago and should have arrived there by now—possibly after you left. I fear that he grew tired of country living.'

'Did he, indeed? I suppose that it is most likely that he would. Very unsatisfactory of him. Did he give you any explanation of why he came here at all?'

'Only that he had come as your agent to oversee how Eddington was being run, you not having been here for so many years.'

The Earl stared at him. 'He said that, did he?' He did not

inform Shaw that Hadleigh had arrived at Eddington without his father's knowledge or permission, but went on to pick another bone with the agent.

'Leave Hadleigh to me. I'll deal with him when I see him in London. What I do wish to know now is how it came about that you never informed me of your father's death.'

Shaw gulped. In for a penny, in for a pound. 'Oh, but I am sure that I did, m'lord. I distinctly remember that I wrote a despatch to your secretary, Mr Graves, telling him of my father's sudden and sad end. Hearing nothing, I took it upon myself to act as agent, seeing that I had been my father's assistant in his last and fatal illness.'

'Your father never told me of that, either,' said the Earl severely.

Salvation from this extremely damaging inquisition came from an unexpected quarter in the arrival of Lord Chard and his attendant secretary. From not wishing to entertain him at all, Shaw was now unimaginably grateful for his timely appearance. When the under-butler came in, Briggs having remained with Shaw and the Earl, to announce the Right Honourable, the Earl of Chard, Shaw rushed forward to greet him, all greasy servility again.

His welcome over, he begged both Earls to take a seat. 'Not before you have introduced me to Lord Chard,' said Lord Bretford glacially, 'and him to me. Your manners, sir, are sadly wanting.'

Shaw nearly bent double in doing the honours.

'Delighted to make your acquaintance at last, Bretford,' said Lord Chard. 'And on your home ground, too. You must visit Loudwater before you leave.'

'I should be honoured to do so,' said Bretford, smiling for

the first time. Chard was certainly living up to his reputation as a handsome man with a great deal of presence and abilities out of the ordinary where running an estate was concerned.

He told him so.

Chard smiled. 'I am particularly pleased to meet you after having met your son, Lord Hadleigh. I was most impressed by him and the work he has done here, both on the estate and in the house. Eddington has been quite transformed, has it not, Shaw? I believe that your father had allowed both parts of Lord Bretford's property to become neglected. You, Shaw, must have been most pleased by Lord Hadleigh's arrival, particularly when he proved to be such an able improver of what needed improving. You must also be proud of him, sir,' he said directly to his fellow peer.

If Shaw's mind was not now totally fuddled by Lord Bretford's unannounced arrival, he might have grasped that Lord Chard was subtly baiting him. Instead he muttered 'quite so, quite so', at suitable intervals. Lord Bretford, equally surprised, merely rose and bowed his acknowledgement of the compliment paid to his son.

'From your letter to me arranging this meeting, m'lord,' said Shaw once they were all seated except, of course, for Briggs, who was standing by the double doors, 'I believe that you have come expressly to discuss the rising level of unrest in the county and the necessity for more constables. We have had no unrest or rioting lately at Eddington, but I understand your natural concern over the general position.'

'Indeed,' said Chard, leaning back in his chair, 'but it is not simply rioting and Luddism which perturbs me, but also the rising levels of other kinds of crime—attacks on decent persons, highway robbery and, I am less than happy to say, murder and attempted murder. These, too, must be dealt with—and ruthlessly—as I am sure you will agree.'

'Quite so, m'lord, of course, m'lord,' gabbled Shaw again, the weight of his own guilt heavy on his shoulders.

'But before we discuss these matters, you will allow me a word with my secretary. John,' he said, pulling out his hunter and inspecting it, 'I think that in about ten minutes or so you may leave to fetch the other persons whom I have brought with me to help in our efforts to rid the county of misdoing.'

'So noted, m'lord,' said the secretary, bowing and resuming his seat a little behind his lordship's.

If Shaw was being baffled by Lord Chard's manoeuvres, the Earl was even more so. What the devil is going on here? was his inward comment.

'Excellent,' said Chard, putting his hunter away. 'Now, where were we?'

Before Shaw could answer him there was a rap on the double doors. Briggs opened them to reveal the under-butler who announced, 'Lord Chard's other guests have arrived—do I show the ladies in here?'

'Ah,' said Chard. 'They must be Mrs Wardour and Miss Beauregard. I believe that I mentioned inviting them in my letter to you, Shaw. I particularly wished to meet Mrs Wardour again. She is, as you may already know, an extremely gifted mathematician and, as such, being a female, is a rarity with whom I had great pleasure in conversing. I think that you will agree with me, Shaw that this was not an opportunity to be missed.'

'Quite so, m'lord,' gabbled Shaw again. 'Show them in at once,' he bade the under-butler, who fled before he could commit any further gaucheries.

Lord Bretford, who was no fool, was beginning to wonder

even more what the devil Chard was up to and why Shaw was so obviously in an advanced state of nervous excitement.

He was soon to find out.

Mary, after she had dressed herself in a toilette suitable for a day to be spent with Lord Chard, was wondering what exactly she would find when she arrived at Eddington, and what would happen when she reached there. She hoped to meet Russell and the hermit, of course, but she had no notion of what Lord Chard had planned for this impromptu meeting.

Aunt Beauregard, quite unaware of all the dangerous currents swirling beneath the surface of her normal orderly and somewhat boring life, was all of a-twitter at the notion of meeting Lord Chard. She had heard of him, had, indeed, seen him, having been part of a crowd which had watched him lay the foundation stone of a new Grammar School for Ancoates, but she had never spoken to him.

He was an extraordinarily handsome man, even more so than Russell Hadleigh, but Russell, until he had deserted them, had possessed the common touch while Chard had the reputation of being a little aloof. So both ladies were a little worried about their visit to Eddington, but for quite different reasons.

What neither of them had expected was what they found.

Mary was disappointed to find that Russell was not already there. She wondered where he was. Aunt Beauregard, on the other hand, was surprised to see Lord Bretford rising to greet her when they entered. She knew him immediately, despite all the changes which the passing years had wrought.

She exclaimed, defying all the forms of politeness by doing so before introductions had been made, 'Jackie Chancellor, by all that's holy! What are you doing here?'

Lord Chard, giving the lie to the rumour of his aloofness, began to laugh, before saying, 'I see that you are as surprised as I am to meet the Earl of Bretford in Northumberland. We all thought him wedded to the south of England. He came, I understand, to see his son who, most unfortunately, had left for London before his father arrived. You, I take it, madam, are Miss Beauregard of Ancoates and this charming young lady must be the celebrated Mrs Wardour. Since you already know Lord Bretford, I must do the honours of introducing Mrs Wardour to him. She is, of course, the daughter of the eminent mathematician Dr Beauregard, Miss Beauregard's late brother, and the widow of Dr Henry Wardour.'

Now it was Lord Bretford's turn to fall into a state of nervous excitement when Lord Chard had finished his introduction. Mary, also, was strangely moved to see him. This, then, was Russell's father, who with her own had destroyed their chance of happiness together all those years ago.

She bowed and offered the Earl no welcoming smile. He stared at her, also remembering the distant past. So, this charming, composed beauty with the lovely eyes and tender mouth was the woman whom Hadleigh had wanted to marry. For the first time he wished that he had met her all those years ago for, had he done so, perhaps his attitude to their marriage might have been different.

'Delighted to meet you,' he muttered. 'I am told that you are a gifted mathematician. I believe that my son has some interests in that direction.'

Mary raised her eyebrows and said coolly, 'I would scarcely describe Lord Hadleigh's gifts as lightly as that, m'lord. My late husband was greatly impressed by his prowess and he has been helping me to develop the notion of a clockwork calculating machine. In some respects his abilities are in advance of those of myself, my late father and my husband.'

The Earl stared at her, dumb-struck. Her voice was even more lovely than her face and her graceful body. 'I am most pleased to hear that, madam,' he offered at last.

It took Mary all her strength not to say, And so you should be. She contented herself, however, with a small bow and then listened to her aunt and the Earl recalling that, in the even more long ago, when neither Mary nor Russell had been thought of, they had been part of a merry crowd of friends, now long since dispersed.

'It is years since we last met,' ended Aunt Beauregard, 'and I trust that you will forgive me for calling you Jackie Chancellor—but that is what I always knew you as.'

'Pardon granted,' smiled the Earl, who was beginning to recover himself after the shock of meeting the woman whom his son had wanted to marry and finding her very different from the idea he had of her. It did not hurt that he knew through his association with the Royal Society that Henry Wardour had been the last of a very rich family and that his widow had inherited everything.

That certainly put a different complexion on things! If only that scamp, Hadleigh, had not rushed back to enjoy himself in London.

They all sat down again. Shaw, who had recovered his equanimity a little, rang for refreshments. When they arrived he was so busy ingratiating himself with all the company that he failed to notice that Chard's secretary had disappeared on his master's errand. Mary found herself next to Lord Bretford, who was making great efforts to entertain both her and Aunt Beauregard.

She was so exercised by another matter that she could scarcely pay attention to m'lord's gallant attempts to mend fences between them. Where was Russell? She had understood at their meeting with Lord Chard that he would be accompanying him to Eddington. Instead he and George Russell were absent and Lord Chard appeared to be on reasonably friendly terms with Arthur Shaw. What deep game could he be playing?

'Yes,' she found herself saying distractedly to the Earl when by his subsequent expression she should have been saying 'no'! The Earl was thinking that nervous excitement must be infectious for the lovely Mrs Wardour was showing distinct signs of having caught it.

'And now,' said Lord Chard, 'I believe that we may resume our discussion of the lawlessness obtaining locally and what we ought to do about it. I take it that we are all agreed that we must stamp it out wherever it occurs and whoever indulges in it. Agreed?'

'Agreed,' said everyone. Shaw was particularly loud in his approval of m'lord's statement.

'Excellent,' said Chard. 'And that goes for the ladies, too, I believe.'

'Certainly,' said Mary in a strong voice, thinking of poor Russell and of the would-be murdering monster sitting opposite to her who was virtually licking Lord Chard's boots in his efforts to agree with him.

She was beginning to get an inkling of what Chard might be up to.

'In that case then,' said Chard, 'we may proceed to the next part of the meeting. My secretary should be back shortly with my two assistants.' He turned an ear towards the double doors. 'I believe that I hear them coming.'

He was right. Without benefit of the stunned under-butler the doors opened to admit not only Chard's secretary, but two men at the sight of whom everyone in the company but Lord Chard and Mary stared with dropped jaws and aghast expressions.

They were Viscount Hadleigh and Mr George Russell!

Not only that, but behind them were three large grim-faced men wearing a dark blue livery.

After a brief, somewhat shocked pause, everyone began to speak at once, but not before Briggs, who had gone an odd yellow colour, had pointed at Russell and squeaked, 'You can't be here, you're dead!'

Lord Bretford's exclamation was more commonplace. 'What in the world are *you* doing here, Hadleigh? You are supposed to be in London,' while Aunt Beauregard's lament was,

'Why are you wearing such odd clothes, Russell?'

It was, however, Briggs's anguished cry which had the most effect. Shaw, glaring at the weak fool who had betrayed them both by his inability to keep his silly mouth shut, and knowing that the game was up, bolted for the little door which opened on to the back corridor of the house.

He never reached it. Russell, delighted by Briggs's give-away which meant that two of the uniformed men had made for him immediately, and burning for revenge on the man who had tried to kill him, chased after Shaw and caught him even as he reached for the door-knob.

'I'll teach you not to try to murder me!' he roared and landed him a facer of which Gentleman Jackson would have been proud. Shaw fell to the ground, moaning and clutching at his bleeding nose.

'Damn you, Hadleigh, you've broken my nose,' he moaned thickly.

'Be grateful that it wasn't your neck I did for,' Russell ground out, straightening up and blowing on his bruised knuckles. This was all a great deal more damaging than playing about at Jackson's salon. One of the men in blue began, most roughly, to haul Shaw to his feet.

His father was staring at his son as though he had never seen him before. Mary clapped her hands together in delight at seeing Russell avenge himself on his betrayer, and Lord Chard, intrigued by the turn events had taken, had risen to his feet.

'Well, well,' he drawled. 'Matters have developed even more swiftly and pointedly than I might have hoped. I had not imagined that things would be settled so quickly. Burgess,' he ordered the man in blue who was now holding Shaw in a head lock, 'you may inform your prisoner of what he is accused, and after that you may charge Briggs.'

Briggs, quivering and shaking, began to try to save himself. 'It wasn't me,' he almost wept, 'it was him,' and he pointed at Shaw, who, having had the charges against him read out, was still trying to stanch his bleeding face. 'I didn't want to hurt m'lord, he made me.'

'If you will allow,' Chard said, ignoring Briggs and turning to Lord Bretford, who was trying to come to terms with the fact that Russell had been behaving as though he were Ritchie, 'I will designate this room a magistrates' court and since all witnesses to the crime of which this pair are accused are present, they may give their evidence to me, and to Lord Bretford, who, I believe, is also a magistrate, as to whether or not they should be consigned to prison to await the next Assizes. My secretary will act as clerk to the court.'

The man holding Shaw, disregarding his captive's plea for his nose to be treated, had manacled his wrists behind his back, and pushed him behind a reversed chair. The now sobbing Briggs, also manacled, was shoved beside him. A side table was pulled forward so that the two Earls could sit behind it facing the prisoners. Chard's secretary sat beside them, a ledger open before him, ready to keep a record of the proceedings.

Russell watched them with a grim smile on his face. He had already gone over to speak to Mary and Aunt Beauregard. Aunt Beauregard quavered at him, 'Is it true that they tried to murder you? Were they only pretending that you had gone to London?'

'I suppose that now we are in a courtroom I ought to reveal as little as possible before I give evidence,' Russell replied. 'But I think that I may say that you have come to the right conclusion.'

'How dreadful! And that man with you. Who is he? I think that I have met him somewhere before, but where I cannot remember, except...' and she began to tremble.

Mary who had been registering her pleasure at seeing Russell safe and well, even if he did look like one of his own under-grooms, asked her gently, 'What is it, Aunt?'

'Nothing, except that he reminds me strongly of someone I knew many years ago.'

'He was until recently the hermit who lived in the woods and his name is George Russell,' Russell told her.

The day's surprises were not yet over. Aunt Beauregard gave a little cry and hid her face in her hands. She dropped them to mutter, her face now ashen, 'No, it cannot be, I must be mistaken.'

At this point Lord Chard, who had been privately conferring with his fellow Earl, called the room to order.

'This magistrates' court is now in session. The accused are present and the charge is that they attempted to murder Russell

Chancellor, Lord Hadleigh, by attacking him and throwing him into the quarry off the by-way to Ancoates. All the necessary witnesses to the crime of which they are accused are here present.

'Shaw and Briggs, listen to me carefully. How plead you?'

'Not guilty, m'lord,' Shaw blurted out defiantly. Briggs's reply was almost inaudible, made as it was through his sobs.

'In that case I will call upon the principal witness, Lord Hadleigh, to give evidence. Stand up, Lord Hadleigh, and face the Bench.'

Russell did so. He was happy to note that everything was being carried out in proper form so that none might later claim that Lord Chard had carried out his magistrate's duties incorrectly.

He described, as accurately as he could, the attack made on him by Shaw and Briggs up to the moment when he had been thrown into the quarry. 'After which,' he finished, 'I have no recollection of anything until I recovered consciousness in Mr Russell's cottage. I have no doubt, from what they said and the manner of the attack, that they intended to kill me.'

'It's all a lie,' howled Shaw. 'It's only his word against ours and there are two of us. Who's to say he wasn't larking about round the quarry on his way back to London?'

'Be silent, Shaw,' said Chard severely, 'until you are asked to speak. May I, before you incriminate yourself further, remind you that if Lord Hadleigh was truly on his way to London it would have been exceedingly odd of him to have taken the by-way north past the quarry, rather than the one leading south which joins the main road to London.'

'May I speak to that, m'lord?' asked Russell, who was beginning to enjoy watching Shaw twist and turn in his doomed efforts to defend himself.

'Yes, Lord Hadleigh, continue.'

'I understand that it was given out and can produce witnesses so to confirm that Shaw and Briggs told everyone that I had left Eddington to return to London.'

'Thank you, m'lord. Which brings up another point. The question of his lordship's missing chaise, does it not, Shaw? The constables have already confirmed that it is not in Eddington's stables. One would wish to know where it is, seeing that whatever else he did, Lord Hadleigh did not travel to London in it. We will leave that for the present.

'You may stand down, Lord Hadleigh. I call upon Mr George Russell to give evidence.'

The hermit rose. Like Russell he was still dressed in the clothes in which they had arrived at Loudwater. Lord Chard had decided that their story, which really needed no confirmation, was further supported by Lord Hadleigh's unseemly attire of which his secretary had already made note.

'You, sir, are Mr George Russell, a gentleman who resides in the county of Northumberland.'

'That is true, m'lord.'

'Please describe to the court the circumstances in which you came to find Lord Hadleigh in the quarry.'

'My home is on the edge of the wood in these parts. I was engaged on my daily walk when I heard loud voices and the sound of a scuffle. Through the trees I could see two men attacking a third. I am an old man, m'lord, and to my shame I allowed that fact to prevent me from assisting the poor victim. They overcame him and began to carry him towards the quarry. I watched them throw over the edge the man whom I later recognised as Lord Hadleigh, whose acquaintance I had made shortly after he arrived in Northumberland.

'When I reached the quarry I saw that the villains' victim was caught on some bushes above a ledge in the quarry wall. I was, by great good fortune, able to assist him. Fortunately, although he remembers little of it, he was sufficiently conscious to be able to assist me before he collapsed at the quarry top.'

'Thank you, Mr. Russell. Were you able to see and identify the two men who attacked m'lord?'

'Yes.'

'And are they in the courtroom today?'

'Yes, m'lord, they are standing over there,' and he pointed at Shaw and Briggs.

'Thank you, Mr Russell. You may stand down. I now call on Mrs Henry Wardour to give evidence.'

Aunt Beauregard, who had been making little moaning noises all the time that Mr George Russell had been giving evidence, hissed, 'Why you?' in Mary's ear.

'In a moment,' Mary whispered back before walking over to stand before the two Earls. She passed Russell on the way and, since he was shielded from all the others in the room, he mouthed 'I love you' at her.

It was an odd thing for a lady to give evidence in a court of law. Had she been Russell's wife she would have been unable to do so, but since she was not Lord Chard had chosen to call her as further evidence.

'Mrs Wardour, please tell the court of what you know about this unfortunate affair. You may take your time in answering if you so wish.'

Mary needed to take no time to think of what she ought to say. She had been waiting for some days to give evidence which would help to trap the men who had wished to kill the man she loved and was eager to begin.

'Simply that I understood from Mr Shaw when I called at Eddington House, because Lord Hadleigh had failed to visit me on a day on which he had promised to do so, that he had suddenly left for London. This surprised me because Lord Hadleigh had said nothing of this to me on his last visit.'

She spoke in a clear, unflustered voice and her manner was such that the watching Lord Bretford was sorry all over again about his past conduct towards her.

Lord Chard knew that what Shaw had said to Mary, if repeated at the Assizes, would not have been evidence because it was hearsay, but since everyone around Eddington had been told the same thing by both Shaw and Briggs he allowed it to pass.

'What happened next, Mrs Wardour?'

'I went riding alone several days after that conversation. I was stopped by Mr Russell who asked me to visit his cottage. He would give me no reason and told me that I must not inform anyone else of what I found there. Greatly puzzled I accompanied him, to find Lord Hadleigh in bed, recovering from his injuries, which I later learned he had sustained when he was thrown into the quarry. They asked me to say nothing of his survival, or that he had not gone to London in case the two miscreants came to finish off the villainy which they had already embarked on.'

'Why were the authorities not informed at once?'

'For the reason I have given you and also that Lord Hadleigh was not fit to travel. I did as they asked, secretly brought them food and some old, but clean, clothing, which had belonged to our grooms, that they are wearing now. As soon as Lord Hadleigh had recovered sufficiently to be able to ride, I joined them in leaving secretly for Loudwater to inform you, m'lord, of the attack upon him.'

'Thank you, Mrs Wardour, most lucid, as I am sure, Bretford, you would agree.'

'Yes, indeed,' said Russell's father who had been staring bemused at the poised, beautiful and clever young widow whom he had once summarily dismissed as a possible wife for his heir on the grounds that she was an unmoneyed nobody unfit to become a Viscountess, let alone a future Countess.

Mary bowed gracefully and resumed her seat next to her aunt, who had also been gazing at her in some surprise, having had no notion of the secret life which Mary had been following since Mr George Russell had accosted her near his cottage.

'What a minx you are, my dear,' she muttered at Mary, 'concealing all that from me.'

'For your protection, dear Aunt,' replied Mary.

Once her evidence was over Lord Chard leaned over to Lord Bretford and had a quiet conference with him, after which he spoke to the two defendants in their makeshift dock.

'Do either of you wish to say anything before I order you to be committed for trial at the next Assizes in Newcastle?'

'Yes,' roared Shaw, 'it's all a pack of lies, made up because Lord H. knew that I didn't agree with all the changes he was making at Eddington—and without his pa's knowledge too, as his own man said—'

'That will do,' said Chard severely. 'The evidence against you is overwhelming and you do not help yourself by black-guarding a man whom I understand gave you a second chance after he had discovered that you had been deceiving and cheating his father. You, Briggs, have you anything to say?'

'Yes, m'lord,' wailed Briggs falling on to his knees. 'I only did what Shaw told me because he was my superior. I never meant to kill m'lord, as God's my witness, I didn't.'

'I find that difficult to believe,' said Chard. 'You do not help your cause by lying about your involvement. On the evidence given we have heard that you helped to throw Lord Hadleigh into the quarry and only Mr George Russell's fortunate intervention saved him.

'All rise: constables, remove the prisoners and convey them to Newcastle Gaol to await trial.'

It was over.

The two Earls conversed confidentially with one another for a few moments. The secretary rose, closed his ledger and put the chair, which had stood in as a temporary dock, back in its proper place.

Russell ran over to Mary and, regardless of everything and everyone, threw his arms around her.

'There's my brave girl,' he said. 'Now we can be married!'

He didn't care whether his father, or Lord Chard, or half-Northumberland including Newcastle, heard him: this time he was going to make sure that they ended up in bed together—to enjoy themselves there rather more than they had done in the one in George Russell's cottage!

All Mary knew was that she was at last where she ought to be, but common sense and the public nature of their reunion had her pushing him gently away, murmuring, 'Later, my love, later.'

Meanwhile, Aunt Beauregard had risen and walked hesitantly towards Mr George Russell, who, without his long hair and beard, and even though clothed as a groom, still looked a fine figure of a man.

'George, is it really you?' she asked. 'I recognised Jackie Chancellor with whom I was not greatly friendly, so you may judge how much more easy it was for me to recognise the man whom I was engaged to marry. As that wretched man said of poor Lord Hadleigh, I thought that you were dead—and for over thirty years, too! Was that a cock-and-bull story or are you really not my George at all?'

A look of anguish passed across the hermit's face. 'Not here,' he murmured, 'not here. When we can be alone, I shall explain. Oh, my dear, when I think of all the wasted years…' He dropped his head.

'But why?' Aunt Beauregard was suddenly as distressed as he was. 'No, I must not trouble you. Later will do,' though she privately thought that whatever explanation he cared to give her, nothing would ever do, since nothing could give back to them the years they had lost.

Fortunately for them both, at that moment the door opened and the harassed under-butler walked in.

'M'lords,' he faltered, not quite sure how to address such a distinguished company. 'A young man and a young woman have just arrived and have asked to speak to Lord Hadleigh. Shall I announce them—or shall I tell them that it is not convenient for them to be entertained today?'

'Oh, announce them, by all means,' exclaimed Russell, quite forgetting that now that his father had arrived he was no longer the master at Eddington. 'Two more members added to our party can only serve to enliven it the further.' Belatedly recognising his father's seniority, he turned to him, smiling, adding, 'If that is agreeable to you, sir.'

'Oh, quite agreeable,' said Lord Bretford, who was showing more friendliness to his son that he had done for years. 'Come one, come all, today, apparently. But before you do so,' he said, addressing the butler, 'my friend, Lord Chard, also has an announcement to make.'

He stood back to allow Chard to speak.

'I have nothing to say as momentous as our late proceedings,' said Chard, his smile as broad as Russell's, 'but it occurs to me that, under the circumstances obtaining, Lords Bretford and Hadleigh would find it difficult to entertain us all at Eddington House. In consequence I am inviting you all, including Mr George Russell and the two ladies, to stay at Loudwater for as long or as short as you individually please. I have no doubt that you both…' and he bowed at Russell and his father '…would wish to be near enough to Eddington to begin to restore the place even further now that Shaw has been dealt with, and Loudwater would make a convenient base for that.'

'If I may be allowed a rider to your kind invitation?' said Lord Bretford. 'While I would be delighted to accept your hospitality, the task of continuing the restoration of Eddington and its house must be left in the hands of my son, Lord Hadleigh. I have been informed by Lord Chard that he has been responsible in a very short time for returning it to some of its former glory after many years of neglect. If he is willing to carry on the hard work he has begun, then I am happy to make him my deputy here—if that is what he wishes, of course.'

He paused; Lord Chard had been nodding agreement to his statement about Russell's hard work. Russell himself, thus publicly and kindly acknowledged by his father, who had always previously lost no opportunity to demean him, scarcely knew what to say.

'Certainly, sir. It is, indeed, my dearest wish to be allowed to remain at Eddington as deputy and agent for I have discovered here a way of life which suits me—and which, I hope will also suit the lady who has promised to be my wife. It is most kind of you to allow me to do so.'

He had begun by stammering a little, but as he gained confidence he finished on a high note, and, tenderly turning, took Mary's hand and kissed it.

'Excellent,' said Lord Bretford, before going over to congratulate his son and his bride-to-be. 'You, sir,' he ordered the under-butler, almost as an afterthought, 'may introduce our visitors to us.'

The under-butler disappeared. Conversation, from being formal, became general. The company began to finish off the Madeira and biscuits whose provision had been the last act of Shaw's reign. They were all thus, after the harsh proceedings of the morning, in a much jollier mood, when the under-butler returned.

'M'lords, ladies and gentlemen, I have the honour of presenting to you Mr and Mrs Thomas Bertram.' It was plain that he was beginning to enjoy his new role in which he was no longer subservient to the late Briggs.

'Good God!' exclaimed Russell. 'Where in the world have you popped up from, Tom? And Angelica, too—you both look blooming.'

'Everyone on their honeymoon should look blooming,' declared the Honourable Tom in the tone of one making a witty *bon mot*. 'Can't say the same of you, old chap, not in that odd get-up. I know the butler fellow made a kind of general introduction for us, but I should dearly like to know in whose company I have found myself. Not that you don't all look eminently respectable,' he hastened to add.

The Hon. Tom's artless charm, together with that of

Angelica, who had rushed over to Mary and begun to kiss her as though she were renewing an acquaintance with her dearest friend, thoroughly broke the ice. Even Aunt Beauregard, who had suddenly realised that she was in the same room as the two runaways of whom her old friend had written such piteous letters, was captivated by the Hon. Tom. The other members of the party, by contrast, were amused by him.

Mary invited Angelica to sit beside her. She immediately began to stare at Russell in his shabby clothing. 'I can't tell you how pleased I am that I refused Lord Hadleigh,' she began, 'so old and so under-dressed compared with my dear Tom. He's quite the Corinthian, isn't he? Have you received any proposals yet?'

This last sentence came out belatedly, more as something polite to say than if the speaker really believed what she was saying.

'Lord Hadleigh,' said Mary, amused by Angelica's naïve frankness, and deciding to make her answer as unadorned as possible to spare Angelica embarrassment, 'has asked me to marry him. I have consented and, from the manner in which his father received the news, I am delighted to say we have his blessing.'

It was, apparently, almost impossible to embarrass Angelica. From scorning Russell as both elderly and ill dressed, she now went on to congratulate Mary effusively on having made such a great catch.

'They say he will be enormously rich when his father dies,' she ended, 'which is why Pa and Ma wished me to marry him. But money isn't everything. *I* accepted Tom out of pure love, of course. Wild horses wouldn't have made me marry a man for his money.'

'But I gather,' Mary could not help replying, 'from a letter from your mama that, before you decided to elope with him, Mr. Bertram had recently inherited a reasonably large fortune.'

'Oh, that!' exclaimed Angelica. 'That really made no difference to my decision to marry him—none at all!'

Her voice took on a sharper note. 'Do I understand that you have been corresponding with my mama—how odd!'

'No, she wrote to my aunt, Miss Beauregard, asking us to inform her of your whereabouts—she was quite worried about you.'

Angelica tossed her head. 'I do hope that you won't. Inform her, I mean. I have never been so happy in my life. At home it was always nag, nag, nag. Tom never nags at me.'

Lord Bretford, overhearing this conversation, couldn't help being relieved that his son had had the good sense not to propose to such a featherbrained piece—however pretty she was. It was beginning to look as though Hadleigh had far more to him than he had previously thought. Certainly Mrs Wardour had been something of a surprise.

He was astonished at the regret which swept over him when he thought of his treatment of his son, particularly when he took into consideration the fact that he had been right to query Shaw's accounts and right to come north to find out what was going on. The whole business meant that he had been an absentee landlord of the worst kind and a poor father to his son. As soon as he could have a private word with Hadleigh, he would try to mend the fences which he had spent his life destroying.

And George Russell. Where had he sprung from? How had he been transformed from the heir to Eddington and its lands into a hermit living in a wretched cottage on the edge of the wilderness? At least, if they were all to spend a few days together at Loudwater, some mysteries might be cleared up. He would give his coachman immediate orders to drive there in Chard's wake. The others, particularly his son, would need to return home to collect their luggage for a few days' stay at what was reputed to be one of the most beautiful mansions in the north.

Aunt Beauregard, still in a daze after encountering a man she had thought dead for many years, and for whom she had mourned inconsolably, could also scarcely wait to reach Loudwater and George.

As for Mary and Russell, it mattered little to them where they were so long as they could be together as much as possible.

Living at Loudwater was a little like living in heaven. It was a house of the most tasteful beauty which was so well run that even those visitors who had previously thought themselves pampered by life were surprised by it.

Russell was once more dressed in his usual clothing. Briggs, desperate not to hang, had tried to gain some commutation from his almost certain sentence to do so by continuing to claim that he had been bullied into helping Shaw to attempt to murder Lord Hadleigh. He had also told the authorities where they had hidden his chaise. Not only that, but he had ratted on Graves, telling how he had conspired with Shaw to cheat Lord Bretford. As a result Russell's father, on being informed of this, had decided to leave Loudwater as soon as possible to return south and hand his secretary over to the law.

This revelation made him even more humble vis-à-vis his heir when he remembered how he had reprimanded him when he had claimed that there was something amiss with Eddington's accounts.

* * *

'I feel almost human again,' Russell confessed to Mary while they were walking one afternoon in Eddington's neglected park, so different from Loudwater's beautifully kept grounds. 'Life has ceased to be one long worry that I am not living up to my father's expectations—particularly the one in which he wished me to marry the fair Angelica.'

Mary began to laugh. 'I think that he changed his mind when he met her. She and Tom Bertram are well suited. I was most relieved, though, when they did not take up Lord Chard's invitation to stay at Loudwater. She told me, in confidence, that the idea of being cooped up with a lot of old men did not attract. I tried to persuade her to go home and make peace with her family, but I fear that idea didn't attract either!'

'Agreed,' said Russell. 'Had we married I think that I might have strangled her in the week. Whatever should we have found to talk about?'

'Not chess and calculating machines, that is for sure,' Mary returned, which set him laughing again.

They had spent the morning at Eddington: Russell had been going over the books and had begun advertising for a bailiff while Mary was directing a new housekeeper and her staff in the business of continuing to refurbish the interior of the House.

She had previously brought down more of the paintings from the attic, in particular the portraits of Serena Cheyney and Margaret Russell, which now hung in the little drawing room. Lord Bretford had spent part of the morning at Eddington and on seeing those of his wife and her cousin, had obviously been extremely struck by them. When Mary, showing him the room, told him, quite casually, unaware of any deeper undercurrents, that Serena Cheyney was now a widow and lived not far from Ancoates, he had said nothing, but shortly afterwards had excused himself and left.

'I thought that he had agreed to go over the accounts with me,' Russell said to her over their simple nuncheon. 'Have you any idea why he left so suddenly?'

'Only that I showed him the portraits in the small drawing room, and informed him that Serena Cheyney, now a widow, lives nearby.'

'That explains it, I think. You remember that, according to both Aunt Beauregard and Sir Ralph Cheyney, everyone thought that, when my father came north after his father had inherited the Earldom, he was going to ask Serena to marry him, but instead he proposed to and married her cousin, the Eddington heiress, Margaret Russell, my mother.'

They were both silent for a moment. Mary said slowly, 'Is it possible that his father, your grandfather, compelled him to marry your mother instead because she was the heiress?'

'I am beginning to think so—which would explain many things.' He fell silent and did not enlarge on the matter further.

Mary respected that silence and said, 'Aunt Beauregard told me something yesterday which might throw further light on the business. When your father was a young man visiting in the north Margaret Russell was not the heiress. George Russell was then the heir. Apparently, shortly before his ailing father died and when he was betrothed to my aunt, Margaret's father discovered that he was illegitimate and consequently had no claim either to be the heir, or to the Russell name.

'It seems that it was discovered that, quite unknowingly, George's father had married a woman whose husband was then living, although in some sort of asylum, so the marriage could not be valid. To avoid scandal Margaret's father and his lawyers confronted George with the truth. They could not allow him in law to inherit, but they were prepared to set up a trust for him which would provide him with a small income if he would disappear. To explain the disappearance they would pretend that he had died suddenly and been summarily buried elsewhere.

'George was something of a scholar. He obtained a post in the Bodleian Library at Oxford University. He never married, becoming a recluse and took the name of William George. A few years ago he had some sort of nervous fit, retired from his post and came north again to where he could, from a distance, see Aunt Beauregard whom he had lost so many years ago.'

Mary's eyes filled with tears. 'It is such a sad story and, oh, Russell, ours might so easily have been the same as George and Aunt Beauregard's and your father and Serena Cheyney's. I shall never think myself unlucky again because, although we have lost so many years together, we have found each other in time to marry and have children.'

Russell sat silent for a time until Mary began to wonder what she had said to disturb him. Finally he came out with, 'You are not the only one who has been the subject of strange confidences. Allow me a moment's thought and I will tell you of them.'

'As many moments as you like,' she said gently, wondering what was coming next.

Russell was remembering the early evening of the previous day… He had arrived from Eddington, tired, but exhilarated to have Chard's butler greet him in the Entrance Hall.

'Your father, m'lord, is in his suite of rooms and has

asked that you visit him as soon as you have recovered from your journey.'

Now, what could that be about, he wondered. His father had been uncommonly civil to him ever since the scene in the impromptu magistrate's court and more than civil to Mary, to whom he had taken a great fancy.

'Inform Lord Bretford I will be with him shortly,' he said, and kept his word as he always did. He found his father standing in a window, looking out over Loudwater's beautiful Park. When he turned to greet him Russell thought that he looked tired.

'Ah, Hadleigh, you are prompt: an excellent virtue. I have asked to see you this evening because I need to speak to you and I must not linger in the north much longer: I have duties to carry out in the south. Watching you, talking to Chard and to Mrs Wardour, and thinking of the past, it has been borne in upon me that I owe you an explanation and an apology.

'I have become unhappily aware that I have not behaved to you as a father ought to behave to a son. Only your good nature has prevented you from resenting your brother Richard because of the favour which I have always shown him as opposed to the distance which I have kept between the pair of us. I owe you an explanation and I can only hope that when I have finished you will forgive me a little—I cannot hope for more than that.

'First let me tell you something of my early youth. Like my friend, Ralph Cheyney, I had no great expectations from life. My father was the cousin of the heir of the Earl of Bretford who was years younger than he was, and my branch of the family had little money. I had half-determined to enter the Army, but decided on one last fling before I did so. Ralph, as you know, lived not too far distant from Eddington and he invited me to stay with him after we went down from Oxford. I accepted his invitation—we had been part of a rowdy set—and the result was the most golden summer of my life. I was one of a crowd of young people and we seemed to be perpetually laughing and enjoying ourselves as only the young can do.

'I shall never forget the first time I saw his sister Serena. I had laughed at the notion of love at first sight, but it held true for the pair of us. There seemed to be no reason why we should not marry—once I was gazetted into the Army—so I proposed to her. She was poor, as was Ralph, who was the younger son; his brother was the heir to the baronetcy, and they came from a good family. She accepted me, and I went home with my head in the clouds, dreaming of the future.

'When I reached there it was to discover that my father's cousin had died suddenly from some sort of summer fever. Not only that, but his father was dying, too, and that meant that in a short space of time my father would be the Earl of Bretford and I would be Lord Hadleigh. Any pleasure I might have gained from that flew away when I told him that I wished to marry Serena: he would have none of it.

"'What! Marry a poverty-stricken girl when you could have any heiress that you wanted! No, no, I have other ideas for you. My friend Henry Russell, who inherited Eddington when it was found that his brother's heir was illegitimate through a bigamous marriage, has an only child, a daughter, Margaret, who is his heiress. I met him again recently and he has intimated that he would look kindly on a marriage between you. I have given the notion my blessing and I expect you to return north to offer for her as soon as decently possible, given that we must carry out the due mourning rituals for my cousin."

'In vain I told him that my dearest wish was to marry Serena and join the Army. He told me that I was a fool, that the Bretford heir must marry money and land and Margaret Russell would possess those in abundance. "She's a pretty girl, too," he said. "Her father gave me her miniature to give to you. I believe you must have met her." I had met her, and although it was true that she was a pretty girl, my heart had already been given to Serena.

'She was never to receive it. My great-uncle died shortly afterwards and as Lord Hadleigh I was sent to Eddington to meet and marry the Russell heiress. To my eternal disgrace I did as I was asked. Your poor mother was delighted: it seems that she had worshipped me from afar. Serena I did not see. The word was that she had heard that I was coming to propose to Margaret and went to stay with relatives. I never saw her again. My marriage to your mother was happy enough, although I fear that she soon came to realize that she was always second best.

'The trouble was that my grief at losing Serena was made even more bitter when her brother Ralph inherited and she became so greatly dowered that I could have married her— but alas, that came too late, I had been married a year by then. It was when you and Ritchie were born that the major damage was done.

'The older he grew, the more he looked like Serena, which was not surprising given that she was our blood relative. The more you grew, the more you began to resemble your mother and the Russells in your looks and your tastes. As a result you were the one who suffered the most of my displeasure at being forced to marry against my wishes, and Ritchie received my love in lieu of that which I couldn't give to Serena. I was grossly unfair to you, I now know—and to your poor mother also. You have your own talents, which are different from Ritchie's, and he recently reproached me for my behaviour to you. I can only ask you to forgive me for the many unnecessary unkindnesses which I inflicted on you. I will quite understand it if you cannot forgive me—and also forgive me for colluding with Dr Beauregard to prevent you from marrying the girl you loved.

'I wanted you to marry an heiress because my father had made me marry one, and Dr Beauregard thought that if his daughter married you she would most likely give up his mathematical work through which he hoped to gain posthumous fame. Her marriage to Dr Wardour was supposed to ensure that. I fear our plans went badly awry. She told me when I asked her what had happened to her father's research that Dr Wardour destroyed her father's papers, but used her to continue and support his own work.

'I offer you a heartfelt apology for the wrongs I have done you and ask you to forgive me so that we may try to be a father and son in the truest sense. I will quite understand if you find it difficult for us to be reconciled.'

Russell remembered that he had immediately offered his father the forgiveness which he had asked for, adding, 'Let us agree to forget the unhappy past, Father, and not let it poison the relations between us. Today is a new day for us and so shall it be henceforward.'

His father had said, his voice shaking a little, 'I know now that I do not deserve your forgiveness, Hadleigh, nor the kindness with which you have just spoken. I agree that the past must die—a lesson which I should have learned when I was younger than you are now.'

All of this he now told Mary, ending with, 'It explains why he was so determined that we should not marry. He would not allow me the happiness which had been denied to him. Hence his determination that I should find an heiress—in my case, Angelica Markham—and marry her whether I loved her or not.'

'I am so pleased that you and your father have become re-conciled,' said Mary, 'and only fancy, if you had done as he wished and not refused him, you might have been the lucky man who won Angelica's hand!'

'Wretch,' said Russell, rising from his chair and coming over to her where she had retired to the sofa after their meal. 'You deserve a kiss for that, and another and another. Thank God we are here where there are few servants to interrupt us, unlike Loudwater. I'm afraid that I shall burn for you so hard that I shall be ashes before I reach the altar.'

'And I, too,' sighed Mary, as he took her into his arms. 'I never knew in the past why poets spoke of the flame of love and of burning for the loved one, but I do now.'

The next few minutes saw the flames of love, or of passion, whichever one might like to call them, burn high and bright. Mary traced his face with her hands as though trying to learn it so that she might know him, even if the heavens turned per-manently dark.

Russell for his part stroked and caressed her until his im-patient body brought him near to fulfilment without him ever having possessed his love. The dishevelled nymph and her equally dishevelled satyr finally drew apart, gasping.

'Now I know why young ladies are never allowed to be alone with a man,' Mary laughed, her eyes alight, 'not that I could ever imagine myself making love to a man other than yourself, but, oh, the wicked temptation of being alone with you exceeds my delight in figures, algebra and geometry!'

'So pleased to learn that you prefer me,' Russell teased her, 'otherwise I should be quite cast down to find that one of Newton's equations excited you more than myself. What a naughty wench you are, to be sure, and who would have thought it?'

He took her in his arms again and in their exalted state who knew where *that* might have ended had there not been a hammering on the door which signalled that the under-butler was tactfully informing them of his presence.

Some hasty rearrangement of stock, buttons and bows was necessary before Russell bellowed, 'Enter,' and the under-butler came in and brought the outside world with him, with some tale of one of the tenant-farmers wishing to see m'lord urgently.

'I regret to have need to disturb you, sir and madam,' he ended.

But a damned good thing he did, was Russell's conclusion as he made for the Entrance Hall, or we should certainly have anticipated our wedding night. Never mind, we can have a stroll in the grounds this afternoon, and with luck might even take up where we left off!

At the same time as Russell and Mary were celebrating the love they had rediscovered after so many years, his father was alighting from his coach before a pleasant house not far from Ancoates. From thence he was shown into a room where a woman, still beautiful and strangely resembling his second son, was waiting to receive him.

'So you have come to me at last, Jackie,' she said softly. 'I always thought that, one day, you would.'

'I am here for your forgiveness,' he told her. 'I gave you up in exchange for an easy life and God has been punishing me for it ever since.'

'But not any more,' she murmured. 'You have my forgiveness and I quite understand why you acted as you did.'

'I cannot hope that you love me still, but I have never forgotten you and that last summer which we shared.'

Her smile for him was a sad one. 'Nor I, and now we are old and may, if we wish, enjoy all that lovers in the autumn of their loves can hope for.'

'Which is more than I deserve,' he replied, and for a moment in the pleasant room it almost seemed that time had turned back as they remembered the past...

Russell's luck held, however; no one came to interrupt them, and though, regretfully, they both agreed that final consummation must be left until after their marriage, which was being arranged to take place in London as soon as possible, he was able to initiate his dear love, if not into the wildest shores of passion, at least to somewhere near them.

Lying on a grassy bank among the golden and scarlet colours of autumn they took their fill of one another, Mary discarding Russell's unwanted shirt and Russell loosening Mary's dress so that he could caress the glories of her body even as she celebrated his. Only the memory of their vow to remain virtuous until their wedding day prevented them from consummating their love on friendly mother earth as so many lovers had done before them.

'If I had my way,' Mary gasped, 'I would rather become your true wife here in the open than after a long and arduous day in church—but we must remember those who will be coming to celebrate our long-overdue marriage and will like to think that we have behaved ourselves.'

'We are at one in that as we are in everything,' replied Russell, reaching for his shirt, 'but if we do not stop now, my rosy nymph, we shall be unable to.' So, regretfully, they rose from the grassy bank on which they had been reclining and walked back to the House, passing on the way the workers in the Park who were engaged in trying to restore it to its former glory.

'I meant it when I told my father that our marriage must not be long delayed,' Russell said when they were in the chaise which took them back to Loudwater. 'I asked him not to let the lawyers maunder on overmuch while working out the settlements, for not only am I impatient to make you my wife in the fullest sense, I shall also not be happy until I am back at Eddington.'

'Nor I either,' Mary said. They had reached the top of a small rise from whence they could look out not only over the Park, and the far pasture where Russell's newly acquired sheep were grazing, but also the wilder scenery of Northumberland in all its majestic splendour.

Her eyes suddenly sparkled with mischief. 'I never thought to love a place so much. The only proviso I have to make is that when we finally settle here you must set aside a quiet room where we may work together on our project to design a calculating machine. Since our meeting again has revived your talents I am in hopes that you will not waste them, and that you will be more than another ignorant squire. After all, you have Lord Chard as a splendid example of what may be achieved. I believe that as a young man he was very like the Lord Hadleigh you were in the years when we were apart—and look at him now.'

Russell turned to take her hand in his.

'Anything you want, my darling, anything you want. Ask— and it shall be granted unto you.'

'Hold to that, sir,' she said, merrily, 'and we shall not go far wrong!'

'Minx!' he exclaimed, and took her in his arms to run with her down the little hill, to their shared delight as well as that of the watching workers.

Lord Hadleigh's rebellion had brought him, and those around him, happiness, and Eddington House had found a loving man and woman to guard it and secure its future.

Epilogue

‹‹‹❦›››

'I half thought that we might be attending a double wedding,' said Ritchie Chancellor, who was helping his brother to prepare for his marriage. Russell and Mary were not being married in London, but in Lord Chard's private chapel at Loudwater. 'What with Father having found his lost love and they being nearly as besotted with each other as you and Mary are.'

'To say nothing of you and Pandora,' retorted Russell. 'Why is this damned stock taking so long to tie?'

'Well, you did send your new valet away because he was being so clumsy,' replied Ritchie reasonably. 'Perhaps I ought to lend you a hand,' which he did, creating a thing of such magnificence that Russell stared at it in the mirror before saying gloomily,

'Why are you so damned good at everything and why do I no longer mind that you are?'

'Because you are so damned good at so many things now yourself,' retorted Ritchie, 'and also because it is quite plain why Father made so many mistakes when rearing us. You reminded him of the woman he didn't want to marry and I reminded him of the woman he did, so he favoured me and demeaned you. To crown all that, like the Russells you resemble, you are a countryman while I, God help me, am any damned man you please.'

'Not quite,' said Russell with a grin. 'The cream of the jest is that each of us secretly resented the other, and now, suddenly we don't.'

'No need,' said Ritchie practically. 'Father's so busy making amends to both of us for the past that I feel inclined to tell him to shut up every now and then. Do you intend to dress like this in Northumberland?' he asked, before swinging the big standing-glass round for Russell to see himself in all his glory.

'Good God, no! That's one of the things I like about the place, no one minds if I look like my own gamekeeper!'

'Does Mary mind?' Ritchie's expression was sly. 'Is she going to look like the gamekeeper's wife?'

'What a tongue you have on you, younger brother, and the answer to that is I don't know. What I do know is that she graces everything with her presence whatever she wears.'

'Agreed as to that,' said Ritchie. 'So, after all these years we have come to terms with Father's past and you need not mount any more rebellions. I was so happy to learn t'other night that you had taken my advice and learned that lying occasionally answers. Theoretically honesty may be the best policy, but in reality it does not always answer. The trick lies in knowing when to abandon it, and not too often at that.'

'As I have learned,' Russell said. He knew, though, that he would never be quite such an iron man as his brother. He had shown mercy to Shaw, where Ritchie would not have done, and in return for his kindness he had nearly lost his life. Even so, he had to be true to himself, and the new man he had discovered on and after his journey to the north was a different one from the discontented fellow who had idled around London.

He pulled out his hunter. 'I think that it is time that we went downstairs. My bride will be waiting.'

'And that would never do. Give me your arm, brother, and we'll be off.'

So far as Ritchie was concerned it could not be said that they were reconciled since they had never really been at odds, but time and chance had revealed to them that, beneath their outward differences, they were really very much alike.

Downstairs Mary was being dressed by Jennie, her maid, Aunt Beauregard, Serena Lascelles and Pandora Chancellor, Ritchie's wife. Since Mary was a widow it had been decided by all of them that deep cream would be the most suitable colour for the bride.

'I cannot understand why I feel so nervous,' Mary was saying. 'After all, this is my second wedding, but I really feel more overset than at the first.'

'Quite natural,' said Aunt Beauregard. She and George had decided not to marry—at least, not yet. Companionable friendship would be the best at first, they had thought, like Jackie and Serena. Aunt Beauregard found it difficult to think of him as the Earl. George had bought a pretty little cottage in Ancoates and she had helped him to furnish it so that it did not look at all like the one in which he had played the hermit.

'After all, your first was a marriage of convenience. I never forgave your father for handing you over to that old man. It must all have seemed like a bad dream—if not a nightmare. Now this marriage is quite different. Stand still, love, and let me crown you with this wreath of cream silk rosebuds. It's a pity you weren't married in the spring or summer, but I quite understand why you didn't want to wait until next year.'

'All very true,' sighed Mary. She looked at herself in the mirror Jennie held up for her. Her cream dress, its waist slightly lower after the new fashion, was charming in its simplicity. Her slippers were of silver, and Serena, whom everyone had learned to love, was handing her her small bouquet—again of cream silk roses.

There were times when she felt like pinching herself to prove that this was no longer a happy dream: that she was really about to marry her first and only love.

'Now,' said Pandora in her jolly way, 'you must take these four things and bestow them around your person.' She and Mary were getting on famously—so much so that from their very first meeting they had become bosom bows. They were as unlike as Russell and Ritchie were, but this had not prevented them from establishing an instant rapport.

'Something old,' she announced and she handed Mary a small linen pocket-handkerchief.

'Something new,' said Aunt Beauregard, and she decorated the collar of Mary's dress with a small gold pin.

'Something borrowed,' and Serena handed her a garter to hold up one of her stockings.

'Something blue,' murmured Jennie shyly and she handed her mistress a length of blue ribbon to tie around the little finger of her right hand.

All her attendants stood back and exclaimed at her.

'Now you are ready,' said Aunt Beauregard. 'Let us go downstairs. We must not keep the groom waiting.'

Nor did they. The chapel at Loudwater was not overlarge and it was quite full. Russell and Ritchie stood by the altar waiting for her, but when she entered the chapel Mary only had eyes for Russell.

So much so that when they at last stood side by side, she breathed gently, 'At last!' to feel him squeeze her hand in return.

Aunt Beauregard began to cry: Pandora, ever resourceful, handed her a handkerchief. The groom, looking at the bride, thought that he had never seen anything quite so beautiful. And to think that he had had to wait so long to make her his— but finally he had, and that was all that mattered. Neither of them could remember the ceremony at all. It passed in a dream, not like the nightmare of Mary's first wedding day and, when later they were at last alone, only the ring on Mary's finger was there to prove that the dream was true.

Not all of us achieve our dreams, but Mary and Russell's not only came true, but in the doing they made of Eddington House a place of love, where all the ghosts of the unhappy past were finally laid to rest in the presence of the pair who had found one another against all the odds.

* * * * *

The Sweet Cheat
by
Meg Alexander

After living in southern Spain for many years, **Meg Alexander** now lives in Kent, although, having been born in Lancashire, she feels that her roots are in the north of England. Meg's career has encompassed a wide variety of roles, from professional cook to assistant director of a conference centre. She has always been a voracious reader, and loves to write. Other loves include history, cats, gardening, cooking and travel. She has a son and two grandchildren.

Chapter One

'Georgie, you can't mean it! You must come with me. How can I leave you here alone?' Harry Westleigh gazed at his sister in dismay.

'There is no time to argue, Hal. Lothmore's chaise will be here at any minute. Now sit on this trunk whilst I finish packing for you.' With flying fingers Georgiana continued her task. 'You have money enough for the journey?'

'Yes!' Harry's voice was muffled as he hid his face in his hands. 'But I won't abandon you to face…to face…'

'Your creditors? It won't be pleasant, I'll grant you, but better that than visit you in a debtors' prison. Here, you had best take this.' She handed him a small leather bag chinking with coins.

'You'll not gamble it away before you reach Dover?'

Her bother raised an anguished face. 'It will leave you penniless. I can't… I won't… Oh, my dear, I am so sorry…'

'It's too late for regrets!' His sister's voice was tart, but a glance at Harry's averted profile caused her to continue in a kinder tone. 'I'll join you in France, Hal, but now the important thing is for you to get away.' She glanced through the window. 'Make haste! The chaise is just turning into the street. Quickly now! We cannot know when the first of the duns will be at the door.'

Harry cast a last look around the room.

'I shan't ever see this place again,' he mourned. 'If only there were more time. Had Swarby not made up his mind to ruin me at the club last night… He called me a swindler, you know.'

'Do come along!' Georgiana caught at his sleeve, tugging him towards the doorway in her impatience. 'I'll come to Dessein's in Calais. Send me your direction as soon as you can.'

'I'll stay at Dessein's too.'

'You most certainly will not. Only think…if you are followed it is the obvious place to find you.' She pushed him ahead of her towards the staircase, following until they reached the outer door to the street.

'Wait! Let me go first. There may be someone watching even now.' With anxious eyes she peered out into the darkness, but the only sound was that of the horses snorting and stamping on the cobblestones as the chaise drew to a halt.

'All's well!' she whispered. 'Now hurry! You'll find our own coach waiting across the river!' Standing on tiptoe, she kissed his cheek, and closed the door upon his protestations. Then she sped upstairs and hurried over to the window. Long after the coach had disappeared she strained to see into the darkness, dreading the sound of pursuit, but all was silence.

At last, weak with relief, she sagged into a chair. The nervous energy which had sustained her for the past few hours had disappeared, leaving her feeling tired to death. Dully, she looked about her at a scene of chaos. Drawers lay on the floor, their contents spilling out; the bed was littered with shirts of the finest lawn, embroidered waistcoats, snowy linen stocks, handkerchiefs, and pale buckskins.

She lifted a hand to ring the bell. Then she remembered. She had dismissed the servants that very day.

She forced herself to rise to her feet. What she needed most of all was sleep. She hadn't closed her eyes the previous night, and now she felt that any further action was beyond her. It was an effort to cross the landing to her own room, and a greater one to struggle out of her gown unaided and slip into her bedrobe.

She splashed cold water on to her hands and face, dried them, and then picked up her hairbrush. As she did so she caught sight of her face in the mirror. It didn't seem possible that she could look so unchanged when her whole world had collapsed about her in less than twenty-four hours.

True, she looked tired, the milky whiteness of her skin accentuated by her fashionable crop of burnished copper curls. Against her pallor, huge green eyes glittered like an emerald sea darkened by cloud. Sick with exhaustion, she was close to tears as she threw down the brush and turned towards her bed.

Then she froze at the sound of thunderous knocking. The noise must surely rouse the neighbourhood, and she had no doubt of the likely profession of her late-night visitor. It would most certainly be a dun. Could she pretend that the house was empty? It wasn't possible. Her candles were still alight and would be visible through the chink in the curtains.

Terror banished weariness as she retraced her steps to the front door. Somehow she must throw the man off Harry's trail. She caught up a worn blue cloak hanging in the hall. One of the maids must have forgotten it. Having drawn the hood over her hair, she opened the door the merest fraction.

The thrust of a powerful shoulder sent it crashing wide before she could protest, and she jumped. The man before her was a sinister figure. Immensely tall, he filled the doorway, his bulk accentuated by a riding cloak with many capes. She could not see his face, as the lower part was hidden by his high collar, whilst the brim of his hat served to conceal his eyes.

Georgiana's mind was racing. Even in the darkness she could see that this was no dun, but it did not matter. He was still her enemy, and Harry's too. Who else would call at such an hour? Harry had canvassed all his friends for help the previous day, without success. It seemed unlikely that her visitor had come to offer succour. She must convince him that she knew nothing.

'Can I help you, sir?' She bobbed a curtsy.

'I'm here to see your master, girl.'

Without further ceremony the man pushed past her into the hall. His bearing and the authoritative tone proclaimed him every inch the aristocrat, and she stepped back in dismay. Her own gentle breeding might have been of some service in handling a dun, but this was a different matter. The man was clearly in a thundering rage. All she could do was to play the part of the ignorant servant he imagined her to be.

'Mr Westleigh is not yet returned, sir,' Georgiana bobbed another curtsy. 'Most likely you will find him at his club.'

A short, unpleasant laugh greeted this remark.

'He is not at his club, not any other, I assure you. I propose to wait for him.' The man shouldered past her without a by-your-leave, and slammed the door behind him.

'You may bring me some wine,' he said shortly. 'I'll be in here.' He threw open the nearest door and walked into the salon. 'You had best light the candles.'

Georgiana picked up a flint, but she could not control her shaking fingers as she tried to strike it.

'Here, let me! There's no need to take fright. I mean you no harm.' As he busied himself with the candles Georgiana slipped out of the room.

This was a pretty pass indeed. She could not hope to fool him for long, and she could guess his errand. He must be one of those members of the nobility whom Harry was said to have swindled. Hastily she grabbed a bottle of wine and a glass and placed them on a silver tray. With any luck he might drink deep and perhaps lost interest in an all-night vigil.

When she returned to the salon the man was lounging in a chair beside the dying embers of the fire, long legs stretched out in front of him as he tapped impatiently on a small drum-table. He eyed her without interest.

'Do you always perform your duties in that strange attire?' he questioned.

Georgiana started. She had forgotten the old cloak and the fact that the hood was drawn about her head.

'Beg pardon, sir! I was in my bed when you arrived.'

'You may retire.' He waved a dismissive hand. 'Your master's man shall attend me.'

Panic seized Georgiana. She had no wish to explain that she was alone in the house. In silence she set down the tray, turning away from him. She was unprepared for the shock when a lean brown hand shot out and gripped her by the wrist.

'Sir, please let me go,' she whined. 'I'm only a poor serving wench.'

'Are you indeed? With hands like those? Come, my dear, you can do better than that.' In a single movement he was on his feet, thrusting back the hood of her cloak. A quick tug at the strings caused the garment to fall to the ground, and Georgiana stood before him in her bedrobe.

'Wages must have increased since I was last in England,' he observed smoothly as he fingered the filmy lawn. 'This creation, if I am not much mistaken, is the work of a fashionable modiste, and has cost a fair number of golden guineas.'

He was rewarded with a glance of pure hatred from Georgiana's jade-green eyes as she looked up at him for the first time. Scarlet with confusion, she was not reassured by what she saw.

Her tormentor was a man in his middle thirties, at a guess, and there was something deeply unnerving in the mocking curve of that wide and mobile mouth. He was heavily tanned, and the blue gaze which transfixed her spoke of arrogance, authority, and a total lack of pity. He was not a man of whom she would care to beg for mercy.

She had no intention of doing so. Still rosy with embarrassment, she bent to pick up the cloak.

'Blushing? Great heavens! Is that a part of your stock-in-trade? You do well to cultivate it. It is a lost art among the ladies of the town. I must compliment Westleigh. Whatever his faults, he has taste in women.'

A careless glance swept her from head to toe. 'The figure is voluptuous, and this charming garment does little to conceal it, especially when outlined against the light.' He smiled again as he reached out to finger the neckline of her bedrobe.

Georgiana jumped as if she had been stung. It was true. Seen against the candlelight this garment left little to the imagination. With what dignity she could command she wrapped her cloak about her.

Her tormentor laughed.

'A waste of time, my dear. You cannot conceal the hair. Ah, yes, the hair…'

To Georgiana's utter fury he wound a flame-coloured strand around his fingers. 'Quite exceptional…if a little *outré*. Is the colour your own, my dear?'

Georgiana raised a hand to strike him, but he was too quick for her. Her wrist was held so fast that she gasped with pain.

'I should not consider it,' he advised. 'Now tell me, where is your paramour?'

Dropping all pretence, Georgiana faced him squarely.

'My *brother,*' she emphasised heavily, 'is well beyond your reach. You may say what you have to say to me.'

The stranger stared at her. 'He cannot have left you to face the music? I suppose it is only to be expected…'

'How dare you speak of him so? You know nothing…of the circumstances.'

'I fear I do. I have a younger brother myself. I was not overly pleased, to put it mildly, to return from the West Indies to find him in deep financial trouble, caused, I believe, by Westleigh.'

'They are not the first to make unwise investments.' Georgiana flew at once to her brother's defence. 'Cleverer men than they have come to grief…'

'Through fraud?'

'No, no! That cannot be! Harry would not…could not…'

'How else would you describe a promise to provide annuities in return for a cash lump sum, and then be unable to honour the commitment?'

'But he will… He must…'

'My dear young lady, he cannot. The money is

gone, I suspect, on supporting a lifestyle which neither he nor my brother can afford. It involved gambling, horses, and, if you'll forgive me for mentioning such indelicate matters, the support of certain ladies of the town.'

'I do not believe you,' Georgiana said, wavering. 'Harry could not have planned such a scheme. He is not clever enough.'

The words brought a look of contempt to her companion's face.

'He was clever enough to take the money and use it,' came the biting reply. 'now he must face the consequences.'

Georgiana paled to the lips, swaying where she stood.

'Nay, you shall not pretend that you did not know.' The man put out a hand to steady her, but she pulled away as if his touch would burn her. 'Look about you, Miss Westleigh. You have lived to the hilt, it would appear, at the expense of others.'

Following his gaze, Georgiana stared at the charming little salon as if seeing it for the first time. The walls, painted in palest green, were a perfect foil for the soft colours of the Aubusson carpet. They threw into relief the graceful lines of her much prized furniture made of rosewood and mahogany by the hand of a master craftsman. A china cabinet in the corner held a collection of expensive *bibelots* and Sèvres porcelain.

As her eyes returned to her tormentor the small gold clock on the alabaster mantelshelf struck the hour of three.

'It did not occur to you to question the cost of all this luxury, or to ask how your brother could afford it?'

'Harry won large sums at White's,' she faltered.

'And lost more. Now let us have done with this charade. You will kindly inform me of your brother's whereabouts.'

Georgiana decided to play for time. 'I do not know you, sir, and your manner towards me has given me no cause to trust you.'

'Then allow me to introduce myself. I am Edward, Viscount Lyndhurst. I think you know my brother, Richard Thorpe.'

Georgiana's eyes grew wide. At the discovery of her visitor's identity she felt robbed of the power of speech.

Impatient now, the Viscount awaited her reply. Getting none, he seized her wrist again and his blue eyes hardened further.

'You will tell me, madam, I assure you.' The

deep voice was soft, but it held more menace than if he had shouted aloud. It terrified her.

'Let me go!' she cried in panic. She knew of the Viscount's reputation. According to his brother he was a ruthless tyrant who would stop at nothing to get his way. 'A cold fish', was the kindest description she had heard of him. Only during the Viscount's absence in the Indies had Richard enjoyed a respite from his cruelty.

As she raised her eyes to Lyndhurst's face she could believe his brother's words. Perhaps it was some trick of the light upon those aquiline features, or only the result of her overwrought imagination, but as he bent towards her he reminded her of some great bird of prey closing in upon his kill.

'You have heard of me, I see.' He laughed again, and it was not a pleasant sound. He had read her mind as easily as if she had spoken her thoughts aloud.

Gathering all her courage, Georgiana faced him squarely. 'Your treatment of your brother does you no credit. Your reputation has preceded you—but you shall not injure mine.'

'Others will do that, Miss Westleigh.' Lyndhurst glanced round the room again. 'You know, of course, that all your assets will be sequestered by the sheriff?'

'I…I don't know what you mean.'

'I mean that your home and its contents will be sold to pay your brother's creditors. By this time next week you could be turned out of doors with no roof above your head. What will you do?'

Georgiana felt as if the blood in her veins had turned to ice. Her heart began to thump unpleasantly, and nausea threatened to overwhelm her. She had given Harry her last few guineas, believing that the sale of their home and its contents would raise enough money to provide them with funds for a year or two. Now, it appeared, she would be penniless, and without even the means to travel to France.

'Doubtless it does not concern you,' the mocking voice continued. 'You are, perhaps, an heiress in your own right?'

The sarcasm cut Georgiana to the quick, but it had the opposite effect to that which the Viscount had intended. Her fear of him vanished. This time he had gone too far.

'Do you dare to call yourself a gentleman?' she enquired coolly. 'If so, I hope not to meet another such. You are insulting, sir. I am no heiress, but if there are debts they shall be settled. I do not care about possessions.'

'A praiseworthy sentiment, but foolhardy.'

The fierce eyes glared at her from beneath jutting brows. 'You do not expect me to believe you?'

'You think me a liar as well as a cheat?'

'Add fool to that assessment of your character and we shall agree. There is not a woman alive who does not prize material goods above all else. I give you that information on good authority.'

'You speak from experience, I suppose. Well, let us say, my lord, that in your own case material goods maybe all you have to offer. I have detected neither charm nor basic good manners.'

Lyndhurst's face grew dark with anger. For a second Georgiana quailed, but she would not retract her words. Then, to her surprise, he began to speak in a more reasonable tone.

'Quarrelling will serve no purpose, Miss Westleigh. Your worthy offer to settle your brother's debts is unrealistic. You will not raise above a thousand pounds under the hammer…a mere bagatelle in view of the sums involved. This was not explained to you?'

'N-no.' Georgiana's pallor had intensified.

A low curse escaped the Viscount's lips, but he continued his remorseless inquisition.

'You speak from ignorance when you disclaim

all interest in possessions. Do you know what it is like to be a vagrant, cold and hungry?'

'Do you?' she flung back at him.

'Thank God it has not been my lot, but I have seen enough of it. Enough to convince me of the need to be beforehand with the world.'

In spite of her dislike of him Georgiana was tempted to smile. That must be the understatement of all time. 'As rich as Croesus,' Richard had described his brother and as tight-fisted with his money as any shylock.

Lyndhurst began to pace the room.

'I asked what you would do, and you did not answer me. Can you return to your family home?'

Her silence was so prolonged that he gave her a curious look.

'Well?'

Long dark lashes veiled the green eyes, and Georgiana, to all appearances, was absorbed in studying the pattern on the carpet.

'That would be impossible,' she said at last. 'My father… Well, Harry is disowned… I was angry and I followed him. It was so unfair, you see.'

The silence intensified.

'I do see. The red hair does not lie, it would appear. Shall I add wilfulness to your other delightful qualities?' Lyndhurst answered slowly. He walked over to her, reached out, and allowed a gleaming copper strand to slide through his fingers. 'You are overly young to champion your brother's cause, I fear.'

'I am the elder,' Georgiana said with dignity. 'And pray, my lord, do not concern yourself with my affairs. I shall do very well without your advice.'

'At twenty…or can you be twenty-one? I doubt it.'

'My age can be of no possible interest to you, sir.'

Let him think what he liked. She would not give him the satisfaction of admitting that she was twenty-three.

He drew up a chair and sat down facing her.

'Come, let me make amends,' he said more gently. 'You have my sincere apologies for mistaking your status in this house, and I admire your loyalty. God knows, it is a quality rare enough in women—or men, for that matter. But do consider… These present difficulties are not easily resolved. They are beyond you.'

His voice was almost kind, and Georgiana ventured a look at his downcast head. Sensing her regard, he raised his eyes to hers and smiled. Georgiana's heart turned over. That smile transformed the harsh lines of his face. It lit up the room, warming her troubled soul and giving her the first crumbs of comfort she had known since Harry had told her the awful news of his ruin.

'Will you not trust me?' Lyndhurst continued. 'We may yet save something from the wreckage.'

Georgiana blinked away her tears. She could be brave when faced with anger, but the offer of help threatened to destroy her composure.

'I cannot help you,' she murmured. 'I have no resources. I can be of no use to you.'

'Nonsense! You have information. That is a resource to which I cannot lay claim. Will you share it with me?'

'I don't know. I must have time to think.'

'My dear, there *is* no time. You must see that. Now look at me! This may be your only chance to help your brother.'

A lean brown hand slid beneath her chin, tilting her face to his. Still irresolute, Georgiana looked deep into his eyes, and there she found the solution to the first, and most immediate, of her problems. The Viscount was clearly a man to whom the habit of command came easily. Nothing would be allowed to stand in his way, and with his help she would get to France.

'I will tell you,' she said at last. 'But there are two conditions. First, you must give me your word that you will not call my brother out.'

'That young puppy! What do you take me for? I might give him a whipping…'

'Then you will understand my second condition. When you follow them you must take me with you.'

The Viscount was on his feet at once.

'Impossible! I'll not be saddled with a weeping wench…'

'Thank you so much. Then I fear you must manage as best you may.'

'I beg your pardon, Miss Westleigh. Your suggestion startled me into impropriety. But you must see that it is out of the question.'

'Very well.' Georgiana sat with folded hands. 'You had best set about your enquiries, sir. You are wasting time.'

'How many times do I have to tell you? There *is* no time.' His voice was heavy with exasperation. 'Good God. Miss Westleigh, you can have no idea of the scandal caused by their hare-brained schemes. Are we to add to it?'

'You cannot be thinking of my reputation. A wilful, lying cheat can have no worries on that score.'

His look was inimical. 'Madam, I am thinking of my own. I have had one such experience. I would not willingly risk another.'

'Then there is no more to be said. I bid you goodnight, my lord.'

The Viscount glared at her.

'Blackmail, Miss Westleigh? I wonder why it should come as a surprise? You and your brother must deal famously together. The sooner my brother is removed from his influence, the easier I shall sleep at night.'

'Then you agree?'

'Have your way.' Lyndhurst turned away. 'You had best call your maid.'

'I have no maid.' Georgiana did not look at him. 'The servants were dismissed today.' She was fully prepared for the explosion of wrath which followed.

'Then how in heaven's name are you to travel? As my light-o'-love?'

'I am sure that no one would suspect you of such frivolous behaviour,' Georgiana taunted. She owed him that for his previous rudeness, and was pleased to notice the tightening of his lips. She gave him no time to reply. 'I had considered a more decorous role as your sister, or, perhaps, as your ward.'

'God forbid!' he said with feeling. 'In any case, no female relative of mine would travel without an abigail.'

'Then your tiger? My hair is short enough, in the style of Lady Caroline Lamb, and I am quite small.'

She had intended to shock him and she succeeded. He rounded on her with a look that boded ill.

'Are you out of your mind?' he asked in icy tones. 'Does your folly know no bounds? You would dare to set forth in breeches, madam? You shall not do so in my company.'

Georgiana's lips twitched, and he responded with a haughty look.

'I see. Is this some misplaced attempt to gammon me?'

'I should not dare, my lord.' Georgiana was at her most demure. 'I am in no joking mood, and did you not say yourself that time was of the essence?' She moved towards the door. 'I shall not keep you above a moment.'

'Stay!' For once he seemed nonplussed. 'No breeches, Miss Westleigh, I beg of you. You may travel as my ward.'

'That would seem to be the most appropriate solution, sir.'

His look was full of suspicion, and Georgiana was tempted to giggle. Perhaps he thought she was referring to age, or to his antiquated ideas. If so, she was glad of it. She had suffered enough from his barbed remarks.

What a prude he was! Stiff-backed, stiff-necked, and quite without the saving grace of humour. The journey ahead of her promised to be a trial in his company, but she would suffer it to reach Calais.

As she threw clothing into a bag her thoughts were sombre. Everything had happened so fast. Was it really less than forty-eight hours since Harry had returned ashen-faced to tell her that he was ruined?

Desperate, he had spent the previous day trying to raise funds, but all to no avail. She herself had pocketed her pride and applied to her own friends. They had given what they could, but the sums involved were too great. A fifty-guinea loan here and there went no way at all towards rescuing him from the consequences of his own folly, but she had taken the money with gratitude in order to help him.

She buried her face in her hands. She had intended to repay the money when the house was sold, but now she too would be labelled as a cheat. She rocked to and fro in an agony of mind. The future did not bear thinking of.

She jumped as the door flew open.

'This is no time for a fit of the vapours, Miss Westleigh.' The Viscount's voice was brisk. 'Make haste! We are wasting time.' He seized her bag and started down the stairs. 'Give me our destination. I must instruct my coachman.'

'I shall not tell you.' Georgiana gave him a defiant look. 'If you know it you will abandon me.'

Lyndhurst stared at her for a long moment.

'This may come as a surprise to you, but once I have given my word I keep it. Unlike your brother's assurances, you may rely upon that.' Without more ado he bundled her into the waiting coach.

'Well? I am waiting…' He sat back with an expression of saintly patience.

'We…we should make for the coast.'

'The coastline of England is extensive, Miss Westleigh. Shall we start in Cornwall and work our way around to the Scottish border?'

'Tell your man to make for Dover.' To discourage further conversation Georgiana drew her cloak about her and settled into the corner seat.

'So it is to be France?' her companion mused. 'And not a moment too soon, by the look of matters.'

'What do you mean?' Georgiana abandoned all pretence and sat bolt upright.

'Look there!' Lyndhurst drew aside the leather curtain at the window and nodded towards the corner of the street. Georgiana saw a group of men, dimly visible in the first pale light of dawn, making towards her door.

'So soon?' she breathed. 'Oh, please let us go.'

She did not look back, but as the coach rumbled away over the cobblestones she heard shouts and the sound of knocking.

'They will soon force the door,' the Viscount observed. 'I warned you, did I not? Now be good enough to tell me how the conspirators intended to travel.'

'I will tell you nothing if you persist in referring to my brother as if he were a criminal.'

'Fraud is a criminal offence, my dear. But if the term offends you I will rephrase my question. How do our unfortunate relatives intend to get away?'

'Lord Lothmore sent his chaise for Harry. He was to take it across the river, and there change into our own coach for the journey to Dover.'

'Doubtless collecting Richard on the way.

Damn Lothmore! When I spoke to him last evening he disclaimed all knowledge of Westleigh's whereabouts.'

'Perhaps he values loyalty,' Georgiana said stiffly.

'A quality which is sometimes sadly misplaced, Miss Westleigh.' His brow creased in thought. 'They will be forced to stop for a change of horses. We'll enquire at the post-houses.'

Tapping his gold-topped clouded cane against the roof, he brought the coach to a halt. A brief conference with his coachman ended with an injunction to 'Spring 'em!', and the horses gathered speed.

Chapter Two

Georgiana closed her eyes once more, but any attempt to sleep was out of the question.

With every jolt in the rutted road she was flung about. In vain she felt for a handhold in order to keep her balance, but a small scream escaped her lips as the coach hit a deep pothole and she was thrown into Lyndhurst's arms. Instinctively they closed about her, and he held her close for a moment.

She found the experience oddly disturbing, and for the first time she was aware of his immense strength. His arms might have been made of iron.

Knowing that it would be useless to struggle, she lay in his embrace, aware of the faint smell of tobacco mingled with that of expensive soap, and the lingering scent of salt sea air. The fine stuff of his coat felt smooth against her cheek, and beneath the ruffled shirt she could hear the beating of his heart.

He set her back in her corner with a mocking smile.

'Comfortable, Miss Westleigh?'

Georgiana felt too confused to reply. In silence she set her bonnet straight and shook out the folds of her warm merino cloak.

'Think how you'd have enjoyed the role of tiger,' he continued slyly. 'So bracing…riding aloft exposed to wind and rain.'

'It isn't raining, and if your coachman were not driving like a madman all would be well.' She gave him a bitter look.

'It can't be helped. We have no time to lose.'

Again the coach hit a pothole, and in an involuntary movement she put out her hands towards him. He laughed, but changed his seat at once to settle down beside her. A long arm slid about her waist and drew her close.

'You are too slight in weight,' he reproved. 'Were you twice the size you would not suffer so.'

'I need neither your help nor your advice,' Georgiana said with dignity. She sat bolt upright in the hope that he would move away. Instead he tightened his grip.

'My lord, you are crushing my gown.'

'Better that than a crushed nose! When I restore you to the arms of your loving brother I do not wish him to think that I have been beating you in my uncontrollable fury.'

'That is ridiculous!' Georgiana caught at his hand and tried to disengage his fingers from her waist, without success.

'Is it? I must confess that since we met I've been strongly tempted to beat you. Never in my experience have I encountered such a stubborn, feather-headed creature.'

A feeling of indignation almost robbed Georgiana of speech.

'I am *not* feather-headed!' she retorted in a choked voice.

'No? How else would you describe this present escapade?'

'What would you have had me do?' she cried bitterly. 'Should I have stayed in London to face the duns? You made it clear that they would turn me out of my home.'

'I hope I also made it clear that your most sensible course of action was to return to your parents.

However, we shall not dwell on it. We are thrown together, it would seem, for better or for worse.'

She was tempted to tell him that the worse, in her opinion, far outweighed the better, but she bit back the words. Lyndhurst was her only hope of getting to France, so she must make the best of what promised to be a nightmare journey.

It would be both useless and undignified to struggle further, so she allowed herself to grow limp within the circle of his arms and closed her eyes. She thought she heard a low chuckle, but she ignored it.

'That's better!' he murmured. 'I cannot have you looking as if you have been in the ring with Gentleman Jackson.'

'You have not heard me complain, nor will you.'

'That's true, but consider my difficulty. Should you strike your head and be rendered senseless I shall lose my guide. I shall not know whether to set sail for Bordeaux, La Rochelle, or Calais.' He felt her stiffen at the mention of Calais, but he made no comment.

'At our present rate of travel you will come upon your brother before we reach Dover,' she ground out.

'Possibly. But I doubt it. Our interesting relatives had too good a start on us.'

The sarcasm in his voice was hateful, and Georgiana turned her head away. Honesty compelled her to admit the truth of much of what he had said, and now, lying in his arms, she realised for the first time that she had placed herself in an invidious position.

It had been easy enough to defy him, and even to blackmail him into bringing her along, but there was no denying the fact that she was now in a closed carriage alone with a total stranger.

Her heart began to thump unpleasantly at the thought, but she forced herself to strive for calm. After all, it was clear that the Viscount had no high opinion of women. He had done his best to dissuade her from the journey, and he had been forthright about his opinion of her character.

She stole a glance at him from beneath lowered lids. Far from being aware of her presence he had closed his eyes, and was, to all appearances, falling asleep.

Georgiana smiled at her own fears. She was safe enough with this irritating creature. No woman would meet his exacting standards, least of all herself.

Idly, she found herself wondering about his past. He was unmarried; that she knew from Richard. It seemed strange that a man of his position should not have taken a wife and started his nursery. In spite of her dislike she would allow that he was an imposing figure. She glanced at him again, sure now that he was sound asleep.

She would not term him handsome…the face was too strong for conventional good looks. Those jutting brows, the Roman nose and the clean lines of a square jaw were oddly at variance with the thick mass of dark brown curls, dressed in the fashionable Brutus cut. To her own surprise she was tempted to touch a gleaming lock which had fallen across his forehead.

As if sensing her regard, the blue eyes opened wide.

'Having second thoughts, Miss Westleigh? Very wise! Give me your brother's destination and I'll set you down, with funds, at the first of the posthouses.'

Georgiana was sorely tempted. With funds she could make her own way to France, but a moment's thought convinced her not to accept his offer. She thought she knew her companion well enough to realise that he would not abandon her to her own devices. She decided to put him to the test.

'There are conditions?'

'Naturally! I cannot allow you to follow me to

France, having sent me off on some wild-goose chase. You will give me your word to return to your parents' home, by the coach which I shall order for you.'

'On no account!' Georgiana gave him a mutinous look.

'Very well! It shall be as you wish. I will take you to France…and then?'

Georgiana stared at him in dismay. She had not thought beyond the need to rush to Harry's side.

'My brother will obtain a post,' she faltered. 'He will take care of me.'

'As he has done to date? His tender care did not include taking you with him, I see.'

'That was my decision,' she retorted hotly. 'Harry did not wish to leave me, but I insisted. I thought…well, I thought that I might follow him when all was settled about the house in London.'

'What an innocent you are! Or did you hope to sell your possessions before your creditors could claim what was owed to them?'

Georgiana was silent. His words stung because there was so much truth in them. She *was* an innocent. In a blind panic, she had not stopped to think that everything she and Harry owned belonged, by rights, to his creditors. She had pressed her last few guineas on him, believing that she could raise enough money to follow him and enable them to live until he could find a position. She blushed furiously, feeling acutely uncomfortable.

'You will do well together,' the cynical voice continued. 'Are you to be the Judas goat, and lead the lambs to the slaughter? That look of innocence will serve for a year or two, but when the bloom wears off you will face an uncertain future, I assure you.'

Tears sprang unbidden to Georgiana's eyes. Must this unpleasant creature be so ready to put her own fears into words? She choked back a sob.

'Forgive me!' A large hand reached out to cover her own. 'That was unpardonable. I spoke in haste. Will you make allowances for my natural anger and anxiety?'

Georgiana dashed away a tear. She would not trust herself to speak, but she nodded briefly.

Obsessed by her own worries, she had given little thought to how Lyndhurst must be feeling. To return from a length absence to find his brother involved in scandal was bad enough, but the nature of that scandal made it insupportable. He had every right to feel betrayed by his brother's folly, but if only Harry were not involved…

She straightened her shoulders. Regrets were useless. Nothing she could say or do would alter what was past. She must learn to live for the day if she and Harry were to survive.

'Better?' The Viscount's voice was gentle. 'We are close to the first of the posthouses. We may have some news of them.'

His hopes were quickly realised. Mine host was happy to inform the Viscount that a coach bearing two young gentlemen of fashion had indeed passed through.

The landlord of the inn had good cause to remember them. More gold than he had seen in a twelve-month had accompanied a plea for haste in changing the horses. He had asked no questions. The change had been accomplished in record time, and the coach and its occupants would, by now, be some hours ahead of his lordship.

More gold changed hands, and Lyndhurst swung aboard with a request to his man for no slackening in speed.

'We shall not catch them before they reach Dover, unless they break a trace,' he frowned.

'Pray do not wish for that. They may be injured.'

'I think it unlikely. Those two young sprigs appear to bear charmed lives.' The Viscount's tone was grim. 'You have no idea how they mean to cross the Channel, I suppose? The packet will not take a coach without previous warning. Does your brother intend to leave it at the port?'

'Oh, no! He cannot. It contains all that Harry...I mean that we own in this world.'

'Then Westleigh was not unprepared for flight?'

'He took little enough,' Georgiana flared. 'And he was thinking of me rather than himself.'

'Was he indeed? I wish I had your faith in human nature.'

'Do you have faith in anything, or anyone?' Her look was hostile.

'Merely in a sense of honour and a modicum of intelligence,' he replied.

Georgiana was silenced. She was tired and stiff and in no mood for further exchanges with her unpleasant companion. Exhaustion overcame her at last, and even the constant rocking of the coach could not prevent her from falling asleep.

She awoke to the cries of sea-birds, and the unwelcome realisation that she was resting comfortably against the Viscount's broad shoulder. His chin was against her hair, and for a moment she thought that he too was asleep.

As she attempted to sit upright she found a pair

of keen blue eyes gazing down at her. As the coach drew to a halt he withdrew his arm from about her waist.

'We have reached Dover,' he announced. 'Though I fear we have missed our fugitives. They may have sailed on the morning tide. Will you excuse me? I must enquire for them.'

Once alone, Georgiana ran her fingers through her curls. Her merino cloak had stood the journey well, but her gown was crushed beyond redemption. What a fright she must look! She felt in her reticule for a mirror and a comb, groaning at her reflection in the glass. Dishevelled could scare describe it!

'No need to trouble yourself,' a calm voice observed from the window. 'Only the young look newborn in the morning light.'

It was a pretty compliment, but Lyndhurst's words brought her no comfort. Anxiously she scanned the crowds on the dockside, fearing to see Harry among the bustle of folk. She prayed that he had already sailed for France, and was out of her companion's reach.

She needed time to decide on her future course of action. Somehow she must contrive to mislead Lyndhurst. She dared not risk a confrontation with her brother. The Viscount had spoken of a whipping…

As she watched, he disappeared into an official-looking building, and was gone for so long that she began to fear the worst. She fervently hoped that Harry and Richard were not already taken.

She fixed her eyes on the doorway through which Lyndhurst had vanished, aware of an unpleasant churning in her stomach. Her heart was pounding, and she sensed a curious fluttering in her breast.

Clenching her fists until the knuckles shone white, she forced herself to breathe deeply until the fluttering stopped. She must be calm. To panic would serve no purpose. Above all she needed a clear head if she was to outwit her dangerous companion.

When he reappeared his expression was not encouraging.

'We are too late,' he told her briefly. 'They are gone.'

Inwardly, Georgiana sighed with relief. Harry was safe for the moment, and out of reach of possible pursuers. She looked up at the Viscount with dancing eyes.

Her joy was short-lived. He left her in no doubt of his intentions.

'We shall find them,' he said with certainty. 'Now, Miss Westleigh, to business. We cannot sail until tonight, so I suggest that we break our fast. You will wish to retire to make a toilette, and you must be famished.'

'I could not eat.' At that moment Georgiana felt that food would choke her.

'Yet you will do so. I'll not be burdened by a fainting female…'

Argument died on her lips as she looked at his stern expression, but he had not done with her.

'The sea is looking ugly,' he went on. 'You will find that retching is most unpleasant on an empty stomach.' He sounded as if the thought gave him a great deal of pleasure.

'I am an excellent sailor, thank you,' Georgiana said with dignity.

'You will have need to be.' He did not speak to her again until they entered the portals of the largest inn in the town.

The Viscount's manner was such that no trace of surprise was permitted to appear on the face of mine host, no matter what his private conjecture as to the likely relationship of his guests. If the lady had no attendant and very little luggage it was none of his concern.

A glance at the perfect set of the coat across the Viscount's broad shoulders, the magnificence of his tasselled Hessians, and the fine quality of his snowy linen, assured the man that he was dealing with the Quality. Not that he needed further assurance. He had seen the coach arrive, noted the crested panelling on the doors, and was unsurprised to find that the habit of command came easily to his visitor.

If the lady looked overly young and not a little nervous, it was to be understood. This would not be the first time that some dashing buck had brought a barque of frailty to the shelter of his roof.

'Your room has a private parlour,' the Viscount murmured. 'Wait for me there. I have some matters to attend, but I shall not be long. Have you any preference in the matter of food?'

'Anything. It does not matter.' Georgiana felt uncomfortable. She had not misinterpreted the landlord's bland expression.

'On the contrary! It matters to me.' Lyndhurst turned away, apparently dismissing her from his thoughts.

He was gone for longer than she expected, leaving her a prey to dread. In spite of his promise he might still abandon her without compunction. She had turned down his generous offer of funds and a coach. Perhaps he felt that he owed her nothing further. Now that he knew Harry's destination, why should he not leave her to her fate? At Calais he could search for the fugitives with every hope of success. The town was not large…

She pushed her worrying thoughts to the back of her mind, but niggling doubts remained. Should he not return, this well-furnished bedchamber with its private parlour was well beyond her means. She would be hard-pressed to mollify the landlord, and how could she pay for a passage to France?

Until this moment she had not realised how dependent she was upon the Viscount's protection. A frown creased her brow. With an impatient gesture she rose to her feet and began to pace the room.

She would not meet trouble halfway. By this time tomorrow she would be in France. She must believe that Lyndhurst was a man of his word, and in her heart she was sure of it. She disliked him, it was true. His intimidating manner and his cruel tongue were not designed to charm, but then, she had no claim upon his forbearance.

He thought her some kind of an adventuress…certainly a liar and a cheat. Her cheeks burned as she recalled his words. It should not matter what he thought of her, but it was hard to be misjudged. She found herself wondering what his reaction would have been had they met under other circumstances.

She pulled a face at herself in the mirror. The jade-green eyes, framed with long, dark lashes, mocked her gently. They were tip-tilted at the corners, giving her heart-shaped face a slightly feline appearance. As a child she had been nicknamed 'Puss', and she had learned to dislike that slanting gaze.

Her mouth she considered too wide for beauty. In any case, those flaming curls must quash all pretension to good looks. Blondes and brunettes were all the rage. Georgiana sighed for the fashion of fifty years ago, when hair had been powdered, but it would not have helped. A pair of arching eyebrows, dark as a raven's wing, would have ruined the effect.

She was an oddity, and, as such, the Viscount would have passed her by without a second glance. Her cheeks grew rosy as she considered the direction of her thoughts, but honesty compelled her to admit that she would prefer him to think well of her, if not exactly to be attracted to her appearance. He was a provoking creature, but she could not bear his contempt.

She walked over to the window, hoping to cool her flaming cheeks. The throng in the courtyard below milled about the London coach, which had just arrived. As she watched, the tall figure of the Viscount forced its way through the crowd to greet an elderly man dressed in sombre clothing.

Her sense of relief was overwhelming as she saw the two men enter the inn. Lyndhurst had kept his word as, in her heart, she had known he would. She felt ashamed of her doubts. If only there were some way she could mitigate his anger, justified though it was.

With a sigh she walked through into the private parlour. It was empty although a table had been laid with gleaming silver and glass. An appetising smell of roasting meat floated towards her from below, and suddenly she felt hungry.

She had not long to wait. Seconds later Lyndhurst entered the room. As she looked up, she surprised a curious expression on his face. In another man she might have thought it admiration.

Suddenly she was glad that she had chosen to wear her most becoming gown. Classical in line, the filmy fabric, in palest green, was caught high beneath her bosom with an emerald ribbon. It had been sadly crushed, but she'd held it over a bowl of steaming water to remove the creases. Now she smoothed at it with nervous fingers.

The Viscount did not appear to notice her confusion. With grave courtesy he seated her at the table, and motioned to the waiting servants. They sat in silence as the meal was served and the landlord himself carved thin pink slices of the tender ham in Madeira sauce which followed a delicious fish soup.

The Viscount had a healthy appetite and did full justice to the haunch of mutton which then appeared, raising an eyebrow as Georgiana refused an offer of beef with caramelised onions. Instead she took a serving of young salad greens.

'You have not touched your wine,' Lyndhurst said at last. 'It is not to your taste?'

Georgiana sipped from her glass.

'It is very good, my lord.'

He smiled then and she bridled, knowing full well that he suspected her of caution. He was right. She was not used to taking more than a glass, and she feared that the wine might loosen her tongue.

'At least you will try this mint and lemon ice, madam?' the landlord pleaded. 'Or perhaps a mouthful of this soufflé? It is as light as air.'

Georgiana smiled and shook her head, and Lyndhurst signalled to the man to withdraw.

'I have hired a vessel,' he announced when they were alone. 'We leave on the evening tide.'

Georgiana's heart lifted. At least he did not intend to leave her behind. He gave her a speculative look. 'By tomorrow we shall be in Calais...' He seemed to be waiting for some comment.

'And then?' she breathed.

'Why, then we shall trace our missing relatives, of course.'

'I did not mean quite that. My lord, you have not said what you intend to do if...when we find them.'

'Let us take one day at a time.' His expression was bland. 'Have you everything you need for the journey? Do you wish to go into the town...?'

'I have sufficient for my needs,' she said stiffly. She would not be further beholden to him, but it was an ungracious reply, and she coloured a little. 'It is kind of you to think of it, and I thank you.'

'You will thank me best by getting some sleep.' His face had closed again and his voice was distant.

Georgiana wondered why a simple word of thanks should have annoyed him so. His courtesy had disarmed her, and for a moment she had been in danger of forgetting that she was nothing more to him than a link with Harry.

She had been fed and cared for because she was of use to him, yet she had been foolish enough to imagine that concern for her had prompted his kindness. An irrational wave of anger tempted her to lash out at him. She would not make the same mistake again.

Then common sense prevailed. There was no point in making an enemy of him at the present time. She needed him as much as he needed her, and until now she had handled matters badly. Perhaps if she tried a different approach...?

'You are right, of course.' She gave him her sweetest smile. 'May I thank you first for an excellent meal?' She sat back with a sigh of contentment, and was disconcerted to see that his wide, mobile mouth was twisted in amusement.

'You feel quite well, Miss Westleigh?'

'Why should I not?'

'I thought I detected a certain softening in your manner, yet you refused my offer of a visit to the shops to replenish your wardrobe.'

'I have no need of anything, as I told you.'

'Not even a pair of breeches? I imagined that you might be considering another role...as my cabin-boy.' He gave her a malicious grin.

Georgiana stared at him in amazement. A joke from Lyndhurst? Was he actually teasing her? She struggled to repress a smile.

'You are pleased to jest,' she said sedately. 'Now if you will excuse me I shall retire.'

A cool hand reached out to rest upon her brow.

'What are you doing?' She pulled away from him.

'I suspect a violent fever. When you fall in with my wishes I fear the worst.'

Georgiana glared at him. A sharp retort rose to her lips, but she held her tongue. With head held high, she swept from the room.

Chapter Three

The day was far advanced when she awoke, and
for a few moments she wondered where she was.
A movement in the corner roused her, and she
lifted her head to find a girl of her own age regarding
her with interest.

'Who are you…and what are you doing here?'
Georgiana raised herself on one elbow.

'Beg pardon, madam. His lordship asked me to
see toy our things. I've pressed your gowns.'

'You work here?'

'No, ma'am. My uncle is his lordship's valet.
We came down on the London coach.'

Lyndhurst had not wasted much time, Georgiana thought wryly. He must have sent a message
to his servants from the first of the posthouses on

the Dover road. Had he taken any other action unknown to her? If he had notified the authorities…

Then she remembered. Harry and Richard were
out of reach of the Bow Street Runners.

Throwing aside the coverlet, she slipped out of
bed, glad to find that the girl had laid out a change
of clothing.

'What is your name?' she asked.

'I'm Betsy, ma'am. Shall I ring for hot water?'

'Please.' Georgiana smiled at her. The girl was
small and thin, but she was clearly anxious to be
helpful, and she had a pleasant face. 'Do you go
to France with us?'

'Yes, miss. I'm afeared of the sea, but my uncle
says it will be all right.'

'Of course it will. You have not travelled to
France before?'

Betsy giggled. 'I ain't bin above three mile from
home afore now, but I'm to train as a lady's maid.
His lordship promised.'

'It won't be difficult,' Georgiana murmured.
'Now if you will find my stout half-boots…'

Leaving the girl to rummage through her bag,
she abandoned herself to the luxury of a bath in
warm, scented water.

'Miss, I was to tell his lordship once you was awake,' Betsy offered hesitantly.

'Very well, but first you shall help me into my gown.'

The girl was both clumsy and nervous, but her hands were gentle, if a trifle impatient. Georgiana guessed that, for his servants, Lyndhurst's word was law and, by waiting, Betsy was disobeying his express command.

'Off you go!' She released the girl at last. 'I will do my hair myself.'

Betsy gave her a look of pure gratitude as she hurried away, but she was back at once.

'I'm to help you with your hair.' There was a note of pride in the girl's voice.

Georgiana hid a smile. 'It will not take long,' she said gravely. 'As you see, it is very short.'

She sat patiently as Betsy brushed at her curls.

'It's that springy, ma'am, but it's beautiful.' Betsy touched the flaming mass with reverence. 'Ain't you lucky to have dark brows? Most folk with red hair look like frightened rabbits.'

Georgiana's shoulders shook. Betsy promised to be a most unusual lady's maid, and vastly entertaining.

She dismissed the girl and strolled into the parlour to find it deserted, but in the courtyard below the bustle had not lessened. As she gazed across the rooftops of the little town she could see ships at anchor in the harbour below. Which of them would bear her to France? And, once there, what was to be her fate?

She turned as the door opened. As the Viscount sauntered towards her his manner was as cool as ever, but to her surprise he took her hand and kissed it in greeting. The touch of his warm lips against her skin was strangely disturbing, but she resisted the temptation to betray her unease by snatching it away. After all, the greeting was no more than common courtesy. Frayed nerves must have caused that curious little flicker in the pit of her stomach.

With all the composure at her command, she looked up at him and smiled. She had sworn to herself that she would not antagonise him further, or her plan to persuade him to trust her must fail.

Honesty compelled her to admit that his appearance was a tribute both to his own physique and to the attentions of his valet. The snowy starched cravat was creased to perfection à la Mathématique, and his dark brown hair gleamed in the sunlight streaming through the window. It shone like a newly fallen chestnut. The fit of his coat and breeches bespoke the hand of a master tailor, and no speck of dust marred the surface of his tasselled Hessians.

She felt a small pang of regret. His was a striking figure, though his dress was understated. Anyone unversed in the finer points of style would have found it unremarkable at first glance, but she had been well trained by Harry. How often had she listened to her brother's lamentations as he struggled to achieve a similar standard?

This man was no dandy, but he looked every inch an aristocrat. She sighed outwardly. Under other circumstances she might have found Lyndhurst pleasing.

She turned away, banishing the treacherous thought.

'You are rested?'

'Yes, my lord.'

'Then you are ready to face the rigours of a Channel crossing?'

'Quite ready!' Belatedly, she remembered Betsy. 'I must thank you for sending a maid to me.'

She heard a chuckle.

'It may be some time before Betsy can claim that title. You find her willing enough?'

Georgiana dimpled, and her mouth curved in a smile.

'May I not share the joke?'

'Betsy is pleased because I have dark brows and lashes,' she replied. 'Without them I should most certainly look like a frightened rabbit.'

Lyndhurst's twinkling eyes belied his frown.

'You must not brook impertinence. I will ask Scroggins to speak to her.'

'Please don't! I should not have told you had I thought you would take it amiss. Betsy is a joy.'

'You are easily pleased, Miss Westleigh. Now will you sit down? I have something to say to you.'

With no great hopes that it would be anything she wished to hear, Georgiana sank into a chair as her companion began to pace the room.

'I must make a last appeal to your good sense,' he said at last. 'Your present plans are folly. Will you not reconsider? My man and Betsy will accompany you to your parents' home.'

'Impossible!' Georgiana stiffened and her mouth set in a mutinous line.

'Why so? Sisterly affection may be excused. Your father will forgive you for championing your brother's cause.'

'No!'

'I find your attitude beyond all reason.' Lyndhurst was growing impatient. 'Your decision to live with Westleigh should not have been allowed. Your father, after all, has some claim upon your obedience.'

Hot colour flooded Georgiana's cheeks. She had no wish to offer an explanation to this authoritarian creature, but she had no alternative.

'My father did not know…of my whereabouts…'

The Viscount's eyebrows rose in disbelief, and his frown deepened.

'I…er…allowed everyone to think that I had eloped…'

'Indeed!' Lyndhurst's tone was grim. 'You had best go on.'

'Oh, don't you see?' she pleaded. 'It was the only way. Had Father found us he would have forced me to leave Harry. If he believed me to be married he could not interfere…'

'You have a curious idea of filial affection.' The contempt in Lyndhurst's voice made Georgiana squirm. 'Had you no thought for the distress you must have caused?'

'I did think of it,' she flung back furiously. 'I wrote to reassure my mother, but, of course, I could not tell her the truth.'

'Naturally not,' he agreed in an icy tone. 'At lease you have succeeded in confirming my opinion of you. Once a cheat…'

'How dare you?' she cried. 'Again you judge me without knowing the full story.'

'Then you had best tell me,' he said, with an unpleasant smile. 'As always, your beloved brother appears to be the cause of this separation from your family. He was disowned, I think you said. What had he done to warrant such a fate?'

Georgiana was silent as she glared at him. She would not discuss private family matters with this autocratic creature.

'I can find out, you know.' His lordship took a leisurely pinch of snuff. 'And you might remember that you cannot sink your brother's reputation further in my eyes. That would be impossible.'

'Really?' She faced him then with flashing eyes. 'You shall hear the story, sir. Then you may judge.'

'Go on.'

Georgiana hesitated. She was wondering where to begin. 'Harry was at Cambridge,' she muttered at last. 'He was sent down…'

'Why?'

'He was rather wild…and…and there were gambling debts…' She looked up at Lyndhurst, hating the mocking smile which played about his mouth. 'He was just a boy,' she snapped furiously. 'And whatever he had done it did not warrant…'

Her voice shook and she could not go on. The memory of her father's anger would live in her mind forever. She had not spoken of his behaviour to a living soul until this day.

'This was the cause of your father's displeasure?'

'Displeasure? That is a masterpiece of understatement. My father is a violent man, my lord. He thrashed Harry with his riding crop before our friends and all the servants…'

'A father has the right to chastise his children.'

'To the point of breaking their bones? Harry put up an arm to save his head, but it did not stop the attack. We heard the crack as his arm snapped. My mother was weeping… She tried to stop the punishment but she was thrust away so fiercely that she fell to the ground. Then I…I seized the whip and threw it in the lake.'

'I see.' Lyndhurst's eyes were intent upon her face.

'Do you? I doubt if you can understand… Things were said that day which cannot be forgotten or forgiven.'

'By Harry?'

'Harry could not speak. He tried to crawl away, but my father told him to stand up and take his beating like a man. He picked up a stick of ash-plant, but my mother caught his arm whilst Harry's friends carried him to the surgeon. Father followed them down the drive, still screaming abuse…'

'My dear!' Lyndhurst's voice was gentler than she had heard it for some time. 'What of yourself?'

'I was beaten too, but with a cane.' She gave him a twisted smile. 'Then I was locked in my room for several days. Harry came back just once, to see my mother. Father ordered him out of the house. He said that he had no son. Harry begged to be allowed to say farewell to me, but permission was refused. My mother told me later that Harry had told my father that he would never forgive him.'

'And you?'

'Never! His treatment of Harry was beyond all reason. His anger I could understand…but not the brutality. Later I suppose he was ashamed, but he would not admit it. He hinted of other matters to his friends, saying that he could not bring himself to speak of the true cause of Harry's banishment.'

'Do you know of anything more?'

'There was nothing. Mother made it her business to find out from friends at Cambridge.'

'It must have been hard for you.'

'I was released in time.' Her smile was pitiful. 'But it was too late. I could not stay beneath my father's roof, and I had been given the opportunity to think. A week on bread and water does much to clear the mind. I rode over to see a friend of ours who was leaving for the colonies. He did not object when I told him of my plan.'

'Which was?'

'To say that we had eloped. He was emigrating and could not be traced with ease, at least for a time.'

'A gallant gentleman!' Lyndhurst's voice was dry. 'You had a *tendre* for him?'

'Not in the least!' Georgiana gave him a withering look. 'But he had no love for my father. When he asked for leave to pay his addresses to me, his suit was dismissed in the most insulting way.'

'And he did not renew it when he knew that you wished to leave your home?'

'He did.' Georgiana coloured faintly. 'But I explained that I could not marry him. In the end, he agreed to help me. We travelled to London with his sister and found Harry.'

'And your mother?'

'That is my only regret.' Her lips quivered. 'I left a note…and later I wrote to reassure her about

Harry and myself, but I do not know if she received the letter. My father may have destroyed it…'

'So you are adamant? There is no possibility of a reconciliation?'

'How can you ask?' Her eyes were bright with unshed tears. 'I cannot and will not return home. My lord, you gave me your word that I should accompany you to France, and I believed you.'

'You may live to regret it.' His face was sombre. 'You have my sympathy, Miss Westleigh. I was too hard on you, but I could wish that you had accepted your friend in marriage. It would have solved many of your problems.'

'And created more. I did not love him, and besides, no man shall master me. I had rather die a spinster.'

'Someone must control that stubborn will.' The fierce blue eyes raked her from head to foot with such an insolent look of appraisal that Georgiana felt naked beneath his gaze. 'And I doubt that you will die a spinster. That face and form will save you from such a fate.'

'You are no gentleman to speak so.' She blinked away the tears from her eyes. 'If you think to dissuade me with your insults you will not succeed.'

'Insults, my dear Miss Westleigh? Most women

would regard my tribute to your beauty as a compliment. However, I must point out that beauty in itself can be a handicap. You would travel to France alone with me? Have you no thought of your reputation?'

'My reputation is already lost. You have made that clear. I must bear the taint of scandal equally with my brother, as you were quick to tell me. To travel as your…companion cannot matter now.'

'Be it on your own head.' He turned and left her.

A chill wind was blowing by the time they reached the dock, and Georgiana looked in dismay at the leaden waves. The seas were mountainous.

'Miss, we shall be drownded for sure!' Betsy's eyes were starting from her head.

'Nonsense!' Georgiana spoke with a confidence she was far from feeling. 'The captain will not sail if there is danger.'

The keen wind cut through her warm merino cloak as if it were made of paper, and she looked in concern at her maid's thin garments. The girl was shaking, as much with cold as with fright.

'My lord?' Georgiana turned to the Viscount, who was supervising the loading of his coach aboard the waiting vessel.

'What is it now?' Lyndhurst was apparently oblivious of the inclement weather.

'May we not go aboard at once? You will not wish to have two fainting females on your hands.'

The taunt brought a tightening of his lips, but he nodded his assent. 'Scroggins will show you to your cabin.' A motion of his head brought the valet to their side, but it was with some trepidation that Georgiana stepped up the companionway.

The weather was atrocious, and, even tied up alongside, the ship was pitching unpleasantly. Georgiana remembered her own claim to be an excellent sailor. She hoped it would be justified.

To her relief the cabin was warm and comfortable, and Scroggins was attentive. He took his niece aside to give her further instructions, but Betsy paid him no attention. Her face was ashen, and before they were under way it had taken on a greenish tinge.

'You had best lie down,' Georgiana suggested. 'Then you will find the motion less disturbing.' She gestured towards the bunk.

'My uncle will be cross with me.' Tears poured down Betsy's cheeks. 'I wasn't to be a trouble to you but, miss, I do feel bad.'

'You will be more trouble if you are ill. Now do

as I say.' Georgiana tucked the girl beneath the coverlet. 'You must try to sleep. In no time at all we shall be in France, and on dry land again.'

She waited until the girl had closed her eyes, and then she left the cabin. Her appearance on deck was not welcomed by the Viscount. He gave her an angry look.

'This will not be an easy crossing,' he announced. 'I prefer that you stay below decks.'

'And I prefer fresh air.' Georgiana was finding it difficult to keep her footing in the gale, but she would not admit defeat.

'As you wish, my self-willed friend. A word of warning, though… If you are swept overboard I shall not attempt to save you.'

'Of course not! Such self-sacrifice would be totally out of character.' The effect of the barbed taunt was lost as the ship pitched into the trough of a wave and Georgiana lost her footing on the slippery deck. With a cry she threw out a hand to save herself.

'Now will you need my warning?' A grip of iron encircled her waist as the Viscount held her close. 'You had best seek your cabin.'

Still gasping with shock, Georgiana lifted her head. She had not allowed for the fury of the storm.

The force of the wind had almost thrown her off her feet. Mutely, she nodded, though she doubted if she had the strength to retrace her steps.

Lyndhurst solved the problem by picking her up and tossing her over one shoulder as if she had been a sack of feathers. Then he groped along the deck until they reached the safety of the companionway.

'Please set me down here.' It was difficult to maintain any semblance of dignity with her heels in the air, her bonnet askew, and her head and arms scrabbling vainly at the Viscount's back, but Georgiana did her best.

She might have saved her breath. Ignoring her pleas, he marched along to her cabin door, threw it open, and dumped her on a chair.

'Madam,' he said heavily, 'my patience has been sorely tried. You will oblige me by showing some consideration for your own welfare, if not for mine. It is a long swim back to Dover, even for a woman of your determination.'

Georgiana was pinned in her chair as he leaned towards her. His face was much too close and she shifted uncomfortably, averting her head. The lips which had been close to her ear now brushed her cheek, and she jumped as if she had been stung.

The intimate contact had discomfited Lyndhurst too, she realised. He straightened at once.

'I beg your pardon,' he said stiffly. A slight flush appeared beneath his tan. 'I did not mean…'

A silence fell between them, and the air was heavy with tension. It was unnerving, and Georgiana's mouth grew dry. Her every sense was aware of the man in front of her…his breathing…the smooth firmness of his skin…and the beautifully moulded mouth. How safe she had felt in his embrace, yet it was meaningless. He had reached out to her merely to save her from harm.

What would it be like to have him reach out for her in love, drawing her gently to him to share untold delights?

Her eyes grew soft as she looked into his own but his expression checked her. His face was cold and distant. He bowed and was about to leave her when retching noises from the bed confirmed that Betsy was in the throes of nausea.

'I'll get Scroggins,' he said quickly.

'No!' With swift fingers Georgiana unfastened her cloak. 'Betsy will not wish her uncle to know that she is unwell.' The ghost of a smile touched her lips. 'She was not to be a trouble to me, or to fail in her duty.'

The Viscount hesitated. 'Miss Westleigh, there is no necessity for you to undertake the duties of a nurse.' The cool formality of his tone succeeded in annoying Georgiana.

'For heaven's sake,' she cried impatiently. 'The girl is feeling wretched. Can't you forget your precious code for once?'

She had expected an explosion of wrath, but none was forthcoming.

'Leave us, please,' she cried. 'Your presence can only add to Betsy's discomfort.'

'Is there anything I can do?'

'You may send for cloths and a bowl of water.'

When she looked round she was alone except for the groaning girl on the bed.

Murmuring words of comfort, Georgiana bathed the pale, sweating face. Then she wedged herself into the corner beside the bunk and held on to Betsy's hand. She was feeling none too good herself.

With grim determination she gritted her teeth. She would not succumb to sickness. It was all in the mind, so Harry had told her, but half an hour later she had begun to doubt his words. Perhaps if she kept her head quite still the rolling motion would not trouble her so.

Between the crashing of the waves and the high keening of the wind she did not hear a tap at the door. She looked up in surprise as Lyndhurst entered the cabin.

'Try sucking this!' One look at her face had told him all he wished to know. 'This is a bad crossing, Miss Westleigh. You should lie down.' He handed her the two halves of a cut lemon.

'I… I don't think I could put anything in my mouth.' Georgiana closed her eyes to shut out the sight of the fruit.

'The sharpness will help,' he insisted.

Obediently she lifted the lemon to her lips, preventing herself from vomiting by an act of will.

'Since Betsy is asleep you may use my cabin.' It was an order rather than suggestion, and Georgiana made no demur as he picked her up.

She was feeling too wretched to resist as he laid her upon his bunk.

'Do you wish to loosen your clothing? You will be more comfortable….'

'I wish that the ship would sink,' she groaned. 'Please go away.'

'In a moment.' With hands that were surprisingly gentle he removed her half-boots and tucked the coverlet round her.

'Try to sleep,' he murmured. 'The storm is abating, and the wind is dropping. I believe we are over the worst.'

With these words of comfort he left her. As always, he proved to be right. Within minutes Georgiana sensed that the roll of the vessel was less pronounced. Even the wind had ceased its screaming through the rigging. She closed her eyes and slept.

The ship was at anchor when she awoke, and it was with relief that she heard the clatter of horses' hooves on cobblestones. Beyond the open porthole she was aware of chattering in a foreign tongue. They must be at Calais unless the ship had been blown off course. Wherever they were it was a safe landfall, for which she could only offer up her thanks to the Almighty.

'His lordship presents his compliments, madam.' Scroggins entered with a tray of freshly baked rolls, some fruit and a pot of coffee. 'He begs that you will join him at your earliest convenience.'

The valet's lips were set in a thin line, and Georgiana pulled a face at his retreating back. Every line of his body betrayed a sense of outrage at her behaviour.

'How is Betsy?' she asked quickly.

'My niece is recovered, I thank you. Had madam only thought to send for me, any disturbance might have been avoided.'

'How kind of you to consider my comfort, Scroggins.' Georgiana gave him a deliberate look. He knew, and so did she, that his concern had been not for her but for his master. So the Viscount was not to be turned out of his own cabin for a whim of hers?

The man's eyes fell. He bowed and took his leave. He had not even thanked her for her care of Betsy, she thought ruefully. Lyndhurst, it seemed, was the pivot of his existence.

She shrugged. It was a pity to make an enemy of the Viscount's servant, but it was not of her doing. Doubtless Scroggins regarded her as some lightskirt who had fallen in Lyndhurst's way and would soon be discarded. The man was as stiff-necked and prudish as his master, she thought in disgust. They made a perfect pair.

She knew that she was being unjust. To be quite fair, it was as well for her that Lyndhurst was blessed with iron self-control. He was a man with the same needs as others, and it could not be denied that she was at his mercy.

Last night, for example, he might have taken advantage of her. She had been in no fit state to oppose him, and they had been in this cabin alone.

The humour of the situation struck her. What man would attempt to seduce a woman who was clearly in the throes of *mal de mer?* Such an incautious move might have resulted in the ruin of his fine linen shirt, and those spotless buckskin breeches. She had certainly been looking her worst, and her groans had been no invitation to a night of passionate love.

With a chuckle she threw aside the coverlet and stood before a dressing mirror. The long sleep had refreshed her and her milky skin had lost its greenish tinge. She poured out her coffee and began to nibble at a roll. How good it tasted! She was halfway through a second when Betsy tapped at the cabin door.

'Miss, his lordship wondered if you was ready to go ashore.' The girl looked subdued, and her eyes were red.

Georgiana felt indignant. Had Scroggins berated her? It seemed more than likely. Lyndhurst would not have troubled himself to take her maid to task.

She was tempted to summon the man, but a moment's reflection convinced her that she might do more harm than good by confronting him directly. Doubtless Scroggins' unreasonable behaviour was influenced by that of his master. What an example for anyone to follow!

She laid a sympathetic hand on Betsy's shoulder.

'Are you feeling better?' she enquired.

Betsy nodded, struggling with her tears.

'I'm that sorry, miss,' she choked out at last. 'I didn't mean to turn you out of your bed…'

'It did not signify. I was quite comfortable in here.'

'Yes, but his lordship… Oh miss, my uncle is so cross with me…'

And with me, Georgiana thought to herself. But Scroggins would learn that he had met his match. It was time to change the subject.

'Help me to dress,' she said quickly. 'And cheer up, Betsy. We shall find the best cure in the world for seasickness.'

'What's that, madam?'

'Sitting under a tree,' Georgiana twinkled.

Betsy stared at her. 'I don't understand.' Then her face cleared as Georgiana smiled, and she began to laugh. 'Miss, you are a caution. I can't feel seasick on the land, can I?'

She was still grinning as she slipped a gown of

primrose-yellow cambric over Georgiana's head, but the smile vanished with the sound of knocking at the cabin door.

'May I come in?' Lyndhurst stood in the doorway. With a wave of his hand he motioned Betsy out of the room. 'I believe I mentioned the need for haste, Miss Westleigh. How much longer do you intend to keep me waiting?'

'Longer than if you had not dismissed my maid.' Georgiana's temper rose to match his own.

'She is here to dress you rather than to provide you with amusement,' came the cool reply.

So he had heard them laughing and resented it. What an unpleasant creature he was!

'I am ready.' She seized her cloak, and was about to sweep past him when she recalled his kindness on the previous night. Possibly he had had no sleep, she realised, which might account for his ill humour.

'I thank you for allowing me to use your cabin,' she said stiffly.

Lyndhurst ignored the olive branch.

'I am still waiting, madam. At this rate it will be noon before we disembark.'

Georgiana threw up her eyes to heaven. He was impossible! How she longed for the moment when she could slip away from him. If she never saw him again it would be too soon, but he had served her purpose. She was now in France, and she felt a surge of relief. What a joy it would be to see Harry again!

With a light step she moved towards the door, but as she passed Lyndhurst he swung her round to face him.

'You are in great good humour today, my dear.' The keen eyes scanned her face.

'I am thankful that the sea crossing is behind us, sir.' Long, dark lashes veiled Georgiana's eyes. 'I should not care to repeat that experience.'

'Did you not tell me that you were an excellent sailor?' he challenged.

The sarcasm in his voice was infuriating. Georgiana did not reply. Then a strong hand gripped her chin and lifted her face to his.

'No tricks, madam! Allow me to warn you that if you have any thought of deceiving me you will regret it.'

'Let me go!' She slapped his hand away from her face. 'How dare you touch me?'

He smiled then, but his eyes were cold, and suddenly Georgiana was afraid.

'You presume too much upon my goodwill, Miss Westleigh. I might have seduced you at any time since our first meeting. Do you think I am made of stone?'

Hot colour flooded Georgiana's cheek. 'You would not,' she cried wildly.

'Why not? Your character leaves much to be desired, but your face and figure does not. A man might enjoy those attributes, at least.'

'You are disgusting!' she flung at him.

'But you are not.' Swiftly he bent his head and claimed her lips. She struggled to turn away, but the firm mouth came down on hers, forcing her lips apart. As his tongue caressed her Georgiana felt a curious sensation in the pit of her stomach, and the urge to draw him even closer was overwhelming. Confusion warred with delight as she melted into his arms.

Her pleasure was short-lived. With a muttered exclamation he thrust her away, and bustled her out of the cabin. Once on deck he strode away as if the fiends of hell were at his heels.

Chapter Four

Bewildered and deeply shaken, Georgiana followed the tall figure of the Viscount as he made his way down the gangplank. Once ashore he did not look at her, leaving Scroggins to help her aboard the waiting coach.

Lyndhurst, she noted, had taken his seat aloft beside the coachman. She might have been a leper, she thought with a surge of indignation. After all, she had not encouraged him to take her in his arms.

Her face burned as she remembered the warmth of his lips against her mouth. Had she only imagined the passion which had flared between them? Whether it was true or not, it appeared to have given that infuriating creature a strong distaste for her company.

Perhaps it was as well. This was no time to fall in love with him, and she had no intention of doing so. She composed her features into a smooth mask of indifference, oblivious to a searching look from Scroggins, who occupied the facing seat. Betsy sat beside him, looking subdued.

Georgiana felt a rising tide of irritation. She was tired of both Lyndhurst and his sour-faced valet. Enough was enough. With a brilliant smile she addressed herself to Betsy.

'Well, we are here in France at last, my dear. Now we may start to enjoy ourselves.' A sly look at Scroggins showed her that the man had stiffened. His lips were compressed, but he did not speak.

'You must make the most of your visit here,' Georgiana continued brightly.

She affected not to notice the girl's nervous look at her uncle before she muttered her agreement. Had he threatened to send her back to England? She would put a stop to his threats at once.

'Scroggins, I doubt if I have expressed my thanks for bringing Betsy to me. I can't think how I should go on without her…'

'Madam is too kind, but it was not of my doing. His lordship insisted…' The valet's tone expressed his disapproval of the whole affair.

'Well, then, we must all obey his lordship's express wish, must we not?' Georgiana hid a smile. She had routed Scroggins without difficulty, and he knew it.

'Look Betsy! Do you see the men in sabots? Those are the clog-like shoes they wear upon their feet…' Georgiana chattered artlessly as they drove along the dockside, drawing a shy response from Betsy until the girl was more herself again.

It was but a short journey to the hotel, but she was dismayed to find that they were to stay at Dessein's. She might have known, she thought bitterly. It was the only suitable destination for an English gentleman.

Anxiously she scanned the crowds in the foyer, dreading to see either Harry or Richard. Yet surely the Viscount would not indulge in a public altercation? She shuddered. It was more than likely that they would encounter the two fugitives this very day. If only she could buy time to warn Harry of the Viscount's presence in the town.

Lyndhurst wasted no time. Within minutes of their arrival he questioned Monsieur Quillac, the proprietor.

It was with an overwhelming sense of relief that Georgiana heard the Frenchman disclaim all knowledge of Messieurs Thorpe and Westleigh. Now, with any luck at all, Harry might see the coat-of-arms upon the Viscount's carriage and re-alise the danger.

Her hopes were dashed when Lyndhurst asked for stabling for the night. His coach would soon be out of sight.

She was inspecting her meagre wardrobe when Scroggins brought her a message.

'His lordship wishes you to join him in the par-lour, madam.' The valet avoided her eye and looked at his niece. 'With your permission I will have a word with Betsy.'

'Please do! Did I mention how pleased I am with her?' Georgiana gave him a brilliant smile. Then, having forestalled any criticism of his niece, she went to meet the Viscount.

He was standing by the fireplace when she en-tered the room, a deep frown creasing his brow.

'You will please to tell me of your arrangements with your brother,' he said without preamble. 'I had hoped to find him here with Richard, but there is no word of them. Now, it would appear, we must search the town.'

'Dessein's is expensive,' Georgiana mur-mured in a low voice. 'You forget, my lord, they cannot have much money to hand after their flight.'

'I don't doubt it,' came the dry reply. 'They have scattered gold like chaff in their haste to get away…but you do not answer my question.'

At a loss for words, Georgiana turned away from his penetrating gaze.

'They would not stay here,' she muttered. 'Is this not the first place that anyone would search for them?'

'It is. But do not prevaricate, Miss Westleigh. They are not here, but you must know how to find your brother.'

'You are mistaken. Our arrangement was that he should find me.'

'Then he will come here?' The keen blue eyes searched her face.

'Possibly…'

'I see. You were to stay here in any case. You must have hoped for a handsome return on the sale of your possessions…'

Her green eyes blazed at him. 'There is no need to remind me that I am beholden to you. I will leave whenever you wish.'

She heard a contemptuous laugh.

'I think you are well aware that I shall not do

that. You are the only card I hold, but to be the lure will be no new experience for you, I imagine.'

'You may imagine what you will. Whatever it is, it gave you no right to…to…'

'Assault your person? Come now, don't play the innocent with me. A single kiss, Miss Westleigh, which, I may add, you returned with interest? It was the impulse of a moment, and doubtless meant as little to you as it did to me.'

Georgiana could have struck him.

'Meaningless, I agree,' she said in icy tones. 'How could it be otherwise? My opinion of you is now quite as low as yours of me. Strangely, I expected better of you. I shall not make that mistake again.'

His laugh was derisive.

'Outraged virtue…coming from you? Will you deny that your charms played their part in persuading your brother's victims to agree to his schemes?'

'I do deny it,' Georgiana cried hotly. 'Though I don't expect you to believe me.' Her hands were shaking with rage, and she thrust them out of sight within the folds of her gown.

'Why should I?' came the cynical reply. 'Doubtless you are proud of your ability to deceive.'

'You may think what you wish,' she ground out. 'You know nothing of the matter, yet you are prepared to judge.'

'If necessary I shall be judge, jury and executioner.' The blue eyes were chips of ice, and his expression was forbidding. 'Now get your cloak. We shall take a stroll about the town.'

'I do not care to accompany you.' Georgiana was in no doubt as to his purpose. He was hoping to come upon the fugitives unawares.

'Yet you will do so. I don't intend to leave you here to warn your brother should he appear in my absence.'

Further argument would be fruitless, she knew. She fetched her cloak, and in silence, allowed her companion to lead her into the street. The storm of the previous night had cleared the air, and the first rays of the sun, breaking through cloud, brought the promise of a fine June day.

Georgiana's heart lifted, in spite of her fear that they might come upon Harry and Richard in the course of their promenade about the narrow streets. She would keep her wits about her. If the worst came to the worst, she could distract Lyndhurst's attention by pretending to faint. There was always the possibility that he would not be taken in. She must think of another stratagem.

She put up her hand to clutch at her bonnet as the wind threatened to tear it from her head. The gusts were fierce, and they stirred up swirling clouds of dust which settled upon bonnet, cloak, and even left a powdery grey deposit on the skirt of her primrose muslin gown. The gritty particles found their way beneath her eyelids, and she averted her head. The stinging sensation was unbearable. With watering eyes she felt in her reticule for a handkerchief.

'Don't rub at them. You will make matters worse.' Lyndhurst took the scrap of lace-edged cambric from her. 'Come here.' He drew her into the shelter of a doorway. 'Now let me see.'

His fingers were surprisingly gentle as he lifted her upper lids. 'Now keep quite still,' he ordered. 'Just moisten your handkerchief and give it to me. You have a cinder or something of the kind in your left eye.'

Georgiana did as she was bidden. His face was very close to hers, but she was in too much pain to refuse his help. His fingers were cool and infinitely careful as he held her face steady, prising open the eyelid again.

'Don't blink. There…I have it now. Is that better?'

Georgiana mopped her streaming eyes and blew her nose.

'It's a great relief,' she said with feeling. 'It felt like a mountain.'

'Just a speck of grit.'

There was an odd note in his voice and she looked up quickly to find that he was eyeing her with concern.

'I must look a perfect fright,' she muttered, more to herself than to him.

'Not at all! Apart from two reddened eyes and a swollen nose, you are your usual ravishing self.'

'Thank you!' She threw him an angry look, only to find that he was laughing. 'I fail to see what you find so amusing, my lord.'

'Just your injured dignity, my dear. When your feathers are ruffled you are quite enchanting.' He drew her arm through his. 'Shall we continue our walk?'

Georgiana was tempted to pull away from him, but he sensed her intention and laid his free hand on the arm resting within his own.

'I think not,' he said in a soft voice. 'Even your dignity would not withstand an unseemly fracas in the street.'

She had no alternative but to continue to pace

beside him, aware that he was matching his long stride to her shorter steps.

'Well, this is all very pleasant, Miss Westleigh. Sunshine, the sea air, and a beautiful woman on my arm. What more could a man ask? Such a pity that we are here on an unpleasant errand.'

A solitary figure strolling along the quayside towards them drew her attention. At first sight his dress was unremarkable. There was nothing in it to cause the passer-by to ignore his height, his handsome countenance, and the perfection of his bow as he drew abreast of them.

'Who is that man?' she asked in a low voice.

'That is George Brummell, Miss Westleigh. You are not acquainted with him?' The Viscount did not return the bow.

'I have not seen him before. He is unlike I imagined.'

The Viscount's laugh was unpleasant.

'You should study the set of his coat, the cut of his pantaloons, and the arrangement of his cravat. He is said to have employed two firms to make his gloves…one for the fingers and the other for the thumbs.' His tone left her in no doubt as to his opinion of a fellow who devoted his life to such trivialities.

'Poor soul!' Georgiana looked back at the lonely walker. 'It is sad indeed that after the life he has led he should be forced to flee to escape his creditors. I hear that he was a kindly man, thoughtful for his friends.'

'Save your pity for those he duped,' Lyndhurst said sharply. 'I suppose I should not be surprised at your fellow-feeling for him.'

'I'm sure he meant well.' Georgiana's temper flared. 'Many business ventures go awry.'

'They do. But a clear intention to steal a man's patrimony with the promise in return of an income for life cannot be excused.' His lips curled in contempt as he looked at her. 'You and your kind are leeches upon the gullible.'

He was baiting her again, and her temper rose further. 'That is of your own doing,' she told him. 'This "errand", as you term it, need not continue.'

'I think it must,' he said mildly. 'What would you have me do? Shall I turn tail and return to England, leaving you here to enjoy your ill-gotten gains?'

'We have no gains, and well you know it. We are stripped of everything. Is not that enough for you?'

'Not quite.'

'So you will have your pound of flesh?' It was

meant as an insult, but to her astonishment he threw back his head and roared with laughter.

'I see that I am discovered. Miss Westleigh, you underestimate yourself. I am persuaded that you weigh far more than a mere pound.'

His effrontery took Georgiana's breath away.

'Oh!' she cried. 'I might have known that you would seize every opportunity to insult me. I was quoting Shakespeare, sir. Have you not read *The Merchant of Venice?* The villain Shylock is not swayed by mercy or love of his fellow creatures. He means to destroy his victim utterly.'

'I could be persuaded to love my fellow creatures…or at least one of them.' Lyndhurst's eyes held a mischievous glint. 'And after all, Miss Westleigh, you indicated only an hour ago that my lust for you is obvious.'

'I said no such thing.' Georgiana coloured to the ears. 'It was just that…well, you had no right to…to…'

'To kiss you? But, my dear, you kissed me back. It was quite an experience. Your demure appearance gives no hint of the fires which burn below. Yet I should, perhaps, have guessed. Those flashing jade-green eyes, and that fiery mane of yours… Ah, yes, I should have guessed.'

Georgiana was speechless with embarrassment. She had been a fool to think herself safe with this man. His brother did not know him. This was no cold fish, but a passionate and demanding creature who would take his pleasure with a woman as it suited him.

She felt a twinge of fear, but whether it was fear of him, or of her own undoubted response to his caresses, she could not decide. Either way, she must escape from him at the earliest opportunity, or she would not answer for the consequences.

With an effort she forced herself to speak.

'You are mistaken in me, my lord, and your remarks are insulting. I have no…no experience of an embrace.' She could not look at him, but even as she spoke she knew that her words were a mistake.

Lyndhurst checked his stride and turned to face her. 'Then you must allow me to compliment you. Given an expert teacher an asset such as yours is beyond price.'

Georgiana's eyes filled with tears. It was a cruel gibe. Was she now to be despised for her natural feelings as a woman?

Blindly she threw out a hand as if to ward off a blow, and found it held in a firm clasp.

'We had best go back.' Lyndhurst's voice was raw with an emotion she could not place. He strode along, almost dragging her back to the inn, until she found herself running to keep up with him.

Ignoring the curious faces in the foyer, he hurried her up to their parlour and thrust her into a chair. Weariness overcame her as she looked at the clenched jaw and the grim line of his mouth. What had she done now to displease him?

'My lord, I am tired,' she whispered. 'I should like to go to my room.'

'Presently. But first I have something to say to you.'

Whatever it was, the Viscount seemed to be in some difficulty as to how to begin. He paced the room for several minutes. Then he thrust a clenched fist into the palm of his other hand and swung round to face her.

'You have succeeded in making me ashamed of myself, Miss Westleigh.' His smile was agonised. 'My behaviour was insufferable.'

Georgiana did not reply. She could not gainsay his words, and yet there seemed little point in agreeing with him.

'I cannot think why… Well, yes, I can… There

is nothing quite so ridiculous as a man at war with himself.'

Puzzled, she looked up at him then. The thick brown crop of hair was tousled, and a lock or two had fallen on to his brow. It gave him the look of a penitent schoolboy.

In spite of herself she smiled at the thought. Then he was on his knees beside her chair.

'Sometimes I forget how young you are,' he murmured. 'You had no need to tell me of your inexperience. An older woman would have made sport of me long since. But you…you do not guess?' Another long look and then he rose to his feet.

'Forgive me,' he said abruptly. 'I have no right to burden you with this nonsense. Suffice it to say that I should be horsewhipped for my incivility.'

Georgiana shot him a slanting glance from under her lashes.

'What a passion you have for horsewhips, sir! You have the instrument with you? I wonder if anyone would dare to use it?'

He gave her an uncertain look, and then an unwilling smile.

'You are generous to make a joke of this matter, Miss Westleigh. It is more than I deserve.'

'You are very hard on yourself, my lord. If we

all got what we deserved the world would be a strange place.' She smiled back at him. 'Now, if you will excuse me…?'

As she rose he moved towards her. For a second she thought that he would take her in his arms, but he checked himself, and bowed. Then he raised her hand to his lips.

'You are a pearl among women,' he said thickly. Then he was gone, leaving her with only the memory of his warm mouth against her flesh. Raising the hand to her cheek, she walked slowly into her bedroom.

She would never understand this stranger who had come without warning into her life.

He could be detestable. She was not surprised that his brother feared the flaying power of his tongue. From her own experience she knew that Lyndhurst could be deeply wounding when he suspected low moral standards in others. Her cheeks grew hot as she thought of his words to her.

Yet could she blame him? On the evidence she had supported her own brother without question, and still planned to do so. And, in spite of the Viscount's belief that she was little better than a criminal, he had been quick to apologise when he'd seen her distress.

He was the oddest mixture of contradictions. What on earth could he have meant by speaking of a man at war with himself? He found her physically attractive. He had made that only too clear. Was he fighting his own desire for a woman who had entrusted herself to his care?

Involuntarily Georgiana shook her head. His lordship, blessed as he was with title, wealth, and an imposing appearance, might have any number of women. He would think it beneath his dignity to force himself upon an unwilling partner.

Then what? Had he meant that he was beginning to change his mind as to the punishment he intended for Harry and his own brother? She doubted it. His face closed whenever he spoke of the two fugitives, and his words were openly contemptuous.

She worried at the question again. Why should a man be at war with himself? He seemed to think that she ought to know. It could not be that he was softening towards her...

Georgiana's eyes grew dreamy. It was not that she cared, of course, but it would be pleasant to think that he no longer regarded her as a liar and a cheat. He had looked so different when he had begged her pardon for his cruel words. The grim expression had given way to a look which was almost vulnerable... She had longed to throw her arms about him and hold him close as she forgave him.

She collected her wandering thoughts with a start. Her imagination was running wild. It was just that when he was close she felt an overwhelming urge to touch him, to stroke his cheek, to caress that unruly crop of thick brown hair, and to see the slow smile which began at the back of his eyes and grew until it seemed to envelop her in pleasure.

Great heavens! She was behaving like some foolish miss swept off her feet by a first kiss. The touch of his lips on her mouth had shaken her, but it had been meaningless. He had said so himself, but for her own part she found it hard to believe. Would she ever feel that surging, dizzying rapture with another man?

A growing sense of depression seized her. What a mess she and Harry had made of their lives. It was useless to dwell on what might have been, or even to hope that Lyndhurst thought better of her. When Harry found her she would flee with him, and all the Viscount's suspicion of her motives would be confirmed. Nothing she said or did would persuade him to trust her again, but it did not matter. She would have vanished from his life.

She felt so low in spirits that it was a relief

when Scroggins appeared with a message from Lyndhurst. His lordship had been called away, and she must dine alone.

A prickle of apprehension ran down Georgiana's spine. Had he received news of Richard and Harry?

'Is…is it something important?' she faltered. It went against the grain to question Scroggins, but she must know.

The man looked at her in silence, and she sensed his hostility.

'I asked you a question,' she said coldly.

'His lordship does not confide in me, madam. I fear I cannot help you.'

'Cannot or will not?' With a gesture of impatience she brushed past him. Lyndhurst might not yet have left for his appointment. She hurried along the corridor to the door of the adjoining room, but her quick knock brought no response.

'You will excuse me for addressing you, ma'am, but I believe that Viscount Lyndhurst is at present in the foyer.'

Georgiana looked round in surprise. The speaker was a tall, thin man dressed in the height of fashion. A clever, somewhat narrow face was crowned with a thatch of greying hair, but it was his eyes which held her attention. Their silver gaze was almost hypnotic. Not a man one would care to claim as an enemy, she thought at once.

With an effort she looked away and nodded her thanks. Then she sped down the stairs and into the crowded foyer.

From her vantage point on the bottom stair she scanned the bustling throng. As he was taller and broader than the men about him, she saw the Viscount at once, but to her dismay he was strolling towards the doorway which led into the street.

With muttered apologies for her haste she thrust her way towards him, attracting curious glances from those close to her.

'My lord?'

He turned at once and reached her side in a couple of swift strides.

'Is something wrong?'

'No, no…at least…when Scroggins gave me your message I thought you might have heard…'

A faint look of annoyance crossed his face. Her breathless words had carried to other ears, and for the moment they were the centre of attention.

Lyndhurst took her elbow and drew her into the relative privacy of a recess.

'You will not wish to conduct our conversation in public, I imagine, Miss Westleigh.' His eyes swept over her, and Georgiana was aware that she must present a dishevelled appearance, without bonnet or cloak, and still panting from her efforts to push through the crowd. She brushed such considerations aside.

'You would tell me, wouldn't you?' she pleaded.

'I have heard nothing.' His voice was cold initially. Then it softened in the face of her evident anxiety. 'I received an invitation to dine at the British Consulate. I take it I have your permission to see my friends there?'

Georgiana hung her head and her cheeks grew rosy.

'I'm sorry,' she whispered. 'I would not have you think that I spy upon your every movement.'

'That would be foolish,' he agreed. 'Now may I suggest that you return to your room? You are looking fagged and much in need of rest...' He took her arm in a firm grip and steered her back through the crowds towards the staircase.

As he raised his hat to leave her she made a final plea.

'My lord, should you hear of Harry and Richard, will you give me your word that you will do nothing until you have spoken to me?'

Lyndhurst gave her a long, considering look. Then his lips twitched. 'What will you do, my pretty tigress, to save them from my wrath?'

She could not answer him.

'Think about it,' he advised. 'Meantime, you may have my word that when they are discovered you shall be the first to hear of it.'

It was scant comfort, but at least she had his promise. As she started up the stairs she had a curious sensation of being watched. She turned, to find that the man who had spoken to her earlier was standing in the shadow of the stairwell.

A little shiver ran down her spine. Somehow his presence in Calais troubled her. How had the stranger known that she was seeking Lyndhurst? He must have asked the landlord for the direction of the Viscount's room, yet he had not claimed acquaintance of his lordship.

It was a mystery. The man was no dun, she was sure of it. He looked every inch the gentleman. Could he be one of Harry's victims? It seemed unlikely. The stranger had a predatory look about him. At a guess he would be the attacker rather than the victim.

She could feel his eyes following her as she climbed the stairs, and suddenly she longed for the comfort of Lyndhurst's presence. In his company she always felt so safe.

She should have told him at once about the stranger, but there had been no time. In any case he most probably would have laughed her to scorn for allowing her imagination to run wild. The man's rooms could well be on the same corridor, and he might have seen Lyndhurst leaving his room. What more natural that he should ask the name of a fellow Englishman? That the stranger was English she had no doubt.

Having reasoned away her fears, she entered her private parlour to find that a light nuncheon had been laid for her. Still lost in thought, she took a little of the cold meats and salad, but it tasted like ashes in her mouth. She must be over-tired. Lyndhurst himself had said that she was looking fagged.

She was amused in spite of her indignation at the frank remark. One might expect nothing but the plain, unvarnished truth from his lordship.

She pushed her plate away and wandered into her bedroom. There she looked thoughtfully at her reflection in the glass. Lyndhurst had not exaggerated. Her eyes looked larger than ever in the piquant face, but dark circles had appeared beneath them.

She felt unutterably weary, and without troubling to remove her gown she lay upon the bed. She should have been making plans, but how could she plan when she had no word of Harry? Lyndhurst would keep her close, and how was she to escape his vigilance?

It was strange that the thought of leaving him gave her no pleasure. After all, she had accomplished the first part of her mission. She was here in Calais, but what was she to do now?

She closed her eyes, allowing her thoughts to drift. It was all too much effort, and she was very tired. If she rested now her mind would clear.

It was early evening when she awoke, and the bustle in the street outside had lessened. She struggled to sit up as the door opened and Betsy arrived with a pile of clothing over her arm.

'I've washed your underclothing, miss, and pressed your gowns.' Betsy's cheeks were flushed and her eyes were sparkling. She had evidently recovered her spirits.

Georgiana smiled her thanks. 'Will you ring for hot water, Betsy? I feel so grubby. Then you may help me dress.'

With the girl's help she made her toilette, shaking her head as she looked at her meagre wardrobe. She had packed so quickly in her haste to get away. Had she really only brought three thin gowns? She shrugged. The leaf-green muslin would have to do again. It did not matter. She would be alone for the rest of what promised to be a long and dreary evening.

Never had the time seemed to go so slowly. Georgiana attempted to do justice to the excellent meal which was served at nine, but she could do no more than toy with the food.

Then she picked up a copy of *La Belle Assemblée,* thoughtfully provided by the landlord, but the fashions did not interest her. Half-heartedly she made an effort to translate the text. If she and Harry were to live in France she must improve her halting, schoolgirl efforts to understand the language.

It was in vain. She could not concentrate, and the room seemed so stuffy. Did the French never open their windows?

She remembered the balcony outside her bedroom window. There, at least, she could enjoy the fresh air. She returned to her room and flung the windows wide. It was a heavenly night, with a crescent moon and a scattering of stars in the summer sky.

Georgiana dragged a chair outside and sat lost in thought for what seemed like hours. What was to become of Harry and herself? She could find no comforting solution to her problems, but she must not think of the long, lonely years ahead. She had not thought to end her days as a spinster, but she and Harry were inextricably tied together. She could never leave him.

The air was growing chill. She left her seat on the balcony, leaving the window open. She was about to ring for Betsy when a sudden noise alerted her.

'Don't touch the bell!' Harry was smiling as he stepped through the open windows. 'How are you, my dear?'

Chapter Five

'Harry!' With a muffled sob Georgiana stumbled towards him, holding out both her hands. 'I've been so worried about you.'

Harry gave her a brotherly hug, and tweaked at a copper curl. 'No need to get into a taking, Georgie. All is well.'

'All is far from well,' she cried in exasperation. 'You do not realise…Lyndhurst is here in Calais. He is searching for Richard, and for you too.'

'I had heard, but I'm not afraid of him.' His words lacked conviction, and his bravado cost him an effort, but he forced another smile. 'What can he do? He could scarce carry us bodily back to England.'

'Don't be foolish! At the very least he has promised you a horsewhipping.'

Harry's smile vanished and he paled. 'Why did you lead him to us?' he demanded. 'And what are you doing in his company anyway?'

'I had no choice. Without him I could not have come here.' She gave him the gist of her story in pithy terms and he had the grace to look ashamed.

'I had no idea, else I would not have left you.'

'That is the trouble, Harry. To say that you had no idea is not an excuse worth considering. Is it not time you showed some common sense?'

'Don't preach!' His face grew sullen. 'Your sound like Lyndhurst himself.'

Georgiana bit back the words which were upon her tongue. There was no point in quarrelling with him.

'How did you find me?' she asked.

'I have my sources.' The injured expression still lingered on his face. It had come as a shock to be criticised so sharply by his adoring elder sister.

Georgiana ignored it. She felt too irritated to attempt to wheedle him into a better humour. Instead she changed the subject.

'Lyndhurst is not our only worry,' she said quietly. 'There is another Englishman in the hotel. I fear he has been watching me.'

To her surprise he smiled. 'Tall and thin, with greying hair?'

'Why, yes! Do you know him?'

'I told you I had sources.' He had not given her a direct answer, and his evasive reply did nothing to reassure her.

'Did you meet him in London? What is his name?' Every instinct warned her against the mysterious stranger. She sensed that he was a dangerous man. If he was an example of Harry's latest friends her brother's future, and her own, promised to be disastrous.

Harry made a gesture of impatience. 'Must you quiz me now? Lyndhurst may be back at any moment.' He glanced towards the door. In spite of his protestations she guessed that he would not relish a meeting with the Viscount.

'His lordship dines at the British Consulate,' she said in a cool tone. 'We shall be undisturbed. Now, Harry, what are we to do?'

'We must get away, of course. Calais is too close to England, and too dangerous. In Paris we might lose ourselves among the crowd.'

'Lyndhurst will follow you,' Georgiana observed quietly.

'Well, then Rome…or Vienna… It cannot signify. In a large city we may hide…'

'A hole-and-corner existence? How are we to live?'

An angry retort rose to his lips, but a glance at her face stemmed the bitter words before he spoke.

'You are tired, dear love.' Privately he was appalled to see the dark circles beneath her eyes and her look of strain. He sat down suddenly and buried his face in his hands.

'Oh, Georgie, I am so sorry,' he said in a muffled voice. 'I did not intend to drag you down with me.'

She laid a hand upon the flaming curls so like her own. 'I fear we shall have to dye our hair, my dear. This colour is like a beacon in a crowd.'

Harry looked up then, to see a faint smile on her face. She bent and kissed his brow.

'When do we leave?' she asked.

He was on his feet at once, his eyes alight with eagerness.

'Tomorrow night,' he announced. 'There is no time to lose, and Richard is in a state because of Lyndhurst.'

'I can imagine.' Georgiana's voice was dry, but Harry did not notice.

'I believe old sourpuss keeps you close,' he continued. 'You must plead illness or some such thing. Then you may keep to your room, although we cannot travel in daylight. I'll come for you about this time tomorrow.'

Strangely, the thought gave her no pleasure.

'Is there no other way?' she asked without much hope. 'The Viscount must have some family feeling. If Richard were to see him and explain…'

Harry stared at her. 'Have you run quite mad? You told me yourself that he thinks only in terms of a horsewhipping. Dear God!' He threw his eyes to heaven. 'To expect a hearing from that prune-faced…'

Georgiana lost her temper then, and her face grew white with anger. 'Must you be so childish?' she demanded coldly. 'Name-calling? You might be five years old…'

'Never say that he has brought you to his way of thinking. That stiff-necked model of rectitude… He is filled with righteous anger, I suppose?'

'And has he not cause? Harry, he mentioned fraud.'

'Stuff! What does he know of our affairs?'

'Quite a lot, it would appear. Is it true that you took large sums of money on a promise of annual payments?'

'It is accepted practice.' His face was sullen. 'Brummell and his friends had a similar scheme…'

'And Brummell is now in a similar position to you. We saw him today. He is disgraced. No one will acknowledge him.'

'By that I imagine you mean that Lyndhurst found it necessary to cut him dead in case a simple greeting might pollute his noble character?'

Georgiana ignored the taunt. 'Brummell can never return to England, Harry. He is forced into exile, as we are ourselves. Oh, my dear, how could you have been so foolish? And to cheat people of their savings…'

A dark flush stained Harry's cheeks. He was unused to such plain speaking from his sister. In her eyes he could do non wrong—or at least he'd thought so until now…

'How do you think we lived?' he said defensively. 'We had the house in London. You enjoyed the balls and entertainments…to say nothing of your dressmakers' bills.'

'I had rather have gone in rags.' She turned away from him. 'You deceived me, Harry. Did you not say that you won thousands at the tables?'

He was saved from the need to reply by a tap at the door. Georgiana looked at him in dismay.

'Quickly!' She pushed him towards the window. 'Hide behind the curtains. I'll send Betsy away.'

But her late-night visitor was the Viscount. He stood in the doorway smiling down at her.

'Forgive me for troubling you at this hour, but I saw your light from the street. I thought you might sleep better for the knowledge that our erring relatives have been seen in Calais…'

Georgiana was silent.

'My dear, you are trembling. Am I such an ogre, then?'

Her eyes were huge with fright as she looked into his own, and a troubled frown creased his brow.

'I see that I am,' he said abruptly. 'Believe me, Miss Westleigh, I wish only what is best for both our families. May I ask you to give me your trust?'

Speechless, she nodded her assent.

'Then I will wish you a good night's rest.' He looked beyond her to the open window, and as if in a trance she followed his gaze. Was it a breeze that stirred the curtains?

'You should close your window,' he murmured. 'The air is chill.'

As Georgiana closed her door her brother appeared from behind the curtains.

'I hope you don't believe a word of that charming speech,' he snapped. 'Trust him to do what is best indeed!'

'I do trust him.' Georgiana lost the last traces of her self-control. 'He, at least, is a man who keeps his word.'

Harry went very white about the lips. The blow had struck home.

'No, please!' She put a weary hand to her head. 'I did not mean that to sound so harsh, but, you see, I cannot complain of the Viscount's care for me.'

'With at least one purpose in mind…that of finding us. I wonder if he had another…?'

He was unprepared for her stinging slap across his cheek.

'How dare you?' she cried furiously. 'You left me to fend for myself.'

Harry had the grace to look ashamed. 'I was angry, and I spoke in haste,' he muttered. 'Of course I did not think that you…that he… That dry stick! I doubt if he's ever looked at a woman in his life. I beg your pardon. Georgie, dear, I'm not myself tonight.'

When she did not reply he stole a glance at her, but she averted her head.

'I didn't mean that he wouldn't be tempted by you,' he offered. 'That would be an insult…but…'

'Harry, you are making matters worse.' Georgiana was torn between laughter and tears. 'You had best go before you get deeper into the mire...'

'Then I am forgiven?' He threw an arm about her shoulders. 'We must stick together, love. You are all I have in the world.'

'I know.' She put up her face for a kiss, though her heart was filled with despair. 'Don't worry... I shall be ready when you come.'

She heard a faint scuffle as he lowered himself by the creeper outside her window, and then a low thud as he dropped into the street. With a sigh she closed the curtains, and began to struggle out of her gown. It was much too late to ring for Betsy. The girl would be long asleep, and she hadn't the heart to wake her. In any case, she needed time to collect her thoughts.

Since his unreserved apology earlier in the day, Lyndhurst's manner towards her had been different. It was softer, gentler and more tolerant. Oh, if only she'd had more time. She might have persuaded him to forgive Harry and his brother.

It was too late now. The die was cast. She would have but one more day in his company, and then he would vanish from her life forever.

She slipped into her bedrobe and lay down, but sleep would not come. To her horror she found that slow tears were beginning to trickle down her cheeks. What a fool she was! She should have been elated. Had she not achieved her object in coming to France? She had found Harry, and now they were to start their new life together, safe in some European city.

The prospect had no power to lift her spirits. She could think only of the long years ahead, living from hand to mouth, and relying only on Harry's ability to provide for her. Would he resort to underhand dealings again?

Sadly, she realised that she could no longer trust him. Her idol had feet of clay, and she herself was partly to blame for his cavalier attitude to life. Her unquestioning support had done him no service. Her affection had blinded her to his faults, but now she saw them only too clearly.

She would have to think for both of them, and keep him on a steady path if possible. It would be a daunting task, and the thought of it was too much for her tired mind.

Weariness overcame her and she drifted into sleep at last with the memory of a pair of clear blue eyes gazing into her own.

* * *

She awoke to find that sunlight was filing the room. In the few seconds before full consciousness returned she stretched luxuriously, fully prepared to enjoy the pleasure of a perfect summer day. Then she remembered, and her spirits sank. Today was to end in a parting which she could only dread. But why?

Swiftly, she tried to control her unguarded thoughts, but it was no longer possible to deceive herself. She loved Lyndhurst with a passion which shook her to the core of her being.

Since Harry's disgrace she had not thought it possible to feel more wretched, but now she could have screamed in agony. Her happiness was to be thrown away...for what? Why had she ever met that cool, imperious figure who could raise her to the heights of rapture with a kiss, or crush her with a frown? She must stop thinking about him, and above all she must not betray herself. He would only despise her the more.

She should have insisted on leaving with Harry on the previous evening, she thought to herself. That way she might have escaped the torture which awaited her in the coming hours. It seemed that she was to be spared none of it.

Betsy confirmed her fears.

'I was to tell his lordship when you wakened, miss.' Betsy had drawn the curtains and was laying out Georgiana's clothes. 'He's waiting for you in the parlour. Must I go now?'

Georgiana drew a deep breath. 'I shall not be long, though he should not wait to break his fast. I find that I am not hungry.'

Her eye fell on the white sprigged muslin hanging by the door. It had always been a favourite gown, but now it looked much too festive for her sombre mood.

'I can't wear that,' she muttered.

Betsy's face fell. 'Miss, it's all you've got. You lay on your bed in one of your gowns, and the other needs a wash.'

'Very well. Come back when you've seen his lordship.'

Quickly she bathed her face and hands, hoping that the warm, scented water would restore her spirits. She did feel a little better as she dressed, but how was she to get through the day without betraying herself? She might hide her emotions with some success, but she feared Lyndhurst's piercing gaze. Surely he would suspect that something was amiss?

When she entered the parlour he was standing

by the window, but he turned at once. His expression was a tribute to her beauty. He walked towards her and took her hand.

'I did not obey your orders,' he said lightly. 'There is something too depressing about dining alone.'

With grave courtesy he seated her at the table, and signalled to the waiting servants.

Georgiana was tempted to refuse the shirred eggs, the pink, succulent slices of ham, and the kidneys in Madeira, but she dared not. He gave her a long, considering glance.

'There is still room for improvement,' he said at last. 'Miss Westleigh, I propose to take you for a drive this morning. The day is fine, the wind has dropped, and you look much in need of a change.'

His words were kindly meant. How could he know that he was turning the knife in the wound? Had she not hoped that he would have other plans, which would take him out of her sight? Her heart gave her the lie. Every moment together would be cherished and remembered for the rest of her life. Still she demurred.

'You do not wish to make further enquiries...about Richard and Harry?'

He gave her a heart-stopping smile.

'My dear Miss Westleigh, our youthful relatives are beginning to bore me. Let us forget them for today. Enough is enough, you will agree?'

'But...'

'No buts... We have concerned ourselves with them for too long. Is it too much to ask that we allow a few hours for ourselves?'

'It is kind in you, but...' She hesitated, and then went on in a rush. 'My lord, you must not feel obliged... I am quite well. It is just that I have not...'

'You have not been sleeping easily? That, my dear, is plain to see. But you promised to trust me, did you not? Will you leave matters in my hands?'

Georgiana could not look at him. His voice was so gentle that she felt like bursting into tears. If only she might have persuaded Harry and Richard to speak to him. They would feel the rough edge of his tongue, and it would be an unpleasant interview, but Lyndhurst, she was now convinced, would find a way out of their difficulties.

When she did not reply he reached across the table and took her hand in his. 'Georgiana, look at me! Do you still believe that I wish you harm?'

It was the first time he had used her given name, and she felt a little glow of happiness. Obediently, she raised her eyes to his and shook her head. That question, at least, she could answer truthfully.

She left her hand in his, longing to curl her fingers about his own. Did he guess at the inner turmoil which swept her every time he touched her? She prayed that he did not. At that moment she could have thrown herself into his arms and told him everything.

But that would mean betraying Harry, and she had given her word to leave with him that very night. She grew cold at the thought of the deception which she planned to carry out against the man she loved so much.

She had been such a fool. She should have pleaded sickness…a headache…anything to avoid the sweet torture of these last few hours with him. It was not too late to make some excuse to return to her room.

She wavered, but as the blue eyes locked with her own she was lost. Just a few more hours of happiness? It was little enough to carry with her in memory through the years ahead.

She was surprised to see a high-perch phaeton at the door, but the Viscount handed her up without comment and took the reins himself.

'You are warm enough?' He tucked a rug about

her knees. Then he guided the team through the narrow streets of Calais towards the open countryside.

Wretched though she was at the thought of her deception, Georgiana felt her spirits lift as they bowled along. The sky was a cloudless blue, and she could smell the salt sea air. High above the wheeling gulls called harshly as they swooped towards the returning fishing boats, and she smiled at their effortless skill.

'I cannot promise you much in the way of scenery.' Lyndhurst had turned inland. 'This part of France is somewhat bleak and featureless, but further south… Ah, there you may see this country at its best.'

'It does not matter.' Georgiana looked up at him shyly. 'I am happy to be here.'

He stopped the carriage at once. A strong hand rested on her shoulder and he turned her round towards him.

'Are you?' The steady eyes searched her face. 'Then so am I.' A lean finger reached up to smooth away a straying copper curl. 'My dear, I have given you no cause to think of me with kindness, but I could wish…'

'Please don't,' she cried in panic. 'Do not say more.'

'Why not?' He had drawn her close, and his lips were nuzzling her cheek. 'Georgiana, my darling, have you not guessed how much I care for you? God knows I have been behaving like a lunatic these last few days, blaming myself for ending my own hopes with my cruelty towards you, and yet hoping that you might see…'

'I did not suspect, else I should not have come,' she told him in a muffled voice. 'Please take me back to Calais.'

This was worse than she could possibly have imagined. To be offered the promise of happiness beyond her dreams only to reject it? The anguish was unbearable.

'My dearest!' He was dropping light kisses upon her brow, her eyelids and her cheeks. 'Can I have been mistaken? Will you deny that when we kissed you felt as I did? There is a bond between us which cannot be broken.'

'You told me that the kiss was meaningless.' It cost her an effort to speak with a lightness she was far from feeling.

'I was lying, as much to myself as to you. I fought my love with all my mind but my heart will be still no longer. My darling Georgiana, will you be my wife?'

'I cannot.' She turned her head too quickly and he claimed her lips. Again she was borne on a dizzying tide of rapture as the warm mouth rested on her own. A warm, unfamiliar sensation swept through her body, urging her to a greater closeness. Of her own volition she threw her arms about his neck, arching her back as he bent over her. By the time he released her she was breathless.

'You are a witch.' He looked down tenderly at her rosy face. 'Will you tease me further by saying that you do not care for me?'

Wildly, Georgiana cast about for some answer that would satisfy him.

'You must give me time,' she pleaded in a low voice.

Even to her own ears the words sounded feeble, but she could think of nothing else to say. It was too late to deny her love. Her own response to him would have given her the lie.

'There is much to consider,' she murmured at last, aware of his sharp eyes on her face.

'Still thinking of your precious Harry?' His tone was sardonic, but she sensed the hurt behind his words.

'I must think of him,' she replied. 'I cannot abandon him. He has no one else who cares…'

'I shall not harm him. That, at least, you must believe.'

'I do.' The temptation to confide in him was overwhelming, but she resisted it. 'I asked only for a little time…'

'As you wish.' He gave her a faint smile, and picked up the reins once more. He was silent for the rest of their drive, and Georgiana was left to the scant comfort of her own thoughts.

She had made up her mind before the returned to the inn. When Harry returned that night she would make him see reason. If she could but convince him that he might trust Lyndhurst he would give up his ridiculous plans to scratch a living in some foreign city.

And Richard would follow his lead. Even on brief acquaintance with the Viscount's brother she had learned that Harry was the stronger character of the two. Though that was not saying much, she would admit.

Her face cleared. The very fact of coming to a decision had lightened her heart. She had no idea how Lyndhurst meant to handle the situation, and he had given her no indication, but she was sure that he would find a solution.

She stole a glance at his clean-cut profile. As if

sensing her regard he looked down at her and the blue eyes held hers captive.

'As I expected, our drive has done you good,' he said gently. 'The shadows have disappeared, my dear. I intend to see that they never return. It breaks my heart to see you in distress.'

'You are very good.' She rested a gloved hand upon his arm. 'You must not believe that I am behaving like some schoolroom miss, my lord. I did not intend to sound so…so formal.'

He swung down and reached up his arms for her. 'Your formality slipped a little, I believe.' He laughed as she began to blush. 'At least you were kind enough not to tell me that my proposal was so sudden, or that you thanked me for the honour I had done you. Words such as those would have ended my hopes at once.'

Georgiana gave him a sweet smile. Her flushed cheeks and her sparkling eyes betrayed her love as clearly as if she had shouted it aloud. Eagerly he moved towards her, but she shook her head and hurried into the hotel. She must speak to Harry first.

The hours which she had dreaded so were now a golden time, and her heart was singing in her breast. Lyndhurst loved her. She marvelled at the thought. She had not imagined such joy could exist.

She felt as if all her worries had been lifted from her shoulders. Harry could be persuaded, she was sure of it. She had always been able to coax him into her way of thinking in the past.

She bathed her face and hands, and tugged a brush through her flaming curls. Her reflection in the mirror showed her a girl in possession of a wonderful secret. So this was love? She had heard of it, even dreamed of it, but none of the poets she had read had come close to describing the rapture which filled her soul.

Lyndhurst moved towards her as she entered the little parlour, but he did not attempt to take her in his arms. It required iron self-control, but he would keep his part of the bargain, she knew. And it was as well. In his arms she could not trust herself to deny him the answer for which he hoped.

'May I hope that you have regained your appetite?' he said lightly. 'The chef, so I hear, is on his mettle today.'

Rumour had not lied. Georgiana allowed herself to be helped to a delicately flavoured fish soup, followed by a timbale of macaroni *à la napolitaine*. Beef with glazed vegetables followed, and, for the first time in days, she was surprised to find that she could do full justice to the meal. Even so, she was forced to refuse the offer of a charlotte, delicious though it looked.

She had feared at first that after the Viscount's words of love she might feel embarrassed in his presence, but it was not so.

With easy camaraderie he kept the conversation going, avoiding dangerous topics, and speaking only of the country in which they found themselves.

It was clear that he knew it well, and she listened avidly as he told her of the castles of the Loire, the rich countryside of the Dordogne, and the sunbaked beauty of Provence.

'One day I will take you there,' he promised. 'The way of life by the Mediterranean Sea has a subtle charm. The moon is huge, and the nights are warm. It is a land for lovers…'

'My lord, you must not…'

'Georgiana, my name is Edward. Will you not bring yourself to use it? I long to hear it on your lips.'

'Very well, then…Edward. Forgive me, but you have not told me what you mean to do about…about Richard and Harry.' She was loath to break the spell in which he held her, but she had to know his answer.

'I have given it much thought.' He did not seem

irritated by the question. 'Richard, I believe, should be removed from the temptations of city life.

'The fault is mine. I should have seen the danger long ago. Idle hands, a fast set of friends, and no responsibilities... It was a recipe for disaster from the first. I propose to send him out to the West Indies. He may learn to manage my estates.'

'And Harry?' she breathed.

'No, not Harry, my dear. Those two striplings are best apart. But I have an interest in the East India Company. Would he consider a position there?'

A wave of relief swept over Georgiana. 'You are much too good,' she cried warmly. 'Oh, Edward, why did you not tell me of your plans? You led me to believe that you would treat them harshly.'

'They may be glad to put an ocean or two between us when they've heard what I have to say,' he murmured drily. 'But, my dear, I could not tell you what I intended before I was certain of your feelings. I would have you love me on your own account. I had no wish to pressure you by offering to help Harry.'

'And you are certain now?' Long lashes veiled her eyes, but she shot him a slanting glance.

'Yes, my lovely minx, I am quite certain.' His

hand rested lightly on her shoulder, and she felt the warmth through the thin fabric of her gown. 'What a temptress you are! Will you still keep me waiting for my answer?'

Before she could reply Scroggins tapped on the door and entered the room. He bore a message on a silver salver, and the contents caused a frown to crease the Viscount's brow. He muttered something beneath his breath, and ordered his carriage at once.

'I must leave you again, I fear,' he said heavily.

'More mysteries?' Secure in the knowledge of his love, Georgiana smiled as she looked up at him. Nothing could harm her now.

'Nothing too dreadful, I assure you, but my business may take some time.'

'Then I shall have an early night.' She allowed him to kiss her hand, returning the pressure of his fingers with her own.

'Until tomorrow, then?' The deep voice was a caress and she could not mistake the glow of tenderness in his eyes.

'Until tomorrow,' she answered shyly. It was at once a farewell and a promise. Tomorrow she would give him his answers She would agree to become his wife.

Chapter Six

For the rest of that long summer evening Georgiana sat dreaming by her window. As day faded into dusk the western skies were suffused with light from the last rays of the sun. Gold and purple, apricot and magenta streaked the heavens, and the glory of the spectacle seemed to match the rapture in her heart.

She looked about her in wonder. She had not thought that the world could look so different. The chair on which she sat, the small table by her side, even the gleaming flowers of the summer jasmine clinging to the balcony, had taken on a new appearance…a new intensity. She felt that she was seeing them fully for the first time.

Edward loved her. Even now she could not quite

believe it. When had he first known? She could re-call each word they had exchanged since their first meeting. There had been quarrels, misunderstand-ings, and at times she had hated him. Yet beneath it all she had never doubted his strength of character.

Was that why she loved him? Now she would always be cherished and protected by a man who put his honour above all else. Yet her own security had never weighed with her.

A little frisson of excitement caused her cheeks to burn. Life with Edward as her lover would never be dull. She adored everything about him. A soft little smile warmed her face. He was infinitely dear to her.

She stirred impatiently in her chair. She could not wait to see him again, and from tomorrow she would not be so cold. She would caress that tou-sled head as she had always longed to do, and kiss each finger of those long, graceful hands in turn.

Was it the deep voice that gave him much of his charm? She could not decide. Perhaps it was the slow smile which began deep in those clear blue eyes and grew until it enveloped both of them in a private world of their own.

A breeze stirred the straying tendrils of her hair, and she came back to reality with a start. It was growing chill. She was about to go indoors when she sensed a movement below her balcony. She turned as Harry's head appeared above the balustrade.

His greeting was brief as he stepped into the room and looked about him.

'Where is your bag?' he asked.

'I haven't packed.' Georgiana faced him squarely. 'Harry, we must talk…'

'Not now, for heaven's sake! Georgie, you must see the need for haste, and you promised to be ready…' Muttering beneath his breath, he strode over to a tall chest, opened a drawer, and began to throw her clothing on the bed.

'Wait! I have something to say to you.'

'You may say it whilst you put your things together. Women!' He threw his eyes to the ceiling.

'Sit down!' his sister said quietly. 'This is important.'

Something in her tone made him pause and stare at her. He knew that expression of old. The determined set of her chin convinced him that he had no choice but to listen to her.

He sighed and made an ostentatious show of consulting his watch. 'What is it?' The words were said with an air of patient resignation.

'Harry, we need not leave. Lyndhurst has offered to help both Richard and yourself if you will but agree to meet him.'

Harry's mouth fell open, and for a moment he seemed to have lost the power of speech. Then Georgiana heard an ugly laugh.

'Some hopes of that! Can't you see that he intends to trick you into betraying us? He would say anything to get his way.' A thought struck him and he paled. 'You did not tell him I was coming here tonight?'

'Of course not! But Harry, you are mistaken in him. I do not believe that he means to harm us.' A faint blush coloured her cheeks.

'So that's it!' Harry's sharp eyes had not missed her slight confusion. 'I might have known. Well, he's a plausible devil, I'll give you that. I could tell you stories…'

'Be quiet!' she snapped. 'I will not have you speak ill of him when he thinks only of my…of our welfare.'

'Good God, Georgie, you can't have formed a *tendre* for him? That would be all we need. My dear, there was a woman years ago… Well, all the world knows that he is a brute.'

'I don't believe you.' Georgiana gave him a long considering glance. 'Did you not assure me that the Viscount was too cold a fish ever to look at a woman?' She spoke bravely, but her voice was shaking. She, above anyone, had cause to know of the Viscount's passionate nature.

'I was angry and I lied.' Harry's face was sullen. 'In any case, I did not wish to frighten you. I could not offer to take you away until tonight, but I was worried, Georgie. It was a shock to find you in his company. I hope… Well, I hope that you have not had to suffer his advances…'

'Edward has asked me to be his wife.' The words were out and the silence in the room grew tangible. 'Harry, I love him. Will you not wish me happiness?'

'It would be a waste of breath.' Her brother's expression was remote. 'I can't say that I blame you, though. He will use you ill, but doubtless the rewards will be worth it. They are more than I can offer you.'

Georgiana was shocked by his bitterness, but she would not reproach him.

'I had not considered the rewards, my dear. Is it so strange that I should wish to marry the man who is my happiness?'

'You are deceived in him. This is first love. It's naught but an illusion. You have no experience…'

'I know my own heart.'

'And I no longer have a place in it?'

She detected the undertone of jealousy.

'My dearest, this is different. As for you and me, we shall always be close.' She gave him a pleading smile. 'We have been through so much together.'

'You need not remind me of your sacrifices on my behalf, even if you choose to throw them up at me.'

'I am doing no such thing!' Georgiana finally lost all patience. 'Harry, you are behaving like a spoilt child. Will you not listen to reason for once in your life?'

Her anger jolted him into a new approach.

'I thought I came first in your affections,' he mourned. 'Georgie, you are all I have. How shall I go on without you?'

'You might learn to stand on your own feet,' came the tart reply. 'Edward has offered to find you a place with the East India Company.'

'I won't take his charity.' Harry's sulky expression deepened. 'You shall not sell yourself on my account.'

Georgiana was tempted to slap him, but she forced herself to stay calm.

'It won't be charity,' she said lightly. 'I understand that conditions are hard in India. The agents of the Company earn their stipend, but it would be an adventure. Do you not long to travel to the East?'

She had caught his interest, and he lifted his head.

'Who knows?' she continued with a cheerful smile. 'You might even become a nabob.'

'And Richard will go too?'

Georgiana shook her head. 'Edward hopes that Richard may learn to manage the family estates in the West Indies.'

'I see. He does not trust us together, is that it?' His sneering tone had returned.

'Harry, this is such an opportunity for you. Will you not take it?'

'I can't.' He had turned away from her, his shoulders hunched in despair.

'Why ever not? At least you might discuss it with Edward.'

'Georgie, you don't understand. Even if I cared to face him, it would be useless.'

'I don't see why...'

'Of course you don't see. How could you? If you must have the truth of it, I am not my own master...'

She could only gaze at him in bewilderment.

'What can you mean? The offer has been made to you...'

'And I am not free to take it.'

'My dearest, what on earth is to stop you doing so?'

'Not what, but who.' He could not meet her eyes. 'There is a man... Well, Richard and I are bound to him in a way...'

A chill struck Georgiana to the heart.

'What have you kept from me?' she cried. 'Who is this man?'

'You have seen him,' he said in a low voice. 'You mentioned him to me last night.'

He had no need to go on. Georgiana remembered only too clearly the still, reptilian gaze of the stranger who had watched her so intently.

'What is he to you?' Terror seized her as she waited for his answer.

Harry buried his face in his hands. 'It was he...Merton...who suggested a way of raising money. At first it seemed above-board. Richard and I...well, we had always intended to honour our commitments. Merton was the banker. He's a wealthy man, and he understands finance. It was just that...well, when we needed the money for the annuities we found that it wasn't there.'

'What was his explanation?' A slow tide of anger rose in Georgiana's breast.

'He mentioned bad investments. And, of course, he had given us some of the money as commission.'

'He is more to blame than you,' she cried hotly. 'That a man of his experience should seek to dupe you! Let me tell Edward. He will know what to do. Merton should be prosecuted.'

'He is too clever for that. His name did not appear in any of our dealings.'

'No matter! Edward will challenge him and force him to return the money.'

'No!' Harry's voice had risen to a shout and for the first time she saw real fear in his eyes. 'Keep Lyndhurst out of this as you value his life. You do not know Merton. He has threatened to kill us if we betray him, and he will keep his word.'

Georgiana needed no convincing. At first sight she had sensed an aura of evil about the mysterious stranger. Her brain was reeling, but she would not give up hope of saving Harry.

'Then you have all the more reason for leaving for the East,' she cried. 'He cannot trace you there, nor would he find Richard in the West Indies.'

'We should never reach the ship.' Harry was very pale. 'Merton has spies… He would murder us without compunction.'

'Even if you promised him your silence? I give you my word that I shall not mention him to Edward, though I should dearly love to do so.'

'He would laugh in your face. Besides, he has other plans for us.'

Her fear now matched his own as she looked at his bent head. She tried to speak, but at first the words would not come.

'Tell me!' she forced out at last.

'He intends to set us up in another city.' Harry would not meet her eyes. 'We can still be useful to him. People trust us, you see, and Merton will not give up the chance of more rich pickings.'

'You shall not do it,' Georgiana said with decision. 'You must have nothing more to do with him. Let him try to harm you and Edward will—'

'Lyndhurst cannot protect us every moment of the day and night. Will you risk his life too?'

Her silence gave him his answer. He rose to his feet, swept her clothing together, and crammed it into her bag.

'I won't go with you.' She snatched it from him. 'Have you thought at all about our future? Are we to live the life of criminals, with the thought of capture always in our minds?'

'I have thought of nothing else.' His face revealed his agony of mind. 'But Georgie, you must come with me. Merton has seen you. He feels that you…'

'That I will help to dupe his victims?' She saw from his expression that she was right. 'I won't do it, Harry.'

'It was not a suggestion. Merton has made up his mind.'

'Then let him try to take me. I promise you he will regret it.'

'And so would you. You have not seen him in a rage. I do not believe him to be quite normal.'

'Splendid!' In her fear and rage Georgiana lashed out at him. 'A lunatic? How carefully you choose your friends, my dear!'

'Georgie, don't.' Harry took her hands in his. 'If we go together now we may yet find a way to escape him.'

'Very well.' She felt as if her heart had turned to stone as she made the decision, but she could see no alternative. She would risk neither Harry's life nor Edward's, though she was throwing away her only hope of happiness.

If she left now, Edward would think that she had gone of her own free will. He would never trust her again. All his previous suspicions would be confirmed, and he would despise her even more for the false promise of love she had offered.

An iron band of anguish constricted her chest

as she took a last look around the pretty room. At that moment she felt that her life was over.

Harry was already at the door. He seemed to be waiting for a signal of some kind. Then he beckoned.

'The coast is clear. Make haste.' As he hurried her towards the back staircase a door closed quietly in the corridor. She looked round fearfully, but there was no sign of the mysterious stranger.

They gained the street without detection, and he hurried her into the waiting coach. Harry drew the curtains closed, but not before she had caught a glimpse of the Viscount strolling towards the hotel in company with another man.

Lyndhurst was resplendent in full evening dress. The perfectly fitting coat set off his broad shoulders to advantage, and Brummell himself could not have bettered the cut of the black satin breeches which clung closely to his long legs. As he passed within a yard of where she sat he turned to his companion with the smile she loved so well. She heard his deep voice though she could not distinguish his words.

The temptation to call out to him was almost irresistible, but she fought back a cry of panic. The knuckles shone white on her clenched fists. Then

Harry tapped on the roof of the coach, the driver whipped up the horses, and the moment was gone.

Hot tears coursed down Georgiana's cheeks as the vehicle gathered speed, putting more distance between herself and the man she loved. How cruel it was to have her happiness snatched away. In that moment she hated Harry.

As if he sensed her feelings he turned to her.

'Will you ever forgive me? I did not intend…'

'You never do,' she cried wildly. 'Don't speak to me, or I might say something that we shall both regret.'

Her bitter words silenced him. She was shivering, though the night was warm, and wordlessly he threw a rug about her knees.

When the coach drew to a halt he handed her down. Money changed hands. Then he took her arm and led her across the street to where another vehicle waited in the shadows. It appeared to be of ancient vintage.

'Where have you been?' Richard jumped down from the box. 'I have waited here this age.'

'Keep your voice down,' Harry ordered. 'You'll wake the neighbourhood. Now let us away before we are pursued.'

A short altercation followed as both of them

wished to drive. Eventually Richard returned to his perch and took the reins. He set off at such an alarming rate that Georgiana protested.

'Do beg him to slow down,' she pleaded. 'If he overturns us we shall be in worse case than ever.'

'Don't fuss, Georgie! You were not used to be such a namby-pamby miss.'

'Hal, I mean it! Tell him to slow down.'

'Richard can handle the ribbons,' Harry told her in an injured tone. 'He's had plenty of practice up and down the public roads in England. For a guinea or two the mail-coach drivers will give up their place to anyone.'

Georgiana shuddered at the thought of coach and passengers in such inexperienced hands. She refused to be convinced.

'Oh, very well. I'll sit beside him.' Harry thrust his head out of the window and called out. He was unprepared for what happened next.

Alarmed by his shout, Richard snatched so sharply at the reins that the horses reared in pain and fright. Georgiana was flung across the coach to the opposite seat, bruising her arms and knees as she fell. It was the outside of enough.

'Get out!' she ordered, and Harry obeyed her, dreading the storm which he knew must follow.

She did not mince her words, and spoke with a force which left both of her companions much subdued. Then she climbed back inside The outburst of anger had relieved her feelings, but she could not shake off a deadening sense of depression. Had not Edward told her once that she was taking on a task beyond her power when she tried to help her brother? She was beginning to believe him.

Suddenly she longed with passion for Lyndhurst's calm good sense. If only he were by her side she would fear nothing and no one. She forced the thought away. She must not dwell on those precious hours in the shelter of his arms, else her courage would fail her.

She looked about her with distaste. The musty smell inside the coach was sickening. Even in the half-light she could see that the padding was almost gone from the seats, and the leather itself was ripped.

What had happened to their family coach? she wondered. In this ramshackle contraption Harry could scarce hope to reach Paris, and Italy would be out of the question.

In great discomfort she suffered the jolting for what seemed like hours. They were travelling more slowly, but it was a relief when Richard brought the coach to a stop. The sound of another argument did not improve her temper.

'Twenty miles is far enough, I tell you.' Harry's voice was raw with strain. 'These broken-down nags will not go further.'

'You chose them,' Richard said sulkily.

'They were all we could afford.'

'I know it, but perhaps at the next inn…'

'They won't do it. Do you want them dropping in their traces?'

Richard made no reply. Muttering under his breath, he climbed down from the box, and together they made their way into the hostelry.

Georgiana was glad to stretch her legs. She felt stiff and sore, and the constant quarrelling had increased her worries. She had not expected perfect accord, but to disagree so soon…? It did not augur well.

After they had ordered refreshments, Harry engaged the landlord in conversation, but when he came back to them he was frowning.

'There are no horses to be had,' he said shortly. 'We are not the first to take this route tonight. We had best bait our own and trust to luck.'

'Did I not tell you so?' Richard's smug expression was infuriating. In triumph he ordered a second bottle of claret.

Georgiana sipped at her coffee. She was more anxious than she dared admit. She feared an explosion of anger if she objected, but when the second bottle was empty and a third ordered she felt it was time to protest.

'Had you not best keep your wits about you?' she murmured. 'The horses are tired, and we do not know the road.'

Harry flushed, but before he could speak Richard intervened.

'We must rest the nags,' he explained kindly. She might have been a backward child, to judge by his tone. 'Pray don't trouble yourself. Why, I have seen drivers so disguised that they could scarce hold the ribbons. It happens frequently. These horses know their way.'

'Stuff! I value my neck if you do not.' She turned to her brother. 'Why are we travelling thus? Where is our own coach?'

Harry had the grace to blush. 'We…er…needed funds, my dear.'

'Could you not ask your friend?' Her voice was heavy with sarcasm. If Merton intended to use them for his own ends, at least he might help them travel in comfort.

'I would not do so.' Harry's face was set, and

she did not pursue the subject, though Richard had left them to order the horses put to.

When he returned she knew at once that something was wrong.

'Here's a pretty pass,' he cried. 'One of the wheels is gone.'

'Gone?' Harry stared at him.

'It is broken clean away. Did I not warn you when you bought the coach? Any fool could have seen…'

'Shut up!' Harry was furious. 'If you recall, you had no wish to stop here. If I'd listened to you we might have found ourselves overturned in some God-forsaken spot—'

'Be quiet, both of you!' Georgiana turned on them, her eyes flashing with anger. 'Will quarrelling solve the problem? For heaven's sake use your heads! There must be someone…a carpenter perhaps?'

'It will take two days.' Thoroughly dispirited, Richard sank into a chair. 'We cannot wait so long.'

'I'll see to it.' Harry stalked off, and after a moment or two Richard followed him.

She was out of all patience with the pair of them. Why was she travelling with these two feckless idiots? If only she'd followed her instinct to tell Edward.

She straightened her shoulders. There was no use in repining. She had made her decision and she must abide by it, though with every hour that passed she recognised her own folly even more.

Worse was yet to come.

When the two men returned Harry laid a purse beside her.

'What is this?'

'You will need the gold for your journey, Georgie.' He looked uncomfortable.

'For *my* journey? What do you mean?'

'We…er…thought you might be more comfortable in the public coach,' Richard offered. 'We cannot stay here in case we are followed.'

'Georgie, we'll take the nags and go ahead to Paris,' Harry said quickly. 'This place is on a public route. You won't have long to wait for the coach, and you will be quite safe. I'll speak to the landlord.'

Rage threatened to choke her, and her look was withering. She could not trust herself to answer him.

'Don't look like that,' Harry pleaded. 'You must agree that it is for the best. Go to the Hôtel Belle Ile in Paris. We'll see you there tonight.'

'It was not our fault, you know.' Richard attempted to placate her. 'It was naught but ill luck.'

'I'll be happy to explain that to your brother if he comes in search of you.' She was unable to resist the taunt and Richard coloured to the ears. She turned away as Harry attempted to kiss her farewell. He shifted uneasily from one foot to the other. Then he sighed and walked away.

Alone with her bitter thoughts, she fell prey once more to her doubts and fears. She was certain of nothing. She might have been upon shifting sands, unable to trust the very ground beneath her feet. The void which had opened before her filled her with despair. What on earth was she to do? Harry could not protect her, she knew that now.

In an agony of mind, she rested her burning face against the cool glass of the window. Outside it was full daylight. In Calais Edward would be awake… She wondered if she had been missed already. There was little doubt of it. Betsy would have given the alarm when she found her mistress vanished.

Georgiana shuddered as she imagined her lover's reaction to the news. He had trusted her and she had betrayed his trust. There was no sign of a struggle in her room. It would be clear that she had left of her own free will. Free will? A bitter smile curved her lips. She had had little choice.

She looked at her watch. There were still some hours to wait before the public coach arrived, and the inn was growing crowded as prospective passengers arrived.

As the noise increased she put up the hood of her cloak, drawing it about her face. She longed to ask for a private room, but that would deplete her meagre funds. She picked up a nearby broadsheet, pretending to be absorbed in it, but her command of French was limited, and the contents did not interest her. Her thoughts returned to her present problems.

She had not been kind to Harry, she thought sadly, but really his behaviour was the outside of enough. He seemed to stumble from one disaster to another. What had happened to the laughing boy she had always loved so much? It did not seem possible that he would leave her here alone.

A burst of laughter from a group of men nearby caused her to lift her head. Then one of them left his friends and came towards her.

'All alone, *mademoiselle?* Will you take a glass with me?'

Georgiana eyed him with distaste. Burly and red-faced, he was old enough to be her father. She gave him a quelling look and turned away.

Taking her silence for assent, he lifted a hand to summon the landlord. 'Wine for the little lady and myself,' he ordered.

Georgiana rose at once, intending to change her seat, but he grasped her arm, forcing her to sit beside him.

'Sir, I am waiting for my friends,' she said with dignity.

'They are over-long in arriving. I've watched you for an hour or more. Now don't be unfriendly, my dear. I've a wager against your kindness.'

Georgiana looked round for the landlord, but he was occupied in serving. She raised an arm to attract his attention.

'Now, now,' her tormentor soothed. 'I mean you no harm.' He glanced towards his erstwhile companions with a grin, nodding to the circle of expectant faces.

'How dare you speak to me?' she hissed. 'Release my arm or I'll make a scene which you won't forget.'

It was the wrong thing to say. Her companion crimsoned. With a swift motion of his hand he threw back her hood.

'A hell-cat, but a beauty too,' he marvelled. Before she could pull away from him he slid an arm about her waist.

'Just one kiss?' he insisted. 'You'll never miss it.'

She swung round then, intending to slap his face, but he was too quick for her. His other hand came down upon her shoulder, forcing her back into her seat and ripping the thin muslin of her gown.

His eyes glistened as they feasted on the smooth expanse of milky flesh. As he bent his face to hers he was breathing hard. She struggled wildly as the slobbering mouth came closer, to the accompaniment of shouts and laughter from his friends.

Then she heard a choking gasp. The man's hands flew to his throat as his eyes began to bulge and his face grew purple. As she watched in horror he was lifted from his seat and flung to the ground.

Half strangled, her attacker tried to crawl away. He was helped along by a swift kick from a booted foot.

Georgiana stared up at the owner of the boot and found herself gazing into Lyndhurst's face. He was very pale, but the blue eyes blazed with anger.

Chapter Seven

A lifted finger brought the landlord to his side. Her command of French was not enough to enable her to follow all he said, but it sufficed to reduce the man to a quivering jelly.

Lyndhurst had not looked at her, but now he took her arm in a brutal grip and marched her through the rapidly thinning crowd. In silence he thrust her ahead of him in the wake of their abject host, and pushed her into a private room.

'Out!' He jerked his head, and the man scuttled off like a frightened rabbit. Then he turned to Georgiana and she quailed at his expression, though his look was impersonal. She might have been a stranger.

'Where are they?' Somehow the quiet tone was

more menacing than if he had stormed at her and she began to tremble.

'Edward, please let me explain!'

'More words, Miss Westleigh? I don't wish to hear them, though you have a gifted tongue. I should not believe you now if you swore on the Bible.'

'You are quick to judge me,' she cried on a sob.

'Spare me your tears. They will not move me. You will give me your brother's direction, if you please.'

'He and Richard are gone,' she faltered. 'You don't understand. They are in danger. Harry told me...'

Lyndhurst's face was thunderous. 'Gone? Do you tell me that they left you here alone?'

'They had no choice. The coach broke down and it could not be repaired...'

'And with your brother's usual tender care for your safety he abandoned you to the mercies of any ill-favoured lout who cares to approach you? It does not surprise me in the least.'

'They...they suggested that I wait for the public coach. Harry spoke with the landlord. He was to see that I was not...not molested.'

'A task which he performed with great efficiency, I note,' Lyndhurst's voice was silky. 'No private room, Miss Westleigh? Your brother must have left you well provided with funds.'

Georgiana's hand closed convulsively on the small bag of coins in her reticule, but Lyndhurst was quick…uncomfortably quick. He took the purse from her nerveless fingers, opened it, and shook out the contents on to the table.

'A fortune indeed!' he observed in a sarcastic tone. 'At least enough to take you on to Paris. And what then?'

Frightened, exhausted and faint from lack of food, Georgiana burst into tears. For a few moments the silence of the room was broken only by her sobbing.

'I will send Betsy to you,' Lyndhurst said abruptly. 'She will help you repair your gown. Then we go on.'

Georgiana felt that her heart must break. She was still in tears when Betsy tapped at the door.

'There, miss, don't take on so.' She threw a comforting arm around Georgiana's shoulders.

'I…I shall be better in a moment.'

'Of course you will. Master has got hisself in a state… He don't know what he's saying, and that's the truth.'

'He…he has every right to be cross.' Georgiana dabbed at her eyes.

'Cross? Miss, he were like a madman when he found you'd gone. We've fairly flown along that road from Calais. I can still feel the bumps.' She rubbed at her hip with a rueful expression.

'I'm very glad to see you,' Georgiana said in a small voice. 'And Betsy, I hope I did not get you into trouble with his lordship.'

'No! He cursed everything and everybody alike, but it weren't meant for me in particler. Will I take a needle to the rip in your gown, miss?'

Georgiana sat in silence as the girl drew the edges of the fabric together.

'It don't show much,' Betsy announced with satisfaction. She turned as a servant entered the room.

'Take it away.' Georgiana waved aside the tray of food.

'Leave it!' Lyndhurst was standing in the doorway. The look on his face was enough to send both Betsy and the waiter scurrying from the room.

'Miss Westleigh, you will eat, or I shall feed you forcibly.' It was clear that he meant what he said.

Miserably, she forced down a few mouthfuls of the food, though she felt that it must choke her.

Lyndhurst did not address her further, but when she had finished he held out her cloak.

In stony silence he led her out to the waiting coach, leaving it to Scroggins to hand her inside.

Neither Betsy nor her uncle dared to speak as they continued on the road to Paris, and after one quick glance at the Viscount's grim expression Georgiana thought it wise to follow their example. His contempt for her was apparent in every line of his rigid frame, and she could only wish that the ground would open and swallow her. She had never been so miserable in her life.

At the end of that dreadful journey he addressed her once. 'The name of your meeting place?' he demanded.

'The Hôtel Belle Ile.'

Without another word, he marched her to her room. It was commodious, but she was quick to notice that there was no balcony. She looked round in surprise as the servants brought in an extra bed.

Lyndhurst answered her unspoken question. 'Betsy will also sleep in here,' he said.

'As my gaoler? I won't have it!' In her misery and frustration Georgiana screamed at him.

'You have no choice, Miss Westleigh. It is either Betsy or myself.'

'You…you hypocrite! You pretend to be scandalised because my brother left me, and now you will take advantage…'

'You flatter yourself. Experience has taught me well. I have not the slightest desire for your company, but you shall not make a fool of me again.'

Hot colour flooded her cheeks, but he affected not to notice.

'Who is it to be?' he demanded. 'Betsy or myself?'

'Need you ask?' She eyed him with a mixture of anger and despair. 'As you find my company so distasteful you may send Betsy to me.'

He bowed, but before he left her he spoke again. 'May I offer you a word of warning? Betsy has her orders. Should anyone approach you, or should you try to leave this room, I shall hear of it at once.'

Her silence was eloquent as she turned her back on him.

'I shall be close at hand,' he continued. 'The adjoining door leads to my rooms.'

'Perhaps you would care to chain my hands and feet?' she cried bitterly.

'It would be no more than you deserve.' He was about to leave her when she turned and threw out her hands to him.

'Edward, will you not listen to me?' she pleaded. 'I had no wish to steal away without a word to you, but Harry told me something…'

He gave a cynical laugh. 'Harry again? When will you learn that your brother will tell you anything to gain his own ends? I suppose he does not care to lose the most valuable member of his infamous group.'

'I thought you fair-minded,' she burst out in rage. 'You won't even listen to what I have to say.'

'Another tissue of lies? You are right. I do not care to listen. You cannot distinguish right from wrong.'

The bitter words struck her to the heart, but she did not reply. It was useless. Nothing she could say or do would make him trust her again. She walked over to the window, hiding her face from him. She would not give him the satisfaction of seeing how cruelly he had wounded her. When she turned round at last she was alone.

A deadly lassitude settled on her spirits. She had achieved nothing by agreeing to Harry's plan. In fact, she had made matters worse if anything. Now she was virtually a prisoner.

She saw nothing of Lyndhurst for the rest of the day, and as the hours passed her apprehension grew. Harry would know by now that she had not taken the public coach. Would he guess that the Viscount had found her? And what of Merton? The thought of that sinister figure made her shudder. She could imagine his rage when he found that his plans had gone awry. If only Edward would listen to her.

Her hopes were vain. On the following day she was allowed out for a short drive, with Scroggins and Betsy in attendance. Lyndhurst sat aloft with his coachman. He neither looked at nor spoke to her. She might have been a leper, she thought sadly. It was clear that he could not bear the sight of her.

She dined alone and the hours dragged endlessly. The solitude weighed heavily on her spirits, but as the day wore on her indignation grew. She was being treated like a child, punished by being sent to her room. The thought served to stiffen her resolve.

When she next saw the Viscount she would give him a piece of her mind. There were laws against abduction, for a nobleman no less than a commoner. He had no right to hold her against her will.

When the door opened she swung round with flashing eyes, but her expression softened when she saw that it was Betsy. The girl looked nervous as she sidled into the room. She reached into her pocket and thrust a note into Georgiana's hand.

'Where did you get this?' Georgiana snatched at the folded paper.

'A man gave it to me. I knowed it was your brother, miss. His hair was the colour of yours. I told him I wasn't supposed to fetch it to you, but he said that my master should not keep you from your family.' She twisted her hands in her apron. 'Oh, miss, you won't tell his lordship, will you? He'd skin me alive.'

Georgiana laid a comforting hand on Betsy's arm and shook her head. The contents of the note were brief. Harry counselled patience. He would find a way to help her escape from Lyndhurst. She sighed. At least he had discovered her whereabouts.

She looked at Betsy's anxious face. 'It is nothing,' she said lightly. 'My brother was worried, but now he knows that I am here. I'm glad to hear from him.'

'Is that all?' Betsy's smile lacked much of its normal gaiety. 'I was that afeared that he'd take you off again.'

'Oh, Betsy, I am so sorry. I did not mean to get

you into trouble with your master. It was not your fault that I left without…without saying anything. The Viscount must know that.'

'You wouldn't have thought so, miss.' Betsy's lip quivered. 'If I hadn't come to your room right early, to see if you wanted me, we might not have knowed till noon.'

'Betsy, I had to go. I'll tell you about it some time.'

Betsy glanced towards the window. 'He…your brother…asked me if you had a balcony.' Her eyes began to sparkle. 'He's brave, Miss Georgiana. To think how he climbed up to see you! But how did you get down? His lordship went mad when he saw the broken creeper. He said you were like to have killed yourself.'

'I left by the staircase,' Georgiana said with dignity.

'Well, my master didn't know that. You should have seen him… The hotel was in an uproar. When he couldn't find you we were out of Calais before you could say knife.' She forbore to mention the Viscount's promises of retribution.

A peremptory knock at the door startled both of them. It could only be Lyndhurst.

'Quick! Help me out of my gown before you

open the door.' Georgiana stuffed the note in her pocket. 'Betsy, you must say that I have retired.'

The knock was repeated.

'One moment!' Georgiana called.

The door was thrown open and the Viscount entered.

'I believe I asked you to wait.' She rounded on him with an angry look, drawing her wrapper close about her.

Lyndhurst ignored her protest. He stood very still in the centre of the room, glancing from one face to the other.

'Betsy?' He turned and held the door wide. The girl need no second bidding to leave the room.

'Please go!' Georgiana turned back to her mirror and began to brush her hair. 'It is late, and, as you see, I intend to seek my bed.'

'Alone? Such a pity! And such a waste!' He had walked across the room and was standing behind her. Reaching out, he twisted a copper curl around his fingers.

In a furious gesture she slapped his hand away. She tried to rise, but his hands came down upon her shoulders, holding her in an iron grip. Even through the flimsy robe she could feel their warmth. It seemed to burn into her flesh.

Panic threatened to overwhelm her. He hated her, she knew that now. Did he intend to take his revenge by raping her? She must stay calm. If she struggled or showed her fear he would enjoy his triumph even more.

'I believe you have dined too well, my lord. You are not yourself, else you would not insult me so.'

'Insult you? Is that possible?' His eyes were glittering with an emotion she did not recognise, but she forced herself not to shrink from him.

She was in no doubt of his intentions, but he would not take her without a struggle. She would need all her wits about her. The love which she had been so ready to offer him should not be debased into a mere animal coupling.

'Abduction and now rape, my lord? You value your honour lightly. As I recall you told me once that you would never force a woman.'

'I have changed, my dear. My honour has been flung back in my face. You will pay for that. As you say, I have dined well, but not too well to do you justice.'

'You disgust me!'

'The feeling is mutual as far as character is concerned, yet there are other consolations…' His hand slid the robe aside, exposing the milky smoothness of her shoulder.

Rigid with anger, she stared into the mirror as he bent and pressed his lips against her flesh. Then he lifted her to her feet, and turned her round to face him. With a soft whisper of silk her robe fell to the ground.

Clad only in her petticoat, Georgiana stood straight and still. Proudly she raised her head and looked at her erstwhile lover. She was very pale, and the great green eyes were huge in her set face.

'I was mistaken in you. You called me a liar and a cheat. Are you any better than I? Worse, I think. What I have done I did for love of my brother. You, my lord, are filled with hatred and self-pity. Take me if you must. I wish you joy of the experience.'

Lyndhurst's face flushed darkly at her stinging words. With a muttered curse he flung her from him and stormed out of the room.

She found that she was trembling as if she had the ague. She stumbled towards the bed, and lay there inert. Was this the man she had vowed to love with all her heart? He could have wounded her no more cruelly if he had raped her there and then. Her hands were like ice. With shaking fingers she pulled the coverlet about her.

He had done her one service, at least. Now she would have no compunction about leaving him. She would live up to his expectations. If she must lie and cheat to get away she would do so. Nothing must be allowed to stand in her way.

Let Merton do his worst. Even his company seemed preferable to that of the man who had just left her. She closed her eyes, but it was almost dawn before she fell asleep.

'Miss, are you all right?' Betsy looked troubled by her mistress's appearance on the following day.

'Quite well, I thank you.' Georgiana managed the briefest of smiles, but Betsy was not reassured.

'You look…different, somehow…not quite yourself.'

'I have been too much indoors.'

'His lordship was saying as much. He's waiting to see you, miss…in the parlour.'

Georgiana marched through at once, to find Lyndhurst standing by the window, apparently lost in thought.

As she entered the room he turned and came towards her.

'Georgiana, I…'

A lifted hand stopped the flow of words. 'Don't

trouble to apologise, my lord. You will not change my opinion of your behaviour.' Her voice was icy. 'You have some instructions for me?'

'None… Will you please listen?'

'As readily as you were prepared to listen to me?'

He winced. 'I deserved that. But, my dear, I was out of my mind with worry. You can have no idea of the danger to which you might have been exposed.'

'I know it now!' She faced him proudly. 'My safety is at much at risk with you as with any other man.'

'That is not true.' He attempted to take her hand. 'I am not made of stone, Georgiana, and you are a very beautiful woman, but I would not harm you.'

'I don't believe you.'

She saw the hurt in his eyes, and the shame. Now, when he was at her feet, was the time to tell him the full story, but anger kept her silent. She would never forgive him. With a stony expression she turned away.

'May I go now?' she asked in a toneless voice.

'Of course. You need not ask my permission. I wish I could make you see why it is necessary to keep you in this place.'

'There is no need to explain. I understand perfectly. I am the bait…the tethered goat. When your victims come to find me you will seize them.'

Lyndhurst realised that he could expect no softening of her attitude. 'Did you tell these so-called victims of my plans for them?' he asked abruptly.

For the first time Georgiana wavered. If she told the truth she would be forced to explain that Harry and Richard were linked inextricably with Merton. She could imagine the outcome. Lyndhurst would seek out that sinister figure, putting himself at risk.

It was no concern of hers, of course. She did not care what happened to him. A vision of his lifeless corpse came unbidden to her mind, and an expression of horror crossed her face. She would not be a party to murder.

'No!' she answered firmly.

'You are the poorest of liars, my dear. Look at me!' Blue eyes locked with green ones. 'There is something wrong, is there not? What had they to say?'

'They did not wish to do as you suggested.' The excuse would serve for the moment, and she prayed that he would not press her further.

'I see.' Lyndhurst looked thoughtful. 'In that case there is no more to be said.' He changed the subject. 'Do you care to take a drive this morning?'

'Why not? The bait must be well advertised, I believe. Doubtless Harry will recognise your carriage and guess that I am here.'

'That was not my first intention. If you must have the truth, you do not look at all the thing…'

'And you are surprised? You astonish me, my lord! Strange though it may seem to you, I am unaccustomed to defending my honour against a brute.'

Lyndhurst's face grew dark. 'I shall trouble you no further, madam.' He gave her a formal bow and walked towards the door.

'Wait!' Georgiana's mind was racing. Harry might be awaiting just this opportunity to rescue her. Indoors she was kept close, but if she could persuade Lyndhurst to walk with her, rather than take the carriage… In the narrow streets of Paris she might slip away from him.

She prayed that Harry was watching the hotel, for she had no desire to find herself alone in a strange city.

'I find myself in need of air, though I have no wish to drive,' she said. 'Perhaps a walk?'

Lyndhurst's face cleared. He came towards her with an eager look, but her cold expression stopped him.

'Pray do not imagine that I seek your company. Your presence is abhorrent to me. You will keep your distance, sir.'

'As you wish.' From the look of pain which crossed his face she might have struck him.

There was silence between them as they strolled towards the river in the summer sunshine. Paris was looking at its best, but Georgiana could find no pleasure in the fine buildings, the avenues of spreading trees, and the bustling crowds about her.

Two lovers came towards them, their faces bright with happiness. This was a city for lovers, someone had told her long ago. She could not help but contrast the joy of others with her own despair. Things might have been so different...

She was intensely aware of the man beside her, and of the glances which he attracted from the women who strolled past them with their escorts. She glared fiercely as she caught a smile or an inviting look, and was mortified when she heard laughter as they passed.

They thought her jealous, and it infuriated her. She was nothing of the kind. They did nit know the Viscount as she did. His striking appearance was a sham.

As always he was perfectly attired, the blue coat

of Bath superfine sitting to advantage on his broad shoulders. He was taller than the men about him, his long legs encased in spotless buckskins. She did not need the lascivious looks to assure her that those heavily muscled calves were unpadded.

I would wish them joy of him, she thought savagely. She alone knew of the false promise in those brilliant eyes. That mobile mouth could spit venom when he chose, and tenderness could turn in a moment to unbridled lust. He would have taken her out of hatred. That she could not forgive.

The thought served to stiffen her resolve. She straightened her shoulders. The past could not be changed. Now she must think of the future. She glanced about her. Figures stirred in the deep shadow of the buildings, but she saw no sign of Harry. She was forced to pause as Lyndhurst threw a coin to a crippled beggar, but no help was at hand.

The cripple shuffled forward until he was directly in their path. 'Blessings on your kind heart, my lord.'

Georgiana's heart was stirred as she looked at him. He'd been sitting on the pavement with outstretched legs. His feet were bare of shoes or stockings, and at first glance it seemed strange that someone of his powerful build should be reduced to begging.

Then she looked at his arms. They were raised in supplication, and with a start she realised that he had no hands. The arms had been severed at the elbows.

Perilously close to tears, she reached into her reticule, but as she bent towards the man she noticed that his eyes were bright.

'Same time tomorrow…at this place?' The words were so low that she could barely catch them.

As she handed him a coin she nodded, glad to see that Lyndhurst had moved on ahead of her. He stopped and turned. Then something in her face caused him to take her arm.

'You are distressed,' he murmured. 'That is a tragic sight, but sadly it is all too common since the recent wars. One sees so much of it in England.'

'Poor fellows!' She allowed him to lead her away. He had not heard the muttered message; that much was clear. With an effort she tried to compose herself. The man's words had been unexpected, and they had shaken her.

'Will you sit down?' Lyndhurst led her to a nearby seat. 'Strange, is it not, that some regard these men as parasites? To relieve their poverty in any way is thought to encourage them in idleness.'

'Better to give to nine undeserving cases for the sake of the tenth who may need help.'

'I agree, yet there are problems. Many of these unfortunates can get no work. If they would eat they must turn to robbery or worse.'

'It is unjust!' she cried. 'The man back there…the cripple…how could he earn his bread?'

'In the only way he knows; he must beg.' Lyndhurst frowned. 'It is a poor reward for bravery.'

'Can nothing be done for them?' Georgiana had forgotten her resolve to keep her companion at a distance. Her face was alight with indignation as she turned to him.

'I fear not. There are thousands in similar case. In England we try… Well, I must not trouble you further with sad tales.'

'Yet his eyes were so bright,' Georgiana murmured. 'I wish…'

'May I give you a word of warning, Georgiana? The man's injuries were shocking, and you will see others in the streets of Paris. Compassion should not blind you to the fact that some of these beggars are dangerous.'

Startled, she rose to her feet. Had he heard the message after all?

'No, don't run away. There is no need to be frightened. You are safe with me. I meant merely that it is not wise to approach such men unless you are well protected.'

'A man without hands? How could he harm me?' she asked scornfully.

'He could trip you for the benefit of his friends. You did not notice? There were others in the background…'

'And I thought you sympathised with him…'

'Pity mingled with caution, my dear. I have seen the lengths to which starving men will go. I don't blame them. In similar circumstances I might do the same.'

'At least you are no hypocrite, my lord.' The words were out before she could consider their possible effect. She had spoken on impulse, and she realised her mistake at once. Lyndhurst took her hand in his.

'Thank you, Georgiana.' His keen eyes searched her face intently. Then he sighed. 'We had best go back. It is growing chill.'

Was it a reference to the fact that she had resumed her unyielding manner towards him? Her lips tightened. She must not weaken now. How close she had come to slipping back into their old relationship… For a few moments she had forgotten how much she despised him.

Yet it was hard to resist his charm. For the rest of the day he was attentive, amusing her with his conversation, and affecting not to notice that her replies were brief.

To throw him off guard she needed guile, and as the hours slipped by she allowed herself to respond more easily. When he left her that evening the look of strain had vanished from his expression, and she was satisfied with her own deception. At all costs she must persuade him to walk with her on the following day.

Lyndhurst fell in at once with her suggestion. As they strolled along the boulevards the next morning he looked so cheerful that her heart misgave her. A knot of anxiety formed in her breast. She had no idea what was to happen when they reached the beggar's corner.

Would Harry arrange some incident to draw Lyndhurst from her side? She glanced at the tall figure beside her. Surely they would not harm him? Her footsteps began to lag.

'Come, my lady of mercy! Did you not tell me that you wished to help the cripple further?' Lyndhurst gave her a fond glance. 'I believe you would like to start a home for such as he.'

She gave him a faint smile, which vanished as

they turned the corner. The cripple was in his usual place, and Georgiana began to tremble.

'Do you stay here. I will give him something.' Lyndhurst released her arm and walked over to the man. Then the alleyway erupted as men came running from the shadows.

A raised cudgel caught Lyndhurst on the shoulder, sending him reeling against the wall. He turned with catlike speed, but he had no weapon, and his fists were of little use against his heavily armed attackers.

As Georgiana watched in horror he went down beneath a flailing mass of bodies. Then she heard a shot. As if by magic the beggars melted away, and Georgiana flew to Lyndhurst's side.

He was still conscious, thought his face was bleeding. As she bent over him he looked beyond her.

'I thank you, sir,' he said with a rueful smile.

Georgiana turned, and then she gasped. Merton was looking down at her. Carefully, he replaced the pistol in his cloak, and reached out a hand to help Lyndhurst to his feet.

Chapter Eight

'You came at an opportune moment, sir.' Lyndhurst was breathing fast. 'This lady and I are in your debt.'

'It was nothing. I was glad to be of some small service to you.' Merton held out his hand as he introduced himself. Then he turned to Georgiana. 'Madam is unharmed, I trust?'

Stupefied, Georgiana could only stare at him.

'The lady appears to be badly shocked, my lord. May I suggest that you make use of my carriage?' He lifted his heavy walking cane to summon a coach which was waiting lower down the street. 'Where are you staying, sir?'

'At the Belle Ile.' Tenderly the Viscount lifted Georgiana in his arms and carried her to the vehicle.

'A lucky coincidence…I am staying there myself.' Merton settled himself in the opposite seat. 'Sir, you are bleeding. You will frighten the lady.' He proffered a snowy handkerchief.

'Miss Westleigh is made of stern stuff.' Lyndhurst held her close within the circle of his arm. 'But had those villains reached her… Lord Merton, I can only blame myself. It was folly to venture forth unarmed.'

'You had no cause to expect an attack, I imagine.' Merton's eyes rested on Georgiana's face with interest. 'No warning…?'

'None at all. Miss Westleigh wished to see something of the city…and we had spoken to one of the beggars yesterday. She hoped to help him in some way.'

'A sad mistake.' Merton shook his head. 'These fellows are no better than animals. Like wild beasts, they will turn and rend you. The lady will have learned her lesson.'

Georgiana could not mistake his meaning. He had made it clear that Lyndhurst's life was at his mercy. Without his intervention, her lover would now be a bloody corpse. She could not begin to understand this terrifying creature. With Lyndhurst unconscious he might have spirited her away. Why had he not done so?

As is he had read her mind Merton gave her a wolfish smile. 'No harm done,' he announced smoothly. 'Those simple-minded fellows sought nothing more than a fat purse. How pleasant it must be to have one's desires satisfied so easily.'

Georgiana could not take her eyes from him. She felt held by that silver gaze. He might have been a coiled snake and she the intended victim. That he had arranged the attack on Lyndhurst she had no doubt, but why had he come to their rescue?

Whatever the reason, she could only be thankful that Lyndhurst had escaped his attackers with nothing more than a cut on his brow. She looked up at him with anxious eyes, relieved to see that the bleeding had stopped. He met her look with a wry smile.

'The price of folly,' he announced lightly. Then he turned to Merton. 'Sir, do you care to dine with us this evening…that is, unless you are otherwise engaged?'

Georgiana's blood ran cold. She laid a restraining hand upon his arm. 'Edward, would it not be best—?'

'Madam is concerned for your health, my lord. She may be right. You have sustained a blow… Neglect of such an injury will often lead to serious consequences.' She heard the mockery in his voice, but Lyndhurst seemed unaware of it.

'It is but a graze.' He renewed his invitation.

'You are quite sure?' Merton was all concern. 'Then since you press me I shall accept with pleasure. It will be an honour.'

With great solicitude he accompanied them into the hotel, walking with them until they reached the Viscount's rooms.

'Until this evening…' With a beaming smile and a wave of his hand he left them.

'Edward, this is not wise.' Georgiana was frantic with terror. 'You should rest. He…Merton…was right. A blow to the head can be dangerous. Let us send word to cancel your invitation. He will understand. Perhaps another day…?'

Lyndhurst had not released his grip upon her arm, and now he drew her close. 'I can only thank those ruffians,' he said softly. 'Can it be that you do care after all?'

'Oh, no!' Georgiana struggled to free herself. 'I mean, of course, I care that you were hurt, as I would with anyone.'

'Anyone, my dearest?' He bent his head to hers, seeking her lips.

'Edward, you must not.' She turned her face away. 'You must be sensible.'

'I don't feel sensible at this moment. Georgiana, my darling, your face gives you away. Will you tell me that you do not love me?'

She could not look at him. Then a lean hand reached out to cup her chin. His lips found hers, and she was swept away on a dizzy tide of love and longing. When at last he released her she was breathless.

'That was not fair,' she protested.

'You have heard the old saying that all is fair in love and war?' He was laughing with pleasure as he looked at her.

'Please… My lord, do you not find something strange about the man who came to our aid?' Georgiana hung on to the last remnants of sanity. 'How did he come to be so close? His coach was waiting in the street.'

'Possibly he had an appointment there.' A cool finger traced the outlined of her lips. 'It was lucky for us…but put it out of your mind, my love.' He rested his face against her hair. 'These last days have been torture, Georgiana. I feared that I had lost you.'

'My lord—'

'Edward, I beg of you…'

'Well, then, Edward, please listen. We know nothing of this man. He could be as great a villain as those who attacked you. We cannot make a friend of him.'

'My dearest, you are overwrought. Your imagination is running away with you. This morning has been a shock, but you must not look for danger everywhere. Merton is an Englishman, of personable address, and you will admit that without his aid we should have been in poor case.'

'I know it, but…but he may have motives other than he claims.'

'Perhaps he plans to abduct you.' Lyndhurst's eyes twinkled. 'I should not blame him for the thought, but I suspect that you would make me jealous.'

'With that creature?' She shuddered. 'I would as soon seek the friendship of an adder.'

She had said too much. She knew it even as she spoke. Lyndhurst frowned, and she was uncomfortably aware of those clear, considering blue eyes intent upon her face.

'What is it?' he asked quietly. 'Have you met this man before?'

'No.' It was a reluctant reply. 'At least…only

briefly. He spoke to me in Calais, at the hotel. It was just to tell me where you were. I was looking for you, you see.'

'He did not insult you, I trust.'

'Of course not. He was all courtesy, but, Edward, I cannot trust him.'

'He should not have spoken to you without an introduction, Georgiana, but I cannot understand why you have taken him in such dislike.'

'Call it a woman's instinct…anything you like,' she cried wildly. 'He was at Dessein's. Now he is staying here at the Belle Ile. Does it not occur to you that he may have followed us?'

'For what purpose, my dear?' Lyndhurst gathered her gently into his arms. 'Most English travellers stay in certain recommended hotels. We might travel across Europe and see the same faces. It is no cause for alarm.'

Georgiana was silent. It was too late to explain. She should have told him of Merton's involvement with Harry and Richard long before this. Now both he and they were in danger. And she could not no longer delude herself. She would go to any lengths to keep Edward safe. A spasm of anguish crossed her face as she recalled the upraised cudgels and the ferocity of the men who had attacked him.

'I cannot bear to see you so distraught, my dearest love.'

'I thought…I thought they had killed you.' She hid her face in his coat.

'I am not so easily disposed of. Unprincipled brutes are difficult to murder.' He was teasing her, hoping to chase away the horror in her eyes. 'Besides, you threatened me with worse. I am scarred for life with the wounds that you inflicted.'

'I am sorry that I hurt you so.'

'The punishment was well deserved.' He took her hand and pressed his lips against her palm. Then he kissed each finger in turn. His mouth moved slowly to rest on the inside of her wrist, and travelled with delicious warmth along her bare arm.

'Please…!' she protested. 'I do not desire…'

'What do you desire? This…and this?' Lyndhurst nuzzled her neck. She jumped as his lips came to rest against the soft swell of her breasts.

In confusion she tugged at the low neckline of her gown, but her hands were held in a firm grip.

'I love you, Georgiana. You must not be afraid of me. In the words of the marriage service, I shall worship you with my body. When you become my wife you will understand that passion can be tender as well as wild.'

Despair threatened to overwhelm her. She could never be his wife, but the sweetness of his caresses tore her heart apart. She could not trust herself to speak.

Lyndhurst hesitated, and his voice was sad as he continued. 'I can only blame myself for your reluctance. When I came to your room the other night I behaved like a lout. Now you cannot bear my touch, and I don't blame you. I frightened you so badly.'

'No!' With an involuntary gesture she reached out to him. 'I am tired and confused, that is all. Will you give me time to compose myself?'

'All the time in the world.' His face lightened. 'And Georgiana, if you really do not wish to dine with Merton I will send a message.'

'It is of no consequence. Let us leave matters as they are.'

She had accepted the inevitable. Much as she disliked the thought of meeting Merton again, she must confront her enemy. It was better to learn something of his plans, if possible, than to continue in this fog of ignorance. Merton was cunning and sharp-witted, but wine might loosen his tongue. With some knowledge of his intentions she would find a way to save both Edward and her brother.

'It will be only for an hour or two,' Lyndhurst assured her. 'But we owe the man a certain courtesy for his help. I promise that he won't outstay his welcome. I shall plead my aching head…'

Georgiana gave him an anxious look. 'Is it very bad?'

'Certainly not, but the excuse will serve, if necessary. If you do not care to join us I'll explain that the shock has been too much for you.'

'I too owe him something,' she replied in a determined tone. 'I would not have him think me faint-hearted.'

'Never that!' Lyndhurst dropped a light kiss upon her brow. 'You are a veritable Amazon.' He was smiling as she left him.

She dressed with extra care that evening, and not only for her own satisfaction. Merton should be made to see that he was not dealing with some timid girl whom he could terrorise into obedience.

'It's pressed up lovely, miss.' Reverently, Betsy laid Georgiana's gown upon the bed. 'My uncle says that there's naught to bet French style for the ladies.'

Georgiana nodded as she slipped into the satin undergown. 'It was a ridiculous garment to pack,' she said ruefully. 'But we left London in haste, and I took the nearest things to hand.'

'Miss, I'm glad you did.' With deft fingers Betsy drew the gauze overdress about her mistress's shoulders. 'All the embroidery…' She shook her head in wonder at the tiny gold stars scattered at random on the flimsy fabric. 'Don't it look well against the white? Why, miss, you look just like a princess.'

Georgiana looked at her reflection in the mirror. The simple column of white satin made her look taller, and gave her an air of dignity, whilst the overdress softened the outlines of her figure. It would do very well for the purpose she had in mind.

She stood in silence as Betsy fastened the gold ribbon beneath her breasts. Then her glance travelled upwards. The last rays of the setting sun were streaming through the window behind her, turning her burnished curls into a flaming halo, but her eyes were steady. As green as the finest jade, they looked back at her, slanting and enormous, but without a trace of fear.

It was strange, but the thought of the ordeal ahead had served to restore her courage. Had she not heard somewhere that the best form of defence was attack? Tonight she would put that saying to the test.

She picked up her scarf and her fan and walked through into the parlour.

Both men rose as she entered the room. Then Lyndhurst walked towards her, his glowing look a tribute to her beauty. He kissed her hand, and the pressure of his fingers claimed her as his own.

'A vision indeed, madam!' Merton confined his greeting to the deepest of bows. 'We are honoured tonight by the company of the most enchanting woman in Paris.'

Georgiana returned the compliment with a slight curtsy. She kept her eyes demurely upon the ground, else her dagger-like look must surely have given her away. It cost her much to murmur some pleasantry in reply, but she would play her part in this charade. Tonight her acting abilities would be tested to the full.

In silence she allowed Lyndhurst to seat her at the table. Then she gave Merton her most ravishing smile.

'How fortunate we were that you happened by this morning in such an opportune way.'

'I beg that you will not speak of it.' Merton waved a dismissive hand. 'These incidents happen. They are best forgotten.'

'They are not easy to forget,' she said carefully. 'One should, perhaps, take them as a warning to be more careful in future.'

'How wise you are.' The silver eyes gazed into hers with meaning. 'I understand your concern, of course. His lordship might have been seriously injured.'

'As you say, the matter is best forgotten.' Lyndhurst's expression was pleasant enough, but there was a slight trace of impatience in his tone. He changed the subject.

'Do you stay long in Paris, sir?'

'A few days only, alas! When my business is concluded here I shall move on...perhaps to Brussels.'

'I have not been there since Waterloo. What a time that was! You will recall that our victory was a close-run thing.'

'Indeed! Had it not been for Blücher's timely arrival on the field we might have lost the day.'

Georgiana paid little attention to their discussion of military tactics. Brussels, she now knew with certainty, was not Merton's intended destination, but that information was of little help. Surreptitiously she signalled to the waiter to refill the gentlemen's glasses.

'We shall bore madam with our dull talk!' Merton exclaimed at last. 'The ladies do not care to think of death and danger.'

He had drunk deep, but the pock-marked face

showed no sign of it. Georgiana looked at the claw-like hand which curved around his glass. The finger-nails were clean and beautifully manicured, but he was older than she had first imagined. Dark brown age-spots showed up clearly against the taut skin.

'I believe we face what must be faced,' she told him quietly.

'With feminine resignation, I have no doubt.' His smile held no amusement. 'On occasion we must accept the inevitable.'

Lyndhurst's eyes roved from one face to the other, and as if aware of his regard Merton turned to his host.

'Madam is a philosopher, I see,' he remarked smoothly. 'She is a worthy antagonist.'

'You may be sure of it.' Lyndhurst laughed aloud. 'You will take a little more wine?'

Merton accepted, and Georgiana sighed with relief. She must be more careful. Edward had been quick to sense the tension in the room. It would not do to alert him further.

'This dish is so very good.' Merton tasted his *fricassée de poulets à l'italienne* with the air of a connoisseur. 'A transformation of the humble chicken! I compliment you upon your choice of menu, madam.'

'The compliments are due surely to the chef.' Georgiana had recovered her composure, and her words, if not warm, were at least civil. She entered as best she could into a discussion of French cooking and the wondrous flavours which resulted from the use of the freshest of ingredients. Yet there were undercurrents beneath the apparently innocuous remarks, and her uneasiness persisted.

Here, in their private room with her love beside her and the servants close at hand, it was folly to imagine that harm might come either to herself or Edward, but Merton's brooding presence cast a pall upon her spirit.

Apparently at ease, he lolled back in his chair, twirling the stem of the wine glass between his fingers.

She was not deceived. He was waiting...waiting...but for what?

She was not long in doubt. When Scroggins appeared with a murmured message Lyndhurst rose to his feet.

'Will you forgive me if I leave you for a moment? There is some trifling matter which will not wait. A fellow below claims to have found my snuff-box. I must have lost it in the struggle.'

His loving look was intended to reassure Georgiana, but her nerves were on edge. This was some trick, she was convinced. She made as if to rise, but Lyndhurst's hand pressed gently upon her shoulder.

'You will entertain our guest for a short time?'

She swallowed and nodded, but inside she felt that she was screaming silently. There was an aura of evil about Merton. Why could not Edward see it? With widened eyes she fought a rising ride of panic as she looked at the man across the table.

He waited until the door had closed upon his host before he spoke.

'A mere stratagem, my dear. You guessed, of course?' He did not wait for her reply. 'We must talk, Miss Westleigh. You are aware of your brother's position, I believe?'

'I know that you have used him for your own ends.'

'Oh, come…we are not speaking of children. Both young men were ready enough to grasp the opportunity of gain. An expensive lifestyle has its charms, especially in London, but pleasure must be paid for, as they came to realise.'

'With robbery? That they did not know.'

'An ugly word, Miss Westleigh, but I see that you are a realist, and we are wasting time. Your brother has told you of my plans. Believe me when I tell you that you have no choice but to agree with them.'

As he bent towards her she was reminded of some great predatory bird, hovering for the kill. Beneath the hooked nose his mouth was thin and cruel, and those strange eyes seemed to bore into the furthest recesses of her mind.

'There is always a choice,' she said coldly. 'As yet, the Viscount knows nothing of your involvement with his brother. Suppose I were to tell him?'

'You will not, I think. This morning's attack was intended to convince you that I have it within my power to kill him. I should not hesitate to do so…and that, my dear, you would not wish.'

'He is nothing to me,' she lied.

'No?' He gave a laugh of pure enjoyment. 'One has only to see you together to know that your regard for him is equal to his for you.'

When she did not reply he spoke again.

'Are you wondering why I saved him? It was for the best of reasons. Fear for his life will guarantee your compliance with my wishes.'

'And they are?'

'That you accompany your brother and his friend to a destination of my choice. There you will work for me.'

'You do not allow for the Viscount's vigilance. Escape is not as easy as you would have me believe.'

'Ah, you are thinking of that bungled first attempt. It was a mistake on my part to listen to your brother. One should not send a boy on a man's errand. Next time I shall handle matters myself.'

'Next time?' she breathed.

'Not quite yet. You may enjoy a few more days with your handsome lover. There are certain arrangements to be made. I intend to leave nothing to chance.'

'What a loathsome creature you are!' Georgiana was breathing fast. 'You may rest assured that I shall do all in my power to destroy you.'

'But, my dear, you have no power of any kind. Now let us have done with this childish nonsense. When I send for you, you will do as you are bidden.' Merton looked up with a smile as Lyndhurst returned to join them.

'Success, my lord? Your property is returned?'

'Surprising, is it not?' The Viscount held up the missing snuff-box. 'The fellow traced me by the crest. An honest rogue! He might have sold it for a few francs.'

'I am sure that he did not lose by his honesty.'

Merton examined the fine workmanship of the precious object. 'Now, my lord, I must beg you to excuse me, with my thanks for a most enjoyable evening. Miss Westleigh has been so gracious…'

Again, he did not attempt to take her hand as he made his farewells, but his bow was low. 'I bid you *au revoir,* rather than goodbye, in the hope that we shall meet again.'

Conscious of Lyndhurst's eyes upon her, she inclined her head. Then, her back rigid, she turned away.

'That was something of a trial for you, I fear.' Lyndhurst took her in his arms as the door closed. 'Merton is a strange creature. We need not see more of him, but we have done our duty.' He dropped a gentle kiss upon her brow. 'I am sorry to have left you alone with him.'

'It did not matter.' Her voice was colourless and he looked at her intently.

'You are very tired, my dearest. I should not have pressed you to join us. The day has been long…'

'And full of incident.' She managed the ghost of a smile though her heart was breaking. 'Oh, Edward, I was so afraid for you…'

'Set your mind at rest. It is over, though I'll admit I shouldn't care to repeat the experience.'

'Next time you will carry a pistol. Will you promise me as much?'

'Of course!' He bent his head and found her lips.

Georgiana clung to him with a passion that matched his own. In a few days' time they would be parted forever. If this was to be their final chance of happiness she would not deny him anything he asked.

'My love!' His hands slid down her arms, drawing her close until their bodies were as one. 'What a temptress you are!' His voice was thick with passion. 'You had best go, else I shall forget my resolution.'

'I wish you would.' She hid her face in his coat.

'What did you say?' He tilted her chin until he could look into her eyes. 'Georgiana, are you sure?'

'Quite sure.' She was blushing, but her voice was steady. 'Edward, I love you dearly. I ask only that we share our love.'

He picked her up then and carried her through into his room. With reverent hands he stroked her hair.

'Let us be married tomorrow,' he said quietly. 'My darling wife, I promise to make you happy.'

His words were bittersweet, and her eyes filled with tears.

'No... This is too sweet a moment for sorrow.

Kiss me, my love!' His mouth closed on hers, gentle but insistent, and her response was immediate. As the soft flesh met her own she gave a cry, and her arms closed about his neck.

Then she was aware of a firm hand cupping her breast, the thumb caressing her nipple through the thin fabric of her gown. She made an inarticulate sound as she felt it harden. Only half-aware of the gauze overdress being slipped from her shoulders, she made no protest as the satin undergarment whispered to the ground.

'Let me look at you.' Lyndhurst held her away from him, his eyes feasting upon her loveliness.

Quite naked, she faced him proudly, secure in the knowledge of her own beauty. Her shyness had left her. Now she was all woman, waiting for the consummation which would bind her forever to her lover.

Murmuring endearments, Lyndhurst laid her upon the bed. She watched quietly as he removed his coat, his shirt and his breeches.

In the candlelight his torso gleamed, highlighting the heavily muscled back and thighs. Perfectly proportioned, his wide shoulders narrowed to a trim waist, and below it his stomach was as flat as that of any athlete. Embarrassed by his arousal, she turned to blow out the last of the candles, but he stayed her with a loving look.

'We have no need of darkness, dearest heart. I want to see your face as you love me. You cannot know how I have longed for you...to see those wondrous eyes fill with desire, and to know that you are mine...'

He tossed away the coverlet and lay beside her, caressing, teasing and stroking until she yearned for fulfilment. When it came she cried out in pain, but it was a precious agony.

Then she was swept away on a tide of passion, her rhythmic movements keeping pace with his until she felt a strange sensation. The tingling began in her toes and consumed her body until it ended in the centre of her being. Fierce cries escaped her lips until the spasmodic pulsing eased.

'Edward...my love!' Spent and exhausted, she drew the dark head to her breast.

'My darling, you are a jewel! To think how I misjudged you!' A teasing note crept into his voice. 'I feared you would shrink from my very touch.'

'But I did not.' Feminine and sure of him, she was triumphant.

'No, you did not. I don't deserve such happiness.' He settled her into the crook of his arm. 'To think that we have a lifetime ahead of us…'

His words brought Georgiana back to reality and she stiffened.

'What is it, my love?' His gentle hands began to stroke her. 'Misgivings? Do you regret…?'

'No!' It was almost a cry of protest. 'I regret nothing. But, Edward, we cannot marry yet.'

'Why not?' His teeth nipped tenderly at her ear. 'You could be pregnant, Georgiana. If passion is the key, then there can be no doubt of it.'

He was laughing as he spoke, and was unprepared for her reaction. The colour drained from her face as she freed herself from his embrace.

'No, no! That cannot be,' she whispered.

'It would be but natural.'

She heard the surprise and the hurt in his voice, but she was silent. To have a child when she must leave him? What a fool she had been! When she had offered him her love she had been heedless of the possible consequences.

'You must not fear childbirth, Georgiana.' Long fingers traced the outline of her spine. 'It can be dangerous, I know, but you would have the best of care. Nothing shall happen to my wife.'

'Edward, I do not fear it,' she said earnestly.

'Nothing would please me more than to give you a son…'

'Or a daughter…but you are my main consideration.' He was looking down at her with the smile she loved so well.

'Even so…' she faltered. 'We should wait. We have not yet resolved…'

'You believe that your brother might object? He has little cause to do so.' Edward slipped out of bed and put on his robe. 'You owe him nothing, Georgiana. He is not your keeper, rather the reverse. He must learn to stand on his own feet.'

'I know, and I have told him so, but may we not tell him before we…before we take this step?'

'We must find him first.' Lyndhurst's voice was ironic. 'Dear Harry…I am beginning to dislike the very sound of his name.'

'You do not know him.' Georgiana hung her head. 'And he is dear to me.'

'I need no convincing of that fact.' Lyndhurst's scowl was replaced by a smile. 'You are loyal, my Venus, but I warn you…when we are married Harry's welfare shall not come before your own.'

Her ready agreement appeared to satisfy him, but it was with a heavy heart that she left him to seek her own room.

Chapter Nine

Georgiana's sorrow could not last. It was banished by the memory of the hours she had spent in her lover's embrace. How sweet it had been to know him fully. Her lips curved in a reminiscent smile as she thought of the old biblical expression. In the past she had considered it a curious phrase, but now she knew its meaning.

She felt bruised and sore, though Edward had been the soul of tenderness. And it had been worth that first sharp pang of agony to soar with him into a world of unimaginable joy.

She would not give him up, if it meant killing Merton herself. That creature would not steal away her happiness, nor harm her loved ones. She had given herself to Edward almost in despair, fearing that she must part from him forever, but the love they had shared had strengthened her courage. Now she would fight Merton with every means at her command. Nothing would stand in her way.

How thin was the veneer of civilisation, she thought ruefully. Were not women supposed to be the gentle sex? Yet the thoughts which filled her mind were far from gentle. She felt like a tigress in defence of her young. Given the opportunity she would destroy her enemy without compunction.

With that comforting prospect in mind, she fell asleep.

It was late morning when she awoke to find Betsy standing by her bed.

'Oh, miss, did I waken you? His lordship said as how you was not to be disturbed… I came in to see if you needed anything.'

'My breakfast…and then hot water.' Georgiana stretched luxuriously. She had never felt more fully alive, and she could not wait to see Edward. 'His lordship has breakfasted already?'

Betsy chuckled. 'He was up betimes. He's been gone out these three hours…'

'Gone where?' Georgiana was puzzled. Edward had said nothing of an appointment.

'I don't know, miss.' Betsy looked at Georgiana's troubled face. 'There's nothing amiss,' she comforted. 'My uncle said as how he'd never seen the master look so cheerful. He promised to be back by noon.'

'Then I had best hurry.' She swallowed the scalding coffee, and nibbled at a croissant. 'Have I anything fit to wear?'

She looked with distaste at the primrose-yellow gown which Betsy had laid across a chair. Careful pressing could not disguise the fact that the fabric was looking tired.

'I should have brought more clothes,' she murmured. Somehow it seemed important that she should look her best for Edward on that particular morning.

'This came for you.' Betsy laid a large green box upon the bed. Her eyes were sparkling as they pleaded with Georgiana to open it without delay.

'For me?'

'Yes, miss. My uncle knows the name…it's famous. And…and I was to give you this.' She produced a small flat parcel from her pocket.

'From whom?' Georgiana asked in surprise.

'It's from his lordship.' With unabashed curiosity Betsy craned her neck to examine the contents of the package. It contained a leather jewel-box.

'Oh! How beautiful!' Georgiana gasped as she looked at a string of perfectly matched pearls which nestled against the velvet lining. Beside them lay a note bearing the simple message 'For my love'. It bore no signature, and none was needed.

'Will you wear it today, miss?' Betsy's eyes were round as she looked at the necklace. 'Pearls takes their glow from a lady's skin, so my uncle says.'

'Yes… Fasten it for me, will you?' Georgiana allowed the milky string to slide through her fingers before she opened the diamond clasp. 'I must take care not to lose it.'

'That you must. But, miss, the other box…?'

With eager fingers Georgiana tore at the wrapping. The box contained a charming gown of snow-white cambric trimmed with palest blue ribbon. Tiny knots adorned the bodice and the flounced hem, and edged the short, puffed sleeves, yet the effect was one of simplicity.

'It will match your chipstraw bonnet,' Betsy cried happily. 'You'll look so fine, Miss Georgiana, and it's such a lovely day. You won't need your cloak.'

'I wasn't planning to go out,' Georgiana said, but she could not resist the temptation to wear her new gown.

She looked at her reflection in the glass. Today her face was vivid, and her skin had a special glow. Her jade-green eyes laughed back at her as if they held some secret known only to herself.

Edward's expression mirrored her mood as he greeted her in the parlour. A brown hand reached up to stroke her hair.

'You are lovelier than ever,' he murmured. 'My darling, I still can't believe that you love me.'

'But you must.' She laughed up at him. 'Look into my eyes! Can you be in any doubt?'

A kiss was her reply, and it took her breath away. Again she was borne on that dizzying tide of rapture as she clung to him. Then he held her at arm's length, and shook her gently.

'Temptress!' he said gaily. 'You shall not divert me from my purpose. Come, my dearest, I have a surprise for you.' He took her hand and was about to lead her from the room.

'Edward, I have not thanked you…' Georgiana's hand went to the pearls about her neck. 'These are so beautiful. I shall treasure them all my life.'

'But not as much as I shall treasure you…' He

bent to kiss her again, but, laughing, she averted her head.

'And my gown… Will you not let me thank you?'

'The way you look is thanks enough. Georgiana, my darling, I would give you everything…'

'There is no need. You have given me yourself. That is all I ask or need.' She lifted her face to his and his mouth came down on hers.

Once more she was lost to everything about her as she responded to the insistent pressure of his lips. With an inarticulate murmur she reached up to throw her arms about his neck, holding him close as she caressed his hair.

'I love you so,' she whispered.

'Witch! You will drive me mad with desire. Let us go, or I won't be responsible for my actions…'

Georgiana could not mistake the look of longing in his eyes and she blushed a little.

'Still shy?' he teased. 'After last night I thought…'

She laid a soft hand over his lips, but she was laughing as she replied. 'My lord, you shall not put me out of countenance.'

'Not yet, perhaps, but tonight…' His fingers wandered the full length of her spine, and it tingled in happy anticipation. 'Tonight, my love, we shall learn more about each other… The bond between us will grow and strengthen, now that we are one flesh.'

'I know it.' She looked at him with perfect trust. 'Edward, I am so happy.'

'And I.' With a loving smile he took her arm. 'My dearest, we must go.'

'But where?'

'That I shall not tell you. It is to be a surprise.'

'A pleasant one?'

'I trust you will think so. The drive to our destination is not far.'

Dreamy-eyed and languorous, Georgiana paid little attention to her surroundings as the carriage bowled through the narrow streets of the French capital. The man beside her occupied her mind to the exclusion of all else.

She was intensely aware of his physical presence, smiling as she thought of the sheer athletic perfection of that powerful frame. As always, his dress was immaculate, if unobtrusive in its elegance. It was no wonder that his striking figure drew all eyes, but she alone could compare him to the Apollo of the Belvedere.

Last night she had seen the wonder of her lover

as nature made him. She had covered the lean, hard body with kisses, stroking the heavily muscled back and thighs, whilst wondering at the smoothness of his tanned skin. The faint male scent of him had excited her, even as he had aroused her with his caresses.

Her glance rested on his hands and her colour rose. Those long, graceful fingers had aroused her to unimaginable heights of passion, questing, exploring and teasing. Even now, as she looked at them, she felt a stirring of desire.

'Georgiana?' Edward was smiling down at her. Then he took her hand in his and pressed his lips against her palm. 'Still tired, my darling? I feel I used you roughly.'

Her blush deepened. 'I…I am not tired… But where are we going, Edward?'

'We are there.' He threw open the carriage door and swung to the ground. Then he reached up to help her down.

Georgiana looked about her in surprise. It was clear that they had reached the outskirts of the city, as green fields stretched on either side. No dwellings of any size lay before them, except for a hostelry and a church.

'What is this place?' she asked.

'It is the home of an old acquaintance.' Edward took her hand and led her along the pathway to the church. At the porch he turned aside and tapped on the door of an adjoining building.

It was opened by a tubby man with twinkling eyes. His tonsure proclaimed his calling.

'Come in, my son.' The priest stood aside to allow his guests to precede him. Then he followed them into a small study.

Georgiana looked at him with interest. His expression was genial, but his bright blue eyes were shrewd as he gazed at her. Then he turned to her companion.

'You wish the ceremony to take place at once, my lord?'

'If Georgiana agrees. My dearest, will you marry me today? I know you have been troubled, but as my wife no harm will come to you…'

Georgiana's mind was in a whirl. This, then, was the reason for the white gown, the pearls…?

'My lord, you should have told me of your plans,' she demurred.

'Would you have agreed?'

She was silent. Suddenly her fears returned. If Merton should discover her marriage he might go to any lengths…

She looked at Edward and his expression broke her heart. In his eyes doubt was mingled with apprehension. On an impulse she reached out to him.

'I wish for nothing more than to be your wife,' she assured him.

'My dearest, you are quite sure? I promised you time to consider but I cannot wait, and I feared that something…someone…might cause you to refuse me.'

His eyes searched her face, and for a moment her heart misgave her. There was so much she had not told him. He believed that her regard for Harry was the sole cause of her hesitation, but there was more…much more. If she agreed to wed him now she might be putting his own life at risk.

'I have overborne your wishes with this stratagem.' Edward clasped her hand with a rueful look. 'I wanted to carry you off…to still your doubts here, in this church. Was I wrong to try to persuade you, Georgiana?'

'No, my love.' She made up her mind on the instant. 'If the good father will marry us I am happy to agree.'

Edward's glowing look was enough to fill her heart with joy. Her doubts vanished like snow in summer, and with a beating heart she allowed him to lead her through into the simple church. When they were married she would tell him everything.

She looked up at the tall, straight figure standing beside her at the altar. He had all her heart and all her trust. How foolish she had been to try to carry her burdens alone. Edward would cherish her and protect her, and she had faith in his judgement.

The ceremony was brief, but as her lover pledged his troth to her she treasured every word. Her own replies were made in a low voice, but they came from her heart. Never before had she understood the full beauty of the marriage service. The vows she made that day she would keep forever.

Those sacred moments ended when Edward kissed her. Then he raised her hand to his lips, saluting her wedding ring.

'May I offer my good wishes for your happiness, Viscountess Lyndhurst?' The tubby little parish priest was beaming with pleasure. 'I have no doubt of it myself. Your husband is a worthy man.'

With many congratulations he ushered them back to the carriage, and waved until they were out of sight.

Edward slipped an arm about Georgiana's waist and drew her close. 'Well, my dear wife, was the ordeal very dreadful?'

'Oh, Edward, it was beautiful! I thought I must disgrace you by bursting into tears of happiness.'

'Dear love!' His kiss was very gentle. 'I had not thought to know such joy. How good you are! It would have served me well if you had refused me out of pique.'

'What can you mean?' Her eyes were very bright.

'I did abduct you,' he teased. 'At least, I did not tell you of my plans. Have you forgiven me the deception?'

'Certainly not! You must know, my lord, that a long betrothal is considered proper.'

'How long?' He buried his face in her neck.

'At least, at the very least, two years.' She kept her eyes demurely on her lap.

'It couldn't be done,' he announced solemnly. 'Why, you will have given me two babes by then…' He kissed her again as she began to blush. 'What a delight you are! A creature of fire and snow! I could not have guessed that my love would be returned in such good part.'

'But you know it now,' she whispered.

'Yes, I know it now. What a life we shall have together, my darling! It will be my pleasure to give you everything your heart can desire. When we return to England we shall go first to Lyndhurst. Then, if you wish it, we may return to Europe, or visit the Indies, if you prefer.'

Georgiana listened in a daze of happiness as he told her of his home, and his estates abroad. Now he would be by her side forever, yet only that morning her future had promised to be bleak in the extreme. These last few hours had transformed her life in a way for which she had not dared to hope.

For the rest of that day the hours flew by. Lyndhurst dismissed the hotel servants, and they were attended only by a smiling Betsy and her uncle.

On being informed of his master's good fortune, Scroggins said all that was proper on the occasion, but his attitude to Georgiana was unbending. He addressed her correctly, but her title seemed to stick in his throat.

'Give him time,' Edward said cheerfully. 'He's a dry stick, but he has a good heart.'

Georgiana sighed to herself. Privately she wondered if Scroggins would ever accept her. Doubtless he thought her an adventuress, who had trapped his master into marriage. Loyalty was all very well in its way, she mused, but in this case she sensed suspicion and hostility.

News of the Viscount's marriage swept the

hotel, and that evening it was clear that the chef had outdone himself. A feast awaited them, but excitement prevented Georgiana from doing justice to the meal. She ate when pressed to do so, but she could not have named the dishes.

Her eyes were on her lover's face, caressing, even in her thoughts, that beautifully curved mouth and the clean lines of his profile. He sensed her regard, and reached across the table to press her hand.

'I could eat you rather than this.' He laughed as he waved a dismissive hand at the viands on the table. 'Have I told you how beautiful you are?'

'You mentioned it,' she teased.

He came round to sit beside her, cupping her face in a firm grip.

'Possibly I did not say that those wonderful eyes remind me of the summer sea, deep green and fathomless.'

'But, my lord, you tell me that you are able always to fathom my innermost thoughts…'

'Not always, Georgiana…' His face grew serious. 'Sometimes I wonder…'

Now, if ever, was the time to speak, the time to unburden herself of the full story of Merton, and his hold upon Harry, but she could not bring herself to do it.

Tonight she would not ruin Edward's happiness. Tomorrow would be time enough to embroil him in the sorry mess of her brother's affairs. Perhaps it was weak of her to put off the moment when she must tell him the full story, but this was her wedding day, and it was precious to her.

'You cannot wonder at my love,' she said gently.

'I shall wonder at it all my life. My dearest wife, I want you so much…'

'And I you, Edward…'

With a muttered exclamation he swept her into his arms and carried her to her room.

His hands were gentle as he untied the ribbon beneath her breasts. Then he drew the flimsy cambric gown over her head and laid it aside. His kisses were urgent as he removed her undergarments. Then he held her away from him, his eyes feasting on her beauty.

'You drive me mad with desire,' he whispered as he bent his head to her naked breasts. 'Tonight, my darling, I will show you what love truly means.'

He threw back the coverlet and laid her on the bed. His coat was quickly thrown aside, but as he began to unbutton his shirt the door burst open.

'Harry!' Georgiana clutched at the coverlet to

hide her naked body as her brother stormed into the room. His face was ashen, but there was murder in his eyes. With a cry of rage he launched himself at Lyndhurst.

Edward sidestepped the sudden charge with ease. As Harry turned, reaching for his throat, he caught the younger man's wrists in an iron grip, forcing him to his knees.

'How dare you burst into your sister's room without a by-your-leave?' he demanded. 'Have you no respect for her privacy?'

'Respect?' It was a shout of rage. 'She deserves none, and nor do you. I'll kill you for this!'

'Be quiet!' the Viscount thundered. 'Another insult to my wife and I'll thrash you within an inch of your life.'

'Your wife?' The fight went out of Harry as he stared at Lyndhurst. 'I...I don't believe you,' he muttered. 'This is some trick. It won't be the first time, will it, my lord?'

Lyndhurst struck him across the mouth. 'You young puppy! I am minded to thrash you anyway.'

'To stop me from speaking the truth? Does my sister know how you dishonoured the woman to whom you were betrothed, and then abandoned her?'

'So you listen to gossip, do you?' Edward released his grip and allowed Edward to rise to his feet. 'That accusation is beneath contempt. I shall not trouble to answer it.'

'Because you can't.' Harry stood very straight and still as he turned to his sister. 'Georgie, come with me now. You can't stay here. I don't care what you have done…'

'That is generous of you, Harry.' Georgiana was furious with him, and her voice was dangerously quiet. 'I have done nothing of which I need be ashamed. Edward is telling the truth. We were married in church this morning.'

'Doubtless by some friend of his, dressed as a parson.' Harry's handsome face was an ugly mask of bitterness. 'He has deceived you for his own ends.' He gasped in pain as steely fingers gripped his arm.

'You will withdraw that remark.' Lyndhurst's eyes glittered with anger.

'I will not withdraw. Name your seconds, sir. I will meet you at a place of your choosing.'

'Stop it!' Georgiana stared at him. 'Harry, you are behaving like an idiot. I am Edward's wife—his *wife,* do you understand? You may believe it or not, as you choose, but nothing will alter the fact that we are married.'

Her words held utter conviction, and Harry made a gesture of despair.

'How could you, Georgie? To go behind my back... I had not thought it of you. You might have warned me...'

'You were always by my side, of course.' She could not resist the taunt.

'I know... I should not have left you. I am to blame for all of this.' He hung his head.

'Oh, Hal!' Georgiana threw up her hands in exasperation. 'How little you know me! Do you think I would marry for any reason other than love?'

'You can't love Lyndhurst,' he said sulkily.

'But I do.' She bestowed a tender glance on Edward and he came to her at once, taking her hand and dropping a kiss upon her fingers.

'He's a monster,' Harry announced. The freckles which stood out against his pale skin served to give him the appearance of a disappointed child.

Lyndhurst's shout of laughter surprised both Georgiana and her brother. He held out a hand to Harry.

'Let us be friends,' he said. 'I do not blame you for your anger. You wished only to defend Georgiana's honour, but she is now in my care.

For her sake, if for no other reason, we must not quarrel. Her happiness will always be my first concern.'

'And Edward is not a monster,' Georgiana said proudly. She gazed into her husband's eyes and Harry could not mistake that look of love.

'Then I suppose I must wish you happy.' His manner was stiff. He did not intend to be mollified too easily.

'Will you give me a kiss?' Georgiana was radiant. 'Harry, I am well content.'

'I am glad of it.' His carefree manner returned as he saluted her, disarmed by her evident joy. 'What a think to happen! Richard won't believe it—!' He stopped and shot an uneasy glance at Lyndhurst.

'Harry, where is my brother?' The Viscount's voice was calm. 'I should like to see him.'

'He isn't far away.' Harry shifted from one foot to the other as he debated with himself. Then he reached a decision. 'I'll take you to him if you wish.'

'At once, if you please!'

'Edward, won't it wait until tomorrow?' Suddenly Georgiana was uneasy. She should have told him of Merton's involvement with the two young men. Now he would learn the story from their own lips. She had no doubt that he would insist on the whole truth. Then he would realise that she had not been frank with him.

'I shall not be long away from you, my dearest.' He blew her a kiss as he accompanied Harry from the room.

She waited for what seemed like hours, until at last she fell asleep, her lips curved in a tender smile. At last it did not matter that Edward had found the fugitives. He had been kind to Harry, in spite of her brother's reluctance to accept his friendship. Now all their problems were in his hands, and he would know what to do.

She stirred as a noise awakened her. Then she sat bolt upright. In the light of a single candle a figure moved towards her.

'Edward?' she murmured.

'Were you expecting someone else? Merton, perhaps…?' Edward's voice was raw with anger.

She could see only the faint outline of his face. Then he held the candle high, and she gave a cry of horror. She was looking into the eyes of a stranger. That mask-like countenance bore no resemblance to the man she loved so well, and she shrivelled at his expression of revulsion.

'You need not shrink from me,' the cynical

voice continued. 'I would not touch you if you were the last woman alive.'

'Edward, please…' Georgiana held out her arms in supplication. 'Only let me explain… I meant to tell you what had happened, but there was no opportunity.'

'No? You lay in my arms…you told me you loved me…whilst you laughed behind my back. When I think of that evening with Merton! How you must both have enjoyed my ignorance of what was afoot!'

'So it is wounded pride which makes you treat me as an enemy…?' Georgiana shivered. She felt icy cold.

'Not pride, my dear, but a sense of betrayal. In my folly I had imagined that you trusted me, yet since we met I have never had your confidence.'

'That is not true, I—'

He silenced her with a look.

'Will you deny that you knew of Merton's villainy? That you have known since we were at Calais?'

'I don't deny it,' she said dully. 'But they told me you would be killed…'

'So your silence was the price of my life?' His laugh was filled with scorn. 'What kind of a man do you think me?'

Georgiana did not reply.

'Unlike your brother I do not care to hide behind your petticoats,' he continued. 'Is it true that you planned to go with Merton?'

'I… We had no choice. It was either your life or that of Harry and your brother.'

'I will take care of my own!' he said savagely. 'If you think so little of me, I wonder why you married me.'

'It was because I love you,' she cried in anguish.

'Love? You don't know the meaning of the word. Love is not simply passion, Georgiana. It demands faith and trust between husband and wife.'

'Like your faith and trust in me?' Georgiana's eyes filled.

'Spare me your tears. This time they will not serve to sway me. You speak of my trust in you?' His laugh was ugly. 'Was it to continue when you disappeared again? The vows you made this morning meant nothing, I suppose?'

'I meant every word of them,' she sobbed. 'I would not have left you, Edward; I had changed my mind. Tonight I meant to tell you all…'

'Another pack of lies and half-truths? Madam, you sicken me. Whether you go or stay is now a matter of indifference to me.'

'You are hateful,' she cried wildly. 'Go! Get out of my sight.'

'It will be a pleasure.' With an ironic bow he left her.

Chapter Ten

Georgiana had never felt so wretched in her life. She buried her head in her pillow and wept until she had no tears left. In a few short hours her world had tumbled about her ears, and on this, her wedding day…

It was so unfair. She had acted with the best of intentions in an effort to protect both Edward and Harry, but she had succeeded in doing neither.

Edward hated her. She would not soon forget the expression in his eyes. They had held contempt, disgust and, above all, anger. He was not a man to forgive or forget an insult to his honour. He would have his revenge, she was sure of it, and now Harry too was at his mercy.

To sleep was impossible. She rose and dressed

and began to pace the room. What on earth was she to do? To be tied for life to a man who loathed her was a fate beyond her worst nightmares, especially as she…as she…

Her lips quivered, then she straightened her shoulders. She did not love him. It was impossible. How could any woman care for someone who had treated her so cruelly? And he had been cruel. Harry was right. Edward was a monster. He had taken her love and flung it back in her face…

She sat by her window for hours until the first pale light of dawn streaked across the sky. Her cheeks were burning, but her hands were icy cold.

She had come to a decision in those lonely hours. She could not stay with Edward; that was clear. He must agree to annul their marriage.

The prospect brought her no comfort, but it was the only solution. She could not bear to see him every day…to be in his presence and to live with his contempt. He had found his brother; perhaps that would be enough to send him back to England.

If she could escape with Harry her husband would think himself well rid of her. Then she remembered Merton and her heart sank. Edward would not leave until he had settled his account with the man who had brought his brother to ruin;

she knew him well enough to know that. And it would be no affair of honour, to be settled between gentlemen. Merton was more likely to resort to a knife in the back.

She sank her head in her hands. It was all very well for Edward to claim that he could take care of himself, but was he prepared for treachery? He did not know Merton as she did.

Yet it was no concern of hers. She must steel herself against any softening towards him. She sat as if turned to stone, and did not turn her head as Betsy entered the room.

'I hope I did right, miss—I mean madam. With his lordship gone I thought you might be wanting your breakfast.'

Georgiana looked at her with brimming eyes. She could not speak.

'There, there, my lady… You must not take on so. Why, you look like a ghost this morning…' With scant regard for ceremony she threw a comforting arm about Georgiana's shoulders.

The presence of a friendly face was the undoing of her mistress. Georgiana began to sob.

'I'm sorry, Betsy. I don't mean to be so foolish.'

'A lovers' quarrel, is it, Miss Georgiana? Well, gentlemen is funny critturs. There's no understanding them.' Betsy's hug was bear-like. 'Leave 'em be, is what I say. They comes round in the end.'

'Betsy, you are wise beyond your years.' Georgiana smiled through her tears. 'But this time you are wrong.'

'Bless you, they're all the same. I ain't no beauty, but the village lads be strong for me…'

'I'm not surprised. Dear Betsy, how kind you are!'

'That's as may be,' came the sturdy reply. 'Now, madam, I was to tell you that his lordship will be back betimes. You are to wait for him in the parlour.'

'I see!' Georgiana was infuriated. How dared Edward send his instructions by the servants?

'My uncle says as how his lordship be on his high ropes this morning,' Betsy ventured.

'Then he may come down from them.' Georgiana was too angry to consider the wisdom of her words.

Betsy giggled, though she endeavoured to look solemn. 'Will you wear the white again?' she asked.

'Certainly not! The yellow will do well enough.'

Betsy was clever enough to hold her tongue. She dressed her mistress in silence.

It was several hours before Edward returned. Meantime Georgiana was a prey to conflicting emotions. Anger gave way to despair, and finally to the faint hope that he might have softened towards her.

One look at his face was enough to disabuse her of that idea. It was expressionless. He came towards her and bowed with formal courtesy. She might have been a stranger.

'I shall not keep you over-long,' he began. 'But there are certain matters to discuss. I intend to remain in Paris for some time. No doubt you will not wish to stay here. I you will tell me of your plans I will provide you with funds…'

'I want nothing from you,' she said coldly.

'You are still my wife, and my responsibility. What do you intend to do?'

'I…I have no plans.'

'You surprise me! That fertile mind must have at least a dozen schemes… Come, madam, we are wasting time. Let us reach an agreement quickly, then I'll relieve you of my company.'

'I shall not leave my brother.' Her eyes were defiant as she faced him squarely.

'I see. What an optimist you are! Neither you nor he will continue your association with Merton. You may be sure of that.'

'What do you mean to do?' Georgiana began to tremble. There was murder in his face.

'I intend to wait for his return. The bird has flown, possibly to attend to the "arrangements" of which he told you. As yet he does not know that I have found his victims.'

'He may not come back,' she breathed.

'He'll come back. Nothing is more certain. Are you not an essential part of his schemes?'

Georgiana did not argue. There was little point. He would not believe a word she said.

'I am concerned only for my brother,' she said. 'You have not told me…'

'He is unharmed. I shall honour his commitments, and those of Richard too.'

'We cannot accept…' Swift colour flooded Georgiana's face.

'Madam, you have no choice. This is my decision and your brother has agreed.'

She was on her feet in an instant. 'Oh, how could he?' she cried. 'He should have asked me first.'

'Still interfering, my dear? When will you learn that your brother is a man grown, if a foolish one? On this occasion he found it reasonable that I, as his brother-in-law, should offer my help. His gratitude was somewhat overwhelming.'

'Then…then he may return to England?'

'Not for the moment. He will go to India, as I suggested. You may, of course, accompany him if you wish, though I would not recommend the climate for a female. England would be a better choice for you. I will write to your father…'

'You will do no such thing!' She gave him a dagger-like look. 'I won't be packed off like some useless baggage.'

'A baggage, certainly,' he purred. 'But useless? Hardly. You are not in your best looks this morning, but that may soon be remedied.'

With a speed which caught her unawares he seized her in his arms.

'Let me go!' she cried. 'Last night you said that you had no wish to touch me.'

'I spoke in haste, my dear. After all, when a man is married he is entitled to expect some comfort from his wife.'

'You will get none from me!' Georgiana struggled in vain to break his grip. 'I hate you!'

'That need not diminish our pleasure, my dear.' His hand cupped her breast, and his thumb caressed her nipple gently.

Her response was instant and could not be denied. Furious in the knowledge that her body could betray her, she bent her head and sank her teeth into his wrist. Then she cried out in pain as he caught at her hair and forced her head back.

'Have you forgotten your marriage vows so soon?' he sneered. 'I seem to remember something about obedience.'

'I will never obey you,' she panted. 'I did not know you when I made those vows.'

'Nor I you, apparently.' He flung her away from him. 'Nevertheless, we are handfasted, and you will do your duty.'

'You…you are trying to frighten me,' she accused. 'If you think to drive me back to England with your threats you will not do it.'

'So it is to be India? As you wish, though I warn you, madam… You bear my name, and I will not have it dragged through the mud.'

'I have no intention of using it. I do not care to be associated with you, or any member of your family.'

'Especially as your own is beyond reproach.'

'That, my lord, is the cheapest of gibes,' Georgiana said with dignity. 'If you have done with me, I shall retire.'

'Oh, I have not done with you, my dear…far from it; but you may go. Incidentally, my brother dines with us this evening, and Harry too.'

Georgiana had reached the door, but his words stopped her. She looked up in surprise, but Edward had turned away and was gazing through the window. She left him without comment.

The evening promised to be a trial, but the reality was worse. Georgiana tried to smile as Richard kissed her shyly and wished her years of happiness. Harry, too, was in buoyant mood, toasting the bride again and again as he chaffed her and congratulated Edward.

Georgiana writhed inwardly. Neither of them could know that they were turning the knife in the wound. She stole a glance at Edward, wondering if he felt as she did, but his face was imperturbable. He plays the part of the loving bridegroom to perfection, she thought bitterly as he pressed her to accept another glass of wine.

'No pearls tonight, my dear?' he enquired.

Georgiana's hand flew to her throat before she remembered. She had laid the pearls back in their case, intending to return them to him.

'They were not suitable with this gown,' she muttered. Her bridal finery, too, was packed away. She could not bear to look at it.

'A pity…but perhaps tomorrow?' There was no warmth in his smile.

Tomorrow you shall have them back, she vowed to herself. She turned away from him and spoke to Richard.

'I hear that you are to go to the West Indies?'

'Yes, Miss Westleigh. I beg your pardon…I should call you sister now that you are Edward's wife.'

'Georgiana will do.' She found that she could not resist his charm. He looked absurdly young as he bent towards her.

'I am to learn to manage the family estates,' he told her with pride. 'I hope I may do well.'

'Of course you will. When do you leave?'

'Quite soon, though Harry goes before me. You will miss him, Georgiana, and so shall I.' His face was wistful. 'I wish we might have gone together, but Edward feels that Harry will do better in the East.'

'I am sure of it.' Edward's voice was bland. 'I have every hope that Harry will become a nabob, if he applies himself.'

Harry beamed upon the assembled company.

'Georgie, I'll make you proud of me.' His eyes sparkled as he looked at her. Then he lowered his voice. 'You don't mind my going, do you?' he asked in an undertone. 'After all, you have Edward now.'

'Yes! I have Edward now.' It took all Georgiana's self-control to utter the words. She shot a swift glance at her husband. It was clear that he had told neither of the young men of their differences. No doubt he was enjoying her discomfiture as she was forced to play out this dreadful charade.

Edward did not look at her. He appeared to be deep in conversation with his brother. She turned again to Harry with a request to be told of his destination in India, and how he would travel there. Later she would be able to remember neither her questions nor his replies.

'Come back, Georgie,' Harry teased. 'You are a world away. I don't believe you've heard a word I've said…'

She made a creditable effort to smile, but her eyes were sad.

'What is it, my dearest? You must not grieve because we are to part for a time. In a year or two you will have your own nursery, and I shall return as the wicked uncle…' He began to laugh.

'I believe you,' she said wryly, though she knew it could never be. His words had served only to remind her of all that she had lost. She blinked back a tear.

'There, there!' Harry patted her hand. 'Edward

will look after you. I was mistaken in him, Georgie. At first I thought you mad, but at bottom he's a stout fellow. He gave us a roasting, though…' His face grew solemn as he recalled the Viscount's biting words.

'He mentioned that he had offered his help,' Georgiana said quietly.

'He will take care of everything. About the money, Georgie… I hope you don't mind. Edward said that as we were brothers now I could accept… He was most insistent.'

'He usually gets his way… But Harry, no more scrapes, do you promise?'

'I give you my word, and I won't break it.'

'Did Edward say what he intended…about Merton?'

'He told us to think no more about the man. I shouldn't care to be in Merton's shoes when Edward meets him. He can be fearsome, can't he? Perhaps he'll manage to get the money back.'

'Perhaps.' Georgiana looked up and caught Richard's eye. He raised his glass to her.

'To the new Viscountess,' he cried gaily. 'When we next see you you'll be at Lyndhurst. I'm beginning to believe the old saw about the ill wind that blows no good.'

'Don't get above yourself, stripling,' Edward's look was enough to cause his brother to subside, but he would not be quelled for long. Relief mingled with excitement as he chattered on about his hopes for both himself and Harry.

Georgiana was bone-weary and depressed, and her head began to ache. For a time she made an effort to join in the conversation, but the pain behind her eyes increased.

'Will you forgive me if I leave you?' she murmured finally.

'Exhausted, my dear?' Edward affected not to notice the smiles of the two young men, but the implication was not lost on Georgiana.

'It has been a long day,' she said stiffly.

'How thoughtless we are!' Harry jumped to his feet. 'Richard, let us go. We may return tomorrow, if Edward will permit...'

'Delighted! You may do me a service, if you will, by acting as Georgiana's escort should she care to see more of the city. I have some matters to attend...'

Georgiana stared at him, and her feeling of depression deepened. Now that Edward had found his brother he had achieved his end in coming to France. She herself was of no further use to him, and she might come and go as she pleased. The knowledge should have brought a feeling of relief, but it left her feeling bereft.

When they were alone she turned to him.

'You have not learned when Merton will return?' she asked coldly.

'Not yet. But let me assure you that you will have no opportunity to warn him…'

'I shall not need to do so. When he seeks out Harry and Richard they will be unable to dissemble.'

'I think not. I have told them what to say.'

'So you have thought of everything? Suppose he should see me in company with my brother in the streets of Paris? He will know at once that something is amiss.'

'You will be in no danger.' Edward's face was imperturbable. 'I have taken steps…'

'So your spies will be at hand? I might have known. I thought it strange that you would set me free.'

He smiled, and she caught her breath.

'I see,' she said slowly. 'You hope that Merton will see us. This is a trap, and I am the bait…'

'Your concern for your friend has quickened your perception, my dear. I congratulate you.'

Green eyes flashing, she took a step towards

him. 'I had not thought that anyone could be so blind,' she cried. 'Merton is not my friend. Would I look kindly on anyone who could harm my brother?'

'You looked rather more than kindly upon me, or have you forgotten your surrender?'

'You need not remind me.' Her colour rose, much to her chagrin. 'There is nothing I regret more bitterly.'

'I do not. It was a most enjoyable experience, and it is more than time that we repeated it.' A vice-like arm slipped about her waist. 'Let me invite you to our bridal bed.'

Georgiana stood like a statue within his grasp.

'I cannot prevent you from taking me, but rape, my lord? You value your honour lightly.'

At that he held her away from him. As the blue eyes looked into hers he was formidable.

'Take care!' he warned. 'You, of all people, may not speak of honour.'

'Of course not! A woman's honour does not weigh with you. What of the lady you betrayed?' She had not forgotten Harry's words, and now she flung them back, too reckless with despair to care for their effect.

Edward's arms fell to his sides. He was white-faced, and his eyes were blazing with anger. Without a word, he strode from the room, leaving Georgiana to enjoy her triumph.

It was a hollow victory. She had wished to drive him away, and she had done so, but it brought her no comfort.

She must get away from him, if only for her own peace of mind. The day when she and Harry sailed for India could not come too soon. I forgot to thank him on Harry's behalf, she thought suddenly. But it did not matter. Doubtless he had some underlying motive for his apparent kindness, even if it was only to separate the two young men.

Her thoughts were bitter as she remembered his courtesy at supper. He could forgive Harry and Richard for their folly, but she herself was not to be excused.

She was well out of her unfortunate marriage, she told herself. Who would wish to be tied for life to such an unpleasant creature? He was arrogant, boorish, unreasonable, and a master of sarcasm. How could she ever have imagined that she loved him? She swallowed the lump in her throat as she rang for Betsy.

Betsy made no comment as her mistress sought

her lonely bed once more, but her face was expressive of surprise.

'His lordship is to make an early start tomorrow.' Georgiana murmured. She did not know if it was true or not, but it would serve as an explanation. At that moment she could not cope with sympathy.

'Then I won't wake you early, madam. You look that fagged…'

'No compliments, Betsy!' Georgiana managed the faintest of smiles. 'A night's sleep will restore me, and my brother is to escort me tomorrow.'

'Mr Harry?' Betsy beamed. It was clear that he had lost none of his ability to charm. 'He'll do you good with his jolly ways.'

Harry's jollity was tested on the following day.

'Notre-Dame? Oh, must we?' He looked dismayed at the prospect. 'You can't wish to poke about a pile of stones, Georgie. We'll have more fun on the river.'

Richard looked relieved at the suggestion, though he had the grace to murmur something about pleasing Georgiana.

'She'll enjoy it,' Harry announced with conviction. 'Won't you, Georgie?'

She did not demur, though the thought crossed

her mind that Edward's spies or bodyguards—whatever he cared to call them—would find it difficult to follow. She did not care.

She looked about her intently as the carriage rolled through the streets, but she saw no signs of pursuit, nor could she distinguish anyone who looked in the least suspicious in the bustling crowds.

As they left the landing-stage several vessels followed in their wake, but they overtook their own slower craft, and Georgiana settled back to enjoy the sensation of the breeze against her face.

'That's better!' Harry glanced at her with approval. 'You looked like a ghost last night. Now you've some colour in your cheeks. Was not this a famous idea?'

'Better than most of yours,' she said drily.

He aimed a playful blow at her. 'No lectures, Georgie. We are both wearing sackcloth today. Richard, ain't that true?'

Richard looked uncomfortable. 'We have both been fools, as Edward pointed out.' He gave her a shy smile. 'But I must thank you for the change in him. He's different somehow. He listened to what we had to say.'

'He'd plenty to say himself.' Harry grimaced. I

may tell you, sister, dear, that he flayed us with his tongue.'

'You may thank your stars that he didn't flay you with a horsewhip.'

'I suppose we deserved it. He was most upset, I believe, by the way I had distressed you, and drawn you in… Oh, Georgie, I am truly sorry.'

She heard his words with some surprise, but, leaning forward, she patted his hand.

'It's over,' she said in an absent tone. 'Now you must think about the future.'

Her words were enough to start both of them into further discussion of their plans, but Georgiana paid them scant attention. As she trailed her fingers in the water she was meditating on Harry's words.

After Edward's rejection of her explanations it seemed strange that he should have berated Harry more for his treatment of his sister than for the fraud which had been the cause of all their troubles. Could she have been mistaken in him?

She pushed the thought aside. Had it not been for her bitter words last night he would have raped her. And he was only too willing to let her go to India with Harry. Those were not the actions of a man in love.

Suddenly she felt chilled.

'It is growing cold,' she said. 'I think we should return.'

They took her back to the hotel, where she presided over a light nuncheon. Then, sensing that they were chafing at the prospect of an afternoon indoors, she announced that she would rest for an hour or two.

'But Edward said…'

'Edward will understand.' She dismissed them and walked into her room.

As she lay down on the bed great waves of sleep came to overwhelm her. She should not have let Harry persuade her to take wine so early in the day, she thought drowsily. Yet it had been only a single glass… She drifted off into slumber.

It was late afternoon when she awoke, and at first she thought she was alone. Then she saw a movement in the chair beside the fireplace.

'Edward?'

'No, my dear. It is not your husband.' Merton rose, stretched, and strolled towards the bed. 'He, I believe, is occupied on some wild-goose chase which I had the foresight to arrange.'

Georgiana lay paralysed. She could not have moved a muscle had she tried.

'What a clever little creature you are!' The silvery eyes were mere slits as they gazed down at her. 'It is a pity that your brother has not more of your intelligence.'

'I don't know what you mean,' she breathed.

'Oh, come now! To marry the Viscount, throwing him off the scent—it was a master-stroke!'

'You may not always think it so. He is no fool.'

'Agreed! That is what makes him such a worthy adversary. Now, my dear, let us to business.'

'I have no business with you.'

'On the contrary, I think you have. My dear Viscountess, do you believe that I will allow your husband to destroy my plans?'

'He knows everything. You cannot keep your villainy a secret.'

'Dead men tell no tales,' he said sententiously. 'An old saw, but a true one…'

Georgiana laughed in his face.

'My lord will not be taken easily…'

'Your faith in him is touching. Such devotion! I believe you would do anything to keep him safe.'

She did not reply, but her eyes never left his face.

'You will not save him, I assure you. Even now it needs but a word from me and he is a dead man.'

'Why do you hate him so?' she cried in anguish.

'Is it not enough that you have ruined his brother and my own?'

'It gave me some satisfaction, but the game is not yet played to its conclusion. Lyndhurst will pay in full for the injury he has done.'

'I don't know what you mean. He has not injured you…'

'No?' The cruel mouth twisted in a grimace. 'You know little of the man you married, my dear. He is a master of deception, as my sister found to her cost.'

Georgiana gazed at him in horror.

'He was to marry her,' Merton continued. 'The announcement appeared in the *Morning Chronicle* and on that promise she allowed herself to be seduced. Your gallant knight then abandoned her and she killed herself.'

'Oh, no!' Georgiana's hand flew to her mouth as if to stifle a cry of anguish. 'You must be mistaken about him. He could not do such a thing.'

'You have not known him long, I believe. In time you will learn the truth.'

'I trust him,' she said with spirit. 'Again I say that you will not find it easy to destroy him.'

'Perhaps not, but then…I have a hostage.'

Georgiana laughed again.

'You are mistaken, sir, if you think this marriage other than a sham. The Viscount does not care for me. His intention was to find his brother.'

'Madam, you are either very clever or a fool.' The silvery eyes were fixed upon her face. 'Shall we put it to the test? Let us approach the Viscount with a proposition; your life or your death...'

'That won't be necessary.' Lyndhurst stepped from behind the concealing curtain. He held a pistol in each hand. 'Stand back, sir. You will please to sit down over there.' He gestured towards a writing table.

Merton shrugged. He had betrayed no surprise at Edward's sudden appearance, but the twitching of an eyelid belied his iron self-control.

'Be careful, Edward! I'm sure he is armed,' Georgiana warned.

'Undoubtedly, my dear. You will take out your pistol very slowly, sir, and lay it on the table.'

Merton did as he was bidden, but he did not speak. Apparently at his ease, he lolled back in his chair, gazing at Edward with a smile of contempt.

Georgiana watched as her husband walked towards him. Edward had never looked more formidable, but she was terrified. As Merton tensed she gave a cry of fright. Keeping a safe distance between himself and the man across the table, Edward picked up the pistol. Then he jerked his head towards the door to the parlour.

'We shall discuss our business elsewhere,' he said coolly. 'I have no wish to distress my wife.' He motioned to Merton to precede him.

The door had scarcely closed behind them before Georgiana was out of bed. She dressed in great haste, almost crying with exasperation as she tugged at recalcitrant ribbons and knots.

Edward had indicated that she must not join them, but she could not wait to find out what might happen. She hurried to the door, half fearing to hear a shot, but only a murmur of conversation was audible. Both men were speaking in low tones, and she could not distinguish a word.

She reached for the handle of the door, hoping to open it the merest crack. Then she stopped. If it creaked and Edward's attention was distracted his enemy would seize the chance to overpower him. Merton, she knew, would snuff out her husband's life without a second thought.

In an agony of mind she waited for what seemed like hours. She knew that she should get help, but Harry and Richard had sought their lodgings hours ago. She did not know where to find them, and in any case she could not roam the streets in the hours of darkness.

Scroggins, perhaps? He was devoted to his master, though she did not know if he could handle a gun. But it might be better than nothing. She reached out for the bell-rope, then hesitated. Edward might not wish to involve the man, and he might not welcome her interference.

The waiting was torture, but there was nothing she could do. She was sick with anxiety; her mind was racing. How much had Edward heard of her conversation with Merton? She tried to recall each word that had passed between them. They had not troubled to lower their voices, and Edward had been there from the start. He must have entered her room whilst she slept.

The tight feeling in her chest began to ease. Now, at least, Edward would know that Merton was as much her enemy as his. He must have suspected that the man would come for her, if not that night then another. But how had he guessed that she would be alone?

The blood in her veins seemed to turn to ice. Perhaps he had not known. He might have hoped to find them both asleep.

She stifled a cry. To take her he must have come

prepared to kill her husband. Even now they might be struggling… She ran to the door again, but the voices had stopped and there was silence.

A vision of Edward's lifeless body lying in the other room spurred her to action, and she flung the door wide. In the candlelight she saw Edward standing by the table reading a document. He was alone. Her relief was so great that she thought her legs would not support her as she stumbled towards him.

'My love!' In two quick strides he was across the room to gather her into his arms.

'I thought he must have killed you,' she sobbed.

'I had the pistols, little goose! Had you forgotten?'

'He might have had another…in his sleeve or in his boot…' She would not be comforted.

'I had not overlooked the possibility, my dearest. I'm only surprised that you did not join us to remind me…' His tone was severe, but when she looked into his eyes she found that he was laughing.

She bridled. 'I don't always interfere, whatever you may think,' she told him stiffly.

'But you were tempted…? Come now, admit it!'

'I was afraid for you,' she said simply. 'Merton is a dangerous man.'

'His fangs are drawn.' Edward sat down and

took her upon his knee. 'He may not return to England. I have his confession, and also a letter to his bankers.' He pointed to the documents.

'But how…?'

'Don't ask, my love. It is better that you do not know the lengths to which your husband is prepared to go to keep you safe.'

'I thought you might have been forced to shoot him.'

'There are other methods of persuasion…and I am not without influence in certain quarters. Like all bullies, he collapsed when faced with the inevitable.'

Georgiana shook her head. 'I can't be easy in my mind,' she murmured. 'He agreed too quickly.'

He silenced her with a long kiss. Then he lifted her in his arms and carried her to her room.

Chapter Eleven

'Georgiana, I have much to say to you. Are you too tired to listen to me tonight?' Edward sat beside her, holding her hand.

She shook her head. 'I should not sleep.'

'Merton has told you an ugly tale. I should have spoke of it myself, but it happened years ago and I had no wish to distress you…'

She put a finger to his lips to silence him. 'Do not go on,' she said. 'There is no need…'

'But I want you to know the truth of it. I did know Merton's sister, though I did not guess at their relationship until tonight. She was a widow, with a husband dead in the Peninsular War.' He hesitated, frowning. 'The lady wished to remarry, and I seemed a suitable candidate, though we were mere acquaintances.'

'My dearest, this is painful for you. I wish you would not…'

'Dear Georgie, hear me out… When I did not come up to scratch she took matters into her own hands. It was she who sent the announcement to the papers and when I desired her to retract she accused me of seduction. It was an ugly business, but I was forced to insist. The next I knew was that she had killed herself.'

'How terrible! She must have been unbalanced.'

'There is some history of insanity in the family, I believe.'

'Yes, Harry told me that Merton himself is sometimes…other than normal.'

'I don't doubt it. Georgie, this is why I had to force his hand.'

'You knew he would come for me tonight?'

'I could not be sure, but I felt that if he heard that we had quarrelled he might seize the opportunity. Betsy was given leave to spread the news.'

'How long had you been behind the curtain?' she asked shyly.

'Long enough to hear how much you love me.'

His look was a tribute to her courage. 'I came in whilst you slept.'

'My darling, I have been guilty of dissembling. I've caused you pain, and for that I shall not easily forgive myself. I could think of no other way to trap Merton than to let him think that I did not share your bed.'

'Your anger was convincing,' she admitted ruefully.

He stroked her cheek. 'It was not entirely simulated. When Harry and Richard told me that you had agreed to Merton's plans I could not believe it.'

'I was trying to save your life.'

'I know that now.' Exasperation mingled with amusement in his expression as he looked at her. 'But could you not trust me enough to tell me what you knew?'

'I wanted to, but I didn't know what to do. Both you and Harry were at risk, and Richard too.'

'So you were prepared to carry the burden alone?' Edward took her hand in his. 'That must not happen in future.'

'Then you have forgiven me?' Her head was bent and she could not look at him.

He tilted her face to his and dropped a kiss upon her nose. 'That question needs no answer. Did it not seem strange to you that I could be on terms with Harry and my brother, and yet so distant with my wife?'

'You were more than distant,' she reproached. 'I hated you for your cruelty.'

'My darling, I ran grave risks, but our marriage was common knowledge. Merton, I knew, would be aware of it as soon as he returned. When he could not find Richard and Harry he would be forced to come to you.'

'But he knew where they lived…'

'I persuaded them to change their lodgings.' He gave her a quizzical look. 'I hoped that he, knowing that we were at odds with each other, would believe that you would be easily convinced…'

'Never!'

'He did not know that, and Betsy followed my instructions. She let it be known that tonight I would not share your bed.'

'To find you here would not have stopped him.' Georgiana's eyes were haunted. 'You might have been asleep…'

'Asleep? With you to tempt me?' His glowing look brought hot colour flooding to her face. Then, with a sigh, he rose. 'You will think about my words? I have treated you so badly, Georgiana. I shall not blame you if you still wish to go with Harry. Remember only that I love you more than life.'

'Dearest Edward, that is all I need to know.' Blindly she reached out for him. 'Don't leave me now. I cannot bear to be without you for a single hour.'

He caught her to him, murmuring endearments as he showered kisses upon her face. That night their passion knew no bounds, and the bond between them grew with each tender word of love. It was full daylight before they slept.

Georgiana awakened first. Carefully she raised herself on one elbow to gaze at Edward's face. In sleep he looked endearingly vulnerable. She was tempted to reach out and brush back the tousled curls which had fallen on to his brow, but she would not disturb him.

She smiled to herself. She had no need to study that beloved face to recall the laughter-lines at the corners of his eyes, the clean line of his jaw, or the curve of that mobile mouth. How long his lashes were…

He stirred, and as he turned towards her the sheet which covered him fell aside. Georgiana looked in wonder at his magnificent physique. She had lost all her shyness at the sight of his naked body. This man was hers alone, and she knew every inch of those perfect contours, from the broad shoulders which tapered to a trim waist, to the long, heavily muscled legs.

Gently she rested her cheek against his chest. Then she gasped as his arms closed round her.

'I thought you were asleep,' she protested. 'You were deceiving me again.' Her eyes were filled with laughter.

'Not so, my temptress!' He held her comfortingly close, and kissed her soundly. 'I have been watching you!' he teased. 'Are you happy with your bargain?'

She blushed. 'I…I did not mean to stare at you, but you are so dear to me. I could not ask for more…'

'Not even more of the same?' He reached out for her and she could not mistake the look in his eyes. She evaded his grasp, slipped out of bed, and fled across the room, still laughing.

'I did not mean…what you thought I meant.' she cried in confusion.

'Come here. You know that you promised to obey me.'

'It is very late. What Betsy will think I can't imagine.'

'I can. And, madam, that demure look is quite

out of place when you are mother-naked.' He was out of bed and striding towards her.

'Edward, please… We ought to make an appearance… Suppose Harry and Richard should arrive?'

'They may go away again.' He made a grab for her, but she ran to stand behind a chair.

'You won't escape me,' he promised as he pushed it aside.

'I will…I will.' She shrieked as he caught her, and collapsed in gales of laughter.

'Such a disobedient wife! What am I to do with you?' He lifted her in his arms.

'Perhaps more of the same?' she murmured, greatly daring, but unashamed of her longing for him.

Betsy, coming to wake her mistress, heard the laughter and went away again.

For Georgiana the rest of the day had a dream-like quality. She dressed and breakfasted and welcomed Harry and Richard when they came to dine, but her thoughts were all of Edward. Her happiness was overwhelming.

Lost in love, she was only half-aware of the conversation of her companions. Then Harry turned to her with sparkling eyes.

'Is it not splendid that Edward routed Merton? He even got the money, Georgie, though I don't know how he did it.' He shot a speculative look at his brother-in-law.

'He will not tell you. I asked, but it seems that we are not to know.' Georgiana smiled at Edward.

'Let me keep my secrets,' Edward teased. 'It is enough that he will trouble us no further.'

'Yet I find it strange… I had not thought he would give in without a struggle.'

Georgiana frowned at her brother's persistence, though she could understand his misgivings. She felt a tiny stirring of apprehension. Had she not felt the same?

She shook her head as if to clear it of unpleasant thoughts. She would trust in Edward's judgement but try as she might she could not forget their enemy. Merton had terrified her beyond all reason, and the memory of those hooded eyes still had the power to turn her blood to ice.

Always, in his presence, she had felt that she was screaming inwardly. From their first meeting she had sensed that there was something strange about him…something which another human being could not reach. A sick mind had to be a cause for pity, but with Merton it was more than that. For the first time in her life she had come face to face with evil. She began to shiver.

'Are you cold, my dearest?' Edward moved to close the open window.

Georgiana shook her head. She must keep a closer guard upon her thoughts. Edward must not guess that the mere mention of Merton's name was enough to terrify her.

His keen eyes searched her face. Then he turned the conversation into lighter channels. It was not until late that night as he lay beside her that he spoke again of Merton.

'My love, are you still afraid?' he began.

Startled, she looked up at him. 'I...I... No, of course not.'

'I wonder how I ever imagined that you could cheat and lie,' he said lightly as he twisted a straying curl about his fingers. 'Your face is the mirror of your thoughts, my darling. When Merton's name is mentioned that haunted look returns. I had hoped to banish it forever.'

'I wish I could believe that he will not return,' she told him wistfully. 'Will you not tell me what you said to him?'

Edward looked at her thoughtfully. 'I had hoped to keep it from you. You will not think well of me, though I had the right…and I would do more, much more, to keep you safe.'

'So…please tell me.'

'I have some papers in my possession,' he said slowly. 'They are from his sister…letters and…and the final suicide note. They prove beyond doubt that she was mad. I kept them long ago to still the gossips' tongues, but I did not. She was gone, and I would not sully the reputation of the dead.'

Georgiana cradled his head upon her breast. 'I love you for that,' she said softly.

'There is more.' Edward's voice was low. 'There was a son…Merton's nephew and the son of her dead husband. The boy is kept hidden at the family home. He is a lunatic. Even as a child there were ugly stories concerning his treatment of various animals. I will not distress you with the details. Now the lad is seventeen and he is dangerous and cunning. He has a keeper, but sometimes he escapes…'

'Oh, Edward…'

'Do you wish me to go on?'

Georgiana nodded though his face was so grim that she dreaded to hear what he would tell her.

'There have been attacks…first upon children and then upon the village girls…'

'How do you know of this?'

'His dead father's estate runs alongside my own. That was how I came to meet the lady. His grandparents live there now, but they are no longer young, and they cannot control the boy.

'I went to see them before I left for the West Indies, and obtained a promise that he would be moved to a place of safety where he could do no further harm, but that did not happen.'

'Why not? It would seem the sensible thing to do.'

'My bailiff tells me that someone stepped in and persuaded them against it.'

'Merton?'

'It must have been Merton. He is the boy's only other living relative. I had never met him, but I'd been aware for some time that someone with influence was covering up the attacks. Now there has been a murder.'

Georgiana sat up suddenly. 'You must speak out at once,' she said with conviction. 'Inform the authorities; they will know what to do.'

'I had every intention of laying the case before them,' Edward told her with a look of pain. 'Then I found out who Merton was. My dear, it was the only weapon I could use against him.'

'The threat of exposure?'

'Yes. I said that I would inform against him.'

'But Edward, you must. Not even to save Richard, Harry or myself shall you leave a lunatic at large, to murder as he wills.'

'He will not be left at large. One of my conditions is that Merton does as I suggest and arranges for the boy to be kept secure. The alternatives are Bedlam, or, at worst, the hangman's rope.'

Georgiana paled. 'Oh, they would not hang him?'

'It is a possibility, and I cannot decide if it would be the better fate…'

She was silent then. How often she had spoken out in indignation against those members of the London *ton* who sought amusement in that infamous place, laughing and scoffing at the spectacle of the Bedlamites and their curious antics. The thought of the gallows outside Newgate made her tremble.

'I understand now,' she whispered. 'You forced him to agree to your terms, but, Edward, you will always be a danger to him, and he has his bully boys. I shall not soon forget the men who attacked you.'

'Yet I too have my "bully boys", as you so rightly term them. Since I knew the truth you have not been out of their sight.'

'I did not notice them.'

'You were not supposed to. I durst not risk another scold for setting spies on you.' His eyes twinkled.

'Do you think me a termagant?' she demanded.

'I think you adorable. Now let me kiss away that troubled look.'

He was as good as his word, and it was some time before they slept.

It was the smell of smoke which roused her. She laid a hand on Edward's shoulder.

'What is it, my love?'

'Smoke! Do you not smell smoke?'

He was out of bed in an instant. 'Get dressed,' he said quickly. He wasted no time in pulling on his shirt, breeches and coat. 'I will find out what is happening.'

As he opened the door she heard shouting and the sound of running feet. Beyond him she could see a mob of struggling figures in the corridor.

Georgiana grabbed her pearls and her reticule. Then she began to stuff clothing into a bag.

'Leave that,' Edward ordered sharply. He stepped into the corridor with outstretched arms, bringing the crowd to a halt.

'You will run less risk of injury if you walk quietly to the staircase,' he said in a calm voice. His words had a steadying effect, and he turned to a man who seemed cooler than the others. 'What has happened?'

'Fire, sir. It started at the far end of the building and is moving fast. You had best go now if you wish to save your skin.'

'The place is alight, my dear.' Edward turned back to Georgiana. 'We must go at once.'

'What of Betsy…and Scroggins? Are they not at the top of the building?'

'I have not forgotten them, Georgie. Let me take you to safety, then I shall go back for them.'

She hesitated.

'Is there not time for you to find them? The smoke is thick, but there are no flames…'

'I won't risk your safety, Georgie. Come with me. For all we know they may already have escaped.' He took her hand and led her into the corridor.

The first wild rush of fleeing guests had ended, and they were passed only by single half-clad figures who hurried by with cloths pressed against their mouths.

Georgiana began to cough and choke. Her eyes were streaming from the effects of smoke. Without pausing in his stride Edward stripped off his coat and threw it about her head.

The fire was gaining on them. She tried to run as she heard crackling and the smell of burning wood. Behind them the tinder-dry wainscoting went up in a shower of sparks.

'Take your time.' Edward caught at her arm to slow her down. 'We are almost there.'

Even as he spoke she heard a crash, accompanied by agonised screaming.

'No, don't look!' Edward buried her face in his shoulder as he glanced into the yawning pit at his feet. 'The staircase has collapsed. We must find another way.'

He could prevent her from seeing the full horror of the tragedy, but the shrieks of the scorched and mutilated victims followed them as they turned back along the corridor. A strange smell hung on the air. It was that of burning flesh, and Georgiana felt her gorge rise.

'This way!' Edward had found another corridor leading to the right. The smoke was thickening fast, but as yet there were no flames. With an arm about her shoulders he urged her along. Then she heard a wave of sound behind her. She looked round and gave a cry of fright as a terror-stricken mob bore down upon them.

In a second she lost her grip on Edward's hand

as the crowd engulfed them. She turned her head and saw him vainly trying to plead for calm, but hysteria had overcome the fleeing guests. His words of entreaty fell upon deaf ears. Then he was by her side again.

'It is useless,' he said quietly. Protecting her with his body, he forced a way to the edge of the crowd. 'In here, my love...' He thrust her into one of the rooms leading off the corridor and closed the door behind him.

'We shall be trapped,' she cried wildly.

'Not so!' He strode across to the window and flung it wide. Then he nodded in satisfaction. 'Thank heavens there is a balcony.'

She hurried across to join him, clutching him to her as she took great gulps of air. Gently he disengaged her fingers.

'I want you to be brave, my love. There is another balcony below. It is not too far for me to lower you closer to the ground.'

'No! I can't do it.' Georgiana looked down to the street below, and the distance to the ground appalled her. 'I'm afraid. I've always been afraid of heights. I shall fall, I know it.'

'You will not fall, I promise.' He pulled a sheet from the bed and tore it into strips. 'See, I will fasten this around your waist and tie it to a chest. Then you will be quite safe.'

'Can't we stay here and wait for help? Look, someone has already fetched a ladder!'

It was true. There was much activity in the watching crowd which filled the street.

'The ladders will not reach to the second floor. Besides, they are made of wood…'

She did not need to be told what would happen if the wood should catch fire.

'But they are bringing water too,' she pleaded. 'I can see men with buckets…'

'They will not douse this conflagration. Georgie, look at me!'

Obediently she raised her eyes to his.

'My love, in this at least you must obey me. Will you do as I say?'

Dumb with terror, she could only nod.

'That's my darling girl!' Deftly he knotted the sheet about her waist, and tied the other end securely to a heavy piece of furniture.

'Edward!' Her soul was in her eyes, and he caught her to him with a muffled groan. 'My love, you will follow me?'

'I will…I promise.' He leaned over the balcony.

'I can see no smoke from below. It seems likely that the fire was started on this floor.'

'But if it is spreading…?'

'When you reach the balcony go at once to the door of the room. If it is open you must close it. The wood will take some time to burn. Soak sheets and covers if you can find some water and pile them against the jamb. That will buy some time.'

'But…but I thought you said that you would follow me.'

'I will…but you must make a start.' To still any further protests he gave her a long kiss. Then he took her in his arms and lifted her over the balcony sill.

'Don't look down,' he ordered. 'Keep your eyes on me.' His hands were like bands of iron as he gripped her wrists. 'Down you go,' he said cheerfully.

Georgiana made her mind a blank as he swung her into space. She could not scream. Her throat was too constricted, but the steady hands still held her, and she was conscious of their immense strength.

'Can you feel the edge of the balcony?' Edward asked in a conversational tone.

'Y-yes,' she whispered.

'Then swing your feet inside it and I'll release you. Tell me when you have done so.'

'Now.' She offered a silent prayer as her wrists were freed. Then she was on solid ground again.

'Are you safe, my love?' Edward's deep voice was reassuring.

'Yes, but please hurry.'

'I shall be with you in a moment. Do you untie the sheet from about your waist.'

It was a struggle to loosen the knots. They had tightened even further as they had taken the strain of her weight, but she managed at last.

'It's free,' she called.

The end of the sheet flapped idly in the breeze, but there was silence from above.

'Edward?' Her voice was high with panic. She leaned out as far as she could, striving to catch a glimpse of him, but the floor of the upper balcony blocked her view.

Where could he be? She could not think what had happened. Had he been overcome by smoke? In an agony of mind she called to him again and again, but he did not reply.

In desperation she looked at the flapping rope of sheets, but she was forced to dismiss the idea of climbing up again. It was beyond her strength.

There might be another way to reach him. She ran to the door and opened it. There was a strong smell of smoke in the corridor, but the air was clear. She stepped outside just as the first grey wisps curled towards her from the angle of the staircase. To her fevered imagination the smoke was like some malevolent spirit, reaching out to claim her life. She closed the door on it.

What could she do? Edward's words came back to her. Had he not said that she must pile up soaking bedding?

Working quickly, she snatched up the coverlet and threw it against the door. Thankfully the enormous waterjug on the dressing stand was full, but she could not lift it. She seized a vase from the mantelshelf, dipping it into the jug again and again until the contents had reduced the bedding to a sodden mass.

Sheets? She took those too, but the waterjug was almost empty. Fiercely she trampled them into the coverlet until they too were soaking. In her haste she tripped and fell against the door, realising with a gasp that the ancient oak panels were hot enough to burn her skin. The fire had travelled more quickly than she could possibly have imagined.

Frantic now, she ran back to the balcony but her shouts to Edward went unanswered. Again she craned her neck out far beyond the balustrade, but a shower of burning debris from above drove her back indoors. Then the upper balcony gave way and fell in a flaming mass to the street below.

Georgiana fought a rising tide of hysteria. She must be calm. If she panicked now it might cost her her life. The smoke in the room was no thicker, and the door, though hot to the touch, was not yet alight.

Edward must have decided to find another way to reach her. She would not believe that he had succumbed to the flames. It wasn't possible. He was wise and resourceful. Perhaps even now he was trying to reach her from the street.

If she could only see him… She eyed her balcony doubtfully. The deadly shower of burning fragments had stopped, and it seemed safe enough to venture out…

She gave a cry. The floor was smouldering. She kicked wildly at the charred debris which was setting it alight, sighing with relief as she realised that she had caught it in time.

Others were not so fortunate. The noise was deafening as screams of terror mingled with an ominous crackling as the fire took hold. Piteous cries for help issued from almost every window, though many were stilled by a crash behind them as the floors gave way.

The upper floor was well alight and smoke and flames belched forth from balconies. Was no one trying to help them?

She looked down into the street. Some ladders had been placed against the building, but they were woefully short. She saw men lashing two or three together in an effort to reach the upper floors, but a sudden burst of flame from one of the windows caught the first climber and sent him screaming to the ground. In seconds the ladder was alight.

Buckets of water were being passed from hand to hand along a chain of sweating men, but she knew that they could not reach her.

She stepped back quickly as something hurtled past her. Then she closed her eyes. Someone had jumped.

The blazing figure was followed by others…all of them missing the outstretched blankets held by willing hands.

Georgiana could not stop shaking. Nausea threatened to overcome her at the thought of those hideous deaths. She would not jump, but perhaps she could lower herself to safety in the way that Edward had lowered her from the floor above.

It was her only chance. She must ignore her

fear of heights. It seemed unimportant when weighed against the prospect of death by fire.

And it was not so very far to the ground from this floor. If she could attract attention the men below might catch her if she fell.

The sodden sheets were difficult to make into a rope but she forced her trembling fingers to obey her. She blessed the day that Harry had shown her how to tie a knot securely.

She used up all the cloth she had and secured one end to the bed. The other she wound about her waist. Silently she prayed that it was long enough and would hold. Then she walked on to the balcony and waved her arms above her head.

Edward would see her, she was sure... But there was no sign of his tall figure in the crowd. Then she caught sight of Betsy's tear-stained face. Half-clad, the girl was standing beside her uncle, sobbing bitterly as she looked up at the building.

As she saw Georgiana her expression changed. She grabbed at Scroggins' arm, pointing upwards in excitement.

Scroggins did not hesitate. He started to run towards the hotel entrance, but a dozen men held him back. Shouting and gesticulating, he could not break their hold, and Georgiana was glad of it. He must not risk his life for her.

At least she had been seen. In seconds a blanket was in place beneath her balcony. The time had come to take her courage in both hands. A hush fell on the crowd below.

She took a deep breath and was about to trust herself to the makeshift rope when she heard shouting from the corridor. The sound was distant, but it could only mean that someone had found a way through. Edward was coming for her, she was sure of it.

With shaking fingers she tore at the rope about her waist, trying to loosen it. The cloth was stiff and intractable, but the knots came apart at last.

She ran to the door, calling as she went. Feverishly she tore at the sodden coverlet which blocked the door, kicking aside pillows and cushions in her haste. Even as she worked the door began to open, slowly at first, as it met the barrier of her makeshift seal, and then more quickly.

Clouds of smoke billowed into the room, causing her to gasp for breath. She ignored the choking sensation in her throat, but her eyes were streaming as she reached out to the dimly seen figure of her rescuer.

'Edward!' she cried on a sob. 'Oh, my love, I thought I had lost you…'

But it was not Edward who came towards her through the smoke. She looked into Merton's face and then she screamed.

Chapter Twelve

Merton's eyes were blank and Georgiana knew then that he was quite mad. He gripped her arm above the elbow and led her back to the balcony.

'Is this not a wonderful sight? A foretaste of hell! I had not thought to see the like when I first lit the kindling.'

'You? It was you who started this?'

'Oh yes! Just a small diversion…but now it is magnificent. I feel like a god!' He threw his arms to heaven in a gesture of triumph.

Georgiana turned to run, but he was too quick for her. Again he caught her arm.

'Don't go! It is not over yet. See, the wall is about to collapse…' He laughed aloud as part of the building bulged and then fell, driving the spectators back.

'But the people…the guests…? Had you no thought for them?'

'They are enjoying it,' he assured her solemnly. 'See how they jump out of the windows. It must be like flying… Would you like to try?'

Georgiana did not shrink from him. She must not show her fear. If she could but keep him talking…

'Not yet,' she said. 'It is not quite over, as you told me.'

'But you were screaming,' he demurred. 'I thought it did not please you…'

'I did not like the flames at first,' she said quickly. 'I thought they must burn me.'

'But they are beautiful!' He sounded puzzled. 'They are the colour of your hair.' He reached up and laid his hand upon her curls.

Georgiana stood very still. Her instinct was to run, but it would be useless. She would not get far.

Merton turned back to the spectacle before him. For a time he watched intently, a cry of pleasure escaping his lips as one wall after another burned and fell. Then he frowned and his face darkened.

'They are spoiling it.' He pointed to a corner of the building where the fire sputtered out as men threw water on the blaze.

'I'll stop them.' He gnawed at his lower lip. 'Yes, I'll stop them just as I stopped the other one.'

Georgiana had a dreadful premonition.

'The...the other one?' she breathed. 'Who was that?'

'He wanted the torch,' Merton muttered vaguely. 'He tried to take it, but I was too clever for him. When he turned to put it out I struck him down.'

Georgiana forgot her fear of him. She tugged at his coat.

'Who was it?' she cried. 'Did you know him?'

At last she had his full attention. He bent his gaze upon her and something moved at the back of the silvery eyes...something as insubstantial as a cloud reflected in a still pool.

Then the thin lips curled back in a travesty of a smile. 'He was my enemy,' he told her. 'And yours as well. I saw him trying to throw you from the balcony. I was standing behind the statue over there...' He pointed across the square.

Georgiana's head was reeling. The floor was behaving oddly. It seemed to be coming up to meet her. Oh, God, she must not faint...

'Why did you come back?' she cried in anguish.

'I wanted to be sure that he would burn in hell.

I killed him, but he did not suffer. I am not cruel, only just…I carried out the sentence…'

Georgiana could not speak. A lump formed in her throat as she gazed at him with horror in her eyes.

Merton gave her a guileless smile. 'I can make a torch for you,' he offered. 'Then we can go together to the other rooms. You will like that. The wood catches fire at once, and then it crackles and speaks to me.'

Despair filled her heart. With Edward gone she had no wish to live, but the instinct for survival was strong. Even in her sorrow she dreaded the thought of death by fire.

In desperation she looked about her for some weapon; the candlesticks on the mantelshelf looked heavy enough…but if she did not succeed with her first blow Merton would kill her there and then. He had all the strength of a madman.

The breeze was freshening now, and it had changed direction. There were cries from below as sparks flew across to the neighbouring buildings.

Merton watched with avid interest. Then he turned and made for the door, dragging her behind him.

'Quickly!' he said. 'We must help them, or our enemies will put it out.'

The corridor was filled with choking smoke. It was so thick that she could not see a yard ahead of her.

'No!' She struggled to break his grip. 'Let us go back. We shall be overcome...'

'Don't be afraid.' Merton's voice was almost kindly. 'I know the way to the other building. See, I have the key.' He opened his clenched fist to show it to her.

'Where did you find that?'

He gave her a cunning smile. 'I stole it before...before... I have forgotten...let me think.' He frowned and then his face cleared. 'I remember now,' he said. 'You promised to come away with me. I stole it so that we could get away.'

Georgiana thought fast. Merton must have had the key for some time.

'I'm glad,' she said simply. 'How clever you are! Is that how you got into the building...from the house next door?'

He did not answer her. He was moving so fast that she had to run to keep up with him. Then she stumbled and fell, breaking his grip as she did so.

He cursed as he raised her to her feet, but the fall had given her an idea. If she could break his grip again she would disappear into the smoke.

She took a few more steps and fell again, squirming out of his grasp. Then she sprang to her feet and began to run in the opposite direction. If she could but find the room again, or even another one, she might yet escape him.

She had no idea where she was. Her eyes were stinging and she could see nothing. Blindly she reached out and touched the wainscoting on one wall. It was hot, but she ignored the pain as she trailed her fingers along, searching for a doorjamb or a latch.

There, she had it… But before she could open the door a hand closed about her mouth and she was held in a fierce grip.

'Georgie!' Edward's arms went round her. 'Thank God I've found you.'

Georgiana peered up at him in disbelief as joy swept through her. Edward was alive, though clearly he was badly injured. The face which she loved so well was now a bloody mask, blackened with smoke.

'Where is Merton?' he asked quickly.

'He is out there somewhere.' She pointed along the corridor. 'Edward, he has a key to the building next door. That is how he comes and goes. It is an escape route.'

'Then let us follow him.' He put his arm about her shoulders, but she saw at once that he could move only with difficulty.

'Would it not be best to go back to the room again?'

'It is an inferno. I jumped down to the balcony, but the flames had taken hold. I thought is must give beneath my weight...'

She did not question him further. Whatever happened now they were together. The danger was great, but she was conscious only of an overwhelming sense of relief. At least he was alive.

Their progress along the corridor was painfully slow. Georgiana had her arm about Edward's waist, but she found it difficult to support his weight as he leaned ever more heavily upon her. She looked at him with anxious eyes.

'Can you go on?' she murmured.

'To the end, if need be,' he assured her. 'See, Georgie, the air is clearing.'

It was true. Perceptibly the smoke was thinning as they moved along.

Georgiana scarcely dared to hope. Could it be that they were close to rescue? Her eyes were shining as she looked at Edward's face.

'Just a few more steps, my darling,' she encouraged. 'Then we shall be safe…' Her words died on her lips as Merton blocked their path. He looked at Edward in wonder.

'I killed you,' he said. 'Why won't you die?'

A pistol appeared in his hand as if by magic as Edward lunged towards him.

'Don't make me shoot you,' Merton pleaded. 'That would be wrong. You are to die in the fire.'

Georgiana's mind was racing. 'How can that be?' she said gently. 'Look about you. There are no flames in this part of the building.'

'That's true!' Merton shook his head as if to clear it. 'The flames are in your hair, but they won't kill him…' He frowned at her. 'I lost you back there…and we were going…we were going…'

'We were going to see the other fire,' Georgiana prompted. 'You promised me that…don't you recall?'

He considered for a moment. 'I think so…'

'Then should we not make haste? Otherwise your enemies will put it out.'

'But he is my enemy.' He waved the pistol at Edward. 'I want to see him burn.'

'Have you forgotten the way to lead us to the other fire?' Georgiana made a desperate attempt to divert his attention from Edward. 'You told me that you had a key.'

'I have…' He swung the heavy object from one finger, holding it tantalisingly out of reach. 'But I must keep it.'

'Of course you must, if you are to use it. Shall we go?'

'I…I don't know…' He sounded puzzled. 'There was something I had to do.' His glance fell on Edward, and again Georgiana saw the strange stirring in his eyes.

'The fire!' she cried in desperation. 'Don't forget the fire…'

'That's it!' He smiled at her. 'I can burn him there… Come…we are wasting time…'

He motioned them ahead of him, his pistol pressed firmly into Edward's spine.

Georgiana still had her arm about her husband's waist, supporting his stumbling steps. He bent towards her.

'Georgie, when you see the chance you must run,' he whispered.

She shook her head. 'I won't leave you.'

'You must. I'm not as weak as I appear.'

She did not look at him. If what he said was true she must not arouse Merton's suspicions. She began to stoop as if Edward's weight were too much for her. Coughing and choking, she staggered along the corridor. In that at least she had no need to dissemble. Her stinging eyes were streaming from the effect of the smoke. Then it began to clear.

Georgiana felt a flicker of hope. To reach the adjoining building Merton would be forced to lead them across the square outside. He could not disguise the fact that Edward was injured, and that she herself was on the verge of collapse. Had he not realised that help would be at hand?

Her hopes were soon dashed. As she turned to the staircase leading to the hotel entrance Merton stopped her.

'Not that way!' His eyes were cunning. 'My enemies are out there…'

He pushed them ahead of him along a corridor leading to the rear, taking a key from his pocket as he did so. The heat was intense and Georgiana winced with each step she took. Her think kid slippers offered no protection from the scorching floorboards.

Edward's arm tightened about her shoulders. 'Be ready!' he warned.

Georgiana needed no persuading. She might have been standing in the open doorway of a furnace. At any moment she feared that the floor and the walls would ignite. She was soaked to the skin in sweat.

Then they were forced to stop at the end of the corridor. A massive door barred their way. Merton walked around them carefully, keeping them at a distance.

With a groan Edward sank to the ground. His collapse was so realistic that Georgiana gave a cry of anguish and fell to her knees beside him.

Merton eyed them without interest. He kicked at the inert figure, but there was no response. Satisfied, he turned to open the door.

'Down!' Edward shouted. He threw his arms about Georgiana and rolled her to one side, covering her with his body as a wall of fire belched out towards them.

Merton stood no chance. His hair and clothing burst into flame as he was caught by the inferno. With arms outstretched he screamed in mortal agony as he fell into the blaze.

Then Edward was on his feet, slamming the door on the horrific sight. Without a word he seized Georgiana's arm and hurried her away.

She felt sick and faint but he did not slow his pace. 'We are almost there,' he encouraged. 'Don't fail me now. The fire can move more quickly than a man can run.'

Terror lent wings to her feet, but even so it seemed an age before they stumbled out into the sunlight. As the sound of cheering reached her ears Georgiana fainted.

She returned to consciousness to find herself resting in the cool luxury of lavender-scented sheets. There was a strange taste in her mouth which she could not recognise. Then full memory returned. She could still taste and smell acrid smoke.

In a panic she sat bolt upright. Where was Edward? Were they safe, or was this building too in the path of the fire? She cried his name aloud.

'I am here, my love.' He was sitting beside her bed, but he rose at once and came to kiss her. Then he stroked her hair. 'You must rest,' he said tenderly. 'You were so brave, but you have had a terrible experience...'

'But you...?' She scanned his face with anxious eyes. 'Edward, you were hurt... I thought... Merton said that he had killed you.' She threw herself into his arms as the tears brimmed over.

'I am very much alive,' he teased. 'I hope to prove it to you when you are well again.'

'Don't joke!' She reached out a hand to touch his cheek. 'You were bleeding…'

'Just a superficial cut. Even the thickest head will bleed profusely; it looked worse than it was.'

'You make light of it, but, my dearest, you looked so dreadful…' She would not be convinced.

'Worse than usual?' The blue eyes twinkled as they looked into her own. 'I'll allow that I was a frightening sight.'

'Where did he strike you?' Gently she touched his head and found an alarming lump. He winced and drew her hand away. 'You should be in bed,' she announced.

'Nothing would please me more,' came the prompt reply. 'But had we not best wait until tonight? You are in no condition to welcome my advances.'

Georgiana's face grew rosy. 'You know I did not mean that you should make love to me,' she protested.

'I am ever hopeful…'

'Edward, be serious.'

'Very well.' He composed his face into an expression of polite interest. 'Madam, what is your will?'

'I want to know what happened. Merton…did he…did he escape the fire?'

He realised then that she had not seen the fearful sight which lived on in his mind, and he was glad of it. That blazing apparition was the stuff of nightmares.

He shook his head. 'He died in the blaze.'

'He was quite mad, you know.'

'I know. The ruin of his plans must have been the last straw.'

He was silent for some time, holding her as if he would never let her go.

'I should have listened to you, my dearest. You were never easy in your mind about him, were you?'

'You could not know that he would set the fire. Oh, Edward…all those people! If only we could have stopped him.' She buried her face against his coat.

'There was nothing we could do, Georgiana. His was an unhinged mind. Reason could not prevail, and he had all the cunning of a madman. I should have suspected treachery when he allowed me to take the torch.'

Georgiana began to shiver, but he soothed her into a calmer frame of mind.

'Betsy wishes to see you,' he said at last. 'Shall I ring for her?'

'Yes, please…and Scroggins too. My love, he tried to save me, but they held him back.'

'Did I not tell you that he was not quite the pillar of stiffness that you thought him?' Edward kissed her again. 'He has a high regard for you.'

Georgiana smiled doubtfully, but when Scroggins and Betsy entered the room she was forced to admit that he was right. The man looked deeply shaken and when he spoke it was with warmth.

'Madam, I am happy to see you safe,' he said. 'If there is anything your ladyship requires…anything I can do…?'

'You tried to do so much.' Georgiana gave him a radiant smile. 'You would have risked your life for me, I think.'

She was surprised to see him flush.

'Madam has been good to me and mine,' he replied. 'Betsy is but a country girl, and much patience is required…' He shot a sharp glance at his niece.

'Nonsense!' Georgiana beamed upon her maid. 'Betsy, you must not cry or you will soak the carpet.' She stretched out a hand and Betsy ran to her.

'Have I anything to wear?' she murmured. 'I still have my pearls…but apart from those…'

Edward rose from his seat beside her, and signalled to his man.

'It is time we left,' he said significantly. 'Madam will not be satisfied until she is allowed to leave her bed.' He looked at Georgiana with a grin. 'Betsy has a surprise for you, my love.' He was laughing as he left the room.

'What is it, Betsy?'

'Oh, miss…I mean madam…there's boxes of it. It was my uncle really… His lordship sent him out with orders… You'll never wear the half of it. Will I open the boxes for you?' In her eagerness the words came tumbling out.

At Georgiana's nod she began to unpack the gowns. Then her hands fell to her sides and she looked at her mistress with brimming eyes.

'What is it, Betsy?'

'Oh, madam, I thought you lost for sure…' She threw her apron over her head as she rocked to and fro in anguish.

'Now, Betsy, I won't have you "taking on" so.' Georgiana used the country expression deliberately, hoping to raise a smile. 'You must help me dress. His lordship tells me that Mr Harry is below…'

'He wanted to come up,' Betsy hiccuped between sobs. 'But the master said as he must wait.'

'Mr Harry is not a patient man,' Georgiana announced. 'If we don't hurry I shall face his wrath.'

'Oh, madam, I'm sorry.' Betsy looked crestfallen. Then she saw a twinkle in Georgiana's eyes, and she managed a reluctant smile. 'My lord would have something to say…'

She returned to her task, piling every surface high with gowns, underlinen, bonnets, ribbons, handkerchiefs and the prettiest of matching slippers.

'Where did it all come from?' Georgiana stared at the mounting heap in amazement. 'I had thought that gowns must be bespoke.'

'My uncle is what his lordship calls resourceful,' Betsy said proudly. 'He knows all the places…'

'I can well believe you. I wonder if the gowns will fit me?'

As she slipped into a pale blue muslin trimmed with matching ribbons she found that Scroggins had assessed both style and fit to perfection.

In wonder she stared at her reflection in the mirror. It didn't seem possible that the terrible events of the last few days had not changed her.

The great green eyes looked back at her. They had lost their haunted expression, but there was something there behind the smile. Sadness? No…not with Edward's love to warm her heart. Then she recognised it for what it was. She had grown up at last. It was a look of maturity.

A deep sense of joy possessed her, but she felt very calm as she made her way downstairs to join the others. Edward and Harry were waiting for her in a private room, and her brother hurried towards her as she entered. He caught her by the shoulders and looked into her eyes.

'Georgie, are you better? I've been out of my mind with worry.'

'I'm not even singed.' She smiled up at him.

'Sit down over here.' He guided her to a chair, still speaking in hushed tones. 'Is there anything I can get for you? Would you prefer to lie on the sofa? Should you be out of bed?' He was very pale and she realised that he was badly shocked.

'Don't be such a noddle-cock, Hal. I'm not at death's door.' The pithy words brought an injured look from Harry.

'You ain't lost your tongue, that's for sure.'

She twinkled at him. 'That's better! There's nothing like a quarrel to bring you to your senses…'

He tried to smile, but his face was grave.

'I have gone through hell in these past hours. It was all my fault, you know. If we had not met Merton this never would have happened.'

'Merton would have sought you out.' Edward regarded him calmly. 'He had reasons other than money to make use of you and Richard.'

'What do you mean?'

'The lady whom you thought I injured was his sister.'

Harry looked acutely uncomfortable. 'You should have told me…'

'I did not know myself until quite recently. And, Harry, I was not the villain you imagined. Georgie will tell you if you care to know.'

'No, no! I'll take your word for it. I expect that the gossips had only half the tale.'

'Thank you.' Edward returned his smile, and Harry's face began to clear.

'That, at least, is a relief,' he sighed. 'But when we heard about the fire…and that Merton had started it… Well, I tell you, neither Richard nor I would go through that again.'

'Don't think about it,' Georgiana pleaded. 'Merton is gone and we are safe.'

'He deserved to die. I won't say that I'm sorry. And it does make all the difference, doesn't it? Now we can return to England.'

Georgiana looked at him in astonishment.

'But…but I thought that you wished…that you had agreed to go to India?'

'I'd rather go back to London, wouldn't you? You must have missed it as I do. When I think of the balls, the parties…and all our friends…!'

Georgiana shot a despairing look at Edward, but he appeared to be absorbed in his newspaper.

Harry sensed her disquiet. 'I shan't be so foolish this time,' he promised. 'I'll choose my friends more carefully and there'll be no gambling. And, Georgie, you mustn't think that I shall always be on your doorstep. I'll visit you, of course, just once or twice a week, but I'll rent a house and—'

'Harry, listen to me. This will not do. You have given your word both to Edward and to me to take this opportunity with the East India Company.'

'But it may be years before I return. I shall not see you. Oh, Georgie, don't you want me…?'

She looked at his downcast head. 'I think you know how dear you are to me,' she replied gently. 'But life has changed for both of us. Did you not promise to make me proud of you? Why, you will come back with a fortune…'

He did not answer her, but she persevered.

'I believed you when you said that you had been through hell, my dear, but now you must look ahead. You are a man, with a man's responsibilities. In time you will take a wife and will have your own establishment…'

She stopped in dismay. She sounded as if she

was reading him a lecture. Edward came to the rescue.

'An interesting prospect,' he said drily. 'But Harry has not chosen his lady yet. Meantime, as a bachelor in India the world will be at his feet. There is racing, polo, excellent fishing in the north of the country, and the hunting is beyond compare. Imagine stalking a tiger…!'

Harry brightened, and his head went up.

'The social round is exhausting.' Edward continued in a bland tone. 'So many levees, dances and receptions… Harry may find them injurious to his health. Perhaps we should persuade him against the idea after all.'

'No, no! I have reconsidered. You may be right after all.' He stood up. 'Have you seen Richard?'

'He is out on some errand for me, but I believe you will find him on the Rue Saint Honore. You will dine with us tonight?'

Harry accepted gratefully and then he left them.

'Well done, my darling.' Edward smiled at his wife. 'I doubt if Harry will waver now.'

'Thanks to you. I sounded as if I was preaching at him, though I did not mean to do so.'

'You were a little circumspect, perhaps even

prim… I can't allow that.' Edward took her in his arms. 'You are much too beautiful to become a solemn matron.'

The slanting eyes gave him a mischievous look. 'You told me once that my appearance was deceptive,' she murmured. 'It is still so.'

'I can't be sure of that.' He held her at arm's length with a teasing look.

'I wonder how I can persuade you?'

'Minx! Would you flirt with your husband? Such improper behaviour calls for strong measures.' He kissed her until she was breathless.

'I could die against your lips,' she whispered.

'Far better to live, my darling, and live to the full. I may worship you with my body, but I love you with all my heart and soul.'

Glowing with happiness, she threw her arms about his neck. 'I wish I could tell you how I feel, but words are not enough.' She pressed a kiss into the hollow of his throat.

'In that we are agreed.' He gathered her close, laughing down at her. 'Perhaps there is another way…'

That night she gave herself to him without reservation. She had not thought it possible to love so fully. Then, with their passion spent, she nestled in the crook of his arm.

'Do you still think me prim, my lord?' she asked in a wicked whisper.

'Madam, you may keep your cool demeanour for the rest of the world. It won't deceive me again.' He bent his head and found her lips.

* * * * *

The Regency

LORDS & LADIES
COLLECTION

More Glittering Regency Love Affairs

VOLUME TWENTY-SEVEN

Lady Sarah's Son by **Gayle Wilson**

Lady Sarah Spenser had once thought that
Justin Tolbert was the most handsome man she knew.
Now Justin was a war hero – and the new Earl
of Wynfield. But he was not the same man
Sarah had once known…

Wedding Night Revenge by **Mary Brendan**

Beautiful, witty Rachel Meredith had jilted handsome
Major Connor Flinte. When her father loses the
house to Connor – now the Earl of Devane, Rachel
is desperate to regain her home. But Connor wants
revenge for the wedding night he never had…

On sale 7th November 2008

www.millsandboon.co.uk

M&B

The ℛegency

LORDS & LADIES
COLLECTION

More Glittering Regency Love Affairs

Volume 17 – 4th January 2008
One Night with a Rake by Louise Allen
The Dutiful Rake by Elizabeth Rolls

Volume 18 – 1st February 2008
A Matter of Honour by Anne Herries
The Chivalrous Rake by Elizabeth Rolls

Volume 19 – 7th March 2008
Tavern Wench by Anne Ashley
The Incomparable Countess by Mary Nichols

Volume 20 – 4th April 2008
Prudence by Elizabeth Bailey
Lady Lavinia's Match by Mary Nichols

Volume 21 – 2nd May 2008
The Rebellious Bride by Francesca Shaw
The Duke's Mistress by Ann Elizabeth Cree

Volume 22 – 6th June 2008
Carnival of Love by Helen Dickson
The Viscount's Bride by Ann Elizabeth Cree

Volume 23 – 4th July 2008
One Night of Scandal & *The Rake's Mistress*
by Nicola Cornick

M&B

The Regency
LORDS & LADIES
COLLECTION

More Glittering Regency Love Affairs

Volume 24 – 1st August 2008
The Reluctant Marchioness by Anne Ashley
Nell by Elizabeth Bailey

Volume 25 – 5th September 2008
Kitty by Elizabeth Bailey
Major Chancellor's Mission by Paula Marshall

Volume 26 – 3rd October 2008
Lord Hadleigh's Rebellion by Paula Marshall
The Sweet Cheat by Meg Alexander

Volume 27 – 7th November 2008
Lady Sarah's Son by Gayle Wilson
Wedding Night Revenge by Mary Brendan

Volume 28 – 5th December 2008
Rake's Reward by Joanna Maitland
The Unknown Wife by Mary Brendan

Volume 29 – 2nd January 2009
Miss Verey's Proposal by Nicola Cornick
The Rebellious Débutante by Meg Alexander

Volume 30 – 6th February 2009
Dear Deceiver by Mary Nichols
The Matchmaker's Marriage by Meg Alexander

Celebrate 100 years of pure reading pleasure with Mills & Boon®

To mark our centenary, each month we're publishing a special 100th Birthday Edition. These celebratory editions are packed with extra features and include a FREE bonus story.

Plus, you have the chance to enter a fabulous monthly prize draw. See 100th Birthday Edition books for details.

Now that's worth celebrating!

September 2008

Crazy about her Spanish Boss by Rebecca Winters
Includes FREE bonus story
Rafael's Convenient Proposal

November 2008

**The Rancher's Christmas Baby
by Cathy Gillen Thacker**
Includes FREE bonus story *Baby's First Christmas*

December 2008

One Magical Christmas by Carol Marinelli
Includes FREE bonus story *Emergency at Bayside*

Look for Mills & Boon® 100th Birthday Editions at your favourite bookseller or visit
www.millsandboon.co.uk